OXFORD WORLD'

BARRY LY

William Makepeace Thackeray was born in 1811 in Calcutta. In 1817 he was sent to England to be educated as a gentleman. From Charterhouse school, he went to Cambridge in 1829. His career at university was undistinguished, and led into an unsettled young-manhood. After false starts in the law, in art (which he studied in Paris), and journalism he compounded his misfortunes with an imprudent marriage in 1835. Tragically, his wife went mad five years later, leaving Thackeray with two young daughters to provide for. His first successes in authorship came with publications (of a largely satirical nature) in *Fraser's Magazine* and *Punch*. Triumph came with the publication of *Vanity Fair* (1847–8). This serialized novel promoted Thackeray to the rank of Dickens's principal rival in fiction. It was followed by the more autobiographical *Pendennis* (1848–50) and the historical *Henry Esmond* (1852), works which consolidated Thackeray's reputation without equalling the runaway popularity of his first full-length novel. Thackeray's energies flagged somewhat in the second half of his writing life. He lectured in America in 1852 and 1865, and stood unsuccessfully for parliament as an Independent Liberal in 1857. His stature as a leading man of letters was confirmed in 1859, when he took over the editorship of the new *Cornhill Magazine* (a post he held until 1862). Thackeray's last years were his most prosperous. But since 1850 his health had never been good, and his writing suffered correspondingly. He died suddenly in December 1863.

Andrew Sanders is Professor of English at the University of Durham. He has edited George Eliot's *Romola* and Dickens's *Dombey and Son* for Penguin Classics and (in the Oxford World's Classics series) Elizabeth Gaskell's *Sylvia's Lovers*, Dickens's *David Copperfield* and *A Tale of Two Cities*, Thackeray's *The Newcomes*, and Thomas Hughes's *Tom Brown's Schooldays*. He is the author of *The Victorian Historical Novel* (1978), *Charles Dickens: Resurrectionist* (1982), a companion to *A Tale of Two Cities*, *The Short Oxford History of Engish Literature* (1994), *Anthony Trollope* (Writers and Their Work series, 1998), and *Dickens and the Spirit of the Age* (forthcoming). He was editor of *The Dickensian* from 1978 to 1986.

OXFORD WORLD'S CLASSICS

For almost 100 years Oxford World's Classics have brought readers closer to the world's great literature. Now with over 700 titles—from the 4,000-year-old myths of Mesopotamia to the twentieth century's greatest novels—the series makes available lesser-known as well as celebrated writing.

The pocket-sized hardbacks of the early years contained introductions by Virginia Woolf, T. S. Eliot, Graham Greene, and other literary figures which enriched the experience of reading. Today the series is recognized for its fine scholarship and reliability in texts that span world literature, drama and poetry, religion, philosophy and politics. Each edition includes perceptive commentary and essential background information to meet the changing needs of readers.

OXFORD WORLD'S CLASSICS

WILLIAM MAKEPEACE
THACKERAY

The Memoirs of Barry Lyndon, Esq.

Edited with an Introduction and Notes by
ANDREW SANDERS

OXFORD
UNIVERSITY PRESS

OXFORD
UNIVERSITY PRESS

Great Clarendon Street, Oxford OX2 6DP

Oxford University Press is a department of the University of Oxford.
It furthers the University's objective of excellence in research, scholarship,
and education by publishing worldwide in

Oxford New York

Athens Auckland Bangkok Bogotá Buenos Aires Calcutta
Cape Town Chennai Dar es Salaam Delhi Florence Hong Kong Istanbul
Karachi Kuala Lumpur Madrid Melbourne Mexico City Mumbai
Nairobi Paris São Paulo Shanghai Singapore Taipei Tokyo Toronto Warsaw

with associated companies in Berlin Ibadan

Oxford is a registered trade mark of Oxford University Press
in the UK and in certain other countries

Published in the United States
by Oxford University Press Inc., New York

This edition first published as a World's Classics paperback 1984
Reissued as an Oxford World's Classics paperback 1999

British Library Cataloguing in Publication Data

Data available

Library of Congress Cataloging in Publication Data

Thackeray, William Makepeace, 1811–1863.
The Memoirs of Barry Lyndon, Esq.
(Oxford world's classics)
Bibliography: p.
I. Sanders, Andrew. II. Title
PR5608.A2S36 1984 823'.8 83–23669

ISBN 0–19–283628–5 (pbk.)

3 5 7 9 10 8 6 4

Printed in Great Britain by
Cox & Wyman Ltd.
Reading, Berkshire

CONTENTS

ACKNOWLEDGEMENTS

My thanks are due to the following for their assistance in various ways: Roy Foster; Graham Handley; Roland Mayer; Sylvère Monod; Leonée Ormond; Graham Parry; Michael Slater; Stephen Wood and Dr. Alan Guy of the National Army Museum.

INTRODUCTION

THE Irish, Thackeray once noted, 'are a nation of liars'. This prejudice which was to inspire and shape *Barry Lyndon* was not, however, based on animosity, antipathy or superiority: Thackeray claimed to feel at home with the Irish character and to know the Irish thoroughly. 'The best friend I ever had in the world', he told David Masson (a Scot) '. . . the nicest and most delightful fellow I ever knew in the world . . . was an Irishman. But, d'ye know he was a great rascal.' In 1855 the former 'Young Irelander', Charles Gavan Duffy, was introduced to the novelist by Thomas Carlyle and found him guardedly sympathetic to Irish nationalism. When Duffy went on to praise 'the accuracy, or rather the fitness, of the Irish names of men and places in *Barry Lyndon*', Thackeray responded that he had 'lived a good deal among Irish people in London and elsewhere'. Nevertheless, his distrust of everything he heard from an Irishman, and a good deal of what he had seen for himself in Ireland in the 1830s and 1840s, was ideally to suit his fictional purposes when he came to compose *Barry Lyndon*, his first substantial work of fiction, in October 1843. The idea of taking an autobiographical narrator, whom readers are led to distrust from the very beginning, clearly appealed to him. It also signals the real originality of the novel. Some fifty years later an Irish writer was to shock many readers by noting: 'A short primer, "When to Lie and How", if brought out in an attractive and not too expensive a form, would no doubt command a large sale, and would prove of real practical service to many earnest and deep-thinking people . . . The only form of lying that is absolutely beyond reproach is lying for its own sake, and the highest development of this is . . . Lying in Art.'

Oscar Wilde's awareness that 'the telling of beautiful untrue things, is the proper aim of Art' has proved prophetic of much twentieth-century aesthetic and critical theory. Though he used different aesthetic terminology, it was an awareness that Thackeray essentially shared. In his earliest published articles and reviews he had attempted to hide behind various personae; that of James Yellowplush (a retired footman) or Michael Angelo Titmarsh (a painter and would-be man of the world) or George Savage Fitz-Boodle (a gentlemanly connoisseur of food, cards, women, snobbery and gossip). When it first appeared in *Fraser's Magazine* in 1844 *Barry Lyndon* purported to be edited by this same G. S. Fitz-Boodle. Although it is clearly told from the point of view of a narrator who exhibits his distortion, exaggeration and egotism, Fitz-Boodle makes us further aware of the artifice by puncturing the narrative with deflating comments or footnotes which become an integral part of the artifice. When Thackeray later cut out many of Fitz-Boodle's annotations to Barry's supposed memoirs he seems to have aspired to tidy up his narrative in the interests of verisimilitude; in many important ways he deprived it of its original ramifications. Just as the changing names of the predominant narrator (Redmond Barry, Barry of Barry-ogue, Captain Barry, Redmond de Balibari, Barry Lyndon) suggest something of his artificiality and unreliability, so the aspersions, asides and attempts at moralizing interposed by an 'editor' remind us that we are reading fiction, a glorious example of lying for its own sake.

The essence of Barry Lyndon's own narrative lies in the fact that he rarely seeks to distinguish between fact and fiction, or between truth and untruth. Late in his memoirs he claims:

> I am of the old school, was always a free liver and speaker and, at least, if I did and said what I liked, was not so bad as many a canting scoundrel I know of who covers his foibles and sins, unsuspected, with a mask of holiness. (Chapter XIX)

Barry is referring to his habit of swearing, but in so doing he is also pleading his frankness of expression. He may be addicted to lying, as he is to swearing, but only rarely is he aware that he can 'ward off the devices of my enemies by an artifice which was not, perhaps, strictly justifiable'. He periodically reminds us that, in his view of himself, he is no hypocrite, that he speaks the truth, and that he has an open nature. He purports to be writing his confessional memoirs as an old and decaying man in the Fleet Prison, but he looks back not with an acquired sadness, or with a desperate need to justify himself, but with the confident assertion that he always was the centre of attention and that he remains so in holding a reader's attention through his narrative. At the beginning of Chapter X he announces:

> I have gout, rheumatism, gravel, and a disordered liver. I have two or three wounds in my body, which break out every now and then, and give me intolerable pain, and a hundred more signs of breaking up. Such are the effects of time, illness and free-living upon one of the strongest constitutions and finest forms the world ever saw. Ah! I suffered from none of these ills in the year '66, when there was no man in Europe more gay in spirits, more splendid in personal accomplishment, than young Redmond Barry.

Rather than dwell on present ills he turns easily to the recall of past triumphs; his decay merely serves to point his former (supposed) splendour. One wonders whether Barry is actually conscious that he has failed. His last words concerning himself proclaim that his ultimate 'miserable existence' is quite unworthy of 'the famous and fashionable Barry Lyndon', for to himself he remains the illusion of success that he constantly interposes between the reader and any possible alternative view of things.

A clue to this swaggering, confident braggadocio can perhaps be found in the delight which Barry's creator found in a popular chap-book on a rainy evening at Galway. Although Thackeray got his idea for the novel's plot a year earlier, his Irish visit and his Irish reading-matter in 1842 seem to have suggested the manner of actually telling the story. The long account of the memoirs of an eighteenth-century highwayman in Chapter XV of *The Irish Sketch Book* indicate not only the diversion and delight Thackeray found on a particular evening but also the rediscovery of a manner of story-telling which served to objectify his own.

> It is a comfort . . . to come on occasions on some of the good old stories and biographies. These books were evidently written before the useful had attained its present detestable popularity. There is nothing useful *here*, that's certain: and a man will be puzzled to

> extract a precise moral out of the adventures of Mr. James Freeny . . . But are we to reject all things that have not a moral tacked to them? . . . Honest Freeny's adventures . . . if they have a moral, have that dubious one which the poet admits may be elicited from a rose; and which every man may select according to his mind. And surely this is a far better and more comfortable system of moralizing than that in the fable-books, where you are obliged to accept the story with the inevitable moral corollary, that *will* stick close to it.

This has a positively Wildean ring, but Thackeray is referring backwards in literary history, not projecting an idea forwards. Freeny's frank, confident, off-hand account of himself seems distinct from the popular criminal literature of the 1840s, however, and Thackeray notes the real divide between modern 'Newgate' novelists like Ainsworth and Bulwer, and a healthier eighteenth-century norm. 'The best part of worthy Freeny's tale', he remarks, 'is the noble *naïveté* and simplicity of the hero as he recounts his own adventures; and the utter unconsciousness that he is narrating anything wonderful.' Captain Freeny may be a criminal as society judges but his instinctive gift for telling his own story frees him of moral inhibition and social censure. His story has 'that simplicity which is beyond the reach of all except the very highest art; and it is not high art certainly that Mr. Freeny can be said to possess'. In this sense art frees itself of the restrictions of moralizing; art makes its own patterns, defines its own rules and constructive principles, and asks the reader, and not the narrative, to supply a moral (if he chooses) 'according to his mind'. As Thackeray had earlier protested in his *Catherine* (1839), novels like Ainsworth's *Rookwood* and Bulwer's *Paul Clifford* had merely romanticized the criminal; the true end of fiction lay not in pointing morals but in the art of representing a subject, whether sordid or pleasing.

The references back to earlier models in Thackeray's account of his reading of Captain Freeny's memoirs suggest the degree to which he was relating this popular chap-book to the work of his favourite novelist, Henry Fielding. He had published an essay proclaiming his long-standing admiration for Fielding in *The Times* in September 1840. In this essay, despite praise for the eighteenth-century novelist's 'benevolence, practical wisdom, and generous sympathy with mankind', Thackeray reveals himself particularly drawn to *The History of the Life of the Late Jonathan Wild the Great*, an ironic study not only of criminality but also of society's definition of the terms 'greatness' and 'heroism'. This comparatively short novel is hailed as 'great comic epic', one which gave 'a more curious picture of the manners of those times than any recognized history of them'. History and biography are drawn together and the theme is broadened out from its starting point, Jonathan Wild the thief, to scathing reflections on the career of the Prime Minister, Sir Robert Walpole, and to general conclusions concerning the definition of a 'great man'. In the concluding chapter of his story Fielding notes of the character of his ostensible hero:

> Jonathan Wild had every qualification necessary to form a great man. As his most powerful and predominant passion was ambition, so nature had, with consummate propriety, adapted all his faculties to the attaining those glorious ends to which this passion directed him. He was extremely ingenious in inventing designs, artful in contriving the means to accomplish his purposes, and resolute in executing them: for as the most exquisite cunning and most undaunted boldness qualified him for any undertaking, so was he not restrained by any of those weaknesses which disappoint the views of mean and vulgar souls, and which are comprehended in one general term of honesty, which is a corruption of HONOSTY, a word derived from what the Greeks call an ass.

The definition works negatively, as do many of Thackeray's, and in so doing it obliges a reader to question the contending values of terms like ambition, power, intelligence, boldness and honesty. Fielding's larger point lies in his questioning why a Caesar or an Alexander are held up to be heroes while a Wild is condemned as a criminal. Wild's vices, like Captain Freeny's, or even Barry Lyndon's, when seen in another perspective, can be viewed as socially desirable virtues.

Thackeray's profound sympathy with Fielding can chiefly be accounted for by noting the parallels between their mutual distrust of moralizing fiction and of conventional attitudes to heroism. The concept of writing 'a novel without a hero' does not, therefore, begin with *Vanity Fair*. There is, however, a strong element in Thackeray's delight in his predecessor which can be related to his distinct taste for the literature and culture of the eighteenth century in general. It would be a mistake to assume, as some critics have done, that his sympathy was unequivocal or that it suggests a nostalgia for a more vivid age than his own. Thackeray cannot be explained away as an 'uneasy Victorian'. Although his excursions into Georgian settings for his novels have been accused of self-indulgence, even of sentimentality, such accusations, especially when directed against the masterly *Henry Esmond*, would seem to stem from a basic misunderstanding of the nature of Thackeray's art. Eighteenth-century history gave him scope to show off his wide and magpie reading, but the use of an historic period in which to set a story also gave him a considerable degree of detachment. In a review of the first Duchess of Marlborough's *Private Correspondence* published in January 1838 he employed the image of the Victorian theatre to suggest his distrust of what others held to be historical judgements:

> The dignity of history sadly diminishes as we grow better acquainted with the materials which compose it. In our orthodox history-books the characters move on as a gaudy playhouse procession, a glittering pageant of kings and warriors, and stately ladies, majestically appearing and passing away. Only he who sits very near to the stage can discover of what stuff the spectacle is made. The kings are poor creatures, taken from the dregs of the company; the noble knights are dirty dwarfs in tin foil; the fair ladies are painted hags with cracked feathers and soiled trains. One wonders how gas and distance could ever have rendered them so bewitching.

It is distance and not proximity which renders history bewitching and the illusion is only broken by the kind of intimate acquaintance which sees beyond a mere impression of dignity, or majesty, or heroism. When Thackeray praises Fielding for suggesting 'a more curious picture of the manners of the eighteenth century than any recognized history' he is in part asserting his own predilection for a fiction without illusions. In his own novels set in the past Thackeray sets himself up as an historian who questions received judgement; the writing of history is not an attempt to interpret the past, it is simply a creation of an impression of what the past was like, a reflection of its manners, tastes and foibles. As G. S. Fitz-Boodle concludes in *Barry Lyndon*, 'it is as right to look at a beauty as at a hunchback; and, if to look, to describe too'. If Thackeray's stories always keep us alert to the fact of their fictionality, his historical stories forcibly remind us that history is the greatest lie of all.

It is this ideal of an illusionless but intimate acquaintance with an age which determines Thackeray's choice of first-person narrator in *Barry Lyndon*. The autobiographical narrator was scarcely a discovery of the early Victorians but it was to prove a fictional device of considerable vogue in the 1840s and 1850s, and one which suited Thackeray's very distinctive ends in his concept of historical fiction. *Barry Lyndon* did not please readers of 1844. *Jane Eyre* of 1847 (which does not, of course, have an historical setting) did very much please its first readers and it would seem to have ushered in a line of related first-person narratives, most significantly *The Tenant of Wildfell Hall* (1848), *David Copperfield* (1849–50), *The History of Henry Esmond* (1852), *Bleak House* (1852–3) and *Villette* (1853). Although it stands apart from this group of novels, *Barry Lyndon* raises critical questions which can be usefully applied to all of them. It conspicuously suggests the degree to which a reader ought to distrust any teller of any tale, and especially a teller who purports both to tell the truth and to justify him- or herself. Rather than ask us simply to distinguish between a narrator whom we can loosely call 'reliable', and one we can type as 'unreliable', Thackeray's story makes us look directly at the shifting levels of meaning in the narrative itself. Perhaps because of its disconcerting narrative tone, *Barry Lyndon* has vexed readers accustomed to steady, and seemingly trustworthy, narrative voices. In his introduction to the 1908 edition of the novel, for example, George Saintsbury complained of Thackeray's 'hampering himself enormously' by adopting an autobiographical form for Barry's life-story. In contrast to *Jonathan Wild* the novelist seemed to have forgotten that he was 'in Barry rather too often' where Fielding kept his cue 'of sardonic showman infallibly and impartially towards every puppet on the stage'. Saintsbury's distinction between a 'detached' narrator and an 'involved' one is perhaps too simple for later twentieth-century critical tastes, but it does lead him on to demand the kind of narrative consistency which adherents of exact verisimilitude continue to admire. He is disturbed, for example, by the supposedly 'inconsistent' moralizing about the ethics of war which pepper Barry's account of his military service during the Seven Years' War. Thackeray, however, would seem to have been very conscious of the unsteadiness of his narrator's perceptions and to have purposefully exploited them; the story's consistency lies not in a sustained use of irony or innuendo, but in a reader's awareness of its artifice. In using his narrator to bring us into a supposedly intimate relationship with the past, he also alerts us to the very uncertainty of our relationship to the narrator himself.

The opening paragraphs of the novel make this clear. The story opens with a generalization, a truth which Barry holds to be universally acknowledged: 'Since the days of Adam, there has been hardly a mischief done in this world but a woman has been at the bottom of it.' The odd syntax presumably represents an Irishism, but once we have grasped what the sentence implies we realize its banality. It is a generalization which, beyond the myth of Adam and Eve, can scarcely be supported (though some of Chaucer's anti-feminists made the attempt). Returning to the sentence once we have completed the whole story it is evident that Barry has based his assumption on the way in which he interprets his own experience, but even then a reader knows that it offers only a partial truth. The proposition is not ironic; it is merely a statement which we must immediately qualify, and, in doing so, must recognize as having alerted us to a basic 'untrustworthiness'. By the time we move on to the second sentence, with its claims to an ancient lineage and the banally valid idea that women 'have played a mighty part with the destinies of our race', we are well aware that we must probe the language for its sense. When Barry proceeds with an 'I presume', moves on to assert that he is 'a man of the world', and then dismisses other 'pretenders' while assuming his own right to a spurious Irish crown, we are capable of appreciating how empty is the notion of being 'compelled' by 'truth'. Pretension and assumption, common enough traits of any autobiographer, are rendered for what they are.

'The marvel of the book', Anthony Trollope noted in his short study of Thackeray, 'is not so much that the hero should evidently think well of himself, as that the author should tell his story as to appear to be altogether on the hero's side.' Trollope admitted to knowing nothing equal to the sustained 'assumed tone' of *Barry Lyndon*, but he was confining his observations to novels and not extending them into the realm of memoirs and autobiographies. Thackeray has found the right style for Barry and, despite Fitz-Boodle's occasional interpolated observations, has allowed Barry to tell his own story. It is probable that a further stimulus to this choice of an autobiographical narrator came from the spate of letters, journals and memoirs published in the opening years of the nineteenth century, a phenomenon which had already inspired Thomas Carlyle to redefine the nature of a purely historical narrative. Rather than bring many voices to bear on the telling of a story, however, Thackeray takes a single story-teller and a single point of view, and then qualifies both by the ruse of Fitz-Boodle's editing and by a reader's likely alertness to the untrustworthiness of Barry's mode of self-expression. The decision to take a first-person narrator cannot be put down exclusively to the chance reading of Captain Freeny's Memoirs; it is more likely to have been formed gradually with Thackeray's acquaintance with the relatively new fashion for first-person accounts of historical events. He is likely to have known, for example, the diary of John Evelyn, first published in 1818, and that of Samuel Pepys, printed in response to the success of Evelyn's in 1825. We can also be reasonably confident that Thackeray drew substantially on memoirs with a more recent historical setting for details of *Barry Lyndon*. Although he had spent several months at Weimar in 1830–1, he seems to have found useful information concerning the petty courts of eighteenth-century Germany in two volumes in particular. 'The Tragical History of the Princess of X——', which takes up Chapters XI and XII of the novel, is largely derived from Baron de la Mothe-Langon's *L'Empire, ou dix ans sous Napoléon* (1836) which Thackeray dismissed as 'a silly book' when he read it in Paris in January 1844 just before he began work on his story. As he later recommends the memoirs of Frederick the Great's sister, the Margravine of Bayreuth, to 'those who are curious about European Court history of the last age' one can assume that he knew the English edition first published in London in 1812. Details of Barry's career as a professional gambler are almost certainly related to the celebrated memoirs of Casanova which had appeared in French at Leipzig between 1826 and 1838, while other aspects of the somewhat *risqué* aristocratic world in which Casanova moved may come from the supposed (and scandalous) *Mémoires* of the duc de Richelieu (Paris, 1790–1). Thackeray's already extensive knowledge of English life in the period was possibly supplemented by reference to the four volumes of the Letters of Pitt the Elder (whose *Life* had been written by the novelist's uncle) (London, 1840) and by the steadily advancing publication of the Letters of the greatest correspondent of the age, Horace Walpole (1820, 1833, 1840, 1843–4).

It was Horace Walpole who in November 1786 had recorded that 'the town was ringing about . . . Countess Strathmore and the enormous barbarities of her husband.' The *cause célèbre* of this same Countess and her barbarous husband gave Thackeray one further crucial strand to his story. During a visit to his friend John Bowes Bowes at Streatlam Castle, Co. Durham, in the summer of 1841, the novelist 'found materials (rather a character) for a story' that he was sure would amuse readers of *Fraser's Magazine*. John Bowes Bowes was an illegitimate descendant of one Andrew Robinson Bowes, alias Stoney-Bowes, whose highly disreputable career had been chronicled in 1810 by Jesse Foot, a career which very obviously parallels that of Redmond Barry, alias Barry Lyndon. The eighteenth-century Bowes had been born Andrew Robinson Stoney of Cold Pig Hill, Co. Durham, and King's Co., Ireland, in 1745. By 1763 he had risen to the rank of lieutenant in the 13th Regiment of Foot, due to the influence of his relatives, and had wooed, and married, an ugly Newcastle heiress. According to Jesse Foot, he proved a subtly cruel husband, knowing 'secret ways of provoking her before company'. Following this first wife's timely death, Stoney moved to London where he frequented raffish, aristocratic gambling houses and where he first noticed the eligible young widow of the ninth Earl of Strathmore, Mary Bowes. The Countess, a noted blue-stocking, was also possessed of a substantial personal fortune, and Stoney, already a practised ladies' man, seized the opportunity of pursuing her. After discountenancing his rivals, and skilfully ingratiating himself with the Countess, Stoney's master-stroke was to get himself wounded in a duel in defence of the lady's honour. Four days after the duel the couple were married and Stoney adopted the ancestral name of Bowes. Despite his attempts at respectability (Bowes was MP for Newcastle 1780–4) the marriage rapidly deteriorated and the Countess's fortune was depleted by the demands of her husband's fast life. Bowes assaulted his wife both verbally and physically, obliging her to escape from him in 1785 and to start legal proceedings against him. In reply Stoney-Bowes forcibly abducted his wife and imprisoned her on their estates in the north. The Countess managed to escape for a second time and promptly had her husband arrested for the crime of abduction. Stoney-Bowes ended his life in the King's Bench Prison in 1810.

The resemblances to the story of the rise and fall of Barry Lyndon are obvious, but Stoney-Bowes's career did not provide Thackeray with all the essentials for his novel. Both men rise from the Irish petty gentry to marry a titled heiress and both end outwitted by their wives. Unlike Stoney-Bowes, however, Barry has a distinctive professional life before his marriage. In its original form in *Fraser's Magazine* the story had a subtle title that Thackeray was obliged to abandon, through no fault of his own, when he revised the book in 1856. 'The Luck of Barry Lyndon', as Thackeray first called his story, expresses both halves of Barry's career—his life as a soldier and gambler, and his life as a gentleman and debtor. The idea of 'luck' is of course crucial to Thackeray's purpose in telling the tale, for luck, fortune and fate are as open to question as concepts as is the idea of heroism. The 'lucky man', like the 'hero', is someone the world has judged as successful; if we shift the terms by which we define, both concepts collapse. The term 'luck' also usefully covers Barry's decided penchant for gambling, an element in the story which is not only confined to his continental career in the company of the Chevalier de Balibari as any acquaintance with the nature of the clubs Barry frequents in London or Dublin suggests. For Barry himself, however, 'luck' seems to mean the games that fate plays with him. The titles of the novel's chapters demonstrate this; there are 'runs of luck' in Chapter X; 'luck' goes against him in Chapter XI; he attains 'the height of his (seeming) Good Fortune' in Chapter XVI and the same fortune 'begins to waver' in Chapter XVIII. When Barry's own narrative closes in Chapter XIX, Fitz-Boodle very properly describes him as an 'ingenious author', a careful but indirect comment on this very idea of luck and fortune. Though Barry Lyndon has sought to excuse his career by means of the terminology of gambling and superstition, Fitz-Boodle's comment permits us to sense that, like the narrative, ingenuity explains more than does chance. Barry has appeared very much as a maker of events rather than a victim of them; when he is a victim, as in his affairs with women, he tends to be caught out by the ingenuity of others (Captain Quin and Nora, Lord George Poynings and Lady Lyndon). The idea of gambling as a systematic calculation (which can, of course, involve cheating), or as a battle of wits, is central to the story. Chance may load the dice, as may an unscrupulous gambler, but that is what an experienced player like Barry, or Thackeray himself, has to take into consideration. Indeed, a mixture of the considered, the calculated and the artful with the arbitrary, the unconscious, and the casual is what gives the narrative much of its piquancy. We are in part alerted to the fact by Barry's own declarations of his 'too easy, generous and careless nature' and its seeming opposite in his evident enough skill in underhandedness and manipulation. The Stoney-Bowes story gave Thackeray a story with a middle and an end; Barry's character, with its penchant for the lie, and for an art, part calculated, part instinctive, gave the novelist his starting point.

A further vital element which Thackeray substantially added to the Stoney-Bowes plot was Barry's eventful career as a soldier. Though both Barry and his original serve in Regiments of Foot, Thackeray's character is perforce obliged to remain a private soldier unblessed with promotion through the influence of relatives. Thus the point of view in regard to the Seven Years' War is very much that of a man with very little influence over the great events he witnesses. Nevertheless, the real fortunes of his war-service are yet again to be largely of his own making. In the celebrated opening to Chapter XXX of *Vanity Fair* Thackeray eschewed the claim to rank among the military novelists. He would seem, in that famous declaration, to be disassociating himself from the manner of the once popular Irish novelist, Charles Lever, whose novels of military life had a particular currency in the 1840s. In *Barry Lyndon*, however, Thackeray seems to be challenging Lever at his own game rather than claiming his place among the non-combatants. Thackeray had met Lever in Dublin in May 1842; he had reviewed his novels favourably, and, despite a notorious spoof of one of them in *Punch*, managed to maintain an amicable relationship with his fellow-writer. It is evident, though, that Thackeray deeply distrusted Lever's tendency to romanticize war. It is probable that original readers of *Barry Lyndon* would have recognized the butt of the somewhat anachronistic, but particularly disarming, declaration of Barry's in Chapter IV:

> Were these memoirs not characterized by truth, and did I deign to utter a single word for which my own personal experience did not give me the fullest authority, I might easily make myself the hero of some strange and popular adventures, and, after the fashion of novel-writers, introduce my readers to the great characters of this remarkable time. These persons (I mean the romance-writers), if they take a drummer or a dustman for a hero, somehow manage to bring him into contact with the greatest lords and most notorious personages of the empire, and I warrant me there's not one of them but, in describing the battle of Minden, would manage to bring

Prince Ferdinand, and my Lord George Sackville, and my Lord Granby into presence.

All Barry manages to see of the battle of Minden, apart from his fellow private soldiers and the enemy attack, is his colonel 'and a couple of orderly officers riding by in the smoke'. Barry kills, witnesses killing and loses his friend and patron Captain Fagan, but that, 'except from books', is all that he actually knows of the conflict. When later, disguised as an officer, he claims to be taking dispatches to a General Rolls, he names a non-existent general. Yet again the nature of Thackeray's narrative alerts us to another way of seeing and another way of recording, and in this sense Barry's viewpoint is clearly one with which the novelist is in full sympathy. Throughout his military career Barry sees little that could be classed as heroic, and no one who could be described as a hero. Although he profusely name-drops in his social progress later in the novel, Barry the soldier seems to notice no one who merits his attention. Even Frederick the Great, whose reputation as 'the Protestant Hero' even the narrator disputes, is only glimpsed once in the novel, as Barry, heavily disguised, leaves Berlin and military service for ever.

Some critics of the novel, most notably those who echo George Saintsbury's preference for psychological consistency, find Barry's brief meditations on the folly of war out of key with his habitual nonchalance and symptomatic of Thackeray's authorial prompting. They forget that Barry has little to boast of in his military career, and a great deal, as a deserter from both the British and the Prussian service, to be wary of. Barry sees war as inglorious, but it is clear that he too has acted ingloriously. Barry may not be the person to 'moralize on the Seven Years' War' but it is surely not inconsistent that he should do so. The offending passage most often cited is generally that with which Chapter IV closes. Having criticized 'the fashion of novel-writers' Barry somewhat ambiguously moves from a succinct account of his actions in battle to a series of scathing observations on the kings and generals who make 'men nursed in poverty . . . take pride in deeds of blood'. In a final anecdote Barry describes the burning of the house of an old woman by the soldiers she had earlier succoured. The anecdote is intended to make his point that men brutalized into being soldiers act brutally. What is significant though is that Barry refers to the perpetrators of the deed as 'some of us', implying that he numbers himself amongst these same brutes. He offers no excuses, merely notes the mindless cruelty without seeing any incongruity in his observation. A further key to this passage is the off-hand description of his killing a French officer and a young ensign in the battle and his addition of the fact that he has robbed the boy's dead body:

> I hate bragging, but I cannot help saying that I made a very close acquaintance with the colonel of the Cravates, for I drove my bayonet into his body, and finished off a poor little ensign, so young, slender, and small, that a blow from my pig-tail would have dispatched him, I think, in place of the butt of my musket, with which I clubbed him down. I killed, besides, four more officers and men, and in the poor ensign's pocket found a purse of fourteen louis-d'or, and a silver box of sugar-plums, of which the former present was very agreeable to me. If people would tell their stories of battle in this simple way, I think the cause of truth would not suffer by it.

There is nothing 'out of character' here just as there is really nothing awkward about Henry Esmond's later 'wearisomely unspecific' (as John Carey so intolerantly puts it) accounts of *his* battles. In both cases Thackeray has carefully allowed his narrators a characteristic perception of how they see war. Esmond is matter-of-fact, flat but exact; Barry's backward glance at brutality, and his frank admission that he was brutalized himself, serve to suggest how little he is inclined to dwell on things and thereafter to apply moral strictures. Perhaps too the momentary tenderness as he notes the boy's slender build before clubbing him to death, and his delicacy in remembering the sugar-plums before robbing the corpse of its louis-d'or, disconcert us by the very fact of their suggestion that the narrator is capable of fine feeling.

Barry truly is stirred by the affections. He loves women romantically and he loves his son, Bryan, as an indulgent parent, but his feelings, however deeply they run, rarely seem to ruffle the impression we have of his ability to live for the moment. He always bounces back from pain, or sentiment, or a check, to an egotistic sense of the rightness of his 'luck' in his relationships. Bryan's death-bed is described with a minimum of sentimentality, and the reconciliation of husband and wife which succeeds it is as brief as it suits Barry to be:

> At last, after two days, he died. There he lay, the hope of my family, the pride of my manhood, the link which had kept me and my Lady Lyndon together. 'O Redmond,' said she, kneeling by the sweet child's body, 'do do let us listen to the truth out of his blessed mouth, and do you amend your life, and treat your poor, loving, fond wife as her dying child bade you.' And I said I would; but there are promises which it is out of a man's power to keep, especially with such a woman as her. But we drew together after that sad event, and we were for several months better friends.

In some ways this glum comment typifies the narrator's refusal to dwell on pain or misfortune and his avoidance of moralization. There is no self-pity, no tender retrospect, no agony of recall, and very little sense of self-awareness.

In her introduction to her father's novel Anne Thackeray notes of *Barry Lyndon* that it is 'scarcely a book to *like*, but one to admire and to wonder at for its consummate power and mastery'. She was clearly reflecting her father's earlier suggestion that she ought not to read the story because she would not like it. Since Anne Thackeray's day the fortunes of *Barry Lyndon* have swung between the neglect to which its author in part condemned it and an excessive admiration which has often emanated from critics who have failed to respond fully to Thackeray's other books. As we gradually begin to reassess the range and variety of his *œuvre*, this his first sustained comic masterpiece may well seem distinct from what came after it. *Barry Lyndon* could scarcely be called an apprentice work, but through it Thackeray seems to have discovered the narrative control which was to produce those two very different masterpieces of his maturity, the hero-less *Vanity Fair* and the unheroic, confessional *History of Henry Esmond*.

NOTE ON THE TEXT

THE first version of the novel, originally entitled *The Luck of Barry Lyndon: A Romance of the Last Century. By Fitz-Boodle*, appeared serially in *Fraser's Magazine* between January and December 1844. There was, however, no monthly number for October 1844 probably as a result of the strains imposed upon author and publisher alike by Thackeray's absence on his voyage around the eastern Mediterranean. Thackeray considerably revised the story in 1856 for publication in Vol. III of his *Miscellanies: Prose and Verse*. On its republication the story was re-entitled *The Memoirs of Barry Lyndon Esq., of the Kingdom of Ireland*. A separate one-volume edition, with an identical text, appeared in the same year. The present text is based on that prepared by George Saintsbury for the Oxford University Press in 1908, to form Vol. VI of *The Oxford Thackeray*. Saintsbury reinstated passages cut from the 1844 text by placing them in square brackets, but retained the most significant of Thackeray's revisions, the amalgamation of the first two of the original chapters and the dropping of the descriptions 'Part I' for Chapters I-XVII and 'Part II' for the last three chapters (now Chapters I-XVI and Chapters XVII-XIX respectively). Saintsbury also retained the chapter titles either altered or added by Thackeray in 1856. The original chapter divisions, and their titles, are given in the Appendix. Saintsbury's sometimes regrettable editorial emendations to Thackeray's eighteenth-century spellings have also been retained. The text of the 1844 edition is reprinted in Martin J. Anisman's *The Luck of Barry Lyndon: A Critical Edition* (New York University Press, New York, 1970).

Asterisks in the text of this edition refer to Andrew Sanders's explanatory notes, printed at the end of the book. The numbered footnotes are either Thackeray's own or Saintsbury's.

SELECT BIBLIOGRAPHY

The Luck of Barry Lyndon was first published serially in *Fraser's Magazine* in 1844. A pirated reprint of this version appeared in New York in 1853, published by D. Appleton & Co. The revised *The Memoirs of Barry Lyndon* formed part of Vol. III of Thackeray's *Miscellanies* which was published in four volumes by Bradbury & Evans in London in 1856. It was reissued in 1862 and 1865. A separate edition of the revised text also appeared in 1856 but it is difficult to determine whether or not it preceded the publication of the *Miscellanies*. *The Memoirs of Barry Lyndon* was translated into French in 1857 and went into a second edition in 1859. The most notable reprints of the revised text are those which form part of the collected editions of Thackeray's *Works* listed below. Martin J. Anisman's critical edition of *The Luck of Barry Lyndon* (New York, 1970) restores the *Fraser's Magazine* text and contains some useful bibliographical information but its annotation is otherwise haphazard and sometimes ill-informed.

COLLECTED EDITIONS: The most valuable collected editions of Thackeray's *Works* are the *Biographical Edition* with introductions by the novelist's daughter Anne Ritchie, 13 vols. (Smith, Elder & Co. 1898–9): *The Memoirs of Barry Lyndon* (with four illustrations by J. E. Millais) forms part of vol. IV; the *Oxford Thackeray*, ed. George Saintsbury, 17 vols. (Oxford University Press, 1908): *The Memoirs of Barry Lyndon* (with Thackeray's later excisions restored) forms part of vol. VI; the *Centenary Biographical Edition* with revised introductions by Anne Thackeray Ritchie, 26 vols. (John Murray, 1910–11): *The Memoirs of Barry Lyndon* forms part of vol. VII.

BIBLIOGRAPHY: 'Lewis Melville's' (L. S. Benjamin's) bibliography of Thackeray's works in his *William Makepeace Thackeray* (2 vols., 1910) remains useful. See also Lionel Stevenson in the *New Cambridge Bibliography of English Literature*, vol. 3, ed. George Watson (Cambridge, 1969); Arthur Pollard in *The English Novel: Select Bibliographical Guides*, ed. A. E. Dyson (Oxford, 1974); Lionel Stevenson in

Victorian Fiction: A Guide to Research, ed. Lionel Stevenson (New York, 1964); Robert A. Colby in *Victorian Fiction: A Second Guide to Research*, ed. George H. Ford (New York, 1978); Dudley Flamm, *Thackeray's Critics: An Annotated Bibliography of British and American Criticism 1836–1901*; John Charles Olmsted, *Thackeray and his Twentieth-Century Critics: An Annotated Bibliography 1900–1975* (New York, 1977).

BIOGRAPHY AND CRITICISM: The primary and invaluable source remains Gordon N. Ray's *The Letters and Private Papers of William Makepeace Thackeray*, 4 vols. (Oxford, 1945–6). Anne Thackeray Ritchie's biographical introductions to her father's *Works* (1898–9, amplified 1910–11) also provide much essential material. Two early biographies retain some interest; 'Lewis Melville's' (L. S. Benjamin's) *William Makepeace Thackeray*, 2 vols. (1899) a rewritten version of which was published in 1910; Herman Merivale and Frank T. Marzials, Life of *W. M. Thackeray* (1891). All earlier biographies were superseded by the work of Gordon N. Ray. *The Buried Life: A Study of the Relation between Thackeray's Fiction and his Personal History* (Oxford, 1952) was a prelude to his great two-volume biography, *Thackeray: The Uses of Adversity 1811–1846* (Oxford, 1955) and *Thackeray: The Age of Wisdom 1847–1863* (Oxford, 1958). Philip Collins's *Thackeray: Interviews and Recollections*, 2 vols. (London, 1983) most usefully assembles a wide range of personal recollections of the novelist. John Sutherland is helpful on Thackeray's working methods in his *Thackeray at Work* (London, 1974).

The best Victorian criticism of *Barry Lyndon* can be found in Anthony Trollope's vigorous study *Thackeray*, published in the 'English Men of Letters Series' in 1879. *Thackeray: The Critical Heritage*, eds. Geoffrey Tillotson and Donald Hawes (London, 1968) reprints James Fitzjames Stephen's review of the novel of 1856. Modern studies include Geoffrey Tillotson, *Thackeray the Novelist* (Cambridge, 1954); Barbara Hardy, *The Exposure of Luxury: Radical Themes in Thackeray* (London, 1972); and John Carey, *Thackeray: Prodigal Genius* (London, 1977), a wayward study which should be read with discrimination. The best book on the literary background to *Barry Lyndon* remains Kathleen Tillotson's *Novels of the Eighteen-Forties* (Oxford, 1954).

Articles include: Robert A. Colby, '*Barry Lyndon* and the Irish Hero', *XIXth Century Fiction*, xxi (September 1966); David Parker, 'Thackeray's *Barry Lyndon*', *Ariel* vi, no. 4 (October 1975).

A film of *Barry Lyndon* was directed by Stanley Kubrick (GB, 1975).

A CHRONOLOGY OF WILLIAM MAKEPEACE THACKERAY

1811 (18 July) William Makepeace Thackeray, only son of Richmond Thackeray and Anne Becher, born at Calcutta

1815 (13 September) Death of Richmond Thackeray

1817 (15 June) Thackeray arrives in England from India. Sent to school in Southampton. Mrs. Richmond Thackeray marries Captain Henry Carmichael-Smyth in India

1819 At school in Chiswick. Mother and step-father return to England

1822–8 At Charterhouse School, London

1829 Matriculates at Trinity College, Cambridge. Visits Paris in long vacation

1830 Leaves Cambridge, without a degree, after heavy gambling losses

1830–1 In Germany, chiefly at Weimar, July–March

1831 (3 June) Admitted to Middle Temple

1832–6 Extended periods of residence at Paris, studying art and contributing to journals (including, from May 1834, *Fraser's Magazine*)

1836 (20 August) Marries Isabella Shawe at the British Embassy at Paris

1837 Settles in London at 18 Albion Street. Birth of daughter, Anne Isabella. *The Yellowplush Correspondence* appears in *Fraser's Magazine* (November 1837–August 1838)

1838 Birth of second daughter, Jane

1839 Death of Jane Thackeray. *Catherine: A Story* published in *Fraser's* (May 1839–February 1840)

1840 Birth of Harriet Marian Thackeray (later Mrs. Leslie Stephen). *A Shabby Genteel Story* published in *Fraser's* (June–October). Publishes *The Paris Sketch Book* (July). His wife's insanity revealed after an attempt to drown herself *en route* from London to Cork (September)

1841 *The Second Funeral of Napoleon* (January). Wife entrusted to a private nurse. Visits John Bowes in Co. Durham and conceives first notion for *Barry Lyndon* (June–July). *The Great Hoggarty Diamond* published in *Fraser's* (September–December)

1842 Wife placed in asylum at Chaillot near Paris. Moves to 13 Great Coram Street. First contribution to *Punch* (June). Visits Ireland (July–November)

1843 Publication of *The Irish Sketch Book* (May). Takes rooms at 27 Jermyn Street

1844 First instalment of *The Luck of Barry Lyndon* in *Fraser's Magazine* (January). Leaves Southampton for Mediterranean and Near Eastern Tour (22 August). Final instalment of *Barry Lyndon* (December)

1845 Returns to London from Rome (February). Moves to 88 St. James's Street. Wife placed in care at Camberwell

1846 *Notes of a Journey from Cornhill to Grand Cairo* published (January). First instalment of *The Book of Snobs* in *Punch* (March). Moves to 13 Young Street, Kensington (June). Publishes first Christmas Book, *Mrs. Perkins's Ball* (December)

1847 First number of *Vanity Fair* (January). Final instalment of *The Book of Snobs* (February). *Our Street* (December)

1848 *Vanity Fair* completed (June). Travels on Continent (July–August). Begins *Pendennis* (3 August) the first number of which appears in November. *Dr. Birch and his Young Friends* (December)

1849 Visits Paris (January–February, August–September). Serious illness disrupts publication of *Pendennis* (October–December). *Rebecca and Rowena* (December)

1850 *Pendennis* completed (November). *The Kickleburys on the Rhine* (December)

1851 Lectures on *The English Humorists* in London (May–July). Begins *Esmond* (August). Resigns from *Punch* (December)

1852 Completes *Esmond* (May). *The History of Henry Esmond* published in 3 vols (October). Leaves Liverpool for Boston (October). Lectures in New York (November–December)

1853 Lectures in eastern United States on *English Humorists* (January–April). Returns to London and visits Paris (May–July). Visits Germany and Switzerland (July–August). Begins *The Newcomes* (9 July). First number of *The Newcomes* published (October). Travels to Rome (November)

1854	Ill at Rome (January–February). Begins *The Rose and the Ring* (February). Moves to 36 Onslow Square, Brompton. *The Rose and the Ring* published (December)
1855	*The Newcomes* finished (June, last monthly number August). Sails from Liverpool to Boston (October). Lectures in United States on *The Four Georges*
1856	Lectures in United States (January–April). Arrives in London (May). Begins *The Virginians* which he shortly abandons (July). Visits Paris. Lectures in Scotland and north of England (November–December)
1857	Lectures in England and Scotland (January–May). Stands unsuccessfully as Independent Liberal in parliamentary election for the City of Oxford (July). First number of *The Virginians* (November)
1858	The 'Garrick Club Affair' provoked by an article by Edmund Yates. Alienation from Dickens (June–July)
1859	Accepts editorship of the *Cornhill Magazine*. Last number of *The Virginians* (October)
1860	First number of the *Cornhill Magazine* (January) containing the first of the *Roundabout Papers* and the first instalment of *Lovel the Widower. The Four Georges* published in the *Cornhill* (July–October)
1861	First instalment of *Philip* in the *Cornhill* (January)
1862	Resigns editorship of *Cornhill Magazine* (March). Moves to 2 Palace Green, Kensington. Last instalment of *Philip* (August)
1863	Begins *Denis Duval* (May). Last *Roundabout Paper* appears in *Cornhill* (November). Dies at Palace Green (24 December). Buried at Kensal Green Cemetery (29 December)
1864	'In Memoriam' by Dickens published in *Cornhill Magazine* (January). The incomplete *Denis Duval* published posthumously in the *Cornhill* (March–June)

CONTENTS

THE MEMOIRS OF BARRY LYNDON, ESQ.

THE MEMOIRS OF

BARRY LYNDON, ESQ.,

OF THE KINGDOM OF IRELAND.

CONTAINING

AN ACCOUNT OF HIS EXTRAORDINARY ADVENTURES; MISFORTUNES; HIS SUFFERINGS IN THE SERVICE OF HIS LATE PRUSSIAN MAJESTY; HIS VISITS TO MANY OF THE COURTS OF EUROPE; HIS MARRIAGE AND SPLENDID ESTABLISHMENTS IN ENGLAND AND IRELAND; AND THE MANY CRUEL PERSECUTIONS, CONSPIRACIES, AND SLANDERS OF WHICH HE HAS BEEN A VICTIM.

THE

MEMOIRS OF BARRY LYNDON, ESQ.

CHAPTER I

MY PEDIGREE AND FAMILY.—UNDERGO THE INFLUENCE OF THE TENDER PASSION

SINCE the days of Adam, there has been hardly a mischief done in this world but a woman has been at the bottom of it. Ever since ours was a family (and that must be very *near* Adam's time,—so old, noble, and illustrious are the Barrys, as everybody knows), women have played a mighty part with the destinies of our race.

I presume that there is no gentleman in Europe that has not heard of the house of Barry of Barryogue, of the kingdom of Ireland, than which a more famous name is not to be found in Gwillim or D'Hozier ;* and though as a man of the world I have learned to despise heartily the claims of some *pretenders* to high birth who have no more genealogy than the lackey who cleans my boots, and though I laugh to utter scorn the boasting of many of my countrymen, who are all for descending from kings of Ireland, and talk of a domain no bigger than would feed a pig as if it were a principality ; yet truth compels me to assert that my family was the noblest of the island, and, perhaps, of the universal world ; while their possessions, now insignificant, and torn from us by war, by treachery, by the loss of time, by ancestral extravagance, by adhesion to the old faith and monarch,* were formerly prodigious, and embraced many counties, at a time when Ireland was vastly more prosperous than now. I would assume the Irish crown* over my coat-of-arms, but that there are so many silly pretenders to that distinction who bear it and render it common.

Who knows, but for the fault of a woman, I might have been wearing it now? You start with incredulity. I say, why not? Had there been a gallant chief to lead my countrymen, instead of puling knaves who bent the knee to King Richard II, they might have been freemen; had there been a resolute leader to meet the murderous ruffian, Oliver Cromwell,* we should have shaken off the English for ever. But there was no Barry in the field against the usurper; on the contrary, my ancestor, Simon de Bary, came over with the first-named monarch, and married the daughter of the then King of Munster, whose sons in battle he pitilessly slew.

In Oliver's time it was too late for a chief of the name of Barry to lift up his war-cry against that of the murderous brewer.* We were princes of the land no longer; our unhappy race had lost its possessions a century previously, and by the most shameful treason. This I know to be the fact, for my mother has often told me the story, and besides had worked it in a worsted pedigree which hung up in the yellow saloon at Barryville where we lived.

That very estate which the Lyndons now possess in Ireland was once the property of my race. Rory Barry of Barryogue owned it in Elizabeth's time, and half Munster beside. The Barry was always in feud with the O'Mahonys in those times; and, as it happened, a certain English colonel passed through the former's country with a body of men-at-arms, on the very day when the O'Mahonys had made an inroad upon our territories, and carried off a frightful plunder of our flocks and herds.

This young Englishman, whose name was Roger Lyndon, Linden, or Lyndaine, having been most hospitably received by the Barry, and finding him just on the point of carrying an inroad into the O'Mahony's land, offered the aid of himself and his lances, and behaved himself so well, as it appeared, that the O'Mahonys were entirely overcome, all the Barrys' property restored, and with it, says the old chronicle, twice as much of the O'Mahonys' goods and cattle.

It was the setting-in of the winter season, and the young soldier was pressed by the Barry not to quit his house of Barryogue, and remained there during several months, his men being quartered with Barry's own gallowglasses,* man by man, in the cottages round about. They conducted themselves, as is their wont, with the most intolerable insolence towards the Irish; so much so, that fights and murders continually ensued, and the people vowed to destroy them.

The Barry's son (from whom I descend) was as hostile to the English as any other man on his domain; and, as they would not go when bidden, he and his friends consulted together and determined on destroying these English to a man.

But they had let a woman into their plot, and this was the Barry's daughter. She was in love with the English Lyndon, and broke the whole secret to him; and the dastardly English prevented the just massacre of themselves by falling upon the Irish, and destroying Phaudrig Barry, my ancestor, and many hundreds of his men. The cross at Barrycross near Carrignadihioul is the spot where the odious butchery took place.

Lyndon married the daughter of Roderick Barry, and claimed the estate which he left; and though the descendants of Phaudrig were alive, as indeed they are in my person,[1] on appealing to the English courts, the estate was awarded to the Englishman, as has ever been the case where English and Irish were concerned.

Thus had it not been for the weakness of a woman, I should have been born to the possession of those very estates which afterwards came to me by merit, as you shall hear. But to proceed with my family history.

My father was well known to the best circles in this kingdom as in that of Ireland, under the name of Roaring Harry Barry. He was bred like many other young sons of genteel families to the profession of the law, being articled to a celebrated attorney of Sackville Street* in the city of Dublin; and, from his great genius and aptitude for learning, there is no doubt he would have made an eminent figure in his profession, had not his social qualities, love of field-sports, and extraordinary graces of manner, marked him out for a higher sphere. While he was attorney's clerk he kept seven race-horses, and hunted regularly both with the Kildare and Wicklow hunts; and rode on his

[1] As we have never been able to find proofs of the marriage of my ancestor Phaudrig with his wife, I make no doubt that Lyndon destroyed the contract, and murdered the priest and witnesses of the marriage.—B. L.

grey horse Endymion that famous match against Captain Punter, which is still remembered by lovers of the sport, and of which I caused a splendid picture to be made and hung over my dining-hall mantelpiece at Castle Lyndon. A year afterwards he had the honour of riding that very horse Endymion before his late Majesty King George II on Epsom Downs, and won the plate there and the attention of the august sovereign.

Although he was only the second son of our family, my dear father came naturally into the estate (now miserably reduced to 400*l*. a year); for my grandfather's eldest son Cornelius Barry (called the Chevalier Borgne,* from a wound which he received in Germany), remained constant to the old religion in which our family was educated, and not only served abroad with credit, but against his Most Sacred Majesty George II in the unhappy Scotch disturbances in '45.* We shall hear more of the Chevalier hereafter.

For the conversion of my father I have to thank my dear mother, Miss Bell Brady, daughter of Ulysses Brady of Castle Brady, county Kerry, Esquire and J.P. She was the most beautiful woman of her day in Dublin, and universally called the Dasher there. Seeing her at the assembly, my father became passionately attached to her; but her soul was above marrying a Papist or an attorney's clerk; and so for the love of her, the good old laws being then in force,* my dear father slipped into my uncle Cornelius's shoes and took the family estate. Besides the force of my mother's bright eyes, several persons, and of the genteelest society too, contributed to this happy change; and I have often heard my mother laughingly tell the story of my father's recantation, which was solemnly pronounced at the tavern in the company of Sir Dick Ringwood, Lord Bagwig, Captain Punter, and two or three other young sparks of the town. Roaring Harry won 300 pieces that very night at faro,* and laid the necessary information the next morning against his brother; but his conversion caused a coolness between him and my uncle Corney, who joined the rebels in consequence.

This great difficulty being settled, my Lord Bagwig lent my father his own yacht, then lying at the Pigeon House,* and the handsome Bell Brady was induced to run away with him to England, although her parents were against the match, and her lovers (as I have heard her tell many thousands of times) were among the most numerous and the most wealthy in all the kingdom of Ireland. They were married at the Savoy,* and my grandfather dying very soon, Harry Barry, Esquire, took possession of his paternal property and supported our illustrious name with credit in London. He pinked the famous Count Tiercelin behind Montague House, he was a member of White's,* and a frequenter of all the chocolate houses; and my mother, likewise, made no small figure. At length, after his great day of triumph before his Sacred Majesty at Newmarket, Harry's fortune was just on the point of being made, for the gracious monarch promised to provide for him. But, alas! he was taken in charge by another monarch, whose will will have no delay or denial,—by Death, namely, who seized upon my father at Chester races, leaving me a helpless orphan. Peace be to his ashes! He was not faultless, and dissipated all our princely family property; but he was as brave a fellow as ever tossed a bumper or called a main, and he drove his coach-and-six like a man of fashion.

I do not know whether his gracious Majesty was much affected by this sudden demise of my father, though my mother says he shed some royal tears on the occasion. But they helped us to nothing; and all that was found in the house for the wife and creditors was a purse of ninety guineas, which my dear mother naturally took, with the family plate, and my father's wardrobe and her own; and, putting them into our great coach, drove off to Holyhead, whence she took shipping for Ireland. My father's body accompanied us in the finest hearse and plumes money could buy; for though the husband and wife had quarrelled repeatedly in life, yet at my father's death his high-spirited widow forgot all her differences, gave him the grandest funeral that had been seen for many a day, and erected a monument over his remains (for which I subsequently paid), which declared him to be the wisest, purest, and most affectionate of men.

In performing these sad duties over her deceased lord, the widow spent almost every guinea she had, and, indeed, would have spent a great deal more, had she discharged one-third of the demands which the ceremonies occasioned. But the people around our old house of Barryogue, although they did not like my father for his change of faith, yet stood by him at this moment, and were for exterminating the mutes sent by Mr. Plumer*of London with the lamented remains. The monument and vault in the church were then, alas! all that remained of my vast possessions; for my father had sold every stick of the property to one Notley, an attorney, and we received but a cold welcome in his house—a miserable old tumbledown place it was.[1]

The splendour of the funeral did not fail to increase the widow Barry's reputation as a woman of spirit and fashion; and when she wrote to her brother Michael Brady, that worthy gentleman immediately rode across the country to fling himself in her arms, and to invite her in his wife's name to Castle Brady.

Mick and Barry had quarrelled, as all men will, and very high words had passed between them during Barry's courtship of Miss Bell. When he took her off, Brady swore he would never forgive Barry or Bell: but coming to London in the year '46, he fell in once more with Roaring Harry, and lived in his fine house in Clarges Street, and lost a few pieces to him at play, and broke a watchman's head or two in his company,—all of which reminiscences endeared Bell and her son very much to the good-hearted gentleman, and he received us both with open arms. Mrs. Barry did not, perhaps wisely, at first make known to her friends what was her condition; but arriving in a huge gilt coach, with enormous armorial bearings, was taken by her sister-in-law and the rest of the county for a person of considerable property and distinction.

For a time, then, and as was right and proper, Mrs. Barry gave the law at Castle Brady. She ordered the servants to and fro, and taught them, what indeed they much wanted, a little London neatness; and 'English Redmond,' as I was called, was treated like a little lord, and had a maid and a footman to himself; and honest Mick paid their wages,—which was much more than he was used to do for his own domestics,—doing all in his power to make his sister decently comfortable under her afflictions. Mamma, in return, determined that, when her affairs were arranged,

[1] In another part of his memoir Mr. Barry will be found to describe this mansion as one of the most splendid palaces in Europe, but this is a practice not unusual with his nation; and with respect to the Irish principality claimed by him, it is known that Mr. Barry's grandfather was an attorney and maker of his own fortune.

she would make her kind brother a handsome allowance for her son's maintenance and her own; and promised to have her handsome furniture brought over from Clarges Street to adorn somewhat the dilapidated rooms of Castle Brady.

But it turned out that the rascally landlord seized upon every chair and table that ought by rights to belong to the widow. The estate to which I was heir was in the hands of rapacious creditors; and the only means of subsistence remaining to the widow and child was a rent-charge of 50*l.* upon my Lord Bagwig's property, who had many turf-dealings with the deceased. And so my dear mother's liberal intentions towards her brother were, of course, never fulfilled.

It must be confessed, very much to the discredit of Mrs. Brady, of Castle Brady, that when her sister-in-law's poverty was thus made manifest, she forgot all the respect which she had been accustomed to pay her, instantly turned my maid and man-servant out of doors, and told Mrs. Barry that she might follow them as soon as she chose. Mrs. Mick was of a low family, and a sordid way of thinking; and after about a couple of years (during which she had saved almost all her little income) the widow complied with Madam Brady's desire. At the same time, giving way to a just, though prudently dissimulated resentment, she made a vow that she would never enter the gates of Castle Brady while the lady of the house remained alive within them.

She fitted up her new abode with much economy and considerable taste, and never, for all her poverty, abated a jot of the dignity which was her due, and which all the neighbourhood awarded to her. How, indeed, could they refuse respect to a lady who had lived in London, frequented the most fashionable society there, and had been presented (as she solemnly declared) at court? These advantages gave her a right which seems to be pretty unsparingly exercised in Ireland by those natives who have it,—the right of looking down with scorn upon all persons who have not had the opportunity of quitting the mother-country and inhabiting England for a while. Thus, whenever Madam Brady appeared abroad in a new dress, her sister-in-law would say, 'Poor creature! how can it be expected that she should know anything of the fashion?' And though pleased to be called the Handsome Widow, as she was, Mrs. Barry was still better pleased to be called the *English* widow.

Mrs. Brady, for her part, was not slow to reply; she used to say that the defunct Barry was a bankrupt and a beggar; and as for the fashionable society which he saw, he saw it from my Lord Bagwig's side-table, whose flatterer and hanger-on he was known to be. Regarding Mrs. Barry, the lady of Castle Brady would make insinuations still more painful. However, why should we allude to these charges, or rake up private scandal of near sixty[1] years old? It was in the reign of George II that the above-named personages lived and quarrelled; good or bad, handsome or ugly, rich or poor, they are all equal now; and do not the Sunday papers and the courts of law supply us every week with more novel and interesting slander?

At any rate, it must be allowed that Mrs. Brady, after her husband's death and her retirement, lived in such a way as to defy slander. For whereas Bell Brady had been the gayest girl in the whole county of Wexford, with half the bachelors at her feet, and plenty of smiles and encouragement for every one of them, Bell Barry adopted a dignified reserve that almost amounted to pomposity, and was as starch as any Quakeress. Many a man renewed his offers to the widow, who had been smitten by the charms of the spinster; but Mrs. Barry refused all offers of marriage, declaring that she lived now for her son only, and for the memory of her departed saint.

'Saint, forsooth!' said ill-natured Mrs. Brady. 'Harry Barry was as big a sinner as ever was known; and 'tis notorious that he and Bell hated each other. If she won't marry now, depend on it, the artful woman has a husband in her eye for all that, and only waits until Lord Bagwig is a widower.'

And suppose she did, what then? Was not the widow of a Barry fit to marry with any lord of England? and was it not always said that a woman was to restore the fortunes of the Barry family? If my mother fancied that *she* was to be that woman, I think it was a perfectly justifiable notion on her part; for the earl (my godfather) was always most attentive to her; and I never knew how deeply this notion of advancing my interests in the world

[1] [Mr. Barry's papers were written about 1800].—Note in *Fraser's Magazine*, omitted in later editions.

had taken possession of mamma's mind, until his lordship's marriage in the year '57 with Miss Goldmore, the Indian nabob's rich daughter.

Meanwhile, we continued to reside at Barryville, and, considering the smallness of our income, kept up a wonderful state. Of the half-dozen families that formed the congregation at Brady's Town, there was not a single person whose appearance was so respectable as that of the widow, who, though she always dressed in mourning, in memory of her deceased husband, took care that her garments should be made so as to set off her handsome person to the greatest advantage; and, indeed, I think, spent six hours out of every day in the week in cutting, trimming, and altering them to the fashion. She had the largest of hoops, and the handsomest of furbelows, and once a month (under my Lord Bagwig's cover) would come a letter from London containing the newest accounts of the fashions there. Her complexion was so brilliant that she had no call to use rouge, as was the mode in those days. No, she left red and white, she said (and hence the reader may imagine how the two ladies hated each other) to Madam Brady, whose yellow complexion no plaster* could alter. In a word, she was so accomplished a beauty, that all the women in the country took pattern by her, and the young fellows from ten miles round would ride over to Castle Brady church to have the sight of her.

But if (like every other woman that ever I saw or read of) she was proud of her beauty, to do her justice she was still more proud of her son, and has said a thousand times to me that I was the handsomest young fellow in the world. This is a matter of taste. A man of sixty may, however, say what he was at fourteen without much vanity, and I must say I think there was some cause for my mother's opinion. The good soul's pleasure was to dress me; and on Sundays and holidays I turned out in a velvet coat with a silver-hilted sword by my side and a gold garter at my knee, as fine as any lord in the land. My mother worked me several most splendid waistcoats, and I had plenty of lace for my ruffles, and a fresh riband to my hair, and as we walked to church on Sundays, even envious Mrs. Brady was found to allow that there was not a prettier pair in the kingdom.

Of course, too, the lady of Castle Brady used to sneer,

because on these occasions a certain Tim, who used to be called my valet, followed me and my mother to church, carrying a huge prayer-book and a cane, and dressed in the livery of one of our own fine footmen from Clarges Street, which, as Tim was a bandy-shanked little fellow, did not exactly become him. But, though poor, we were gentlefolks, and not to be sneered out of these becoming appendages to our rank; and so would march up the aisle to our pew with as much state and gravity as the lord-lieutenant's lady and son might do. When there, my mother would give the responses and amens in a loud, dignified voice that was delightful to hear, and, besides, had a fine loud voice for singing, which art she had perfected in London under a fashionable teacher; and she would exercise her talent in such a way that you would hardly hear any other voice of the little congregation which chose to join in the psalm. In fact, my mother had great gifts in every way, and believed herself to be one of the most beautiful, accomplished, and meritorious persons in the world. Often and often has she talked to me and the neighbours regarding her own humility and piety, pointing them out in such a way that I would defy the most obstinate to disbelieve her.

When we left Castle Brady we came to occupy a house in Brady's Town, which mamma christened Barryville. I confess it was but a small place, but, indeed, we made the most of it. I have mentioned the family pedigree which hung up in the drawing-room, which mamma called the yellow saloon, and my bedroom was called the pink bedroom, and hers the orange-tawny apartment (how well I remember them all!); and at dinner-time Tim regularly rang a great bell, and we each had a silver tankard to drink from, and mother boasted with justice that I had as good a bottle of claret by my side as any squire of the land. So, indeed, I had, but I was not, of course, allowed at my tender years to drink any of the wine, which thus attained a considerable age, even in the decanter.

Uncle Brady (in spite of the family quarrel) found out the above fact one day by calling at Barryville at dinner-time, and unluckily tasting the liquor. You should have seen how he sputtered and made faces! But the honest gentleman was not particular about his wine or the company in which he drank it. He would get drunk, indeed, with the parson or the priest indifferently; with the latter, much to my mother's indignation, for, as a true blue Nassauite,* she heartily despised all those of the old faith, and would scarcely sit down in the room with a benighted Papist. But the squire had no such scruples; he was, indeed, one of the easiest, idlest, and best-natured fellows that ever lived, and many an hour would he pass with the lonely widow when he was tired of Madam Brady at home. He liked me, he said, as much as one of his own sons, and at length, after the widow had held out for a couple of years, she agreed to allow me to return to the castle; though, for herself, she resolutely kept the oath which she had made with regard to her sister-in-law.

The very first day I returned to Castle Brady my trials may be said, in a manner, to have begun. My cousin, Master Mick, a huge monster of nineteen (who hated me, and I promise you I returned the compliment), insulted me at dinner about my mother's poverty, and made all the girls of the family titter. So when we went to the stables, whither Mick always went for his pipe of tobacco after dinner, I told him a piece of my mind, and there was a fight for at least ten minutes, during which I stood to him like a man, and blacked his left eye, though I was myself only twelve years old at the time. Of course he beat me, but a beating makes only a small impression on a lad of that tender age, as I had proved many times in battles with the ragged Brady's Town boys before, not one of whom, at my time of life, was my match. My uncle was very much pleased when he heard of my gallantry; my cousin Nora brought brown paper and vinegar for my nose, and I went home that night with a pint of claret under my girdle, not a little proud, let me tell you, at having held my own against Mick so long.

And though he persisted in his bad treatment of me, and used to cane me whenever I fell in his way, yet I was very happy now at Castle Brady with the company there, and my cousins, or some of them, and the kindness of my uncle, with whom I became a prodigious favourite. He bought a colt for me, and taught me to ride. He took me out coursing and fowling, and instructed me to shoot flying. And at length I was released from Mick's persecution, for his brother, Master Ulick, returning from Trinity College, and hating his elder brother, as is mostly the way in families of fashion, took me under his protection, and from that time, as Ulick was a deal bigger and stronger than Mick, I, English Redmond, as I was called, was left alone, except when the former thought fit to thrash me, which he did whenever he thought proper.

Nor was my learning neglected in the ornamental parts, for I had an uncommon natural genius for many things, and soon topped in accomplishments most of the persons around me. I had a quick ear and a fine voice, which my mother cultivated to the best of her power, and she taught me to step a minuet gravely and gracefully, and thus laid the foundation of my future success in life. The common dances I learned, as, perhaps, I ought not to confess, in the servants' hall, which, you may be sure, was never without a piper, and where I was considered unrivalled both at a hornpipe and a jig.

In the matter of book-learning, I had always an uncommon taste for reading plays and novels, as the best part of a gentleman's polite education, and never let a pedlar pass the village, if I had a penny, without having a ballad or two from him. As for your dull grammar, and Greek, and Latin, and stuff, I have always hated them from my youth upwards, and said, very unmistakably, I would have none of them.

This I proved pretty clearly at the age of thirteen, when my aunt Biddy Brady's legacy of 100*l.* came in to mamma, who thought to employ the sum on my education, and sent me to Doctor Tobias Tickler's famous academy at Ballywhacket—Backwhacket, as my uncle used to call it. But six weeks after I had been consigned to his reverence, I suddenly made my appearance again at Castle Brady, having walked forty miles from the odious place, and left the doctor in a state near upon apoplexy. The fact was, that at taw, prison-bars,* or boxing, I was at the head of the school, but could not be brought to excel in the classics; and after having been flogged seven times without its doing me the least good in my Latin, I refused to submit altogether (finding it useless) to an eighth application of the rod. 'Try some other way, sir,' said I, when he was for horsing me once more; but he wouldn't; whereon, and to defend myself, I flung a slate at him, and knocked down a Scotch usher with a leaden inkstand. All the lads huzzaed at this, and some of the servants wanted to stop me; but taking out a large clasp-knife that my cousin Nora had given me, I swore I would plunge it into the waistcoat of the first man who dared to balk me, and faith, they let me pass on. I slept that night twenty miles off Ballywhacket, at the house of a cottier, who gave me potatoes and milk, and to whom I gave a hundred guineas after, when I came to visit Ireland in my days of greatness. I wish I had the money now. But what's the use of regret? I have had many a harder bed than that I shall sleep on to-night, and many a scantier meal than honest Phil Murphy gave me on the evening I ran away from school. So six weeks was all the schooling I ever got. And I say this to let parents know the value of it, for though I have met more learned bookworms in the world, especially a great hulking, clumsy, blear-eyed old doctor, whom they called Johnson* and who lived in a court off Fleet Street, in London, yet I pretty soon silenced him in an argument (at Button's Coffee-house),* and in that, and in poetry, and in what I call natural philosophy, or the science of life, and in riding, music, leaping, the small-sword, the knowledge of a horse, or a main of cocks, and the manners of an accomplished gentleman and a man of fashion, I may say for myself that Redmond Barry has seldom found his equal. 'Sir,' said I to Mr. Johnson, on the occasion I allude to—he was accompanied by a Mr. Buswell* of Scotland, and I was presented to the club by a Mr. Goldsmith,* a countryman of my own,—'Sir,' said I, in reply to the schoolmaster's great thundering quotation in Greek, 'you fancy you know a great deal more than me, because you quote your *Aristotle* and your *Pluto*, but can you tell me which horse will win at Epsom Downs next week?—Can you run six miles without breathing?—Can you shoot the ace of spades ten times without missing? If so, talk about Aristotle and Pluto to me.'

'D'ye knaw who ye're speaking to?' roared out the Scotch gentleman, Mr. Buswell, at this.

'Hold your tongue, Mr. Boswell,' said the old schoolmaster. 'I had no right to brag of my Greek to the gentleman, and he has answered me very well.'

'Doctor,' says I, looking waggishly at him, 'do you know ever a rhyme for Aris*totle?*'

'Port, if you plaise,' says Mr. Goldsmith, laughing. And we had *six rhymes for Aristotle* before we left the coffee-house that evening. It became a regular joke afterwards when

I told the story, and at White's, or the Cocoa-tree,* you would hear the wags say, 'Waiter, bring one of Captain Barry's rhymes for Aristotle!' Once, when I was in liquor at the latter place, young Dick Sheridan called me a great Staggerite,* a joke which I could never understand. But I am wandering from my story, and must get back to home, and dear old Ireland again.

I have made acquaintance with the best in the land since, and my manners are such, I have said, as to make me the equal of them all; and, perhaps, you will wonder how a country boy, as I was, educated amongst Irish squires, and their dependents of the stable and farm, should arrive at possessing such elegant manners as I was indisputably allowed to have. I had, the fact is, a very valuable instructor in the person of an old gamekeeper, who had served the French king at Fontenoy,* and who taught me the dances, and customs, and a smattering of the language of that country, with the use of the sword, both small and broad. Many and many a long mile I have trudged by his side as a lad, he telling me wonderful stories of the French king, and the Irish brigade, and Marshal Saxe,* and the opera-dancers; he knew my uncle, too, the Chevalier Borgne, and, indeed, had a thousand accomplishments which he taught me in secret. I never knew a man like him for making or throwing a fly, for physicking a horse, or breaking, or choosing one; he taught me manly sports, from birds'-nesting upwards, and I always shall consider Phil Purcell as the very best tutor I could have had. His fault was drink, but for that I have always had a blind eye; and he hated my cousin Mick like poison, but I could excuse him that too.

With Phil, and at the age of fifteen, I was a more accomplished man than either of my cousins; and I think Nature had been, also, more bountiful to me in the matter of person. Some of the Castle Brady girls (as you shall hear presently) adored me. At fairs and races many of the prettiest lasses present said they would like to have me for their bachelor, and yet somehow, it must be confessed, I was not popular.

In the first place, every one knew I was bitter poor; and I think, perhaps, it was my good mother's fault that I was bitter proud too. I had a habit of boasting in company of my birth, and the splendour of my carriages, gardens, cellars, and domestics, and this before people who were perfectly aware of my real circumstances. If it was boys, and they ventured to sneer, I would beat them, or die for it; and many's the time I've been brought home wellnigh killed by one or more of them, on what, when my mother asked me, I would say was 'a family quarrel.' 'Support your name with your blood, Reddy, my boy,' would that saint say, with the tears in her eyes; and so would she herself have done with her voice, aye, and her teeth and nails.

Thus, at fifteen, there was scarce a lad of twenty, for half a dozen miles round, that I had not beat for one cause or other. There were the vicar's two sons of Castle Brady—in course I could not associate with such beggarly brats as them, and many a battle did we have as to who should take the wall in Brady's Town; there was Pat Lurgan, the blacksmith's son, who had the better of me four times before we came to the crowning fight, when I overcame him; and I could mention a score more of my deeds of prowess in that way, but that fisticuff facts are dull subjects to talk of, and to discuss before high-bred gentlemen and ladies.

However, there is another subject, ladies, on which I must discourse, and *that* is never out of place. Day and night you like to hear of it; young and old, you dream and think of it. Handsome and ugly (and, faith, before fifty, I never saw such a thing as a plain woman), it's the subject next to the hearts of all of you; and I think you guess my riddle without more trouble. *Love!* sure the word is formed on purpose out of the prettiest soft vowels and consonants in the language, and he or she who does not care to read about it is not worth a fig to my thinking.

[It may possibly be becoming for ladies to fall in love only once in their lives—viz. with the happy individual on whom their hands are bestowed:—it may, I say, be possibly becoming and virtuous in them to bring virgin hearts to St. George's, Hanover Square;* and it is certain that the jealous, greedy, selfish sultan, Man, would so confine their affections, if he could, nor allow them to think and feel until such time as he chooses to select them as objects of his favour. But for his own part, Man, the whiskered lord and master, is by no means so squeamish, as every man of tolerable sensibilities will aver who reads this, and will take the trouble of computing how many times from his earliest youth up to the perusal of this sentence, he has given way to the tender passion.

Can any man lay his hand upon his waistcoat and conscientiously say, 'Until I saw the present Mrs. Jones, I never was in love in my life?' Can any man say so? He is a poor creature if he can; and I make no doubt he has had at least forty first-loves since he began to be capable of admiring at all. As for the ladies—them, of course, I put out of the question,—they *are* fresh, no doubt: they never fall in love until mamma tells them that Mr. So-and-so is an amiable young man, and in every way eligible; they never flirt with Captain Smith at a ball; and sigh as they lie at home in bed, and think what a charming, dashing fellow he is; they never hear the young curate read his sermon so sweetly, and think how pale and interesting he looks, and how lonely he must feel in his curacy-house, and what a noble work it would be to share the solitude, and soothe the pains, and listen to the delightful doctrine, of so excellent a man; they never think of attaching themselves to any mortal except their brother, until he brings home a young friend from college, and says, 'Mary, Tom Atkinson admires you hugely, and is heir to two thousand a year!' They never begin the attack, as I have heard; but their young hearts wait like so many fortresses, to be attacked and carried after a proper period of siege—by blockade, or by bribery, or by capitulation, or by fiery escalade.

Whilst ladies persist in maintaining the strictly defensive condition, men must naturally, as it were, take the opposite line, that of attack; otherwise, if both parties held aloof, there would be no more marriages; and the two hosts would die in their respective inaction, without ever coming to a battle. Thus it is evident that as the ladies will not, the men must take the offensive. I, for my part, have made in the course of my life, at least a score of chivalrous attacks upon several strongly fortified hearts. Sometimes I began my works too late in the season, and winter suddenly came and rendered further labours impossible; sometimes I have attacked the breach madly, sword in hand, and have been plunged violently from the scaling-ladder into the ditch; sometimes I have made a decent lodgement in the place, when—bang! blows up a mine, and I am scattered to the deuce! and sometimes when I have been in the very heart of the citadel—ah, that I should say it !—a sudden panic has struck me, and I have run like the British out of Carthagena !* One grows tired after a while of such perpetual activity. Is it not time that the ladies should take an innings ? Let us widowers and bachelors form an association to declare that for the next hundred years we will make love no longer. Let the young women come and make love to us ; let them write us verses ; let them ask us to dance, get us ices and cups of tea, and help us on with our cloaks at the hall-door ; and if they are eligible, we may perhaps be induced to yield and say, 'La, Miss Hopkins—I really never—I am so agitated—ask papa ! '

My day is over, however ; my race is run, and the above hint is only thrown out for those who shall come after me. But in the matter of love I showed my genius early ; and if in after-times I achieved, as shall be shown, vast and signal victories over the fair sex, this fact only proves my merit and courage the more ; for in my first affair I was wofully unsuccessful.

Ah ! that first affair, how well one remembers it ! What a noble discovery it is that the boy makes when he finds himself actually and truly in love with some one ! What a delicious magnificent secret it is that he carries about with him ! My first love was like my first gold watch (an elegant French gold repeater). I used to go into corners, and contemplate and gloat over my treasure ; to take it to bed with me, and lay it under my pillow of nights, and wake of mornings with the happy consciousness that it was there. What a change does that blessed first love make in a lad ! You fall in love, say of a Sunday ; a young woman at church modestly hands you the psalm-book, and blushes and droops down her eyes, as she tremulously sings the Old Hundredth.* By the time the music is done, you have passed over into a new state of existence, and your childhood lies far away from you. It was only on Saturday that you had made a party for cricket, and were longing for Monday to be a fine day. It was but last Friday, Heaven bless us ! that you and Harry Hunter had been examining curiously a certain apple-tree in Farmer Smith's orchard, and had settled (after knocking down one of the fruits with a stone, and trying each of you a slice of it) that the apples would be ripe in about a fortnight, and the tree in a fit state for robbing. Psha! is it possible that only three days since you had an ambition for robbing orchards, and looked forward to the pleasure of hiding a store of the stolen pippins under your bed? Is it possible that the setting up of three yellow stumps upon a meadow, and the dexterous knocking down of them, should have been the chief ambition of your life? There lies the cricket-ball, which you greased carefully overnight; before going to church even, you looked at it to examine its condition, and I believe spent the best part of the half-hour during sermon in the morning in cutting a pair of bails for the wickets. Evening service is over—Fanny Edwards and her mother have slowly strolled home over the fields to tea; and as you pass by Smith's apple-tree you blush to think that you could ever have had a longing for the silly green codlins shining among the leaves, and put away your wicket-sticks in a rage. And what is the cause of all this? You and Fanny have been holding on by one hymn-book; you have done it any time these six years; but what made her blush and you tremble so this time? She is eight years older than you (that follows, of course); and if there was a humiliation for you in the world some few months back, it was to be obliged to walk with her. You cried for rage one day when she gave you a kiss, and called you a pretty little boy; after dinner, when you were told by your papa to walk off to the ladies, you sat in the very farthest corner of the room away from her, or passed the evening with the gardener's boy, or with Tom in the stables, or with making ducks and drakes on the ponds,—anyhow rather than with Fanny Edwards, whom you abominated next to the schoolmaster.

What a change now!—ah, gods, what a royal change! How different is Fanny Edwards! What has happened to her that she has become an angel since yesterday, or what strange enchantment has fallen upon you, that she should seem like one? Shall we go on in this strain, and discourse through this entire chapter upon the nature and peculiarities of love, and its influences upon the youthful bosom? No, no! such things had best be thought about, not spoken of. Let any man who has a mind to do so, fall back in his chair, dropping the book out of his hand—fall back into his chair, and call back the sleeping sweet reminiscences of his early love-days, long before he ever saw Mrs. Jones. She, good woman, has sent down half a dozen times already to say that tea is waiting. Never mind; sit still, Jones, and dream on. Call back again that early, brilliant, immortal first love. What matters what the object of it was? Perhaps a butcher's daughter down the village; perhaps a great, skinny, ogling French governess; perhaps a fat, meek, fair-haired clergyman's daughter, that was ten years older than yourself, as a matter of course.

Never mind who it was: it is not of the least consequence. As a general rule, nothing comes of a first love; and a wise and lucky chance it is, too; for ten to one the object of it is unworthy, and the gratification of it would make a poor lad miserable for life. And it has always appeared to me that the tender passion in due season gushes instinctively out of a man's heart; and that he loves as a bird sings or a rose blows, from nature, and because he cannot help it. As I have read in a Persian song-book,*—

The nightingale sings in the garden: perhaps it is a princess who hears his music.
The rose blushes in the parterre: perhaps it is gathered by the black cook, who has come to cut pot-herbs for dinner.

Fate sports with us, my friends; women have ruled us since the days of Adam. With this sentiment I began, and with it will end my chapter.][1]

My uncle's family consisted of ten children; who, as is the custom in such large families, were divided into two camps, or parties; the one siding with their mamma, the other taking the part of my uncle in all the numerous quarrels which arose between that gentleman and his lady. Mrs. Brady's faction was headed by Mick, the eldest son, who hated me so, and disliked his father for keeping him out of his property: while Ulick, the second brother, was his father's own boy; and, in revenge, Master Mick was desperately afraid of him. I need not mention the girls' names; I had plague enough with them in after-life, Heaven knows; and one of them was the cause of all my early troubles; this was (though to be sure all her sisters denied it) the belle of the family, Miss Honoria Brady by name, [—the remembrance of whom inspired all those

[1] Omitted in later editions; in *Fraser's Magazine*, chapter i ended here.

remarks concerning love, with which I finished off the foregoing chapter, and which I hope all fair young ladies and youths entering life have well considered.][1]

She said she was only nineteen at the time; but I could read the fly-leaf in the family Bible as well as another (it was one of the three books which, with the backgammon-board, formed my uncle's library), and know that she was born in the year '37, and christened by Dr. Swift,* Dean of St. Patrick's, Dublin: hence she was three-and-twenty years old at the time she and I were so much together.

When I come to think about her now, I know she never could have been handsome; for her figure was rather of the fattest, and her mouth of the widest; she was freckled over like a partridge's egg, and her hair was the colour of a certain vegetable which we eat with boiled beef, to use the mildest term. Often and often would my dear mother make these remarks concerning her; but I did not believe them then, and somehow had gotten to think Honoria an angelical being far above all the other angels of her sex.

And as we know very well that a lady who is skilled in dancing or singing never can perfect herself without a deal of study in private, and that the song or the minuet which are performed with so much graceful ease in the assembly-room have not been acquired without vast labour and perseverance in private; so it is with the dear creatures who are skilled in coquetting. Honoria, for instance, was always practising, and she would take poor me to rehearse her accomplishment upon; or the exciseman, when he came his rounds, or the steward, or the poor curate, or the young apothecary's lad from Brady's Town, whom I recollect beating once for that very reason. If he is alive now I make him my apologies. Poor fellow! as if it was *his* fault that he should be a victim to the wiles of one of the greatest coquettes (considering her obscure life and rustic breeding) in the world.

If the truth must be told, and every word of this narrative of my life is of the most sacred veracity, my passion for Nora began in a very vulgar and unromantic way. I did not save her life; on the contrary, I once very nearly killed her, as you shall hear. I did not behold her by moonlight playing on the guitar, or rescue her from the

[1] Omitted in later editions.

hands of ruffians, as Alfonso does Lindamira* in the novel; but one day after dinner at Brady's Town in summer, going into the garden to pull gooseberries for my dessert, and thinking only of gooseberries, I pledge my honour, I came upon Miss Nora and one of her sisters, with whom she was friends at the time, who were both engaged in the very same amusement.

'What's the Latin for gooseberry, Redmond?' says she. She was always 'poking her fun,' as the Irish phrase it.

'I know the Latin for goose,' says I.

'And what's that?' cries Miss Mysie, as pert as a peacock.

'Bo to you!' says I (for I had never a want of wit); and so we fell to work at the gooseberry-bush, laughing and talking as happy as might be. In the course of our diversion Nora managed to scratch her arm, and it bled, and she screamed, and it was mighty round and white, and I tied it up, and I believe was permitted to kiss her hand; and though it was as big and clumsy a hand as ever you saw, yet I thought the favour the most ravishing one that was ever conferred upon me, and went home in a rapture [the exact condition of the young lad described in the last chapter.][1]

I was much too simple a fellow to disguise any sentiment I chanced to feel in those days; and not one of the eight Castle Brady girls but was soon aware of my passion, and joked and complimented Nora about her bachelor.

The torments of jealousy the cruel coquette made me endure were horrible. Sometimes she would treat me as a child, sometimes as a man. She would always leave me if ever there came a stranger to the house,

'For after all, Redmond,' she would say, 'you are but fifteen, and you hav'n't a guinea in the world;' at which I would swear that I would become the greatest hero ever known out of Ireland, and vow that before I was twenty I would have money enough to purchase an estate six times as big as Castle Brady. All which vain promises, of course, I did not keep; but I make no doubt they influenced me in my very early life, and caused me to do those great actions for which I have been celebrated, and which shall be narrated presently in order.

[1] Omitted in later editions.

I must tell one of them, just that my dear young lady readers may know what sort of a fellow Redmond Barry was, and what a courage and undaunted passion he had. I question whether any of the jenny-jessamines of the present day would do half as much in the face of danger.

About this time it must be premised the United Kingdom was in a state of great excitement from the threat generally credited of a French invasion. The Pretender*was said to be in high favour at Versailles, a descent upon Ireland was especially looked to, and the noblemen and people of condition in that and all other parts of the kingdom showed their loyalty by raising regiments of horse and foot to resist the invaders. Brady's Town sent a company to join the Kilwangan regiment, of which Master Mick was the captain; and we had a letter from Master Ulick at Trinity College, stating that the university had also formed a regiment, in which he had the honour to be a corporal. How I envied them both! especially that odious Mick, as I saw him in his laced scarlet coat with a ribbon in his hat march off at the head of his men. He, the poor spiritless creature, was a captain, and I nothing,—I who felt I had as much courage as the Duke of Cumberland*himself, and felt, too, that a red jacket would mightily become me! My mother said I was too young to join the new regiment; but the fact was, that it was she herself who was too poor, for the cost of a new uniform would have swallowed up half her year's income, and she would only have her boy appear in a way suitable to his birth, riding the finest of racers, dressed in the best of clothes, and keeping the genteelest of company.

Well, then, the whole country was alive with war's alarums, the three kingdoms ringing with military music, and every man of merit paying his devoirs at the court of Bellona,* whilst poor I was obliged to stay at home in my fustian jacket and sigh for fame in secret. Mr. Mick came to and fro from the regiment, and brought numerous of his comrades with him. Their costume and swaggering airs filled me with grief, and Miss Nora's unvarying attentions to them served to make me half wild. No one, however, thought of attributing this sadness to the young lady's score, but rather to my disappointment at not being allowed to join the military profession.

Once the officers of the Fencibles*gave a grand ball at

Kilwangan, to which, as a matter of course, all the ladies of Castle Brady (and a pretty ugly coachful they were) were invited. I knew to what tortures the odious little flirt of a Nora would put me with her eternal coquetries with the officers, and refused for a long time to be one of the party to the ball. But she had a way of conquering me, against which all resistance of mine was in vain. She vowed that riding in a coach always made her ill. 'And how can I go to the ball,' said she, 'unless you take me on Daisy behind you on the pillion ?' Daisy was a good blood mare of my uncle's, and to such a proposition I could not for my soul say no ; so we rode in safety to Kilwangan, and I felt myself as proud as any prince when she promised to dance a country-dance with me.

When the dance was ended, the little ungrateful flirt informed me that she had quite forgotten her engagement, and actually danced the set with an Englishman ! I have endured torments in my life, but none like that. She tried to make up for her neglect, but I would not. Some of the prettiest girls there offered to console me, for I was the best dancer in the room. I made one attempt, but was too wretched to continue, and so remained alone all night in a state of agony. I would have played but I had no money, only the gold piece that my mother bade me always keep in my purse as a gentleman should. I did not care for drink, or know the dreadful comfort of it in those days ; but I thought of killing myself and Nora, and most certainly of making away with Captain Quin !

At last, and at morning, the ball was over. The rest of our ladies went off in the lumbering creaking old coach ; Daisy was brought out, and Miss Nora took her place behind me, which I let her do without a word. But we were not half a mile out of town when she began to try with her coaxing and blandishments to dissipate my ill humour.

'Sure it's a bitter night, Redmond dear, and you'll catch cold without a handkerchief to your neck.' To this sympathetic remark from the pillion, the saddle made no reply.

'Did you and Miss Clancy have a pleasant evening, Redmond ? You were together, I saw, all night.' To this the saddle only replied by grinding his teeth, and giving a lash to Daisy.

'Oh ! mercy, you make Daisy rear and throw me, you

careless creature, you; and you know, Redmond, I'm so timid.' The pillion had by this got her arm round the saddle's waist, and, perhaps, gave it the gentlest squeeze in the world.

'I hate Miss Clancy, you know I do!' answers the saddle; 'and I only danced with her because—because—the person with whom I intended to dance chose to be engaged the whole night.'

'Sure there were my sisters,' said the pillion, now laughing outright in the pride of her conscious superiority; 'and for me, my dear, I had not been in the room five minutes before I was engaged for every single set.'

'Were you obliged to dance five times with Captain Quin?' said I; and, oh! strange delicious charm of coquetry, I do believe Miss Nora Brady at twenty-three years of age felt a pang of delight in thinking that she had so much power over a guileless lad of fifteen.

Of course she replied that she did not care a fig for Captain Quin; that he danced prettily, to be sure, and was a pleasant rattle of a man; that he looked well in his regimentals, too; and if he chose to ask her to dance, how could she refuse him?

'But you refused me, Nora.'

'Oh! I can dance with you any day,' answered Miss Nora, with a toss of her head; 'and to dance with your cousin at a ball looks as if you could find no other partner. Besides,' said Nora—and this was a cruel, unkind cut, which showed what a power she had over me, and how mercilessly she used it,—'besides, Redmond, Captain Quin's a man, and you are only a boy!'

'If ever I meet him again,' I roared out with an oath, 'you shall see which is the best man of the two. I'll fight him with sword or with pistol, captain as he is. A man, indeed! I'll fight any man—every man! Didn't I stand up to Mick Brady when I was eleven years old?—Didn't I beat Tom Sullivan, the great hulking brute, who is nineteen?—Didn't I do for the French usher? Oh, Nora, it's cruel of you to sneer at me so!'

But Nora was in the sneering mood that night, and pursued her sarcasms, and pointed out that Captain Quin was already known as a valiant soldier, famous as a man of fashion in London, and that it was mighty well of Redmond to talk and boast of beating ushers and farmers' boys, but to fight an Englishman was a very different matter.

Then she fell to talk of the invasion, and of military matters in general, of King Frederick (who was called, in those days, the Protestant hero [—apt title!][1]), of Monsieur Thurot and his fleet, of Monsieur Conflans* and his squadron, of Minorca, how it was attacked, and where it was, and both agreed it must be in America, and hoped the French might be soundly beaten there.

I sighed after a while (for I was beginning to melt), and said how much I longed to be a soldier; on which Nora recurred to her infallible, 'Ah! now, would you leave me, then? But, sure, you're not big enough for anything more than a little drummer.' To which I replied, by swearing that a soldier I would be, and a general too.

As we were chattering in this silly way, we came to a place that has ever since gone by the name of Redmond's Leap Bridge. It was an old high bridge, over a stream sufficiently deep and rocky, and as the mare Daisy with her double load was crossing this bridge, Miss Nora, giving a loose to her imagination, and still harping on the military theme (I would lay a wager that she was thinking of Captain Quin), Miss Nora said, 'Suppose, now, Redmond, you, who are such a hero, was passing over the bridge, and the inimy on the other side?'

'I'd draw my sword, and cut my way through them.'

'What, with me on the pillion? Would you kill poor me?' (This young lady was perpetually speaking of 'poor me!')

'Well, then, I'll tell you what I'd do. I'd jump Daisy into the river, and swim you both across, where no enemy could follow us.'

'Jump twenty feet! you wouldn't dare to do any such thing on Daisy. There's the Captain's horse, Black George, I've heard say that Captain Qui——'

She never finished the word, for, maddened by the continual recurrence of that odious monosyllable, I shouted to her to 'hold tight by my waist,' and, giving Daisy the spur, in a minute sprang with Nora over the parapet into the deeper water below. I don't know why now, whether it was I wanted to drown myself and Nora, or to perform an

[1] Omitted in later editions.

act that even Captain Quin should crane at, or whether I fancied that the enemy actually was in front of us, I can't tell now ; but over I went. The horse sank over his head, the girl screamed as she sank, and screamed as she rose, and I landed her, half fainting, on the shore, where we were soon found by my uncle's people, who returned on hearing the screams. I went home, and was ill speedily of a fever, which kept me to my bed for six weeks, and I quitted my couch prodigiously increased in stature, and, at the same time, still more violently in love than I had been even before.

At the commencement of my illness, Miss Nora had been pretty constant in her attendance at my bedside, forgetting, for the sake of me, the quarrel between my mother and her family, which my good mother was likewise pleased, in the most Christian manner, to forget. And, let me tell you, it was no small mark of goodness in a woman of her haughty disposition, who, as a rule, never forgave anybody, for my sake to give up her hostility to Miss Brady, and to receive her kindly. For, like a mad boy as I was, it was Nora I was always raving about and asking for ; I would only accept medicines from her hand, and would look rudely and sulkily upon the good mother, who loved me better than anything else in the world, and gave up even her favourite habits, and proper and becoming jealousies, to make me happy.

As I got well, I saw that Nora's visits became daily more rare : 'Why don't she come ?' I would say, peevishly, a dozen times in the day ; in reply to which query, Mrs. Barry would be obliged to make the best excuses she could find,—such as that Nora had sprained her ankle, or that they had quarrelled together, or some other answer to soothe me. And many a time has the good soul left me to go and break her heart in her own room alone, and come back with a smiling face, so that I should know nothing of her mortification. Nor, indeed, did I take much pains to ascertain it ; nor should I, I fear, have been very much touched even had I discovered it, for the commencement of manhood, I think, is the period of our extremest selfishness. We get such a desire then to take wing, and leave the parent-nest, that no tears, entreaties, or feelings of affection will counterbalance this overpowering longing after independence. She must have been very sad, that poor mother of mine—

Heaven be good to her!—at that period of my life; and has often told me since what a pang of the heart it was to her to see all her care and affection of years forgotten by me in a minute, and for the sake of a little, heartless jilt, who was only playing with me while she could get no better suitor. For the fact is, that during the last four weeks of my illness, no other than Captain Quin was staying at Castle Brady, and making love to Miss Nora in form; and my mother did not dare to break this news to me, and you may be sure that Nora herself kept it a secret. It was only by chance that I discovered it.

Shall I tell you how? The minx had been to see me one day, as I sat up in my bed, convalescent, and was in such high spirits, and so gracious and kind to me, that my heart poured over with joy and gladness, and I had even for my poor mother a kind word and a kiss that morning. I felt myself so well that I ate up a whole chicken, and promised my uncle, who had come to see me, to be ready, against partridge-shooting, to accompany him, as my custom was.

The next day but one was a Sunday, and I had a project for that day which I determined to realize, in spite of all the doctors and my mother's injunctions, which were that I was on no account to leave the house, for the fresh air would be the death of me.

Well, I lay wondrous quiet, composing a copy of verses, the first I ever made in my life, and I give them here spelt as I spelt them in those days when I knew no better. And though they are not so polished and elegant as *Ardelia, ease a love-sick swain*: and, *When Sol bedecks the Daisied Mead*; and other lyrical effusions of mine which obtained me so much reputation in after-life, I still think them pretty good for a humble lad of fifteen:—

THE ROSE OF FLORA

Sent by a Young Gentleman of Quality to Miss Br—dy, of C—stle Br—dy

On Brady's tower there grows a flower,
  It is the loveliest flower that blows,—
At Castle Brady there lives a lady,
  (And how I love her no one knows);
Her name is Nora, and the goddess Flora
  Presents her with this blooming rose.

'O Lady Nora,' says the goddess Flora,
'I've many a rich and bright parterre;
In Brady's towers there's seven more flowers,
But you're the fairest lady there:
Not all the county, nor Ireland's bounty,
Can projuice a treasure that's half so fair!'

What cheek is redder? sure roses fed her!
Her hair is maregolds, and her eye of blew
Beneath her eyelid, is like the vi'let,
That darkly glistens with gentle jew!
The lily's nature is not surely whiter
Than Nora's neck is,—and her arrums too.

'Come, gentle Nora,' says the goddess Flora,
'My dearest creature, take my advice,
There is a poet, full well you know it,
Who spends his life-time in heavy sighs,—
Young Redmond Barry, 'tis him you'll marry,
If rhyme and raisin you'd choose likewise.'

On Sunday, no sooner was my mother gone to church, than I summoned Phil the valet, and insisted upon his producing my best suit, in which I arrayed myself (although I found that I had shot up so in my illness that the old dress was wofully too small for me), and, with my notable copy of verses in my hand, ran down towards Castle Brady, bent upon beholding my beauty. The air was so fresh and bright, and the birds sang so loud amidst the green trees, that I felt more elated than I had been for months before, and sprang down the avenue (my uncle had cut down every stick of the trees, by the way) as brisk as a young fawn. My heart began to thump as I mounted the grass-grown steps of the terrace, and passed in by the rickety hall-door. The master and mistress were at church, Mr. Screw, the butler, told me, after giving a start back at seeing my altered appearance, and gaunt, lean figure, and so were six of the young ladies.

'Was Miss Nora one?' I asked.

'No, Miss Nora was not one,' said Mr. Screw, assuming a very puzzled, and yet knowing look.

'Where was she?' To this question he answered, or rather made believe to answer, with usual Irish ingenuity, and left me to settle whether she was gone to Kilwangan on the pillion behind her brother, or whether she and her sister had gone for a walk, or whether she was ill in her room; and while I was settling this query Mr. Screw left me abruptly.

I rushed away to the back court, where the Castle Brady stables stand, and there I found a dragoon whistling the 'Roast Beef of Old England,'* as he cleaned down a cavalry horse. 'Whose horse, fellow, is that?' cried I. 'Feller, indeed!' replied the Englishman; 'the horse belongs to my captain, and he's a better *feller* nor you any day.'

I did not stop to break his bones, as I would on another occasion, for a horrible suspicion had come across me, and I made for the garden as quickly as I could.

I knew somehow what I should see there. I saw Captain Quin and Nora pacing the alley together. Her arm was under his, and the scoundrel was fondling and squeezing the hand which lay closely nestling against his odious waistcoat. Some distance beyond them was Captain Fagan of the Kilwangan regiment, who was paying court to Nora's sister Mysie.

I am not afraid of any man or ghost; but as I saw that sight my knees fell a-trembling violently under me, and such a sickness came over me, that I was fain to sink down on the grass by a tree against which I leaned, and lost almost all consciousness for a minute or two; then I gathered myself up, and, advancing towards the couple on the walk, loosened the blade of the little silver-hilted hanger I always wore in its scabbard; for I was resolved to pass it through the body of the delinquents, and spit them like two pigeons. I don't tell what feelings else besides those of rage were passing through my mind, what bitter blank disappointment, what mad wild despair, what a sensation as if the whole world was tumbling from under me: I make no doubt that my reader hath been jilted by the ladies many times, and so bid him recall his own sensations when the shock first fell upon him.

'No, Norelia,' said the captain (for it was the fashion of those times for lovers to call themselves by the most romantic names out of novels), 'except for you and four others, I vow before all the gods, my heart has never felt the soft flame!'

'Ah! you men, you men, Eugenio!'* said she (the beast's name was John), 'your passion is not equal to ours. We are like—like some plant I've read of—we bear but one flower, and then we die!'

'Do you mean you never felt an inclination for another?' said Captain Quin.

'Never, my Eugenio, but for thee! How can you ask a blushing nymph such a question?'

'Darling Norelia!' said he, raising her hand to his lips.

I had a knot of cherry-coloured ribands, which she had given me out of her breast, and which somehow I always wore upon me. I pulled these out of my bosom and flung them in Captain Quin's face, and rushed out with my little sword drawn, shrieking, 'She's a liar—she's a liar, Captain Quin! Draw, sir, and defend yourself, if you are a man!' and with these words I leaped at the monster, and collared him, while Nora made the air echo with her screams; at the sound of which the other captain and Mysie hastened up.

Although I sprang up like a weed in my illness, and was now nearly attained to my full growth of six feet, yet I was but a lath by the side of the enormous English captain, who had calves and shoulders such as no chairman at Bath ever boasted. He turned very red, and then exceedingly pale at my attack upon him, and slipped back and clutched at his sword—when Nora, in an agony of terror, flung herself round him, screaming, 'Eugenio! Captain Quin, for Heaven's sake spare the child—he is but an infant!'

'And ought to be whipped for his impudence,' said the captain; 'but never fear, Miss Brady, I shall not touch him; your *favourite* is safe from me.' So saying, he stooped down and picked up the bunch of ribands which I had flung at Nora's feet, and handing it to her, said in a sarcastic tone, 'When ladies make presents to gentlemen, it is time for *other* gentlemen to retire.'

'Good heavens, Quin!' cried the girl, 'he is but a boy.'

'I'm a man,' roared I, 'and will prove it.'

'And don't signify any more than my parrot or lap-dog. Mayn't I give a bit of riband to my own cousin?'

'You are perfectly welcome, miss,' continued the captain, 'as many yards as you like.'

'Monster!' exclaimed the dear girl; 'your father was a tailor, and you are always thinking of the shop. But I'll have my revenge, I will! Reddy, will you see me insulted?'

'Indeed, Miss Nora,' says I, 'I intend to have his blood as sure as my name's Redmond.'

'I'll send for the usher to cane you, little boy,' said the

captain, regaining his self-possession; 'but as for you, miss, I have the honour to wish you a good day.'

He took off his hat with much ceremony, and made a low *congé*, and was just walking off, when Mick, my cousin, came up, whose ear had likewise been caught by the scream.

'Hoity-toity! Jack Quin, what's the matter here?' says Mick; 'Nora in tears, Redmond's ghost here with his sword drawn, and you making a bow?'

'I'll tell you what it is, Mr. Brady,' said the Englishman; 'I have had enough of Miss Nora here and your Irish ways. I ain't used to 'em, sir.'

'Well, well! what is it?' said Mick, good-humouredly (for he owed Quin a great deal of money, as it turned out); 'we'll make you used to our ways, or adopt English ones.'

'It's not the English way for ladies to have two lovers' (the 'Henglish way,' as the captain called it), 'and so, Mr. Brady, I'll thank you to pay me the sum you owe me, and I resign all claims to this young lady. If she has a fancy for schoolboys, let her take 'em, sir.'

'Pooh, pooh! Quin, you are joking,' said Mick.

'I never was more in earnest,' replied the other.

'By Heaven, then look to yourself!' shouted Mick. 'Infamous seducer! infernal deceiver!—you come and wind your toils round this suffering angel here—you win her heart and leave her—and fancy her brother won't defend her? Draw this minute, you slave! and let me cut the wicked heart out of your body!'

'This is regular assassination,' said Quin, starting back; 'there's two on 'em on me at once. Fagan, you won't let 'em murder me?'

'Faith!' said Captain Fagan, who seemed mightily amused, 'you may settle your own quarrel, Captain Quin;' and coming over to me, whispered, 'At him again, you little fellow.'

'As long as Mr. Quin withdraws his claim,' said I, 'I, of course, do not interfere.'

'I do, sir,—I do,' said Mr. Quin, more and more flustered.

'Then defend yourself like a man,—curse you!' cried Mick again. 'Mysie, lead this poor victim away—Redmond and Fagan will see fair play between us.'

'Well, now—I don't—give me time—I'm puzzled—I—I don't know which way to look.'

'Like the donkey betwixt the two bundles of hay,' said Mr. Fagan, dryly, 'and there's pretty pickings on either side.'

CHAPTER II

IN WHICH I SHOW MYSELF TO BE A MAN OF SPIRIT

DURING this dispute, my cousin Nora did the only thing that a lady, under such circumstances, could do, and fainted in due form. I was in hot altercation with Mick at the time, or I should have, of course, flown to her assistance, but Captain Fagan (a dry sort of fellow this Fagan was) prevented me, saying, 'I advise you to leave the young lady to herself, Master Redmond, and be sure she will come to.' And so, indeed, after a while, she did, which has shown me since that Fagan knew the world pretty well, for many's the lady I've seen in after times recover in a similar manner. Quin did not offer to help her, you may be sure, for, in the midst of the diversion, caused by her screaming, the faithless bully stole away.

'Which of us is Captain Quin to engage?' said I to Mick; for it was my first affair, and I was as proud of it as of a suit of laced velvet. 'Is it you or I, cousin Mick, that is to have the honour of chastising this insolent Englishman?' And I held out my hand as I spoke, for my heart melted towards my cousin under the triumph of the moment.

But he rejected the proffered offer of friendship. 'You—you!' said he, in a towering passion; 'hang you for a meddling brat, your hand is in everybody's pie. What business had you to come brawling and quarrelling here, with a gentleman who has fifteen hundred a year?'

'Oh,' gasped Nora, from the stone bench, 'I shall die; I know I shall. I shall never leave this spot.'

'The Captain's not gone yet,' whispered Fagan, on which Nora, giving him an indignant look, jumped up and walked towards the house.

'Meanwhile,' Mick continued, 'what business have you, you meddling rascal, to interfere with a daughter of this house?'

'Rascal yourself!' roared I; 'call me another such name, Mick Brady, and I'll drive my hanger into your weasand. Recollect, I stood to you when I was eleven years old. I'm your match now, and, by Jove, provoke me, and I'll beat you like—like your younger brother always did.' That was a home-cut, and I saw Mick turn blue with fury.

'This is a pretty way to recommend yourself to the family,' said Fagan, in a soothing tone.

'The girl's old enough to be his mother,' growled Mick.

'Old or not,' I replied: 'you listen to this, Mick Brady' (and I swore a tremendous oath, that need not be put down here), 'the man that marries Nora Brady must first kill me—do you mind that?'

'Pooh, sir,' said Mick, turning away, 'kill you,—flog you, you mean! I'll send for Nick the huntsman to do it;' and so he went off.

Captain Fagan now came up, and, taking me kindly by the hand, said I was a gallant lad, and he liked my spirit. 'But what Brady says is true,' continued he; 'it's a hard thing to give a lad counsel who is in such a far-gone state as you; but, believe me, I know the world, and if you will but follow my advice, you won't regret having taken it. Nora Brady has not a penny; you are not a whit richer. You are but fifteen, and she's four-and-twenty. In ten years, when you're old enough to marry, she will be an old woman; and, my poor boy, don't you see—though it's a hard matter to see—that she's a flirt, and does not care a pin for you or Quin either?'

But who in love (or in any other point, for the matter of that) listens to advice? I never did, and I told Captain Fagan fairly, that Nora might love me or not, as she liked, but that Quin should fight me before he married her—that I swore.

'Faith,' says Fagan, 'I think you are a lad that's likely to keep your word;' and, looking hard at me for a second or two, he walked away likewise, humming a tune; and I saw he looked back at me as he went through the old gate out of the garden. And when he was gone, and I was quite alone, I flung myself down on the bench where Nora had made believe to faint, and had left her handkerchief; and, taking it up, hid my face in it, and burst into such a passion of tears, as I would then have had nobody see for the world. The crumpled riband which I had flung at Quin lay in the walk, and I sat there for hours, as wretched as any man in Ireland, I believe, for the time being. But it's a changeable world! When we consider how great our sorrows *seem*, and how small they *are*;

how we think we shall die of grief, and how quickly we forget, I think we ought to be ashamed of ourselves and our fickle-heartedness. For, after all, what business has Time to bring us consolation ? I have not, perhaps, in the course of my multifarious adventures and experience, hit upon the right woman; and have forgotten, after a little, every single creature I adored; but I think, if I could but have lighted on the right one, I would have loved her *for ever*.

I must have sat for some hours bemoaning myself on the garden-bench, for it was morning when I came to Castle Brady, and the dinner-bell clanged as usual at three o'clock, which wakened me up from my reverie. Presently I gathered up the handkerchief, and once more took the riband. As I passed through the offices, I saw the captain's saddle was still hanging up at the stable-door, and saw his odious red-coated brute of a servant swaggering with the scullion-girls and kitchen-people. 'The Englishman's still there, Master Redmond,' said one of the maids to me (a sentimental black-eyed girl, who waited on the young ladies). 'He's there in the parlour, with the sweetest fillet of *vale;* go in, and don't let him browbeat you, Master Redmond.'

And in I went, and took my place at the bottom of the big table, as usual, and my friend the butler speedily brought me a cover.

'Hallo, Reddy, my boy ! ' said my uncle, 'up and well ?—that's right.'

'He'd better be home with his mother,' growled my aunt.

'Don't mind her,' says uncle Brady ; 'it's the cold goose she ate at breakfast didn't agree with her. Take a glass of spirits, Mrs. Brady, to Redmond's health.' It was evident he did not know of what had happened ; but Mick, who was at dinner too, and Ulick, and almost all the girls, looked exceedingly black, and the captain foolish ; and Miss Nora, who was again by his side, ready to cry. Captain Fagan sat smiling ; and I looked on as cold as a stone. I thought the dinner would choke me, but I was determined to put a good face on it ; and when the cloth was drawn, filled my glass with the rest ; and we drank the King and the Church, as gentlemen should. My uncle was in high good humour, and especially always joking with Nora and the captain. It was, 'Nora, divide that merrythought with the captain! see who'll be married first.' 'Jack Quin, my dear boy, never mind a clean glass for the claret, we're short of crystal at Castle Brady; take Nora's and the wine will taste none the worse;' and so on. He was in the highest glee,—I did not know why. Had there been a reconciliation between the faithless girl and her lover since they had come into the house?

I learned the truth very soon. At the third toast, it was always the custom for the ladies to withdraw; but my uncle stopped them this time, in spite of the remonstrances of Nora, who said, 'O, pa! do let us go!' and said, 'No, Mrs. Brady and ladies, if you plaise; this is a sort of toast that is drunk a great dale too seldom in my family, and you'll please to receive it with all the honours. Here's CAPTAIN AND MRS. JOHN QUIN, and long life to them. Kiss her, Jack, you rogue; for, faith, you've got a treasure!'

'He has already,' . . . I screeched out, springing up.

'Hold your tongue, you fool—hold your tongue!' said big Ulick, who sat by me; but I wouldn't hear.

'He has already,' I screamed, 'been slapped in the face this morning, Captain John Quin; he's already been called coward, Captain John Quin; and this is the way I'll drink his health. "Here's your health, Captain John Quin:"' and I flung a glass of claret into his face. I don't know how he looked after it, for the next moment I myself was under the table, tripped up by Ulick, who hit me a violent cuff on the head as I went down; and I had hardly leisure to hear the general screaming and scurrying that was taking place above me, being so fully occupied with kicks, and thumps, and curses, with which Ulick was belabouring me. 'You fool!' roared he—'you great blundering marplot—you silly beggarly brat' (a thump at each), 'hold your tongue!' These blows from Ulick, of course, I did not care for, for he had always been my friend, and had been in the habit of thrashing me all my life.

When I got up from under the table all the ladies were gone; and I had the satisfaction of seeing the captain's nose was bleeding, as mine was—*his* was cut across the bridge, and his beauty spoiled for ever. Ulick shook himself, sat down quietly, filled a bumper, and pushed the bottle to me. 'There, you young donkey,' said he, 'sup that; and let's hear no more of your braying.'

'In Heaven's name, what does all the row mean?' says my uncle. 'Is the boy in the fever again?'

'It's all your fault,' said Mick, sulkily: 'yours and those who brought him here.'

'Hold your noise, Mick!' says Ulick, turning on him; 'speak civil of my father and me, and don't let me be called upon to teach you manners.'

'It *is* your fault,' repeated Mick. 'What business has the vagabond here? If I had my will, I'd have him flogged and turned out.'

'And so he should be,' said Captain Quin.

'You'd best not try it, Quin,' said Ulick, who was always my champion; and, turning to his father, 'The fact is, sir, that the young monkey has fallen in love with Nora, and finding her and the captain mighty sweet in the garden to-day, he was for murdering Jack Quin.'

'Gad, he's beginning young,' said my uncle, quite good-humouredly. 'Faith, Fagan, that boy's a Brady, every inch of him.'

'And I'll tell you what, Mr. B,' cried Quin, bristling up; 'I've been insulted grossly in this '*ouse*. I ain't at all satisfied with these here ways of going on. I'm an Englishman, I am, and a man of property: and I—I——'

'If you're insulted, and not satisfied, remember there's two of us, Quin,' said Ulick, gruffly. On which the captain fell to washing his nose in water, and answered never a word.

'Mr. Quin,' said I, in the most dignified tone I could assume, 'may also have satisfaction any time he pleases, by calling on Redmond Barry, Esquire, of Barryville.' At which speech my uncle burst out a-laughing (as he did at everything); and in this laugh, Captain Fagan, much to my mortification, joined. I turned rather smartly upon him, however, and bade him to understand, that though I was a boy, for my cousin Ulick, who had been my best friend through life, I could put up with rough treatment from him; yet, even that sort of treatment I would bear from him no longer; and that any other person who ventured on the like would find me a man to their cost. 'Mr. Quin,' I added, 'knows that fact very well; and, if *he's* a man, he'll know where to find me.'

My uncle now observed that it was getting late, and that my mother would be anxious about me. 'One of you had better go home with him,' said he, turning to his sons, 'or the lad may be playing more pranks.' But Ulick said, with a nod to his brother, 'Both of us ride home with Quin here.'

'I'm not afraid of Freeny's people,'* said the captain, with a faint attempt at a laugh; 'my man is armed, and so am I.'

'You know the use of arms very well, Quin,' said Ulick; 'and no one can doubt your courage; but Mick and I will see you home for all that.'

'Why, you'll not be home till morning, boys. Kilwangan's a good ten mile from here.'

'We'll sleep at Quin's quarters,' replied Ulick: '*we're going to stop a week there.*'

'Thank you,' says Quin, very faint; 'it's very kind of you.'

'You'll be lonely, you know, without us.'

'Oh, yes, very lonely!' says Quin.

'And in *another week*, my boy,' says Ulick (and here he whispered something in the captain's ear, in which I thought I caught the words 'marriage,' 'parson,' and felt all my fury returning again).

'As you please,' whined out the captain; and the horses were quickly brought round, and the three gentlemen rode away.

Fagan stopped, and, at my uncle's injunction, walked across the old treeless park with me. He said that, after the quarrel at dinner, he thought I would scarcely want to see the ladies that night, in which opinion I concurred entirely; and so we went off without an adieu.

'A pretty day's work of it you have made, Master Redmond,' said he. 'What! you, a friend to the Bradys, and knowing your uncle to be distressed for money, try and break off a match which will bring fifteen hundred a year into the family? Quin has promised to pay off the four thousand pounds which is bothering your uncle so. He takes a girl without a penny—a girl with no more beauty than yonder bullock. Well, well, don't look furious; let's say she *is* handsome—there's no accounting for tastes,—a girl that has been flinging herself at the head of every man in these parts these ten years past, and *missing* them all. And you, as poor as herself, a boy of fifteen—well, sixteen, if you insist—and a boy who ought to be attached to your uncle as to your father——'

'And so I am,' said I.

'And this is the return you make him for his kindness! Didn't he harbour you in his house when you were an orphan, and hasn't he given you rent-free your fine mansion of Barryville yonder? And now, when his affairs can be put into order, and a chance offers for his old age to be made comfortable, who flings himself in the way of him and competence?—You, of all others; the man in the world most obliged to him. It's wicked, ungrateful, unnatural. From a lad of such spirit as you are, I expected truer courage.'

'I am not afraid of any man alive,' exclaimed I (for this latter part of the captain's argument had rather staggered me, and I wished, of course, to turn it, as one always should when the enemy's too strong); 'and it's *I* am the injured man, Captain Fagan. No man was ever, since the world began, treated so. Look here—look at this riband. I've worn it in my heart for six months. I've had it there all the time of the fever. Didn't Nora take it out of her own bosom and give it me? Didn't she kiss me when she gave it me, and call me her darling Redmond.'

'She was *practising*,' replied Mr. Fagan, with a sneer. 'I know women, sir. Give them time, and let nobody else come to the house, and they'll fall in love with a chimney-sweep. There was a young lady in Fermoy——'

'A young lady in flames,' roared I (but I used a still hotter word). 'Mark this, come what will of it, I swear I'll fight the man who pretends to the hand of Nora Brady. I'll follow him, if it's into the church, and meet him there. I'll have his blood, or he shall have mine; and this riband shall be found dyed in it. Yes! and if I kill him, I'll pin it on his breast, and then she may go take back her token.' This I said because I was very much excited at the time, and because I had not read my novels and romantic plays for nothing.

'Well,' says Fagan after a pause, 'if it must be, it must. For a young fellow, you are the most bloodthirsty I ever saw. Quin's a determined fellow, too.'

'Will you take my message to him?' said I, quite eagerly.

'Hush!' said Fagan: 'your mother may be on the look-out. Here we are, close to Barryville.'

'Mind! not a word to my mother,' I said; and went

into the house swelling with pride and exultation to think that I should have a chance against the Englishman I hated so.

Tim, my servant, had come up from Barryville on my mother's return from church, for the good lady was rather alarmed at my absence, and anxious for my return. But he had seen me go in to dinner, at the invitation of the sentimental lady's-maid; and when he had had his own share of the good things in the kitchen, which was always better furnished than ours at home, had walked back again to inform his mistress where I was, and, no doubt, to tell her, in his own fashion, of all the events that had happened at Castle Brady. In spite of my precautions to secrecy, then, I half suspected that my mother knew all, from the manner in which she embraced me on my arrival, and received our guest, Captain Fagan. The poor soul looked a little anxious and flushed, and every now and then gazed very hard in the captain's face, but she said not a word about the quarrel, for she had a noble spirit, and would as lief have seen any one of her kindred hanged as shirking from the field of honour. What has become of those gallant feelings nowadays? Sixty years ago a man was a *man*, in old Ireland, and the sword that was worn by his side was at the service of any gentleman's gizzard, upon the slightest difference. But the good old times and usages are fast fading away. One scarcely ever hears of a fair meeting now, and the use of those cowardly pistols, in place of the honourable and manly weapon of gentlemen, has introduced a deal of knavery into the practice of duelling that cannot be sufficiently deplored.

When I arrived at home I felt that I was a man in earnest, and welcoming Captain Fagan to Barryville, and introducing him to my mother, in a majestic and dignified way, said the captain must be thirsty after his walk, and called upon Tim to bring up a bottle of the yellow-sealed Bordeaux, and cakes and glasses, immediately.

Tim looked at the mistress in great wonderment; and the fact is, that six hours previous I would as soon have thought of burning the house down as calling for a bottle of claret on my own account; but I felt I was a man now, and had a right to command; and my mother felt this too, for she turned to the fellow and said, sharply, 'Don't you hear, you rascal, what *your master* says? Go, get the wine, and the cakes and glasses, directly.' Then (for you may be sure she did not give Tim the keys of our little cellar) she went and got the liquor herself; and Tim brought it in, on the silver tray, in due form. My dear mother poured out the wine, and drank the captain welcome; but I observed her hand shook very much as she performed this courteous duty, and the bottle went clink, clink, against the glass. When she had tasted her glass, she said she had a headache, and would go to bed; and so I asked her blessing, as becomes a dutiful son—(the modern *bloods* have given up the respectful ceremonies which distinguished a gentleman in my time)—and she left me and Captain Fagan to talk over our important business.

'Indeed,' said the captain, 'I see now no other way out of the scrape than a meeting. The fact is, there was a talk of it at Castle Brady, after your attack upon Quin this afternoon, and he vowed that he would cut you in pieces; but the tears and supplications of Miss Honoria induced him, though very unwillingly, to relent. Now, however, matters have gone too far. No officer, bearing his Majesty's commission, can receive a glass of wine on his nose—this claret of yours is very good, by the way, and by your leave we'll ring for another bottle—without resenting the affront. Fight you must, and Quin is a huge strong fellow.'

'He'll give the better mark,' said I. 'I am not afraid of him.'

'In faith,' said the captain, 'I believe you are not; for a lad I never saw more game in my life.'

'Look at that sword, sir,' says I, pointing to an elegant silver-mounted one, in a white shagreen*case, that hung on the mantelpiece, under the picture of my father, Harry Barry. 'It was with that sword, sir, that my father pinked Mohawk O'Driscol, in Dublin, in the year 1740: with that sword, sir, he met Sir Huddlestone Fuddlestone, the Hampshire baronet, and ran him through the neck. They met, on horseback, with sword and pistol, on Hounslow Heath, as, I dare say, you have heard tell of, and those are the pistols (they hung on each side of the picture) which the gallant Barry used. He was quite in the wrong, having insulted Lady Fuddlestone, when in liquor, at the Brentford assembly. But like a gentleman, he scorned to apologize, and Sir Huddlestone received a ball through his hat, before they engaged with the sword. I am Harry

Barry's son, sir, and will act as becomes my name and my quality.'

'Give me a kiss, my dear boy,' said Fagan, with tears in his eyes. 'You're after my own soul. As long as Jack Fagan lives, you shall never want a friend or a second.'

Poor fellow! he was shot six months afterwards, carrying orders to my Lord George Sackville, at Minden,* and I lost thereby a kind friend. But we don't know what is in store for us, and that night was a merry one at least. We had a second bottle, and a third too (I could hear the poor mother going downstairs for each, but she never came into the parlour with them, and sent them in by the butler, Mr. Tim); and we parted at length, he engaging to arrange matters with Mr. Quin's second that night, and to bring me news in the morning as to the place where the meeting should take place. I have often thought since, how different my fate might have been, had I not fallen in love with Nora at that early age; and had I not flung the wine in Quin's face, and so brought on the duel! I might have settled down in Ireland but for that (for Miss Quinlan was an heiress, within twenty miles of us, and Peter Burke, of Kilwangan, left his daughter Judy 700*l*. a year, and I might have had either of them, had I waited a few years). But it was in my fate to be a wanderer, and that battle with Quin sent me on my travels at a very early age, as you shall hear anon.

I never slept sounder in my life, though I woke a little earlier than usual, and you may be sure my first thought was of the event of the day, for which I was fully prepared. I had ink and pen in my room—had I not been writing these verses to Nora but the day previous, like a poor fond fool as I was? And now I sat down and wrote a couple of letters more; they might be the last, thought I, that I ever should write in my life. The first was to my mother. 'Honoured Madam'—I wrote—'This will not be given you unless I fall by the hand of Captain Quin, whom I meet this day in the field of honour, with sword and pistol. If I die, it is as a good Christian and a gentleman,—how should I be otherwise when educated by such a mother as you? I forgive all my enemies—I beg your blessing, as a dutiful son. I desire that my mare Nora, which my uncle gave me, and which I called after the most faithless of her sex, may be returned to Castle Brady, and beg you will give my silver-hilted hanger to Phil Purcell, the gamekeeper. Present my duty to my uncle and Ulick, and all the girls of *my* party there. And I remain your dutiful son,—REDMOND BARRY.'

To Nora I wrote,—'This letter will be found in my bosom along with the token you gave me. It will be dyed in my blood (unless I have Captain Quin's, whom I hate, but forgive), and will be a pretty ornament for you on your marriage day. Wear it, and think of the poor boy to whom you gave it, and who died (as he was always ready to do) for your sake.—REDMOND.'

These letters being written, and sealed with my father's great silver seal of the Barry arms, I went down to breakfast, where my mother was waiting for me, you may be sure. We did not say a single word about what was taking place; on the contrary, we talked of anything but that; about who was at church the day before, and about my wanting new clothes now I was grown so tall. She said, I must have a suit against winter, if—if—she could afford it. She winced rather at the 'if,' Heaven bless her! I knew what was in her mind. And then she fell to telling me about the black pig that must be killed, and that she had found the speckled hen's nest that morning, whose eggs I liked so, and other such trifling talk. Some of these eggs were for breakfast, and I ate them with a good appetite; but in helping myself to salt I spilled it, on which she started up with a scream. '*Thank God*,' said she, '*it's fallen towards me*.' And then, her heart being too full, she left the room. Ah! they have their faults, those mothers; but are there any other women like them?

When she was gone I went to take down the sword with which my father had vanquished the Hampshire baronet, and, would you believe it, the brave woman had tied *a new riband* to the hilt, for indeed she had the courage of a lioness and a Brady united. And then I took down the pistols, which were always kept bright and well oiled, and put some fresh flints I had into the locks, and got balls and powder ready against the captain should come. There was claret and a cold fowl put ready for him on the sideboard, and a case-bottle of old brandy too, with a couple of little glasses on the silver tray with the Barry arms emblazoned. In after-life, and in the midst of my fortune and splendour, I paid thirty-five guineas, and almost as much more interest, to the London goldsmith who supplied my father with that very tray. A scoundrel pawnbroker would only give me sixteen for it afterwards, so little can we trust the honour of rascally tradesmen !

At eleven o'clock Captain Fagan arrived, on horseback, with a mounted dragoon after him. He paid his compliments to the collation which my mother's care had provided for him, and then said, 'Look ye, Redmond, my boy ; this is a silly business. The girl will marry Quin, mark my words ; and as sure as she does you'll forget her. You are but a boy. Quin is willing to consider you as such. Dublin's a fine place, and if you have a mind to take a ride thither and see the town for a month, here are twenty guineas at your service. Make Quin an apology, and be off.'

'A man of honour, Mr. Fagan,' says I, 'dies, but never apologizes. I'll see the captain hanged before I apologize.'

'Then there's nothing for it but a meeting.'

'My mare is saddled and ready,' says I, 'where's the meeting, and who's the captain's second ?'

'Your cousins go out with him,' answered Mr. Fagan.

'I'll ring for my groom to bring my mare round,' I said, 'as soon as you have rested yourself.' Tim was accordingly dispatched for Nora, and I rode away, but I didn't take leave of Mrs. Barry. The curtains of her bedroom windows were down, and they didn't move as we mounted and trotted off. . . . *But two hours afterwards*, you should have seen her as she came tottering downstairs, and heard the scream which she gave as she hugged her boy to her heart, quite unharmed and without a wound in his body.

What had taken place I may as well tell here. When we got to the ground, Ulick, Mick, and the captain were already there, Quin, flaming in red regimentals, as big a monster as ever led a grenadier company. The party were laughing together at some joke of one or the other, and I must say I thought this laughter very unbecoming in my cousins, who were met, perhaps, to see the death of one of their kindred.

'I hope to spoil this sport,' says I to Captain Fagan, in a great rage, 'and trust to see this sword of mine in yonder big bully's body.'

'Oh ! it's with pistols we fight,' replied Mr. Fagan. 'You are no match for Quin with the sword.'

'I'll match any man with the sword,' said I.

'But swords are to-day impossible; Captain Quin is—is lame. He knocked his knee against the swinging park gate last night, as he was riding home, and can scarce move it now.'

'Not against Castle Brady gate,' says I, 'that has been off the hinges these ten years.' On which Fagan said it must have been some other gate, and repeated what he had said to Mr. Quin and my cousins, when, on alighting from our horses, we joined and saluted those gentlemen.

'Oh, yes! dead lame,' said Ulick, coming to shake me by the hand, while Captain Quin took off his hat and turned extremely red. 'And very lucky for you, Redmond, my boy,' continued Ulick; 'you were a dead man else, for he is a devil of a fellow—isn't he, Fagan?'

'A regular Turk,' answered Fagan; adding, 'I never yet knew the man who stood to Captain Quin.'

'Hang the business!' said Ulick; 'I hate it. I'm ashamed of it. Say you're sorry, Redmond; you can easily say that.'

'If the young *feller* will go to *Dubling*, as proposed—' here interposed Mr. Quin.

'I am *not* sorry—I'll *not* apologize—and I'll as soon go to *Dubling* as to ——!' said I, with a stamp of my foot.

'There's nothing else for it,' said Ulick, with a laugh to Fagan. 'Take your ground, Fagan,—twelve paces, I suppose?'

'Ten, sir,' said Mr. Quin, in a big voice; 'and make them short ones, do you hear, Captain Fagan?'

'Don't bully, Mr. Quin,' said Ulick, surlily; 'here are the pistols.' And he added, with some emotion, to me, 'God bless you, my boy; and when I count three, fire.'

Mr. Fagan put my pistol into my hand,—that is, not one of mine (which were to serve, if need were, for the next round), but one of Ulick's. 'They are all right,' said he. 'Never fear: and, Redmond, fire at his neck—hit him there under the gorget. See how the fool shows himself open.'

Mick, who had never spoken a word, Ulick, and the captain retired to one side, and Ulick gave the signal. It was slowly given, and I had leisure to cover my man well. I saw him changing colour and trembling as the numbers were given. At 'three,' both our pistols went off. I heard something whiz by me, and my antagonist, giving a most horrible groan, staggered backwards and fell.

'He's down—he's down!' cried the seconds, running towards him. Ulick lifted him up—Mick took his head.

'He's hit here, in the neck,' said Mick; and laying open his coat, blood was seen gurgling from under his gorget, at the very spot at which I aimed,

'How is it with you?' said Ulick. 'Is he really hit?' said he, looking hard at him. The unfortunate man did not answer, but when the support of Ulick's arm was withdrawn from his back, groaned once more, and fell backwards.

'The young fellow has begun well,' said Mick, with a scowl. 'You had better ride off, young sir, before the police* are up. They had wind of the business before we left Kilwangan.'

'Is he quite dead?' said I.

'Quite dead,' answered Mick.

'Then the world's rid of *a coward*,' said Captain Fagan, giving the huge prostrate body a scornful kick with his foot. 'It's all over with him, Reddy,—he doesn't stir.'

'*We* are not cowards, Fagan,' said Ulick, roughly, 'whatever he was! Let's get the boy off as quick as we may. Your man shall go for a cart, and take away the body of this unhappy gentleman. This has been a sad day's work for our family, Redmond Barry, and you have robbed us of 1500*l.* a year.'

'It was Nora did it,' said I; 'not I.' And I took the riband she gave me out of my waistcoat, and the letter, and flung them down on the body of Captain Quin. 'There!' says I—'take her those ribands. She'll know what they mean; and that's all that's left to her of two lovers she had and ruined.'

I did not feel any horror or fear, young as I was, in seeing my enemy prostrate before me; for I knew that I had met and conquered him honourably in the field, as became a man of my name and blood.

'And now, in Heaven's name, get the youngster out of the way,' said Mick.

Ulick said he would ride with me, and off accordingly we galloped, never drawing bridle till we came to my mother's door. When there, Ulick told Tim to feed my mare, as I would have far to ride that day, and I was in the poor mother's arms in a minute.

I need not tell how great were her pride and exultation when she heard from Ulick's lips the account of my behaviour at the duel. He urged, however, that I should go into hiding for a short time; and it was agreed between them that I should drop my name of Barry, and, taking that of Redmond, go to Dublin, and there wait until matters were blown over. This arrangement was not come to without some discussion; for why should I not be as safe at Barryville, she said, as my cousin and Ulick at Castle Brady?—bailiffs and duns never got near *them;* why should constables be enabled to come upon me? But Ulick persisted in the necessity of my instant departure, in which argument, as I was anxious to see the world, I must confess I sided with him; and my mother was brought to see that in our small house at Barryville, in the midst of the village, and with the guard but of a couple of servants, escape would be impossible. So the kind soul was forced to yield to my cousin's entreaties, who promised her, however, that the affair would soon be arranged, and that I should be restored to her. Ah! how little did he know what fortune was in store for me!

My dear mother had some forebodings, I think, that our separation was to be a long one; for she told me that all night long she had been consulting the cards regarding my fate in the duel; and that all the signs betokened a separation; and, taking out a stocking from her escritoire, the kind soul put twenty guineas in a purse for me (she had herself but twenty-five), and made up a little valise, to be placed at the back of my mare, in which were my clothes, linen, and a silver dressing-case of my father's. She bade me, too, to keep the sword and the pistols I had known to use so like a man. She hurried my departure now (though her heart, I know, was full), and almost in half an hour after my arrival at home I was once more on the road again, with the wide world, as it were, before me. I need not tell how Tim and the cook cried at my departure, and, mayhap, I had a tear or two myself in my eyes; but no lad of sixteen is *very* sad who has liberty for the first time, and twenty guineas in his pocket; and I rode away, thinking, I confess, not so much of the kind mother left alone, and of the home behind me, as of to-morrow, and all the wonders it would bring.

CHAPTER III

I MAKE A FALSE START IN THE GENTEEL WORLD

I RODE that night as far as Carlow, where I lay at the best inn; and being asked what was my name by the landlord of the house, gave it as Mr. Redmond, according to my cousin's instructions, and said I was of the Redmonds of Waterford county, and was on my road to Trinity College, Dublin, to be educated there. Seeing my handsome appearance, silver-hilted sword, and well-filled valise, my landlord made free to send up a jug of claret without my asking, and charged, you may be sure, pretty handsomely for it in the bill. No gentleman in those good old days went to bed without a good share of liquor to set him sleeping, and on this my first day's entrance into the world, I made a point to act the fine gentleman completely, and, I assure you, succeeded in my part to admiration. The excitement of the events of the day, the quitting my home, the meeting with Captain Quin, were enough to set my brains in a whirl, without the claret, which served to finish me completely. I did not dream of the death of Quin, as some milksops, perhaps, would have done; indeed, I have never had any of that foolish remorse consequent upon any of my affairs of honour; always considering, from the first, that where a gentleman risks his own life in manly combat, he is a fool to be ashamed because he wins. I slept at Carlow as sound as man could sleep; drank a tankard of small beer and a toast to my breakfast; and exchanged the first of my gold pieces to settle the bill, not forgetting to pay all the servants liberally, and as a gentleman should. I began so the first day of my life, and so have continued. No man has been at greater straits than I, and has borne more pinching poverty and hardship; but nobody can say of me that, if I had a guinea, I was not free-handed with it, and did not spend it as well as a lord could do.

I had no doubts of the future; thinking that a man of my person, parts, and courage could make his way anywhere. Besides, I had twenty gold guineas in my pocket, a sum which (although I was mistaken) I calculated would last me for four months at least, during which time something would be done towards the making of my fortune. So I rode on, singing to myself, or chatting with the passers-by; and all the girls along the road said, 'God save me, for a clever gentleman!' As for Nora and Castle Brady, between to-day and yesterday there seemed to be a gap as of half a score of years. I vowed I would never re-enter the place but as a great man; and I kept my vow too, as you shall hear in due time.

There was much more liveliness and bustle on the king's high road in those times than in these days of stage-coaches,* which carry you from one end of the kingdom to another in a few score hours. The gentry rode their own horses or drove in their own coaches, and spent three days on a journey which now occupies ten hours; so that there was no lack of company for a person travelling towards Dublin. I made part of the journey from Carlow towards Naas with a well-armed gentleman from Kilkenny, dressed in green and a gold cord, with a patch on his eye, and riding a powerful mare. He asked me the question of the day, and whither I was bound, and whether my mother was not afraid on account of the highwaymen to let one so young as myself to travel? But I said, pulling out one of them from a holster, that I had a pair of good pistols that had already done execution, and were ready to do it again; and here, a pock-marked man coming up, he put spurs into his bay mare and left me. She was a much more powerful animal than mine, and, besides, I did not wish to fatigue my horse, wishing to enter Dublin that night, and in reputable condition.

As I rode towards Kilcullen, I saw a crowd of the peasant people assembled round a one-horse chair,* and my friend in green, as I thought, making off half a mile up the hill. A footman was howling 'stop thief' at the top of his voice; but the country fellows were only laughing at his distress, and making all sorts of jokes at the adventure which had just befallen.

'Sure, you might have kept him off with your blunder-*bush!*' says one fellow.

'Oh, the coward! to let the captain *bate* you; and he only one eye!' cries another.

'The next time my lady travels, she'd better lave you at home!' said a third.

'What is this noise, fellows?' said I, riding up amongst

them, and, seeing a lady in the carriage very pale and frightened, gave a slash of my whip, and bade the red-shanked ruffians keep off. 'What has happened, madam, to annoy your ladyship?' I said, pulling off my hat, and bringing my mare up in a prance to the chair-window.

The lady explained. She was the wife of Captain Fitz-simons, and was hastening to join the captain at Dublin. Her chair had been stopped by a highwayman; the great oaf of a servant-man had fallen down on his knees armed as he was; and though there were thirty people in the next field working when the ruffian attacked her, not one of them would help her, but, on the contrary, wished the captain, as they called the highwayman, good luck.

'Sure he's the friend of the poor,' said one fellow, 'and good luck to him!'

'Was it any business of ours?' asked another. And another told, grinning, that it was the famous Captain Freeny,* who, having bribed the jury to acquit him, two days back, at Kilkenny assizes, had mounted his horse at the jail door, and the very next day had robbed two barristers who were going the circuit.[1]

I told this pack of rascals to be off to their work, or they should taste of my thong, and proceeded, as well as I could, to comfort Mrs. Fitzsimons under her misfortunes. 'Had she lost much?' 'Everything: her purse, containing upwards of a hundred guineas; her jewels, snuff-boxes, watches, and a pair of diamond shoe-buckles of the captain's.' These mishaps I sincerely commiserated; and knowing her by her accent to be an Englishwoman, deplored the difference that existed between the two countries, and said that in *our* country (meaning England) such atrocities were unknown.

'You, too, are an Englishman?' said she, with rather a tone of surprise. On which I said, I was proud to be such, as, in fact, I was; and I never knew a true Tory gentleman of Ireland who did not wish he could say as much.

[1] [Mr. Barry's story may be correct; but we find in the autobiography of Captain Freeny that it was not he, but a couple of his associates, who were acquitted from a bribe of five guineas distributed amongst the jury. He describes the robbery of a lady under precisely similar circumstances. In the present day the peasantry of Tipperary look on at murders.]—Note in ***Fraser's Magazine***, omitted in later editions.

I rode by Mrs. Fitzsimons' chair all the way to Naas; and, as she had been robbed of her purse, asked permission to lend her a couple of pieces to pay her expenses at the inn, which sum she was graciously pleased to accept, and was, at the same time, kind enough to invite me to share her dinner. To the lady's questions regarding my birth and parentage, I replied that I was a young gentleman of large fortune (this was not true; but what is the use of crying bad fish? My dear mother instructed me early in this sort of prudence) and good family in the county of Waterford; that I was going to Dublin for my studies, and that my mother allowed me five hundred per annum. Mrs. Fitzsimons was equally communicative. She was the daughter of General Granby Somerset, of Worcestershire, of whom, of course, I had heard (and though I had not, of course I was too well-bred to say so); and had made, as she must confess, a runaway match with Ensign Fitzgerald Fitzsimons. Had I been in Donegal?—No! That was a pity. The captain's father possesses a hundred thousand acres there, and Fitzsimonsburgh Castle 's the finest mansion in Ireland. Captain Fitzsimons is the eldest son; and, though he has quarrelled with his father, must inherit the vast property. She went on to tell me about the balls at Dublin, the banquets at the Castle, the horse races at the Phoenix, the ridottos and routs,* until I became quite eager to join in those pleasures; and I only felt grieved to think that my position would render secrecy necessary, and prevent me from being presented at the court, of which the Fitzsimonses were the most elegant ornaments. How different was her lively rattle to that of the vulgar wenches at the Kilwangan assemblies. In every sentence she mentioned a lord or a person of quality. She evidently spoke French and Italian, of the former of which languages I have said I knew a few words; and, as for her English accent, why, perhaps, I was no judge of that, for, to say the truth, she was the first *real* English person I had ever met. She recommended me, further, to be very cautious with regard to the company I should meet at Dublin, where rogues and adventurers of all countries abounded; and my delight and gratitude to her may be imagined, when, as our conversation grew more intimate (as we sat over our dessert), she kindly offered to accommodate me with lodgings in her own house, where her Fitzsimons, she said, would welcome with delight her gallant young preserver.

'Indeed, madam,' said I, 'I have preserved nothing for you.' Which was perfectly true; for had I not come up too late after the robbery to prevent the highwayman from carrying off her money and pearls?

'And sure, ma'am, them wasn't much,' said Sullivan, the blundering servant, who had been so frightened at Freny's approach, and was waiting on us at dinner. 'Didn't he return you the thirteenpence in copper, and the watch, saying it was only pinchbeck?'

But his lady rebuked him for a saucy varlet, and turned him out of the room at once, saying to me when he had gone, 'that the fool didn't know what was the meaning of a hundred-pound bill, which was in the pocket-book that Freeny took from her.'

Perhaps had I been a little older in the world's experience, I should have begun to see that Madam Fitzsimons was not the person of fashion she pretended to be; but, as it was, I took all her stories for truth, and, when the landlord brought the bill for dinner, paid it with the air of a lord. Indeed, she made no motion to produce the two pieces I had lent to her; and so we rode on slowly towards Dublin, into which city we made our entrance at nightfall. The rattle and splendour of the coaches, the flare of the linkboys, the number and magnificence of the houses, struck me with the greatest wonder; though I was careful to disguise this feeling, according to my dear mother's directions, who told me that it was the mark of a man of fashion never to wonder at anything, and never to admit that any house, equipage, or company he saw, was more splendid or genteel than what he had been accustomed to at home.

We stopped, at length, at a house of rather mean appearance, and were let into a passage by no means so clean as that at Barryville, where there was a great smell of supper and punch. A stout, redfaced man, without a periwig, and in rather a tattered nightgown and cap, made his appearance from the parlour, and embraced his lady (for it was Captain Fitzsimons) with a great deal of cordiality. Indeed, when he saw that a stranger accompanied her, he embraced her more rapturously than ever. In introducing me, she persisted in saying that I was her preserver, and complimented my gallantry as much as if I had killed Freeny, instead of coming up when the robbery was over. The captain said he knew the Redmonds of Waterford intimately well, which assertion alarmed me, as *I* knew nothing of the family to which I was stated to belong. But I posed him, by asking *which* of the Redmonds he knew, for I had never heard his name in our family. He said, he 'knew the Redmonds of Redmondstown.' 'Oh,' says I, 'mine are the Redmonds of Castle Redmond;' and so I put him off the scent. I went to see my nag put up at a livery stable hard by, with the captain's horse and chair, and returned to my entertainer.

Although there were the relics of some mutton-chops and onions on a cracked dish before him, the captain said, 'My love, I wish I had known of your coming, for Bob Moriarty and I just finished the most delicious venison pasty, which his grace the Lord Lieutenant sent us, with a flask of sillery* from his own cellar. You know the wine, my dear? But as bygones are bygones, and no help for them, what say ye to a fine lobster and a bottle of as good claret as any in Ireland? Betty, clear these things from the table, and make the mistress and our young friend welcome to our home.'

Not having small change, Mr. Fitzsimons asked me to lend him a tenpenny-piece to purchase the dish of lobsters; but his lady, handing out one of the guineas I had given her, bade the girl get the change for that, and procure the supper, which she did presently, bringing back only a very few shillings out of the guinea to her mistress, saying that the fishmonger had kept the remainder for an old account. 'And the more great, big, blundering fool you, for giving the gold piece to him,' roared Mr. Fitzsimons. I forget how many hundred guineas he said he had paid the fellow during the year.

Our supper was seasoned, if not by any great elegance, at least by a plentiful store of anecdotes, concerning the highest personages of the city, with whom, according to himself, the captain lived on terms of the utmost intimacy. Not to be behindhand with him, I spoke of my own estates and property as if I was as rich as a duke. I told all the stories of the nobility I had ever heard from my mother, and some that, perhaps, I had invented; and ought to have been aware that my host was an impostor himself, as he did not find out my own blunders and misstatements.

But youth is ever too confident. It was some time before I knew that I had made no very desirable acquaintance in Captain Fitzsimons and his lady, and, indeed, went to bed congratulating myself upon my wonderful good luck in having, at the outset of my adventures, fallen in with so distinguished a couple.

The appearance of the chamber I occupied might, indeed, have led me to imagine that the heir of Fitzsimonsburgh Castle, county Donegal, was not as yet reconciled with his wealthy parents, and, had I been an English lad, probably my suspicion and distrust would have been aroused instantly. But, perhaps, as the reader knows, we are not so particular in Ireland on the score of neatness as people are in this precise country, hence the disorder of my bed-chamber did not strike me so much. For were not all the windows broken and stuffed with rags even at Castle Brady, my uncle's superb mansion? Was there ever a lock to the doors there, or if a lock a handle to the lock, or a hasp to fasten it to? So, though my bedroom boasted of these inconveniences, and a few more, though my counterpane was evidently a greased brocade dress of Mrs. Fitzsimons's, and my cracked toilet-glass not much bigger than a half-crown, yet I was used to this sort of ways in Irish houses, and still thought myself in that of a man of fashion. There was no lock to the drawers, which, when they *did* open, were full of my hostess's rouge-pots, shoes, stays, and rags, so I allowed my wardrobe to remain in my valise, but set out my silver dressing apparatus upon the ragged cloth on the drawers, where it shone to great advantage.

When Sullivan appeared in the morning, I asked him about my mare, which he informed me was doing well; I then bade him bring me hot shaving-water, in a loud, dignified tone.

'Hot shaving-water!' says he, bursting out laughing (and I confess not without reason). 'Is it yourself you're going to shave?' said he. 'And maybe when I bring you up the water I'll bring you up the cat too, and you can shave her.' I flung a boot at the scoundrel's head in reply to this impertinence, and was soon with my friends in the parlour for breakfast. There was a hearty welcome, and the same cloth that had been used the night before, as I recognized by the black mark of the Irish-stew dish, and the stain left by a pot of porter at supper.

My host greeted me with great cordiality; Mrs. Fitzsimons said I was an elegant figure for the Phoenix; and, indeed, without vanity, I may say of myself that there were worse-looking fellows in Dublin than I. I had not the powerful chest and muscular proportion which I have since attained (to be exchanged, alas! for gouty legs and chalk-stones in my fingers, but 'tis the way of mortality), but I had arrived at near my present growth of six feet, and with my hair in buckle, a handsome lace *jabot*[*] and wristbands to my shirt, and a red plush waistcoat, barred with gold, looked the gentleman I was born. I wore my drab[*] coat with plate buttons, that was grown too small for me, and quite agreed with Captain Fitzsimons that I must pay a visit to his tailor, in order to procure myself a coat more fitting my size.

'I needn't ask whether you had a comfortable bed,' said he. 'Young Fred Pimpleton (Lord Pimpleton's second son) slept in it for seven months, during which he did me the honour to stay with me, and if *he* was satisfied, I don't know who else wouldn't be.'

After breakfast we walked out to see the town, and Mr. Fitzsimons introduced me to several of his acquaintances whom we met, as his particular young friend Mr. Redmond, of Waterford county; he also presented me at his hatter's and tailor's as a gentleman of great expectations and large property; and although I told the latter that I should not pay him ready cash for more than one coat, which fitted me to a nicety, yet he insisted upon making me several, which I did not care to refuse. The captain, also, who certainly wanted such a renewal of raiment, told the tailor to send him home a handsome military frock, which he selected.

Then we went home to Mrs. Fitzsimons, who drove out in her chair to the Phoenix Park, where a review was, and where numbers of the young gentry were round about her, to all of whom she presented me as her preserver of the day before. Indeed, such was her complimentary account of me, that before half an hour I had got to be considered as a young gentleman of the highest family in the land, related to all the principal nobility, a cousin of Captain Fitzsimons, and heir to 10,000*l.* a year. Fitzsimons said he had ridden over every inch of my estate; and faith, as he chose to tell these stories for me, I let him have his way—indeed was not a little pleased (as youth is) to be made much of, and to pass for a great personage. I had little notion then that I had got among a set of impostors—that Captain Fitzsimons was only an adventurer, and his lady a person of no credit; but such are the dangers to which youth is perpetually subject, and hence let young men take warning by me.[1]

I purposely hurry over the description of my life, in which the incidents were painful, of no great interest except to my unlucky self, and of which my companions were certainly not of a kind befitting my quality. The fact was, a young man could hardly have fallen into worse hands than those in which I now found myself. I have been to Donegal since, and have never seen the famous Castle of Fitzsimonsburgh, which is, likewise, unknown to the oldest inhabitants of that county; nor are the Granby Somersets much better known in Hampshire.* The couple into whose hands I had fallen were of a sort much more common than those at present, for the vast wars of later days have rendered it very difficult for noblemen's footmen or hangers-on to procure commissions, and such, in fact, had been the original station of Captain Fitzsimons. Had I known his origin, of course I would have died rather than have associated with him; but in those simple days of youth I took his tales for truth, and fancied myself in high luck at being, in my outset into life, introduced into such a family. Alas! we are the sport of destiny. When I consider upon what small circumstances all the great events of my life have turned, I can hardly believe myself to have been anything but a puppet in the hands of Fate, which has played its most fantastic tricks upon me.

The captain had been a gentleman's gentleman, and his lady of no higher rank. The society which this worthy pair kept was at a sort of ordinary which they held, and at which their friends were always welcome on payment

[1] [The Editor of the Memoirs of Barry Lyndon cannot help pointing out here a truth which seems to have escaped the notice of the amiable autobiographer, viz. that there *were more than two* impostors present at Captain and Mrs. Fitzsimons's table, when they and their young guest dined there. It never seems to have struck Mr. Barry that had he not represented himself to be a man of fortune none of the difficulties here described would have occurred [to him.—Note in *Fraser's Magazine*, omitted in later editions.

of a certain moderate sum for their dinner. After dinner, you may be sure that cards were not wanting, and that the company who played did not play for love merely. To these parties persons of all sorts would come; young bloods from the regiments garrisoned in Dublin; young clerks from the Castle; horse-riding, wine-tippling, watchman-beating men of fashion about town, such as existed in Dublin in that day more than in any other city with which I am acquainted in Europe. I never knew young fellows make such a show, and upon such small means. I never knew young gentlemen with what I may call such a genius for idleness; and whereas an Englishman, with fifty guineas a year, is not able to do much more than to starve, and toil like a slave in a profession, a young Irish buck, with the same sum, will keep his horses, and drink his bottle, and live as lazy as a lord. Here was a doctor who never had a patient, cheek by jowl with an attorney who never had a client; neither had a guinea—each had a good horse to ride in the park, and the best of clothes to their backs. A sporting clergyman without a living; several young wine-merchants, who consumed much more liquor than they had or sold; and men of similar character, formed the society at the house into which, by ill luck, I was thrown. What could happen to a man but misfortune from associating with such company? (I have not mentioned the ladies of the society, who were, perhaps, no better than the males)—and in a very, very short time I became their prey.

As for my poor twenty guineas, in three days I saw, with terror, that they had dwindled down to eight; theatres and taverns having already made such cruel inroads in my purse. At play I had lost, it is true, a couple of pieces, but seeing that every one round about me played upon honour and gave their bills, I, of course, preferred that medium to the payment of ready money, and when I lost paid on account.

With the tailors, saddlers, and others, I employed similar means; and in so far Mr. Fitzsimons' representation did me good, for the tradesmen took him at his word regarding my fortune (I have since learned that the rascal pigeoned several other young men of property), and for a little time supplied me with any goods I might be pleased to order. At length, my cash running low, I was compelled to pawn some of the suits with which the tailor had provided me; for I did not like to part with my mare, on which I daily rode in the park, and which I loved as the gift of my respected uncle. I raised some little money, too, on a few trinkets which I had purchased of a jeweller who pressed his credit upon me, and thus was enabled to keep up appearances for yet a little time.

I asked at the post office repeatedly for letters for Mr. Redmond, but none such had arrived; and, indeed, I always felt rather relieved when the answer of 'No,' was given to me; for I was not very anxious that my mother should know my proceedings in the extravagant life which I was leading at Dublin. It could not last very long, however; for when my cash was quite exhausted, and I paid a second visit to the tailor, requesting him to make me more clothes, the fellow hummed and ha'd, and had the impudence to ask payment for those already supplied; on which, telling him I should withdraw my custom from him, I abruptly left him. The goldsmith, too (a rascal Jew), declined to let me take a gold chain to which I had a fancy, and I felt now, for the first time, in some perplexity. To add to it, one of the young gentlemen who frequented Mr. Fitzsimons' boarding-house had received from me, in the way of play, an I O U for eighteen pounds (which I lost to him at piquet), and which, owing Mr. Curbyn, the livery-stable keeper, a bill, he passed into that person's hands. Fancy my rage and astonishment, then, on going for my mare, to find that he positively refused to let me have her out of the stable, except under payment of my promissory note! It was in vain that I offered him his choice of four notes that I had in my pocket—one of Fitzsimons' for 20*l.*, one of Counsellor Mulligan's, and so forth,—the dealer, who was a Yorkshireman, shook his head, and laughed at every one of them; and said, 'I tell you what, Master Redmond, you appear a young fellow of birth and fortune, and let me whisper in your ear that you have fallen into very bad hands—it's a regular gang of swindlers; and a gentleman of your rank and quality should never be seen in such company. Go home, pack up your valise, pay the little trifle to me, mount your mare, and ride back again to your parents,—it's the very best thing you can do.'

In a pretty nest of villains, indeed, was I plunged! It

seemed as if all my misfortunes were to break on me at once; for, on going home and ascending to my bedroom in a disconsolate way, I found the captain and his lady there before me, my valise open, my wardrobe lying on the ground, and my keys in the possession of the odious Fitzsimons. 'Whom have I been harbouring in my house?' roared he, as I entered the apartment. 'Who are you, sirrah?'

'*Sirrah!* Sir,' said I, 'I am as good a gentleman as any in Ireland.'

'You're an impostor, young man, a schemer, a deceiver!' shouted the captain.

'Repeat the words again, and I will run you through the body,' replied I.

'Tut, tut! I can play at fencing as well as you, Mr. Redmond Barry. Ah! you change colour, do you—your secret is known, is it? You come like a viper into the bosom of innocent families: you represent yourself as the heir of my friends the Redmonds of Castle Redmond; I inthrojuice you to the nobility and genthry of this methropolis' (the captain's brogue was large, and his words, by preference, long); 'I take you to my tradesmen, who give you credit, and what do I find? That you have pawned the goods which you took up at their houses.'

'I have given them my acceptances, sir,' said I with a dignified air.

'*Under what name*, unhappy boy—under what name?' screamed Mrs. Fitzsimons; and then, indeed, I remembered that I had signed the documents Barry Redmond instead of Redmond Barry; but what else could I do? Had not my mother desired me to take no other designation? After uttering a furious tirade against me, in which he spoke of the fatal discovery of my real name on my linen—of his misplaced confidence and affection, and the shame with which he should be obliged to meet his fashionable friends, and confess that he had harboured a swindler, he gathered up the linen clothes, silver toilette articles, and the rest of my gear, saying, that he should step out that moment for an officer, and give me up to the just revenge of the law.

During the first part of his speech, the thought of the imprudence of which I had been guilty, and the predicament in which I was plunged, had so puzzled and confounded me, that I had not uttered a word in reply to the fellow's abuse, but had stood quite dumb before him. The sense of danger, however, at once roused me to action. 'Hark ye, Mr. Fitzsimons,' said I; 'I will tell you why I was obliged to alter my name, which *is* Barry, and the best name in Ireland. I changed it, sir, because, on the day before I came to Dublin, I killed a man in deadly combat—an Englishman, sir, and a captain in his Majesty's service; and if you offer to let or hinder me in the slightest way, the same arm which destroyed him is ready to punish you; and, by Heaven, sir, you or I don't leave this room alive!'

So saying, I drew my sword like lightning, and giving a 'ha, ha!' and a stamp with my foot, lunged it within an inch of Fitzsimons's heart, who started back and turned deadly pale, while his wife, with a scream, flung herself between us.

'Dearest Redmond,' she cried, 'be pacified. Fitzsimons, you don't want the poor child's blood. Let him escape—in Heaven's name let him go.'

'He may go hang for me,' said Fitzsimons, sulkily; 'and he'd better be off quickly, too, for the jeweller and the tailor have called once, and will be here again before long. It was Moses the pawnbroker that peached; I had the news from him myself.' By which I conclude that Mr. Fitzsimons had been with the new-laced frock-coat which he procured from the merchant-tailor on the day when the latter first gave me credit.

What was the end of our conversation? Where was now a home for the descendant of the Barrys? Home was shut to me by my misfortune in the duel. I was expelled from Dublin by a persecution occasioned, I must confess, by my own imprudence. I had no time to wait and choose. No place of refuge to fly to. Fitzsimons, after his abuse of me, left the room growling, but not hostile; his wife insisted that we should shake hands, and he promised not to molest me. Indeed, I owed the fellow nothing; and, on the contrary, had his acceptance actually in my pocket for money lost at play. As for my friend, Mrs. Fitzsimons, she sat down on the bed and fairly burst out crying. She had her faults, but her heart was kind; and though she possessed but three shillings in the world, and fourpence in copper, the poor soul made me take it before I left her—to go—whither? My mind was made up: there was a score of recruiting parties in the town beating up for men to join our gallant armies in America and Germany; I knew where to find one of these, having stood by the sergeant at a review in the Phoenix Park, where he pointed out to me characters on the field, for which I treated him to drink.

I gave one of my shillings to Sullivan, the butler of the Fitzsimonses, and, running into the street, hastened to the little ale-house at which my acquaintance was quartered, and before ten minutes had accepted his Majesty's shilling. I told him frankly that I was a young gentleman in difficulties; that I had killed an officer in a duel, and was anxious to get out of the country. But I need not have troubled myself with any explanations; King George was too much in want of men then to heed from whence they came, and a fellow of my inches, the sergeant said, was always welcome. Indeed, I could not, he said, have chosen my time better. A transport was lying at Dunleary, waiting for a wind, and on board that ship, to which I marched that night, I made some surprising discoveries, which shall be told in the next chapter.

CHAPTER IV

IN WHICH BARRY TAKES A NEAR VIEW OF MILITARY GLORY

I NEVER had a taste for anything but genteel company, and hate all descriptions of low life. Hence my account of the society in which I at present found myself must of necessity be short, and indeed, the recollection of it is profoundly disagreeable to me. Pah! the reminiscences of the horrid black-hole of a place in which we soldiers were confined, of the wretched creatures with whom I was now forced to keep company, of the ploughmen, poachers, pickpockets, who had taken refuge from poverty, or the law, as, in truth, I had done myself, is enough to make me ashamed even now, and it calls the blush into my old cheeks to think I was ever forced to keep such company. I should have fallen into despair but that, luckily, events occurred to rouse my spirits, and in some measure to console me for my misfortunes.

The first of these consolations I had was a good quarrel, which took place on the day after my entrance into the transport-ship, with a huge red-haired monster of a fellow —a chairman, who had enlisted to fly from a vixen of a wife, who, boxer as he was, had been more than a match for him. As soon as this fellow—Toole, I remember, was his name—got away from the arms of the washerwoman, his lady, his natural courage and ferocity returned, and he became the tyrant of all round about him. All recruits, especially, were the object of the brute's insult and ill-treatment.

I had no money, as I said, and was sitting very disconsolately over a platter of rancid bacon and mouldy biscuit, which was served to us at mess, when it came to my turn to be helped to drink, and I was served, like the rest, with a dirty tin noggin, containing somewhat more than half a pint of rum-and-water. The beaker was so greasy and filthy that I could not help turning round to the messman and saying, 'Fellow, get me a glass!' At which all the wretches round about me burst into a roar of laughter, the very loudest among them being, of course, Mr. Toole. 'Get the gentleman a towel for his hands, and serve him a basin of turtle-soup,' roared the monster, who was sitting, or rather squatting, on the deck opposite me, and as he spoke he suddenly seized my beaker of grog and emptied it, in the midst of another burst of applause.

'If you want to vex him, ax him about his wife, the washerwoman, who *bates* him,' here whispered in my ear another worthy, a retired link-boy,* who, disgusted with his profession, had adopted the military life.

'Is it a towel of your wife's washing, Mr. Toole?' said I. 'I'm told she wiped your face often with one.'

'Ax him why he wouldn't see her yesterday, when she came to the ship,' continued the link-boy. And so I put to him some other foolish jokes about soap-suds, henpecking, and flat-irons, which set the man into a fury, and succeeded in raising a quarrel between us. We should have fallen-to at once, but a couple of grinning marines, who kept watch at the door, for fear we should repent of our bargain and have a fancy to escape, came forward and interposed between us with fixed bayonets, and the serjeant, coming down the ladder and hearing the dispute, condescended to say that we might fight it out like men with *fistes* if we chose, and that the fore-deck should be free to us for that purpose. But the use of *fistes*, as the Englishman called them, was not then general in Ireland, and it was agreed that we should have a pair of cudgels, with one of which weapons I finished the fellow in four minutes, giving him a thump across his stupid sconce which laid him lifeless on the deck, and not receiving myself a single hurt of consequence.

This victory over the cock of the vile dunghill obtained me respect among the wretches of whom I formed part, and served to set up my spirits, which otherwise were flagging; and my position was speedily made more bearable by the arrival on board our ship of an old friend. This was no other than my second in the fatal duel which had sent me thus early out into the world, Captain Fagan. There was a young nobleman who had a company in our regiment (Gale's Foot),* and who, preferring the delights of the Mall and the clubs to the dangers of a rough campaign, had given Fagan the opportunity of an exchange, which, as the latter had no fortune but his sword, he was glad to make. The sergeant was putting us through our exercise on deck (the seamen and officers of the transport looking grinning on) when a boat came from the shore bringing our captain to the ship, and though I started and blushed red as he recognized me—a descendant of the Barrys—in this degrading posture, I promise you that the sight of Fagan's face was most welcome to me, for it assured me that a friend was near me. Before that I was so melancholy that I would certainly have deserted had I found the means, and had not the inevitable marines kept a watch to prevent any such escapes. Fagan gave me a wink of recognition, but offered no public token of acquaintance, and it was not until two days afterwards, and when we had bidden adieu to old Ireland and were standing out to sea, that he called me into his cabin, and then, shaking hands with me cordially, gave me news, which I much wanted, of my family. 'I had news of you in Dublin,' he said. 'Faith, you've begun early, like your father's son, and I think you could not do better than as you have done. But why did you not write home to your poor mother? She has sent a half-dozen letters to you at Dublin.'

I said I had asked for letters at the post-office, but there were none for Mr. Redmond. I did not like to add that I had been ashamed after the first week to write to my mother.

'We must write to her by the pilot,' said he, 'who will leave us in two hours, and you can tell her that you are safe, and married to Brown Bess.'* I sighed when he talked about being married; on which he said, with a laugh, 'I see you are thinking of a certain young lady at Brady's Town.'

'Is Miss Brady well?' said I, and indeed could hardly utter it, for I certainly *was* thinking about her; for, though I had forgotten her in the gaieties of Dublin, I have always found adversity makes man very affectionate.

'There's only seven Miss Bradys now,' answered Fagan, in a solemn voice, 'poor Nora——'

'Good Heavens! what of her?' I thought grief had killed her.

'She took on so at your going away that she was obliged to console herself with a husband. She's now Mrs. John Quin.'

'Mrs. John Quin! Was there *another* Mr. John Quin?' asked I, quite wonder-stricken.

'No, the very same one, my boy. He recovered from his wound. The ball you hit him with was not likely to hurt him. It was only made of tow. Do you think the Bradys would let you kill fifteen hundred a year out of the family?' And then Fagan further told me that, in order to get me out of the way, for the cowardly Englishman could never be brought to marry from fear of me, the plan of the duel had been arranged. 'But hit him you certainly did, Redmond, and with a fine thick plugget of tow, and the fellow was so frightened that he was an hour in coming to. We told your mother the story afterwards, and a pretty scene she made; she dispatched a half-score of letters to Dublin after you, but I suppose addressed them to you in your real name, by which you never thought to ask for them.'

'The coward!' said I (though, I confess, my mind was considerably relieved at the thoughts of not having killed him). 'And did the Bradys of Castle Brady consent to admit a poltroon like that into one of the most ancient and honourable families of the world.'

'He has paid off your uncle's mortgage,' said Fagan,

'he gives Nora a coach-and-six, he is to sell out, and Lieutenant Ulick Brady of the militia is to purchase his company. That coward of a fellow has been the making of your uncle's family. Faith! the business was well done.' And then, laughing, he told me how Mick and Ulick had never let him out of their sight, although he was for deserting to England, until the marriage was completed, and the happy couple off on their road to Dublin. 'Are you in want of cash, my boy?' continued the good-natured captain. 'You may draw upon me, for I got a couple of hundred out of Master Quin for my share, and while they last you shall never want.'

And so he bade me sit down and write a letter to my mother, which I did forthwith in very sincere and repentant terms, stating that I had been guilty of extravagances, that I had not known until that moment under what a fatal error I had been labouring, and that I had embarked for Germany as a volunteer. And the letter was scarcely finished when the pilot sang out that he was going on shore; and he departed, taking with him, from many an anxious fellow besides myself, our adieus to friends in old Ireland.

Although I was called Captain Barry for many years of my life, and have been known as such by the first people of Europe, yet I may as well confess I had no more claim to the title than many a gentleman who assumes it, and never had a right to an epaulet, or to any military decoration higher than a corporal's stripe of worsted. I was made corporal by Fagan during our voyage to the Elbe, and my rank was confirmed on terra firma. I was promised a halbert, too, and afterwards, perhaps, an ensigncy,* if I distinguished myself; but Fate did not intend that I should remain long an English soldier, as shall appear presently. Meanwhile, our passage was very favourable; my adventures were told by Fagan to his brother officers, who treated me with kindness; and my victory over the big chairman procured me respect from my comrades of the fore-deck. Encouraged and strongly exhorted by Fagan, I did my duty resolutely; but, though affable and good-humoured with the men, I never at first condescended to associate with such low fellows, and, indeed, was called generally amongst them 'my lord.' I believe it was the ex-linkboy, a facetious knave, who gave me the title, and

I felt that I should become such a rank as well as any peer in the kingdom.

It would require a greater philosopher and historian than I am to explain the causes of the famous Seven Years' War* in which Europe was engaged; and, indeed, its origin has always appeared to me to be so complicated, and the books written about it so amazingly hard to understand, that I have seldom been much wiser at the end of a chapter than at the beginning, and so shall not trouble my reader with any personal disquisitions concerning the matter. All I know is, that after his Majesty's love of his Hanoverian dominions had rendered him most unpopular in his English kingdom, with Mr. Pitt* at the head of the anti-German war-party, all of a sudden, Mr. Pitt becoming minister, the rest of the empire applauded the war as much as they had hated it before. The victories of Dettingen and Crefeld* were in everybody's mouths, and 'the Protestant hero,' as we used to call the godless old Frederick of Prussia, was adored by us as a saint a very short time after we had been about to make war against him, in alliance with the empress-queen.* Now, somehow, we were on Frederick's side; the empress, the French, the Swedes, and the Russians were leagued against us; and I remember, when the news of the battle of Lissa* came even to our remote quarter of Ireland, we considered it as a triumph for the cause of Protestantism, and illuminated, and bonfired, and had a sermon at church, and kept the Prussian's king's birthday, on which my uncle would get drunk, as indeed on any other occasion. Most of the low fellows enlisted with myself were, of course, Papists (the English army was filled with such out of that never-failing country of ours), and these, forsooth, were fighting the battles of Protestantism with Frederick, who was belabouring the Protestant Swedes and the Protestant Saxons, as well as the Russians of the Greek Church, and the Papist troops of the emperor and the King of France. It was against these latter that the English auxiliaries were employed, and we know that, be the quarrel what it may, an Englishman and a Frenchman are pretty willing to make a fight of it.

We landed at Cuxhaven, and before I had been a month in the Electorate* I was transformed into a tall and proper young soldier, and, having a natural aptitude for military exercise, was soon as accomplished at the drill as the oldest sergeant in the regiment. It is well, however, to dream of glorious war in a snug arm-chair at home, aye, or to make it as an officer, surrounded by gentlemen, gorgeously dressed, and cheered by chances of promotion. But those chances do not shine on poor fellows in worsted lace; the rough texture of our red coats made me ashamed when I saw an officer go by; my soul used to shudder when, on going the rounds, I would hear their voices as they sat jovially over the mess-table; my pride revolted at being obliged to plaster my hair with flour and candle-grease, instead of using the proper pomatum for a gentleman. Yes, my tastes have always been high and fashionable, and I loathed the horrid company in which I was fallen. What chances had I of promotion? None of my relatives had money to buy me a commission, and I became soon so low-spirited that I longed for a general action and a ball to finish me, and vowed that I would take some opportunity to desert.

When I think that I, the descendant of the kings of Ireland, was threatened with a caning by a young scoundrel who had just joined from Eton College—when I think that he offered to make me his footman, and that I did not, on either occasion, murder him! On the first occasion I burst into tears, I do not care to own it, and had serious thoughts of committing suicide, so great was my mortification. But my kind friend Fagan came to my aid in the circumstance with some very timely consolation. 'My poor boy,' said he, 'you must not take the matter to heart so. Caning is only a relative disgrace. Young Ensign Fakenham was flogged himself at Eton School only a month ago. I would lay a wager that his scars are not yet healed. You must cheer up, my boy; do your duty, be a gentleman, and no serious harm can fall on you.' And I heard afterwards that my champion had taken Mr. Fakenham very severely to task for this threat, and said to him that any such proceedings for the future he should consider as an insult to himself, whereon the young ensign was, for the moment, civil. As for the sergeants, I told one of them, that if any man struck me, no matter who he might be, or what the penalty, I would take his life. And, faith! there was an air of sincerity in my speech which convinced the whole bevy of them; and as long as I remained in the English service no rattan was ever laid on the shoulders of Redmond Barry. Indeed, I was in that savage, moody state, that my mind was quite made up to the point, and I looked to hear my own dead march played as sure as I was alive. When I was made a corporal, some of my evils were lessened; I messed with the sergeants by special favour, and used to treat them to drink, and lose money to the rascals at play, with which cash my good friend Mr. Fagan punctually supplied me.

Our regiment, which was quartered about Stade and Lüneburg, speedily got orders to march southwards towards the Rhine, for news came that our great general, Prince Ferdinand of Brunswick,* had been defeated—no, not defeated, but foiled in his attack upon the French under the Duke of Broglio, at Bergen,* near Frankfort-on-the-Main, and had been obliged to fall back. As the allies retreated, the French rushed forward, and made a bold push for the Electorate of our gracious monarch in Hanover, threatening that they would occupy it as they had done before when D'Estrées beat the hero of Culloden, the gallant Duke of Cumberland, and caused him to sign the capitulation of Closter Zeven.* An advance upon Hanover always caused a great agitation in the royal bosom of the King of England, more troops were sent to join us, convoys of treasure were passed over to our forces, and to our ally's the King of Prussia; and although, in spite of all assistance, the army under Prince Ferdinand was very much weaker than that of the invading enemy, yet we had the advantage of better supplies, one of the greatest generals in the world, and, I was going to add, of British valour, but the less we say about *that* the better. My Lord George Sackville* did not exactly cover himself with laurels at Minden, otherwise there might have been won there one of the greatest victories of modern times.

Throwing himself between the French and interior of the Electorate, Prince Ferdinand wisely took possession of the free town of Bremen, which he made his store-house and place of arms, and round which he gathered all his troops, making ready to fight the famous battle of Minden.

Were these memoirs not characterized by truth, and did I deign to utter a single word for which my own personal experience did not give me the fullest authority, I might easily make myself the hero of some strange and popular adventures, and, after the fashion of novel-writers, introduce my readers to the great characters of this remarkable time.

These persons (I mean the romance-writers), if they take a drummer or a dustman for a hero, somehow manage to bring him in contact with the greatest lords and most notorious personages of the empire, and I warrant me there's not one of them but, in describing the battle of Minden, would manage to bring Prince Ferdinand, and my Lord George Sackville, and my Lord Granby into presence. It would have been easy for me to have *said* I was present when the orders were brought to Lord George to charge with the cavalry and finish the rout of the Frenchmen, and when he refused to do so, and thereby spoiled the great victory. But the fact is, I was two miles off from the cavalry when his lordship's fatal hesitation took place, and none of us soldiers of the line knew of what had occurred until we came to talk about the fight over our kettles in the evening, and repose after the labours of a hard-fought day. I saw no one of higher rank that day than my colonel and a couple of orderly officers riding by in the smoke—no one on *our* side, that is. A poor corporal (as I then had the disgrace of being) is not generally invited into the company of commanders and the great; but, in revenge, I saw, I promise you, some very good company on the *French* part, for their regiments of Lorraine and Royal Cravate* were charging us all day; and in *that* sort of *mêlée* high and low are pretty equally received. I hate bragging, but I cannot help saying that I made a very close acquaintance with the colonel of the Cravates, for I drove my bayonet into his body, and finished off a poor little ensign, so young, slender, and small, that a blow from my pig-tail would have dispatched him, I think, in place of the butt of my musket, with which I clubbed him down. I killed, besides, four more officers and men, and in the poor ensign's pocket found a purse of fourteen louis-d'or, and a silver box of sugar-plums, of which the former present was very agreeable to me. If people would tell their stories of battles in this simple way, I think the cause of truth would not suffer by it. All I know of this famous fight of Minden (except from books) is told here above. The ensign's silver *bonbon* box and his purse of gold; the livid face of the poor fellow as he fell; the huzzas of the men of my company as I went out under a smart fire and rifled him; their shouts and curses as we came hand in hand with the Frenchmen,—

these are, in truth, not very dignified recollections, and had best be passed over briefly. When my kind friend Fagan was shot, a brother captain, and his very good friend, turned to Lieutenant Rawson, and said, 'Fagan's down; Rawson, there's your company.' It was all the epitaph my brave patron got. 'I should have left you a hundred guineas, Redmond,' were his last words to me, 'but for a cursed run of ill luck last night at faro;' and he gave me a faint squeeze of the hand; and, as the word was given to advance, I left him. When we came back to our old ground, which we presently did, he was lying there still, but he was dead. Some of our people had already torn off his epaulets, and, no doubt, had rifled his purse. Such knaves and ruffians do men in war become! It is well for gentlemen to talk of the age of chivalry; but remember the starving brutes whom they lead—men nursed in poverty, entirely ignorant, made to take a pride in deeds of blood—men who can have no amusement but in drunkenness, debauch, and plunder. It is with these shocking instruments that your great warriors and kings have been doing their murderous work in the world; and while, for instance, we are at the present moment admiring the 'Great Frederick,' as we call him, and his philosophy, and his liberality, and his military genius, I, who have served him, and been, as it were, behind the scenes of which that great spectacle is composed, can only look at it with horror. What a number of items of human crime, misery, slavery, to form that sum-total of glory! I can recollect a certain day, about three weeks after the battle of Minden, and a farm-house in which some of us entered; and how the old woman and her daughters served us, trembling, to wine; and how we got drunk over the wine, and the house was in a flame, presently: and woe betide the wretched fellow afterwards who came home to look for his house and his children!

CHAPTER V

IN WHICH BARRY TRIES TO REMOVE AS FAR FROM MILITARY GLORY AS POSSIBLE

After the death of my protector, Captain Fagan, I am forced to confess that I fell into the very worst of courses and company. Being a rough soldier of fortune himself, he had never been a favourite with the officers of his regiment; who had a contempt for Irishmen, as Englishmen sometimes will have, and used to mock his brogue, and his blunt, uncouth manners. I had been insolent to one or two of them, and had only been screened from punishment by his intercession; and especially his successor, Mr. Rawson, had no liking for me, and put another man into the sergeant's place vacant in his company after the battle of Minden. This act of injustice rendered my service very disagreeable to me; and, instead of seeking to conquer the dislike of my superiors, and win their goodwill by good behaviour, I only sought for means to make my situation easier to me, and grasped at all the amusements in my power. In a foreign country, with the enemy before us, and the people continually under contribution from one side or the other, numberless irregularities were permitted to the troops which would not have been allowed in more peaceable times. I descended gradually to mix with the sergeants, and to share their amusements; drinking and gambling were, I am sorry to say, our principal pastimes; and I fell so readily into their ways that, though only a young lad of seventeen, I was the master of them all in daring wickedness; though there were some among them who, I promise you, were far advanced in the science of every kind of profligacy. I should have been under the provost-marshal's* hands, for a dead certainty, had I continued much longer in the army: but an accident occurred which took me out of the English service in rather a singular manner.

The year in which George II died,* our regiment had the honour to be present at the battle of Warburg (where the Marquis of Granby and his horse fully retrieved the discredit which had fallen upon the cavalry since Lord George

Sackville's defalcation at Minden), and where Prince Ferdinand once more completely defeated the Frenchmen. During the action, my lieutenant, Mr. Fakenham, of Fakenham, the gentleman who had threatened me, it may be remembered, with the caning, was struck by a musket-ball in the side. He had shown no want of courage in this or any other occasion where he had been called upon to act against the French; but this was his first wound, and the young gentleman was exceedingly frightened by it. He offered five guineas to be carried into the town which was hard by; and I and another man, taking him up in a cloak, managed to transport him into a place of decent appearance, where we put him to bed, and where a young surgeon (who desired nothing better than to take himself out of the fire of the musketry) went presently to dress his wound.

In order to get into the house, we had been obliged, it must be confessed, to fire into the locks with our pieces, which summons brought an inhabitant of the house to the door, a very pretty and black-eyed young woman, who lived there with her old half-blind father, a retired Jagdmeister of the Duke of Cassel,* hard by. When the French were in the town, meinherr's house had suffered like those of his neighbours; and he was at first exceedingly unwilling to accommodate our guests. But the first knocking at the door had the effect of bringing a speedy answer; and Mr. Fakenham, taking a couple of guineas out of a very full purse, speedily convinced the people that they had only to deal with a person of honour.

Leaving the doctor (who was very glad to stop) with his patient, who paid me the stipulated reward, I was returning to my regiment with my other comrade, after having paid, in my German jargon, some deserved compliments to the black-eyed beauty of Warburg, and thinking, with no small envy, how comfortable it would be to be billeted there, when the private who was with me cut short my reveries, by suggesting that we should divide the five guineas that the lieutenant had given me.

'There is your share,' said I, giving the fellow one piece, which was plenty, as I was the leader of the expedition. But he swore a dreadful oath that he would have half; and, when I told him to go to a quarter which I shall not name, the fellow, lifting his musket, hit me a blow with the butt-end of it which sent me lifeless to the ground; and, when I awoke from my trance, I found myself bleeding with a large wound in the head, and had barely time to stagger back to the house where I had left the lieutenant, when I again fell fainting at the door.

Here I must have been discovered by the surgeon on his issuing out; for when I awoke a second time I found myself in the ground-floor room of the house, supported by the black-eyed girl, while the surgeon was copiously bleeding me at the arm. There was another bed in the room where the lieutenant had been laid,—it was that occupied by Gretel, the servant; while Lischen, as my fair one was called, had, till now, slept in the couch where the wounded officer lay.

'Who are you putting into that bed?' said he, languidly, in German; for the ball had been extracted from his side with much pain and loss of blood.

They told him it was the corporal who had brought him.

'A corporal?' said he, in English; 'turn him out.' And you may be sure I felt highly complimented by the words. But we were both too faint to compliment or to abuse each other much, and I was put to bed carefully; and, on being undressed, had an opportunity to find that my pockets had been rifled by the English soldier after he had knocked me down. However, I was in good quarters; the young lady who sheltered me presently brought me a refreshing drink; and, as I took it, I could not help pressing the kind hand that gave it me; nor, in truth, did this token of my gratitude seem unwelcome.

This intimacy did not decrease with further acquaintance. I found Lischen the tenderest of nurses. Whenever any delicacy was to be provided for the wounded lieutenant, a share was always sent to the bed opposite his, and to the avaricious man's no small annoyance. His illness was long. On the second day the fever declared itself; for some nights he was delirious; and I remember it was when a commanding officer was inspecting our quarters, with an intention, very likely, of billeting himself on the house, that the howling and mad words of the patient overhead struck him, and he retired rather frightened. I had been sitting up very comfortably in the lower apartment, for my hurt was quite subsided; and it was only when the officer asked me, with a rough voice, why I was not at my regiment, that I began to reflect how pleasant my quarters were to me, and that I was much better here than crawling under an odious tent with a parcel of tipsy soldiers, or going the night-rounds, or rising long before daybreak for drill.

The delirium of Mr. Fakenham gave me a hint, and I determined forthwith to *go mad*. There was a poor fellow about Brady's Town called 'Wandering Billy,' whose insane pranks I had often mimicked as a lad, and I again put them in practice. That night I made an attempt upon Lischen, saluting her with a yell and a grin which frightened her almost out of her wits; and when anybody came I was raving. The blow on the head had disordered my brain; the doctor was ready to vouch for this fact. One night I whispered to him that I was Julius Caesar, and considered him to be my affianced wife Queen Cleopatra, which convinced him of my insanity. Indeed, if her Majesty had been like my Aesculapius,* she must have had a carroty beard, such as is rare in Egypt.

A movement on the part of the French speedily caused an advance on our part. The town was evacuated, except by a few Prussian troops, whose surgeons were to visit the wounded in the place; and, when we were well, we were to be drafted to our regiments. I determined that I never would join mine again. My intention was to make for Holland, almost the only neutral country of Europe in these times, and thence to get a passage somehow to England, and home to dear old Brady's Town.

If Mr. Fakenham is now alive [(I have lost sight of him since the year 1814, when I met him at Brixton),][1]* I here tender him my apologies for my conduct to him. He was very rich; he used me very ill. I managed to frighten away his servant who came to attend him after the affair of Warburg, and from that time would sometimes condescend to wait upon the patient, who always treated me with scorn; but it was my object to have him alone, and I bore his brutality with the utmost civility and mildness, meditating in my own mind a very pretty return for all his favours to me. Nor was I the only person in the house to whom the worthy gentleman was uncivil. He ordered the fair Lischen hither and thither, made impertinent love to her, abused her soups, quarrelled with her omelets,

[1] Omitted in later editions.

and grudged the money which was laid out for his maintenance, so that our hostess detested him as much as, I think, without vanity, she regarded me.

For, if the truth must be told, I had made very deep love to her during my stay under her roof, as is always my way with women, of whatever age or degree of beauty. To a man who has to make his way in the world, these dear girls can always be useful in one fashion or another; never mind if they repel your passion; at any rate, they are not offended with your declaration of it, and only look upon you with more favourable eyes in consequence of your misfortune. As for Lischen, I told her such a pathetic story of my life (a tale a great deal more romantic than that here narrated,—for I did not restrict myself to the exact truth in that history, as in these pages I am bound to do) that I won the poor girl's heart entirely, and, besides, made considerable progress in the German language under her instruction. Do not think me very cruel and heartless, ladies; this heart of Lischen's was like many a town in the neighbourhood in which she dwelt, and had been stormed and occupied several times before I came to invest it; now mounting French colours, now green-and-yellow Saxon, now black-and-white Prussian, as the case may be. A lady who sets her heart upon a lad in uniform must prepare to change lovers pretty quickly, or her life will be but a sad one.

The German surgeon who attended us after the departure of the English only condescended to pay our house a visit twice during my residence; and I took care, for a reason I had, to receive him in a darkened room, and much to the annoyance of Mr. Fakenham, who lay there: but I said the light affected my eyes dreadfully since my blow on the head; and so I covered up my head with clothes when the doctor came, and told him that I was an Egyptian mummy, or talked to him some insane nonsense, in order to keep up my character.

'What is that nonsense you were talking about an Egyptian mummy, fellow?' asked Mr. Fakenham, peevishly.

'Oh! you'll know soon, sir,' said I.

The next time that I expected the doctor to come, instead of receiving him in a darkened room, with handkerchiefs muffled, I took care to be in the lower room, and was having a game at cards with Lischen as the surgeon entered. I had taken possession of a dressing-jacket of the lieutenant's, and some other articles of his wardrobe, which fitted me pretty well, and, I flatter myself, was no ungentlemanlike figure.

'Good morrow, corporal,' said the doctor, rather gruffly, in reply to my smiling salute.

'Corporal! Lieutenant, if you please,' answered I, giving an arch look at Lischen, whom I had not yet instructed in my plot.

'How lieutenant?' asked the surgeon. 'I thought the lieutenant was——'

'Upon my word, you do me great honour,' cried I, laughing; 'you mistook me for the mad corporal upstairs. The fellow has once or twice pretended to be an officer, but my kind hostess here can answer which is which.'

'Yesterday he fancied he was Prince Ferdinand,' said Lischen; 'the day you came he said he was an Egyptian mummy.'

'So he did,' said the doctor; 'I remember; but, ha! ha! do you know, lieutenant, I have in my notes made a mistake in you two?'

'Don't talk to me about his malady; he is calm now.'

Lischen and I laughed at this error as at the most ridiculous thing in the world; and, when the surgeon went up to examine his patient, I cautioned him not to talk to him about the subject of his malady, for he was in a very excited state.

The reader will be able to gather from the above conversation what my design really was. I was determined to escape, and to escape under the character of Lieutenant Fakenham, taking it from him to his face, as it were, and making use of it to meet my imperious necessity. It was forgery and robbery, if you like; for I took all his money and clothes,—I don't care to conceal it; but the need was so urgent, that I would do so again; and I knew I could not effect my escape without his purse, as well as his name. Hence it became my duty to take possession of one and the other.

As the lieutenant lay still in bed upstairs, I did not hesitate at all about assuming his uniform, especially after taking care to inform myself from the doctor whether any men of ours who might know me were in the town. But there were none that I could hear of; and so I calmly took my walks with Madame Lischen, dressed in the lieutenant's uniform, made inquiries as to a horse that I wanted to purchase, reported myself to the commandant of the place as Lieutenant Fakenham, of Gale's English regiment of foot, convalescent, and was asked to dine with the officers of the Prussian regiment at a very sorry mess they had. How Fakenham would have stormed and raged had he known the use I was making of his name!

Whenever that worthy used to inquire about his clothes, which he did with many oaths and curses that he would have me caned at the regiment for inattention, I, with a most respectful air, informed him that they were put away in perfect safety below; and, in fact, had them very neatly packed, and ready for the day when I proposed to depart. His papers and money, however, he kept under his pillow; and, as I had purchased a horse, it became necessary to pay for it.

At a certain hour, then, I ordered the animal to be brought round, when I would pay the dealer for him. (I shall pass over my adieus with my kind hostess, which were very tearful indeed), and then, making up my mind to the great action, walked upstairs to Fakenham's room attired in his full regimentals, and with his hat cocked over my left eye.

'You g*w*eat scound*w*el!' said he, with a multiplicity of oaths; 'you mutinous dog; what do you mean by d*w*essing yourself in my *w*egimentals? As sure as my name's Fakenham, when we get back to the *w*egiment, I'll have your soul cut out of your body.'

'I'm promoted lieutenant,' said I, with a sneer; 'I'm come to take my leave of you;' and then going up to his bed, I said, 'I intend to have your papers and purse.' With this I put my hand under his pillow, at which he gave a scream that might have called the whole garrison about my ears. 'Hark ye, sir!' said I, 'no more noise, or you are a dead man!' and, taking a handkerchief, I bound it tight around his mouth so as wellnigh to throttle him, and, pulling forward the sleeves of his shirt, tied them in a knot together, and so left him, removing the papers and the purse, you may be sure, and wishing him politely a good day,

'It is the mad corporal,' said I to the people down below

who were attracted by the noise from the sick man's chamber ; and so taking leave of the old blind Jagdmeister, and an adieu I will not say how tender of his daughter, I mounted my newly purchased animal, and, as I pranced away, and the sentinels presented arms to me at the town-gates, felt once more that I was in my proper sphere, and determined never again to fall from the rank of a gentleman.

I took at first the way towards Bremen, where our army was, as bringing reports and letters from the Prussian commandant of Warburg to head quarters ; but, as soon as I got out of sight of the advanced sentinels, I turned bridle and rode into the Hesse-Cassel territory,* which is luckily not very far from Warburg, and I promise you I was very glad to see the blue-and-red stripes on the barriers, which showed me that I was out of the land occupied by our countrymen. I rode to Hof, and the next day to Cassel, giving out that I was the bearer of dispatches to Prince Henry,* then on the Lower Rhine, and put up at the best hotel of the place, where the field-officers of the garrison had their ordinary. These gentlemen I treated to the best wines that the house afforded, for I was determined to keep up the character of the English gentleman, and I talked to them about my English estates with a fluency that almost made me believe in the stories which I invented. I was even asked to an assembly at Wilhelmshöhe, the Elector's palace,* and danced a minuet there with the Hofmarschall's lovely daughter, and lost a few pieces to his excellency the first hunt-master of his highness.

At our table at the inn there was a Prussian officer who treated me with great civility, and asked me a thousand questions about England, which I answered as best I might. But this best, I am bound to say, was bad enough. I knew nothing about England, and the court, and the noble families there ; but, led away by the vaingloriousness of youth (and a propensity which I possessed in my early days, but of which I have long since corrected myself, to boast and talk in a manner not altogether consonant with truth), I invented a thousand stories which I told him ; described the king and the ministers to him, said the British ambassador at Berlin was my uncle, and promised my acquaintance a letter of recommendation to him. When the officer asked me my uncle's name, I was not able to give him the real name, and so said his name was O'Grady:* it is as good a name as any other, and those of Kilballyowen, county Cork, are as good a family as any in the world, as I have heard. As for stories about my regiment, of these, of course, I had no lack. I wish my other histories had been equally authentic.

On the morning I left Cassel, my Prussian friend came to me with an open, smiling countenance, and said he too was bound for Düsseldorf, whither I said my route lay; and so laying our horses' heads together, we jogged on. The country was desolate beyond description. The prince in whose dominions we were was known to be the most ruthless seller of men in Germany.* He would sell to any bidder, and, during the five years which the war (afterwards called the Seven Years' War) had now lasted, had so exhausted the males of his principality, that the fields remained untilled, even the children of twelve years old were driven off to the war, and I saw herds of these wretches marching forwards, attended by a few troopers, now under the guidance of a red-coated Hanoverian sergeant, now with a Prussian sub-officer accompanying them, with some of whom my companion exchanged signs of recognition.

'It hurts my feelings,' said he, 'to be obliged to commune with such wretches, but the stern necessities of war demand men continually, and hence these recruiters whom you see market in human flesh. They get five-and-twenty dollars a man from our government for every man they bring in. For fine men—for men like you,' he added, laughing, 'we would go as high as a hundred. In the old king's time we would have given a thousand for you, when he had his giant regiment that our present monarch disbanded.'

'I knew one of them,' said I, 'who served with you: we used to call him Morgan Prussia.'*

'Indeed! and who was this Morgan Prussia?'

'Why, a huge grenadier of ours, who was somehow snapped up in Hanover by some of your recruiters.'

'The rascals!' said my friend, 'and did they dare take an Englishman?'

'Faith, this was an Irishman, and a great deal too sharp for them, as you shall hear. Morgan was taken, then, and drafted into the giant guard, and was the biggest man almost among all the giants there. Many of these monsters used to complain of their life, and their caning, and their long drills, and their small pay, but Morgan was not one of the grumblers. "It's a deal better," said he, "to get fat here in Berlin than to starve in rags in Tipperary!"'

'Where is Tipperary?' asked my companion.

'That is exactly what Morgan's friends asked him. It is a beautiful district in Ireland, the capital of which is the magnificent city of Clonmel;* a city, let me tell you, sir, only inferior to Dublin and London, and far more sumptuous than any on the Continent. Well, Morgan said that his birthplace was near that city, and the only thing which caused him unhappiness, in his present situation, was the thought that his brothers were still starving at home, when they might be so much better off in his Majesty's service.

'"Faith," says Morgan to the sergeant, to whom he imparted the information, "it's my brother *Bin* that would make the fine sergeant of the guards, entirely!"

'"Is Ben as tall as you are?" asked the sergeant.

'"As tall as *me*, is it? Why, man, I'm the shortest of my family! There's six more of us, but Bin's the biggest of all. Oh! out and out the biggest. Seven feet in his stockin-*fut*, as sure as my name's Morgan!"

'"Can't we send and fetch them over, these brothers of yours?"

'"Not you. Ever since I was seduced by one of you gentlemen of the cane, they've a mortal aversion to all sergeants," answered Morgan: "but it's a pity they cannot come, too. What a monster Bin would be in a grenadier's cap!"

'He said nothing more at the time regarding his brothers, but only sighed as if lamenting their hard fate. However, the story was told by the sergeant to the officers, and by the officers to the king himself; and his Majesty was so inflamed by curiosity that he actually consented to let Morgan go home in order to bring back with him his seven enormous brothers.'

'And were they as big as Morgan pretended?' asked my comrade. I could not help laughing at his simplicity.

'Do you suppose,' cried I, 'that Morgan ever came back? No, no; once free, and he was too wise for that. He has bought a snug farm in Tipperary with the money that was given him to secure his brothers, and I fancy few men of the guards ever profited so much by it.'

The Prussian captain laughed exceedingly at this story, said that the English were the cleverest nation in the world, and, on my setting him right, agreed that the Irish were even more so ; and we rode on very well pleased with each other, for he had a thousand stories of the war to tell, and the skill and gallantry of Frederick, and the thousand escapes, and victories, and defeats scarcely less glorious than victories, through which the king had passed. Now that I was a gentleman, I could listen with admiration to these tales ; and yet the sentiment recorded at the end of the last chapter was uppermost in my mind but three weeks back, when I remembered that it was the great general got the glory, and the poor soldier only insult and the cane.

'By the way, to whom are you taking dispatches ?' asked the officer.

It was another ugly question which I determined to answer at haphazard ; and so I said, 'To General Rolls.'* I had seen the general a year before, and gave the first name in my head. My friend was quite satisfied with it, and we continued our ride until evening came on ; and, our horses being weary, it was agreed that we should come to a halt.

'There is a very good inn,' said the captain, as we rode up to what appeared to me a very lonely-looking place.

'This may be a very good inn for Germany,' said I, 'but it would not pass in Old Ireland. Corbach is only a league off : let us push on for Corbach.'

'Do you want to see the loveliest woman in Europe ?' said the officer. 'Ah ! you sly rogue, I see *that* will influence you ;' and, truth to say, such a proposal *was* always welcome to me, as I don't care to own. 'The people are great farmers,' said the captain, 'as well as innkeepers ;' and, indeed, the place seemed more a farm than an innyard. We entered by a great gate into a court walled round, and at one end of which was the building, a dingy ruinous place. A couple of covered wagons were in the court, their horses were littered under a shed hard by, and lounging about the place were some men, and a pair of sergeants in the Prussian uniform, who both touched their hats to my friend the captain. This customary formality struck me as nothing extraordinary, but the aspect of the inn had something exceedingly chilling and forbidding in it, and I observed the men shut to the great yard-gates as soon as we were entered. Parties of French horsemen, the captain said, were about the country, and one could not take too many precautions against such villains.

We went in to supper, after the two sergeants had taken charge of our horses; the captain, also, ordering one of them to take my valise to my bedroom. I promised the worthy fellow a glass of schnapps for his pains.

A dish of fried eggs and bacon was ordered from a hideous old wench that came to serve us, in place of the lovely creature I had expected to see; and the captain, laughing, said, 'Well, our meal is a frugal one, but a soldier has many a time a worse;' and, taking off his hat, sword-belt, and gloves, with great ceremony, he sat down to eat. I would not be behindhand with him in politeness, and put my weapon securely on the old chest of drawers where his was laid.

The hideous old woman before mentioned brought us in a pot of very sour wine, at which and at her ugliness I felt a considerable ill humour.

'Where's the beauty you promised me?' said I, as soon as the old hag had left the room.

'Bah!' said he, laughing, and looking hard at me: 'it was my joke. I was tired, and did not care to go farther. There's no prettier woman here than that. If she won't suit your fancy, my friend, you must wait awhile.'

This increased my ill humour.

'Upon my word, sir,' said I, sternly, 'I think you have acted very coolly!'

'I have acted as I think fit!' replied the captain.

'Sir,' said I, 'I'm a British officer!'

'It's a lie!' roared the other, 'you're a DESERTER! You're an impostor, sir; I have known you for such these three hours. I suspected you yesterday. My men heard of a man escaping from Warburg, and I thought you were the man. Your lies and folly have confirmed me. You pretend to carry dispatches to a general who has been dead these ten months; you have an uncle who is an ambassador, and whose name forsooth, you don't know. Will you join and take the bounty, sir, or will you be given up?'

'Neither!' said I, springing at him like a tiger. But,

agile as I was, he was equally on his guard. He took two pistols out of his pocket, fired one off, and said, from the other end of the table where he stood dodging me, as it were,—

'Advance a step, and I send this bullet into your brains!' In another minute the door was flung open, and the two sergeants entered armed with musket and bayonet to aid their comrade.

The game was up. I flung down a knife with which I had armed myself, for the old hag on bringing in the wine had removed my sword.

'I volunteer,' said I.

'That's my good fellow? What name shall I put on my list?'

'Write Redmond Barry of Bally Barry,' said I, haughtily; 'a descendant of the Irish kings!'

'I was once with the Irish brigade, Roche's,'* said the recruiter, sneering, 'trying if I could get any likely fellows among the few countrymen of yours that are in the brigade, and there was scarcely one of them that was not descended from the kings of Ireland.'

'Sir,' said I, 'king or not, I am a gentleman, as you can see.'

'Oh! you will find plenty more in our corps,' answered the captain, still in the sneering mood. 'Give up your papers, Mr. Gentleman, and let us see who you really are.'

As my pocket-book contained some bank-notes as well as papers of Mr. Fakenham's, I was not willing to give up my property, suspecting very rightly that it was but a scheme on the part of the captain to get and keep it.

'It can matter very little to you,' said I, 'what my private papers are: I am enlisted under the name of Redmond Barry.'

'Give it up, sirrah!' said the captain, seizing his cane.

'I will not give it up!' answered I.

'*Hound!* do you mutiny?' screamed he, and, at the same time, gave me a lash across the face with the cane, which had the anticipated effect of producing a struggle. I dashed forward to grapple with him, the two sergeants flung themselves on me, I was thrown to the ground and stunned again, being hit on my former wound in the head. It was bleeding severely when I came to myself, my laced coat was already torn off my back, my purse and papers gone, and my hands tied behind my back.

The great and illustrious Frederick had scores of these white slave-dealers all round the frontiers of his kingdom, debauching troops or kidnapping peasants and hesitating at no crime to supply those brilliant regiments of his with food for powder; and I cannot help telling here with some satisfaction the fate which ultimately befell the atrocious scoundrel who, violating all the rights of friendship and good fellowship, had just succeeded in entrapping me. This individual was a person of high family and known talents and courage, but who had a propensity to gambling and extravagance, and found his calling as a recruit-decoy far more profitable to him than his pay of second captain in the line. The sovereign, too, probably found his services more useful in the former capacity. His name was Monsieur de Galgenstein,* and he was one of the most successful of the practisers of his rascally trade. He spoke all languages, and knew all countries, and hence had no difficulty in finding out the simple braggadocio of a young lad like me.

About 1765, however, he came to his justly merited end. He was at this time living at Kehl, opposite Strasburg, and used to take his walk upon the bridge there, and get into conversation with the French advanced sentinels, and to whom he was in the habit of promising 'mountains and marvels,' as the French say, if they would take service in Prussia. One day there was on the bridge a superb grenadier, whom Galgenstein accosted, and to whom he promised a company at least if he would enlist under Frederick.

'Ask my comrade yonder,' said the grenadier; 'I can do nothing without him. We were born and bred together, we are of the same company, sleep in the same room, always go in pairs. If he will go and you will give him a captaincy, I will go too.'

'Bring your comrade over to Kehl,' said Galgenstein, delighted, 'I will give you the best of dinners, and can promise to satisfy both of you.'

'Had you not better speak to him on the bridge?' said the grenadier. 'I dare not leave my post, but you have but to pass, and talk over the matter.'

Galgenstein, after a little parley, passed the sentinel;

but presently a panic took him, and he retraced his steps. But the grenadier brought his bayonet to the Prussian's breast and bade him stand, that he was his prisoner.

The Prussian, however, seeing his danger, made a bound across the bridge and into the Rhine, whither flinging aside his musket, the intrepid sentry followed him. The Frenchman was the better swimmer of the two, seized upon the recruiter, and bore him to the Strasburg side of the stream, where he gave him up.

'You deserve to be shot,' said the general to him, 'for abandoning your post and arms, but you merit reward for an act of courage and daring. The king prefers to reward you,' and the man received money and promotion.

As for Galgenstein, he declared his quality as a nobleman and a captain in the Prussian service, and applications were made to Berlin to know if his representations were true. But the king, though he employed men of this stamp (officers to seduce the subjects of his allies), could not acknowledge his own shame. Letters were written back from Berlin to say that such a family existed in the kingdom, but that the person representing himself to belong to it must be an impostor, for every officer of the name was at his regiment and his post. It was Galgenstein's death-warrant, and he was hanged as a spy in Strasburg.

. . . .

'Turn him into the cart with the rest,' said he, as soon as I awoke from my trance.

CHAPTER VI

THE CRIMP-WAGON—MILITARY EPISODES

The covered wagon to which I was ordered to march was standing, as I have said, in the courtyard of the farm, with another dismal vehicle of the same kind hard by it. Each was pretty well filled with a crew of men, whom the atrocious crimp, who had seized upon me, had enlisted under the banners of the glorious Frederick; and I could see by the lanterns of the sentinels, as they thrust me into the straw, a dozen dark figures huddled together in the horrible moving prison where I was now to be confined.

A scream and a curse from my opposite neighbour showed me that he was most likely wounded, as I myself was; and, during the whole of the wretched night, the moans and sobs of the poor fellows in similar captivity kept up a continual, painful chorus, which effectually prevented my getting any relief from my ills in sleep. At midnight (as far as I could judge) the horses were put to the wagons, and the creaking, lumbering machines were put in motion. A couple of soldiers, strongly armed, sat on the outer bench of the cart, and their grim faces peered in with their lanterns every now and then through the canvas curtains, that they might count the number of their prisoners. The brutes were half drunk, and were singing love and war songs, such as, '*O Gretchen, mein Täubchen, mein Herzenstrompet, Mein Kanon, mein Heerpauk und meine Musket,*' '*Prinz Eugen der edle Ritter,*'* and the like; their wild whoops and *Jodels* making doleful discord with the groans of us captives within the wagons. Many a time afterwards have I heard these ditties sung on the march, or in the barrack-room, or round the fires as we lay out at night.

I was not near so unhappy, in spite of all, as I had been on my first enlisting in Ireland. At least, thought I, if I am degraded to be a private soldier, there will be no one of my acquaintance who will witness my shame, and that is the point which I have always cared for most. There will be no one to say, 'There is young Redmond Barry, the descendant of the Barrys, the fashionable young blood of Dublin, pipeclaying his belt, and carrying his brown Bess.' Indeed, but for that opinion of the world, with which it is necessary that every man of spirit should keep upon equal terms, I, for my part, would have always been contented with the humblest portion. Now here, to all intents and purposes, one was as far removed from the world as in the wilds of Siberia, or in Robinson Crusoe's island. And I reasoned with myself thus:—'Now you are caught, there is no use in repining; make the best of your situation, and get all the pleasure you can out of it. There are a thousand opportunities of plunder, &c., offered to the soldier in war-time, out of which he can get both pleasure and profit; make use of these, and be happy. Besides, you are extraordinarily brave, handsome, and clever: and who knows but you may procure advancement in your new service?'

In this philosophical way I looked at my misfortunes, determining not to be cast down by them; and bore my woes and my broken head with perfect magnanimity. The latter was, for the moment, an evil against which it required no small powers of endurance to contend; for the jolts of the wagon were dreadful, and every shake caused a throb in my brain which I thought would have split my skull. As the morning dawned, I saw that the man next me, a gaunt, yellow-haired creature, in black, had a cushion of straw under his head.

'Are you wounded, comrade?' said I.

'Praised be the Lord,' said he, 'I am sore hurt in spirit and body, and bruised in many members; wounded, however, am I not. And you, poor youth?'

'I am wounded in the head,' said I, 'and I want your pillow: give it me—I've a clasp-knife in my pocket!' and with this I gave him a terrible look, meaning to say (and mean it I did, for look you, *à la guerre c'est à la guerre*, and I am none of your milksops), that, unless he yielded me the accommodation, I would give him a taste of my steel.

'I would give it thee without any threat, friend,' said the yellow-haired man, meekly, and handed me over his little sack of straw.

He then leaned himself back as comfortably as he could against the cart, and began repeating, 'Ein' feste Burg ist unser Gott,'* by which I concluded that I had got into the company of a parson. With the jolts of the wagon, and accidents of the journey, various more exclamations and movements of the passengers showed what a motley company we were. Every now and then a countryman would burst into tears; a French voice would be heard to say, '*O mon Dieu!—mon Dieu!*' a couple more of the same nation were jabbering oaths and chattering incessantly; and a certain allusion to his own and everybody else's eyes, which came from a stalwart figure at the far corner, told me that there was certainly an Englishman in our crew.

But I was spared soon the tedium and discomforts of the journey. In spite of the clergyman's cushion, my head, which was throbbing with pain, was brought abruptly in contact with the side of the wagon; it began to bleed afresh; I became almost light-headed. I only recollect having a draught of water here and there; once stopping at a fortified town, where an officer counted us:—all the rest of the journey was passed in a drowsy stupor, from which, when I awoke, I found myself lying in a hospital bed, with a nun in a white hood watching over me.

'They are in sad spiritual darkness,' said a voice from the bed next to me, when the nun had finished her kind offices and retired; 'they are in the night of error, and yet there is the light of faith in those poor creatures.'

It was my comrade of the crimp-wagon, his huge, broad face looming out from under a white nightcap, and ensconced in the bed beside.

'What! you there, Herr Pastor?' said I.

'Only a candidate, sir,' answered the white nightcap. 'But, praised be Heaven! you have come to. You have had a wild time of it. You have been talking in the English language (with which I am acquainted), of Ireland, and a young lady, and Mick, and of another young lady, and of a house on fire, and of the British Grenadiers, concerning whom you sang us parts of a ballad, and of a number of other matters appertaining, no doubt, to your personal history.'

'It has been a very strange one,' said I; 'and, perhaps, there is no man in the world, of my birth, whose misfortunes can at all be compared to mine.'

I do not object to own that I am disposed to brag of my birth and other acquirements, for I have always found that if a man does not give himself a good word, his friends will not do it for him.

'Well,' said my fellow-patient, 'I have no doubt yours is a strange tale, and shall be glad to hear it anon; but, at present, you must not be permitted to speak much, for your fever has been long, and your exhaustion great.'

'Where are we?' I asked; and the candidate informed me that we were in the bishopric and town of Fulda,* at present occupied by Prince Henry's troops. There had been a skirmish with an out-party of French near the town, in which, a shot entering the wagon, the poor candidate had been wounded.

As the reader knows already my history, I will not take the trouble to repeat it here, or to give the additions with which I favoured my comrade in misfortune. But I confess that I told him ours was the greatest family and finest palace in Ireland, that we were enormously wealthy, related to all the peerage, descended from the ancient kings, &c.; and, to my surprise, in the course of our conversation, I found that my interlocutor knew a great deal more about Ireland than I did. When, for instance, I spoke of my descent,—

'From which race of kings?' said he.

'Oh!' said I (for my memory for dates was never very accurate), 'from the old ancient kings of all.'

'What! can you trace your origin to the sons of Japhet?' said he.

'Faith, I can,' answered I, 'and farther too,—to Nebuchadnezzar, if you like.'

'I see,' said the candidate, smiling, 'that you look upon those legends with incredulity. These Partholans and Nemedians,* of whom your writers fondly make mention, cannot be authentically vouched for in history. Nor do I believe that we have any more foundation for the tales concerning them, than for the legends relative to Joseph of Arimathea, and King Brute,* which prevailed two centuries back in the sister island.'

And then he began a discourse about the Phoenicians, the Scyths, or Goths, the Tuath de Danans, Tacitus, and King MacNeil,* which was, to say the truth, the very first news I had heard of those personages. As for English, he spoke it as well as I, and had seven more languages, he said, equally at his command; for, on my quoting the only Latin line that I knew, that out of the poet Homer, which says,—

As in praesenti perfectum fumat in avi,*

he began to speak to me in the Roman tongue; on which I was fain to tell him that we pronounced it in a different way in Ireland, and so got off the conversation.

My honest friend's history was a curious one, and it may be told here in order to show of what motley materials our levies were composed:—

'I am,' said he, 'a Saxon by birth, my father being pastor of the village of Pfannkuchen,* where I imbibed the first rudiments of knowledge. At sixteen (I am now twenty-three), having mastered the Greek and Latin tongues, with the French, English, Arabic, and Hebrew; and, having come into possession of a legacy of a 100 rixdalers,* a sum amply sufficient to defray my university courses,

I went to the famous academy of Göttingen, where I devoted four years to the exact sciences and theology. Also, I learned what worldly accomplishments I could command; taking a dancing-tutor at the expense of a groschen a lesson, a course of fencing from a French practitioner, and attending lectures on the great horse and the equestrian science at the hippodrome of a celebrated cavalry professor. My opinion is that a man should know everything as far as in his power lies, that he should complete his cycle of experience, and, one science being as necessary as another, it behoves him, according to his means, to acquaint himself with all. For many branches of personal knowledge (as distinguished from spiritual, though I am not prepared to say that the distinction is a correct one), I confess I have found myself inapt. I attempted tight-rope dancing, with a Bohemian artist who appeared at our academy, but in this I failed lamentably, breaking my nose in the fall which I had. I also essayed to drive a coach-and-four, which an English student, Herr Graf Lord von Martingale, drove at the university. In this, too, I failed; oversetting the chariot at the postern, opposite the Berliner gate, with his lordship's friend, Fräulein Miss Kitty Coddlins within. I had been instructing the young lord in the German language when the above accident took place, and was dismissed by him in consequence. My means did not permit me further to pursue this *curriculum**(you will pardon me the joke), otherwise, I have no doubt, I should have been able to take a place in any hippodrome in the world, and to handle the ribands (as the high-well-born lord used to say) to perfection.

'At the university I delivered a thesis on the quadrature of the circle, which, I think, would interest you; and held a disputation in Arabic against Professor Strumpff,* in which I was said to have the advantage. The languages of Southern Europe, of course, I acquired; and, to a person well grounded in Sanskrit, the Northern idioms offer no difficulty. If you have ever attempted the Russian you will find it child's play, and it will always be a source of regret to me that I have been enabled to get no knowledge (to speak of) of Chinese; and, but for the present dilemma, I had intended to pass over into England for that purpose, and get a passage in one of the English company's ships to Canton.

'I am not of a saving turn, hence my little fortune of a 100 rixdalers, which has served to keep many a prudent man for a score of years, barely sufficed for a five years' studies; after which my studies were interrupted, my pupils fell off, and I was obliged to devote much time to shoe-binding in order to save money, and, at a future period, resume my academic course. During this period I contracted an attachment' (here the candidate sighed a little) 'with a person, who, though not beautiful, and forty years of age, is yet likely to sympathize with my existence; and, a month since, my kind friend and patron, university Prorector Doctor Nasenbrumm,* having informed me that the Pfarrer of Rumpelwitz* was dead, asked whether I would like to have my name placed upon the candidate list, and if I were minded to preach a trial sermon? As the gaining of this living would further my union with my Amalia, I joyously consented, and prepared a discourse.

'If you like I will recite it to you—No?—Well, I will give you extracts from it upon our line of march. To proceed, then, with my biographical sketch, which is now very near a conclusion, or, as I should more correctly say, which has very nearly brought me to the present period of time, I preached that sermon at Rumpelwitz, in which I hope that the Babylonian question was pretty satisfactorily set at rest. I preached it before the Herr Baron and his noble family, and some officers of distinction who were staying at his castle. Mr. Doctor Moser of Halle followed me in the evening discourse; but, though his exercise was learned, and he disposed of a passage of Ignatius,* which he proved to be a manifest interpolation, I do not think his sermon had the effect which mine produced, and that the Rumpelwitzers much relished it. After the sermon, all the candidates walked out of church together, and supped lovingly at the Blue Stag in Rumpelwitz.

'While so occupied, a waiter came in and said that a person without wished to speak to one of the reverend candidates, "the tall one." This could only mean me, for I was a head and shoulders higher than any other reverend gentleman present. I issued out to see who was the person desiring to hold converse with me, and found a man whom I had no difficulty in recognizing as one of the Jewish persuasion.

'"Sir," said this Hebrew, "I have heard from a friend,

who was in your church to-day, the heads of the admirable discourse you pronounced there. It has affected me deeply, most deeply. There are only one or two points on which I am yet in doubt, and if your honour could but condescend to enlighten me on these, I think—I think Solomon Hirsch would be a convert to your eloquence."

'"What are these points, my good friend?" said I; and I pointed out to him the twenty-four heads of my sermon, asking him in which of these his doubts lay.

'We had been walking up and down before the inn while our conversation took place, but the windows being open, and my comrades having heard the discourse in the morning, requested me, rather peevishly, not to resume it at that period. I, therefore, moved on with my disciple, and, at his request, began at once the sermon, for my memory is good for anything, and I can repeat any book I have read thrice.

'I poured out, then, under the trees, and in the calm moonlight, that discourse which I had pronounced under the blazing sun of noon. My Israelite only interrupted me by exclamations indicative of surprise, assent, admiration, and increasing conviction. "Prodigious!" said he; —"*Wunderschön!*" would he remark at the conclusion of some eloquent passage; in a word, he exhausted the complimentary interjections of our language, and to compliments what man is averse? I think we must have walked two miles when I got to my third head, and my companion begged I would enter his house, which we now neared, and partake of a glass of beer, to which I was never averse.

'That house, sir, was the inn at which you, too, if I judge aright, were taken. No sooner was I in the place than three crimps rushed upon me, told me I was a deserter, and their prisoner, and called upon me to deliver up my money and papers, which I did with a solemn protest as to my sacred character. They consisted of my sermon in MS., Prorector Nasenbrumm's recommendatory letter, proving my identity, and three groschen four pfennigs in bullion. I had already been in the cart twenty hours when you reached the house. The French officer, who lay opposite you, he who screamed when you trod on his foot, for he was wounded, was brought in shortly before your arrival. He had been taken with his epaulets and regimentals, and declared his quality and rank; but he was alone (I believe it was some affair of love with a Hessian lady which caused him to be unattended); and as the persons into whose hands he fell will make more profit of him as a recruit than as a prisoner, he is made to share our fate. He is not the first by many scores so captured. One of M. de Soubise's*cooks, and three actors out of a troupe in the French camp, several deserters from your English troops (the men are led away by being told that there is no flogging in the Prussian service), and three Dutchmen were taken besides.'

'And you,' said I,—'you who were just on the point of getting a valuable living,—you who have so much learning, are you not indignant at the outrage?'

'I am a Saxon,' said the candidate, 'and there is no use in indignation. Our government is crushed under Frederick's heel*these five years, and I might as well hope for mercy from the Grand Mogul.* Nor am I, in truth, discontented with my lot; I have lived on a penny bread for so many years, that a soldier's rations will be a luxury to me. I do not care about more or less blows of a cane, all such evils are passing, and therefore endurable. I will never, God willing, slay a man in combat, but I am not unanxious to experience on myself the effect of the war-passion, which has had so great an influence on the human race. It was for the same reason that I determined to marry Amalia, for a man is not a complete *Mensch**until he is the father of a family, to be which is a condition of his existence, and therefore a duty of his education. Amalia must wait; she is out of the reach of want, being, indeed, cook to the Frau Prorectorin Nasenbrumm, my worthy patron's lady. I have one or two books with me, which no one is likely to take from me, and one in my heart which is the best of all. If it shall please Heaven to finish my existence here, before I can prosecute my studies further, what cause have I to repine? I pray God I may not be mistaken, but I think I have wronged no man, and committed no mortal sin. If I have, I know where to look for forgiveness; and if I die, as I have said, without knowing all that I would desire to learn, shall I not be in a situation to learn *everything*, and what can human soul ask for more?

'Pardon me for putting so many *I's* in my discourse,'

said the candidate, 'but when a man is talking of himself, 'tis the briefest and simplest way of talking.'

In which, perhaps, though I hate egotism, I think my friend was right. Although he acknowledged himself to be a mean-spirited fellow, with no more ambition than to know the contents of a few musty books, I think the man had some good in him, especially in the resolution with which he bore his calamities. Many a gallant man of the highest honour is often not proof against these, and has been known to despair over a bad dinner, or to be cast down at a ragged-elbowed coat. *My* maxim is to bear all, to put up with water if you cannot get burgundy, and if you have no velvet, to be content with frieze. But burgundy and velvet are the best, *bien entendu*, and the man is a fool who will not seize the best when the scramble is open.

The heads of the sermon which my friend the theologian intended to impart to me were, however, never told; for, after our coming out of the hospital, he was drafted into a regiment quartered as far as possible from his native country, in Pomerania; while I was put into the Bülow regiment,* of which the ordinary head quarters were Berlin. The Prussian regiments seldom change their garrisons as ours do, for the fear of desertion is so great that it becomes necessary to know the face of every individual in the service, and, in time of peace, men live and die in the same town. This does not add, as may be imagined, to the amusements of the soldier's life. It is lest any young gentleman like myself should take a fancy to a military career, and fancy that of a private soldier a tolerable one, that I am giving these, I hope, moral descriptions of what we poor fellows in the ranks really suffered.

As soon as we recovered, we were dismissed from the nuns and the hospital to the town prison of Fulda, where we were kept like slaves and criminals, with artillerymen with lighted matches* at the doors of the courtyards and the huge black dorm tory where some hundreds of us lay, until we were dispatched to our different destinations. It was soon seen by the exercise which were the old soldiers amongst us, and which the recruits; and for the former, while we lay in prison, there was a little more leisure, though, if possible, a still more strict watch kept than over the broken-spirited yokels who had been forced or coaxed into the service. To describe the characters here assembled would require Mr. Gillray's*own pencil. There were men of all nations and callings. The Englishmen boxed and bullied; the Frenchmen played cards, and danced, and fenced; the heavy Germans smoked their pipes, and drank beer if they could manage to purchase it. Those who had anything to risk gambled, and at this sport I was pretty lucky, for, not having a penny when I entered the dépôt (having been robbed of every farthing of my property by the rascally crimps),* I won near a dollar in my very first game at cards with one of the Frenchmen, who did not think of asking whether I could pay or not upon losing. Such, at least, is the advantage of having a gentlemanlike appearance; it has saved me many a time since by procuring me credit when my fortunes were at their lowest ebb.

Among the Frenchmen there was a splendid man and soldier, whose real name we never knew, but whose ultimate history created no small sensation, when it came to be known in the Prussian army. If beauty and courage are proofs of nobility, as (although I have seen some of the ugliest dogs and the greatest cowards in the world in the *noblesse*) I have no doubt courage and beauty are, this Frenchman must have been of the highest families in France, so grand and noble was his manner, so superb his person. He was not quite so tall as myself, fair, while I am dark, and, if possible, rather broader in the shoulders. He was the only man I ever met who could master me with the small-sword, with which he would pink me four times to my three. As for the sabre, I could knock him to pieces with it, and I could leap farther and carry more than he could. This, however, is mere egotism. This Frenchman, with whom I became pretty intimate, for we were the two cocks, as it were, of the dépôt, and neither had any feeling of low jealousy, was called, for want of a better name, Le Blondin, on account of his complexion. He was not a deserter, but had come in from the Lower Rhine and the bishoprics, as I fancy, fortune having proved unfavourable to him at play probably, and other means of existence being denied him. I suspect that the Bastille was waiting for him in his own country, had he taken a fancy to return thither.

He was passionately fond of play and liquor, and thus we had a considerable sympathy together, and when excited by one or the other, [he] became frightful. I, for my part, can bear, without wincing, both ill luck and wine; hence my advantage over him was considerable in our bouts, and I won enough money from him to make my position tenable. He had a wife outside (who, I take it, was the cause of his misfortunes and separation from his family), and she used to be admitted to see him twice or thrice a week, and never came empty-handed—a little, brown, bright-eyed creature, whose ogles had made the greatest impression upon all the world.

This man was drafted into a regiment that was quartered at Neiss,* in Silesia, which is only at a short distance from the Austrian frontier; he maintained always the same character for daring and skill, and was, in the secret republic of the regiment which always exists, as well as the regular military hierarchy, the acknowledged leader. He was an admirable soldier, as I have said, but haughty, dissolute, and a drunkard. A man of this mark, unless he takes care to coax and flatter his officers (which I always did), is sure to fall out with them. Le Blondin's captain was his sworn enemy, and his punishments were frequent and severe.

His wife and the women of the regiment (this was after the peace) used to carry on a little commerce of smuggling across the Austrian frontier, where their dealings were winked at by both parties; and in obedience to the instructions of her husband, this woman, from every one of her excursions, would bring in a little powder and ball, commodities which are not to be procured by the Prussian soldier, and which were stowed away in secret till wanted. They *were* to be wanted, and that soon.

Le Blondin had organized a great and extraordinary conspiracy. We don't know how far it went, how many hundreds or thousands it embraced; but strange were the stories told about the plot amongst us privates, for the news was spread from garrison to garrison, and talked of by the army in spite of all the government efforts to hush it up—hush it up, indeed! I have been of the people myself, I have seen the Irish rebellion, and I know what is the freemasonry of the poor.

He made himself the head of the plot. There were no writings nor papers. No single one of the conspirators communicated with any other but the Frenchman; but personally he gave his orders to them all. He had arranged matters for a general rising of the garrison, at twelve o'clock on a certain day; the guard-houses in the town were to be seized, the sentinels cut down, and—who knows the rest? Some of our people used to say that the conspiracy was spread through all Silesia, and that Le Blondin was to be made a general in the Austrian service.

At twelve o'clock, and opposite the guard-house by the Böhmer-Thor of Neiss, some thirty men were lounging about in their undress, and the Frenchman stood near the sentinel of the guard-house, sharpening a wood-hatchet on a stone. At the stroke of twelve, he got up, split open the sentinel's head with a blow of his axe, and the thirty men rushing into the guard-house, took possession of the arms there, and marched at once to the gate. The sentry there tried to drop the bar, but the Frenchman rushed up to him, and, with another blow of the axe, cut off his right hand with which he held the chain. Seeing the men rushing out armed, the guard without the gate drew up across the road to prevent their passage; but the Frenchman's thirty gave them a volley, charged them with the bayonet, and brought down several, and, the rest flying, the thirty rushed on. The frontier is only a league from Neiss, and they made rapidly towards it.

But the alarm was given in the town, and what saved it was that the clock by which the Frenchman went was a quarter of an hour faster than any of the clocks in the town. The *générale** was beat, the troops called to arms, and thus the men who were to have attacked the other guard-houses were obliged to fall into the ranks, and their project was defeated. This, however, likewise rendered the discovery of the conspirators impossible, for no man could betray his comrade, nor of course would he criminate himself.

Cavalry was sent in pursuit of the Frenchman and his thirty fugitives, who were by this time far on their way to the Bohemian frontier. When the horse came up with them, they turned, received them with a volley and the bayonet, and drove them back. The Austrians were out at the barriers, looking eagerly on at the conflict. The women, who were on the look-out too, brought more ammunition to these intrepid deserters, and they engaged and drove back the dragoons several times. But in these gallant and fruitless combats much time was lost, and a battalion presently came up, and surrounded the brave thirty, when the fate of the poor fellows was decided. They fought with the fury of despair; not one of them asked for quarter. When their ammunition failed, they fought with the steel, and were shot down or bayoneted where they stood. The Frenchman was the very last man who was hit. He received a bullet in the thigh, and fell, and in this state was overpowered, killing the officer who first advanced to seize him.

He and the very few of his comrades who survived were carried back to Neiss, and immediately, as the ringleader, he was brought before a council of war. He refused all interrogations which were made as to his real name and family. 'What matters who I am?' said he; 'you have me and will shoot me. My name would not save me were it ever so famous.' In the same way he declined to make a single discovery regarding the plot. 'It was all my doing,' he said; 'each man engaged in it only knew me, and is ignorant of every one of his comrades. The secret is mine alone, and the secret shall die with me.' When the officers asked him what was the reason which induced him to meditate a crime so horrible? 'It was your infernal brutality and tyranny,' he said. 'You are all butchers, ruffians, tigers, and you owe it to the cowardice of your men that you were not murdered long ago.'

At this his captain burst into the most furious exclamations against the wounded man, and rushing up to him, struck him a blow with his fist. But Le Blondin, wounded as he was, as quick as thought seized the bayonet of one of the soldiers who supported him, and plunged it into the officer's breast. 'Scoundrel and monster,' said he, 'I shall have the consolation of sending you out of the world before I die.' He was shot that day. He offered to write to the king, if the officers would agree to let his letter go sealed into the hands of the postmaster; but they feared, no doubt, that something might be said to inculpate themselves, and refused him the permission. At the next review Frederick treated them, it is said, with great severity, and rebuked them for not having granted the Frenchman his request. However, it was the king's interest to conceal the matter, and so it was, as I have said before, hushed up—so well hushed up, that a hundred thousand soldiers in the army knew it, and many's the one of us that has drunk to the Frenchman's memory over our wine, as a martyr for the cause of the soldier. I shall have, doubtless, some readers who will cry out at this, that I am encouraging insubordination and advocating murder. If these men had served as privates in the Prussian army from 1760 to 1765, they would not be so apt to take objection. This man destroyed two sentinels to get his liberty; how many hundreds of thousands of his own and the Austrian people did King Frederick kill because he took a fancy to Silesia?* [How many men, in later days, did Napoleon Bonaparte cause to die by shot or steel, or cold or hunger, because he wished to make himself master of Russia?][1]* It was the accursed tyranny of the system that sharpened the axe which brained the two sentinels of Neiss; and so let officers take warning, and think twice ere they visit poor fellows with the cane.

I could tell many more stories about the army, but as, from having been a soldier myself, all my sympathies are in the ranks, no doubt my tales would be pronounced to be of an immoral tendency, and I had best, therefore, be brief. Fancy my surprise while in this dépôt, when one day a well-known voice saluted my ear, and I heard a meagre young gentleman, who was brought in by a couple of troopers and received a few cuts across the shoulders from one of them, say in the best English, 'You infernal *wascal*, I'll be *wevenged* for this. I'll *wite* to my ambassador, as sure as my name's Fakenham of Fakenham.' I burst out laughing at this: it was my old acquaintance in *my* corporal's coat. Lischen had sworn stoutly that he was really and truly the private, and the poor fellow had been drafted off, and was to be made one of us. But I bear no malice, and having made the whole room roar with the story of the way in which I had tricked the poor lad, I gave him a piece of advice, which procured him his liberty. 'Go to the inspecting officer,' said I; 'if they once get you into Prussia it is all over with you, and they will never give you up. Go now to the commandant of the dépôt, promise him a hundred—five hundred guineas to set you free; say that the crimping captain has your papers and portfolio' (this was true); 'above all, show him that you have the means of paying him the promised money, and I will

[1] Omitted in later editions.

warrant you are set free.' He did as I advised, and when we were put on the march Mr. Fakenham found means to be allowed to go into hospital, and while in hospital the matter was arranged as I had recommended. He had nearly, however, missed his freedom by his own stinginess in bargaining for it, and never showed the least gratitude towards me, his benefactor.

I am not going to give any romantic narrative of the Seven Years' War. At the close of it, the Prussian army, so renowned for its disciplined valour, was officered and under-officered by native Prussians, it is true, but was composed for the most part of men hired or stolen, like myself, from almost every nation in Europe. The deserting to and fro was prodigious. In my regiment (Bülow's) alone, before the war here, had been no less than 600 Frenchmen, and as they marched out of Berlin for the campaign, one of the fellows had an old fiddle on which he was playing a French tune, and his comrades danced almost, rather than walked, after him, singing '*Nous allons en France.*' Two years after, when they returned to Berlin, there were only six of these men left, the rest had fled or were killed in action. The life the private soldier led was a frightful one to any but men of iron courage and endurance. There was a corporal to every three men, marching behind them, and pitilessly using the cane: so much so that it used to be said that in action there was a front rank of privates and a second rank of sergeants and corporals to drive them on. Many men would give way to the most frightful acts of despair under these incessant persecutions and tortures, and amongst several regiments of the army a horrible practice had sprung up, which for some time caused the greatest alarm to the government. This was a strange frightful custom of *child-murder*. The men used to say that life was unbearable, that suicide was a crime, in order to avert which, and to finish with the intolerable misery of their position, the best plan was to kill a young child, which was innocent, and therefore secure of heaven, and then to deliver themselves as guilty of the murder. The king himself, the hero, sage, and philosopher, the prince who had always liberality on his lips, and who affected a horror of capital punishments, was frightened at this dreadful protest on the part of the wretches whom he had kidnapped, against his monstrous tyranny, and his only means of remedying the evil was strictly to forbid that such criminals should be attended by any ecclesiastic whatever, and denied all religious consolation.

The punishment was incessant. Every officer had the liberty to inflict it, and in peace it was more cruel than in war. For when peace came the king turned adrift such of his officers as were not noble, whatever their services might have been. He would call a captain to the front of his company, and say, 'He is not noble, let him go.' We were afraid of him somehow, and were cowed before him like wild beasts before their keeper. I have seen the bravest men of the army cry like children at a cut of the cane; I have seen a little ensign of fifteen call out a man of fifty from the ranks, a man who had been in a hundred battles, and he has stood presenting arms, and sobbing and howling like a baby while the young wretch lashed him over the arms and thighs with the stick. In a day of action this man would dare anything. A button might be awry *then* and nobody touched him; but when they had made the brute fight then they lashed him again into subordination. Almost all of us yielded to the spell—scarce one could break it. The French officer I have spoken of as taken along with me, was in my company and caned like a dog. I met him at Versailles twenty years afterwards, and he turned quite pale and sick when I spoke to him of old days. 'For God's sake,' said he, 'don't talk of that time; I wake up from my sleep trembling and crying even now.'

As for me, after a very brief time, in which it must be confessed I tasted, like my comrades, of the cane, and after I had found opportunities to show myself to be a brave and dexterous soldier, I took the means I had adopted in the English army to prevent any further personal degradation. I wore a bullet around my neck, which I did not take the pains to conceal, and I gave out that it should be for the man or officer who caused me to be chastised. And there was something in my character which made my superiors believe me, for that bullet had already served me to kill an Austrian colonel, and I would have given it to a Prussian with as little remorse. For what cared I for their quarrels, or whether the eagle under which I marched had one head or two?* All I said was, 'No man shall find me tripping in my duty; but no man shall ever lay a hand upon me.'

And by this maxim I abided as long as I remained in the service.

I do not intend to make a history of battles in the Prussian any more than in the English service. I did my duty in them as well as another, and by the time that my moustache had grown to a decent length, which it did when I was twenty years of age, there was not a braver, cleverer, handsomer, and I must own, wickeder soldier in the Prussian army. I had formed myself to the condition of the proper fighting beast; on a day of action I was savage and happy; out of the field I took all the pleasure I could get, and was by no means delicate as to its quality or the manner of procuring it. The truth is, however, that there was among our men a much higher tone of society than among the clumsy louts in the English army, and our service was generally so strict that we had little time for doing mischief. I am very dark and swarthy in complexion, and was called by our fellows the 'Black Englander,' the 'Schwarzer Engländer,' or the English devil. If any service was to be done I was sure to be put upon it. I got frequent gratifications of money, but no promotion; and it was on the day after I had killed the Austrian colonel (a great officer of Uhlans,* whom I engaged singly and on foot) that General Bülow, my colonel, gave me two frédérics-d'or* in front of the regiment, and said, 'I reward thee now, but I fear I shall have to hang thee one day or other.' I spent the money, and that I had taken from the colonel's body, every groschen, that night with some jovial companions; but as long as war lasted was never without a dollar* in my purse.

CHAPTER VII

BARRY LEADS A GARRISON LIFE, AND FINDS MANY FRIENDS THERE

After the war, our regiment was garrisoned in the capital, the least dull, perhaps, of all the towns of Prussia; but that does not say much for its gaiety. Our service, which was always severe, still left many hours of the day disengaged, in which we might take our pleasure had we the means of paying for the same. Many of our mess got leave to work in trades, but I had been brought up to none, and besides, my honour forbade me, for as a gentleman, I could not soil my fingers by a manual occupation. But our pay was barely enough to keep us from starving, and as I have always been fond of pleasure, and as the position in which we now were, in the midst of the capital, prevented us from resorting to those means of levying contributions which are always pretty feasible in war-time, I was obliged to adopt the only means left me of providing for my expenses, and, in a word, became the *Ordonnanz*, or confidential military gentleman, of my captain. I spurned the office four years previously, when it was made to me in the English service; but the position is very different in a foreign country: besides, to tell the truth, after five years in the ranks, a man's pride will submit to many rebuffs, which would be intolerable to him in an independent condition.

The captain was a young man and had distinguished himself during the war, or he would never have been advanced to rank so early. He was, moreover, the nephew and heir of the Minister of Police, Monsieur de Potzdorff, a relationship which no doubt aided in the young gentleman's promotion. Captain de Potzdorff was a severe officer enough on parade or in barracks, but he was a person easily led by flattery. I won his heart in the first place by my manner of tying my hair in queue (indeed it was more neatly dressed than that of any man in the regiment), and subsequently gained his confidence by a thousand little arts and compliments, which as a gentleman myself, I knew how to employ. He was a man of pleasure, which he pursued more openly than most men in the stern court of the king: he was generous and careless with his purse, and he had a great affection for Rhine wine, in all which qualities I sincerely sympathized with him, and from which I, of course, had my profit. He was disliked in the regiment because he was supposed to have too intimate relations with his uncle, the police minister, to whom, it was hinted, he carried the news of the corps.

Before long I had ingratiated myself considerably with my officer, and knew most of his affairs. Thus I was relieved from many drills and parades, which would otherwise have fallen to my lot, and came in for a number of perquisites which enabled me to support a genteel figure and to appear with some *éclat* in a certain, though it must be confessed very humble, society in Berlin. Among the ladies I was always an especial favourite, and so polished was my behaviour amongst them that they could not understand how I should have obtained my frightful nickname of the Black Devil in the regiment. 'He is not so black as he is painted,' I laughingly would say, and most of the ladies agreed that the private was quite as well bred as the captain, as indeed how should it be otherwise, considering my education and birth?

When I was sufficiently ingratiated with him, I asked leave to address a letter to my poor mother in Ireland, to whom I had not given any news of myself for many, many years, for the letters of the foreign soldiers were never admitted to the post for fear of appeals or disturbances on the part of their parents abroad. My captain agreed to find means to forward the letter, and as I knew that he would open it, I took care to give it him sealed, thus showing my confidence in him. But the letter was, as you may imagine, written so that the writer should come to no harm were it intercepted. I begged my honoured mother's forgiveness for having fled from her. I said that my extravagance and folly in my own country I knew rendered my return thither impossible; but that she would, at least, be glad to know that I was well and happy in the service of the greatest monarch in the world, and that the soldier's life was most agreeable to me. And, I added, that I had found a kind protector and patron who I hoped would some day provide for me as I knew it was out of her power to do. I offered remembrances to all the girls at Castle Brady, naming them from Biddy to Becky downwards, and signed myself, as in truth I was, her affectionate son, Redmond Barry, in Captain Potzdorff's company of the Bülowisch regiment of foot in garrison at Berlin. Also I told her a pleasant story about the king kicking the chancellor and three judges downstairs, as he had done one day when I was on guard at Potsdam, and said I hoped for another war soon, when I might rise to be an officer. In fact, you might have imagined my letter to be that of the happiest fellow in the world, and I was not on this head at all sorry to mislead my kind parent.

I was sure my letter was read, for Captain Potzdorff began asking me some days afterwards about my family, and I told him the circumstances pretty truly, all things considered. I was a cadet of a good family, but my mother was almost ruined and had barely enough to support her eight daughters, whom I named. I had been to study for the law at Dublin, where I had got into debt and bad company, had killed a man in a duel, and would be hanged or imprisoned by his powerful friends if I returned. I had enlisted in the English service, where an opportunity for escape presented itself to me such as I could not resist, and hereupon I told the story of Mr. Fakenham of Fakenham in such a way as made my patron to be convulsed with laughter, and he told me afterwards that he had repeated the story at Madame de Kameke's[*] evening assembly, where all the world was anxious to have a sight of the young Englander.

'Was the British ambassador there?' I asked, in a tone of the greatest alarm, and added, 'For Heaven's sake, sir, do not tell my name to him, or he might ask to have me delivered up, and I have no fancy to go to be hanged in my dear native country.' Potzdorff, laughing, said he would take care that I should remain where I was, on which I swore eternal gratitude to him.

Some days afterwards, and with rather a grave face, he said to me, 'Redmond, I have been talking to our colonel about you, and as I wondered that a fellow of your courage and talents had not been advanced during the war, the general said they had had their eye upon you; that you were a gallant soldier, and had evidently come of a good stock; that no man in the regiment had had less fault found with him; but that no man merited promotion less. You were idle, dissolute, and unprincipled; you had done a deal of harm to the men; and, for all your talents and bravery, he was sure would come to no good.'

'Sir!' said I, quite astonished that any mortal man should have formed such an opinion of me, 'I hope General Bülow is mistaken regarding my character. I have fallen into bad company, it is true; but I have only done as other soldiers have done; and, above all, I have never had a kind friend and protector before to whom I might show that I was worthy of better things. The general may say I am a ruined lad, and send me to the d—l; but be sure of this, I would go to the d—l to serve *you*.' This speech I saw pleased my patron very much; and, as I was very discreet and useful in a thousand delicate ways to him, he soon came to have a sincere attachment for me. One day, or rather night, when he was *tête à tête* with the lady of the Tabaks-Rat von Dose* for instance, I . . . . but there is no use in telling affairs which concern nobody now.

Four months after my letter to my mother, I got, under cover to the captain, a reply, which created in my mind a yearning after home, and a melancholy which I cannot describe. I had not seen the dear soul's writing for five years. All the old days, and the fresh happy sunshine of the old green fields in Ireland, and her love, and my uncle, and Phil Purcell, and everything that I had done and thought, came back to me as I read the letter; and when I was alone I cried over it, as I hadn't done since the day when Nora jilted me. I took care not to show my feelings to the regiment or my captain; but that night, when I was to have taken tea at the garden-house outside Brandenburg Gate, with Fräulein Lottchen (the Tabaks-Rätin's gentlewoman of company), I somehow had not the courage to go; but begged to be excused, and went early to bed in barracks, out of which I went and came now almost as I willed, and passed a long night weeping and thinking about dear Ireland.

Next day, my spirits rose again, and I got a ten-guinea bill cashed, which my mother sent in the letter, and gave a handsome treat to some of my acquaintance. The poor soul's letter was blotted all over with tears, full of texts, and written in the wildest incoherent way. She said she was delighted to think I was under a Protestant prince, though she feared he was not in the right way: that right way, she said, she had the blessing to find, under the guidance of the Rev. Joshua Jowls, whom she sat under. She said he was a precious, chosen vessel; a sweet ointment, and precious box of spikenard;* and made use of a great number more phrases that I could not understand; but one thing was clear in the midst of all this jargon, that the good soul loved her son still, and thought and prayed day and night for her wild Redmond. Has it not come across many a poor fellow, in a solitary night's watch, or in sorrow, sickness, or captivity, that at that very minute, most likely, his mother is praying for him? I often have had these thoughts; but they are none of the gayest, and it's quite as well that they don't come to you in company; for where would be a set of jolly fellows then?—as mute as undertakers at a funeral, I promise you. I drank my mother's health that night in a bumper, and lived like a gentleman whilst the money lasted. She pinched herself to give it me, as she told me afterwards; and Mr. Jowls was very wroth with her.

Although the good soul's money was pretty quickly spent, I was not long in getting more; for I had a hundred ways of getting it, and became a universal favourite with the captain and his friends. Now, it was Madame von Dose who gave me a frédéric-d'or for bringing her a bouquet or a letter from the captain [1]; now it was, on the contrary, the old privy councillor who treated me with a bottle of Rhenish, and slipped into my hand a dollar or two, in order that I might give him some information regarding the *liaison* between my captain and his lady. But though I was not such a fool as not to take his money, you may be sure I was not dishonourable enough to betray my benefactor; and he got very little out of *me*. When the captain and the lady fell out, and he began to pay his addresses to the rich daughter of the Dutch minister, I don't know how many more letters and guineas the unfortunate Tabaks-Räthin handed over to me, that I might get her lover back again. But such returns are rare in love, and the

[1] [In the original MS. the words 'my master' have often been written, but afterwards expunged, by Mr. Barry, and 'my captain' written in their stead. If we have allowed the passage which describes his occupation under Monsieur de Potzdorff to remain, it is not, we beseech the reader to suppose, because we admire the autobiographer's principles or professions.]—Note in *Fraser's Magazine*, omitted in later editions.

captain used only to laugh at her stale sighs and entreaties. In the house of Mynheer van Guldensack I made myself so pleasant to high and low, that I came to be quite intimate there; and got the knowledge of a state secret or two which surprised and pleased my captain very much. These little hints he carried to his uncle, the minister of police, who, no doubt, made his advantage of them; and thus I began to be received quite in a confidential light by the Potzdorff family, and became a mere nominal soldier, being allowed to appear in plain clothes (which were, I warrant you, of a neat fashion), and to enjoy myself in a hundred ways, which the poor fellows, my comrades, envied. As for the sergeants, they were as civil to me as to an officer; it was as much as their stripes were worth to offend a person who had the ear of the minister's nephew. There was in my company a young fellow by the name of Kurz, who was six feet high in spite of his name,* and whose life I had saved in some affair of the war. What does this lad do, after I had recounted to him one of my adventures, but call me a spy and informer, and beg me not to call him *Du* any more, as is the fashion with young men when they are very intimate. I had nothing for it but to call him out; but I owed him no grudge. I disarmed him in a twinkling; and, as I sent his sword flying over his head, said to him, 'Kurz, did ever you know a man guilty of a mean action who can do as I do now?' This silenced the rest of the grumblers; and no man ever sneered at me after that.

No man can suppose that, to a person of my fashion, the waiting in antechambers, the conversation of footmen and hangers-on was pleasant. But it was not more degrading than the barrack-room, of which I need not say I was heartily sick. My protestations of liking for the army were all intended to throw dust into the eyes of my employer. I sighed to be out of slavery. I knew I was born to make a figure in the world. Had I been one of the Neiss garrison, I would have cut my way to freedom by the side of the gallant Frenchman; but here I had only artifice to enable me to attain my end, and was not I justified in employing it? My plan was this: I may make myself so necessary to M. de Potzdorff that he will obtain my freedom. Once free, with my fine person and good family, I will do what ten thousand Irish gentlemen have done before, and will marry a lady of fortune and condition. And the proof that I was, if not disinterested, at least actuated by a noble ambition, is this. There was a fat grocer's widow in Berlin with six hundred thalers of rent, and a good business, who gave me to understand that she would purchase my discharge if I would marry her; but I frankly told her that I was not made to be a grocer, and thus absolutely flung away a chance of freedom which she offered me.

And I was grateful to my employers, more grateful than they to me. The captain was in debt, and had dealings with the Jews, to whom he gave notes of hand payable on his uncle's death. The old Herr von Potzdorff, seeing the confidence his nephew had in me, offered to bribe me to know what the young man's affairs really were. But what did I do? I informed Monsieur George von Potzdorff of the fact; and we made out, in concert, a list of little debts, so moderate, that they actually appeased the old uncle instead of irritating, and he paid them, being glad to get off so cheap.

And a pretty return I got for this fidelity. One morning, the old gentleman being closeted with his nephew (he used to come to get any news stirring as to what the young officers of the regiments were doing; whether this or that gambled; who intrigued, and with whom; who was at the ridotto on such a night; who was in debt, and what not; for the king liked to know the business of every officer in his army), I was sent with a letter to the Marquis d'Argens*(that afterwards married Mademoiselle Cochois, the actress), and, meeting the marquis at a few paces off in the street, gave my message, and returned to the captain's lodging. He and his worthy uncle were making my unworthy self the subject of conversation.

'He is noble,' said the captain.

'Bah!' replied the uncle (whom I could have throttled for his insolence). 'All the beggarly Irish who ever enlisted tell the same story.'

'He was kidnapped by Galgenstein,' resumed the other.

'A kidnapped deserter,' said M. Potzdorff, '*la belle affaire!*'

'Well, I promised the lad I would ask for his discharge; and I am sure you can make him useful.'

'You *have* asked his discharge,' answered the elder,

laughing. '*Bon Dieu!* You are a model of probity! You'll never succeed to my place, George, if you are no wiser than you are just now. Make the fellow as useful to you as you please. He has a good manner and a frank countenance. He can lie with an assurance that I never saw surpassed, and fight, you say, on a pinch. The scoundrel does not want for good qualities: but he is vain, a spendthrift, and a *bavard*. As long as you have the regiment *in terrorem* over him, you can do as you like with him. Once let him loose, and the lad is likely to give you the slip. Keep on promising him; promise to make him a general, if you like. What the deuce do I care? There are spies enough to be had in this town without him.'

It was thus that the services I rendered to M. Potzdorff were qualified by that ungrateful old gentleman; and I stole away from the room extremely troubled in spirit, to think that another of my fond dreams was thus dispelled; and that my hopes of getting out of the army, by being useful to the captain, were entirely vain. For some time my despair was such that I thought of marrying the widow; but the marriages of privates are never allowed without the direct permission of the king; and it was a matter of very great doubt whether his Majesty would allow a young fellow of twenty-two, the handsomest man of his army, to be coupled to a pimple-faced old widow of sixty, who was quite beyond the age when her marriage would be likely to multiply the subjects of his majesty. This hope of liberty was therefore vain; nor could I hope to purchase my discharge, unless any charitable soul would lend me a large sum of money; for, though I made a good deal, as I have said, yet I have always had through life an incorrigible knack of spending, and (such is my generosity of disposition) have been in debt ever since I was born.

My captain, the sly rascal! gave me a very different version of his conversation with his uncle to that which I knew to be the true one; and said smilingly to me, 'Redmond, I have spoken to the minister regarding thy services,[1] and thy fortune is made. We shall get thee out

[1] The service about which Mr. Barry here speaks has, and we suspect purposely, been described by him in very dubious terms. It is most probable that he was employed to wait at the table of

of the army, appoint thee to the police bureau, and procure for thee an inspectorship of customs; and, in fine, allow thee to move in a better sphere than that in which Fortune has hitherto placed thee.'

Although I did not believe a word of this speech, I affected to be very much moved by it, and, of course, swore eternal gratitude to the captain for his kindness to the poor Irish castaway.

'Your service at the Dutch minister's has pleased me very well. There is another occasion on which you may make yourself useful to us; and if you succeed, depend on it your reward will be secure.'

'What is the service, sir?' said I; 'I will do anything for so kind a master.'

'There is lately come to Berlin,' said the captain, 'a gentleman in the service of the Empress Queen, who calls himself the Chevalier de Balibari, and wears the red riband and star of the Pope's order of the Spur.* He speaks Italian or French indifferently; but we have some reason to fancy this Monsieur de Balibari is a native of your country of Ireland. Did you ever hear such a name as Balibari in Ireland?'

'Balibari! Balyb..?' A sudden thought flashed across me. 'No, sir,' said I, 'never heard the name.'

'You must go into his service. Of course, you will not know a word of English; and if the chevalier asks as to the particularity of your accent, say you are a Hungarian. The servant who came with him will be turned away to-day, and the person to whom he has applied for a faithful fellow will recommend you. You are a Hungarian; you served in the Seven Years' War. You left the army on account of weakness of the loins. You served Monsieur de Quellenberg two years; he is now with the army in Silesia, but there is your certificate signed by him. You

strangers in Berlin, and to bring to the police minister any news concerning them which might at all interest the government. The great Frederick never received a guest without taking these hospitable precautions; and as for the duels which Mr. Barry fights, may we be allowed to hint a doubt as to a great number of these combats? It will be observed, in one or two other parts of his Memoirs, that whenever he is at an awkward pass, or does what the world does not usually consider respectable, a duel, in which he is victorious, is sure to ensue; from which he argues that he is a man of undoubted honour.

afterwards lived with Dr. Mopsius, who will give you a character, if need be; and the landlord of the Star will, of course, certify that you are an honest fellow; but his certificate goes for nothing. As for the rest of your story, you can fashion that as you will, and make it as romantic or as ludicrous as your fancy dictates. Try, however, to win the chevalier's confidence by provoking his compassion. He gambles a great deal, and *wins*. Do you know the cards well?'

'Only a very little, as soldiers do.'

'I had thought you more expert. You must find out if the chevalier cheats; if he does, we have him. He sees the English and Austrian envoys continually, and the young men of either ministry sup repeatedly at his house. Find out what they talk of; for how much each plays, especially if any of them play on parole. If you can read his private letters, of course you will; though about those which go to the post, you need not trouble yourself, we look at them there. But never see him write a note without finding out to whom it goes, and by what channel or messenger. He sleeps with the keys of his dispatch-box with a string round his neck. Twenty frederics, if you get an impression of the keys. You will, of course, go in plain clothes. You had best brush the powder out of your hair, and tie it with a riband simply; your moustache you must of course shave off.'

With these instructions, and a very small gratuity, the captain left me. When I again saw him, he was amused at the change in my appearance. I had, not without a pang (for they were as black as jet, and curled elegantly), shaved off my moustache; had removed the odious grease and flour, which I always abominated, out of my hair; had mounted a demure French grey coat, black satin breeches, and a maroon plush waistcoat, and a hat without a cockade. I looked as meek and humble as any servant out of place could possibly appear; and I think not my own regiment, which was now at the review at Potsdam, would have known me. Thus accoutred, I went to the Star Hotel, where this stranger was,—my heart beating with anxiety, and something telling me that this Chevalier de Balibari was no other than Barry, of Ballybarry, my father's eldest brother, who had given up his estate in consequence of his obstinate adherence to the Romish superstition.

Before I went in to present myself, I went to look in the *remises* at his carriage. Had he the Barry arms? Yes, there they were, argent, a bend gules, with four escallops of the field,—the ancient coat of my house. They were painted in a shield about as big as my hat, on a smart chariot handsomely gilded, surmounted with a coronet, and supported by eight or nine cupids, cornucopias, and flower-baskets, according to the queer heraldic fashion of those days. It must be he! I felt quite faint as I went up the stairs. I was going to present myself before my uncle in the character of a servant!

'You are the young man whom M. de Seebach recommended?'

I bowed, and handed him a letter from that gentleman, with which my captain had taken care to provide me. As he looked at it I had leisure to examine him. My uncle was a man of sixty years of age, dressed superbly in a coat and breeches of apricot-coloured velvet, a white satin waistcoat embroidered with gold like the coat. Across his breast went the purple riband of his order of the Spur; and the star of the order, an enormous one, sparkled on his breast. He had rings on all his fingers, a couple of watches in his fobs, a rich diamond *solitaire* in the black riband round his neck, and fastened to the bag of his wig; his ruffles and frills were decorated with a profusion of the richest lace. He had pink silk stockings rolled over the knee, and tied with gold garters; and enormous diamond buckles to his red-heeled shoes. A sword mounted in gold, and with a white fish-skin scabbard; and a hat richly laced, and lined with white feathers, which were lying on a table beside him, completed the costume of this splendid gentleman. In height he was about my size, that is, six feet and half an inch; his cast of features singularly like mine, and extremely *distingué*. One of his eyes was closed with a black patch, however; he wore a little white and red paint, by no means an unusual ornament in those days; and a pair of moustachios, which fell over his lip, and hid a mouth that I afterwards found had rather a disagreeable expression. When his beard was removed, the upper teeth appeared to project very much; and his countenance wore a ghastly fixed smile, by no means pleasant.

It was very imprudent of me; but when I saw the splendour of his appearance, the nobleness of his manner, I felt it impossible to keep disguise with him; and when he said, 'Ah, you are a Hungarian, I see!' I could hold no longer.

'Sir,' said I, 'I am an Irishman, and my name is Redmond Barry, of Bally-Barry.' As I spoke, I burst into tears; I can't tell why; but I had seen none of my kith or kin for six years, and my heart longed for some one.

CHAPTER VIII

BARRY BIDS ADIEU TO THE MILITARY PROFESSION

You who have never been out of your country, know little what it is to hear a friendly voice in captivity; and there's many a man that will not understand the cause of the burst of feeling which I have confessed took place on my seeing my uncle. He never for a minute thought to question the truth of what I said. 'Mother of God!' cried he, 'it's my brother Harry's son.' And I think in my heart he was as much affected as I was at thus suddenly finding one of his kindred; for he, too, was an exile from home, and a friendly voice, a look, brought the old country back to his memory again, and the old days of his boyhood. 'I'd give five years of my life to see them again,' said he, after caressing me very warmly. 'What?' asked I. 'Why,' replied he, 'the green fields, and the river, and the old round tower, and the burying-place at Ballybarry. 'Twas a shame for your father to part with the land, Redmond, that went so long with the name.'

He then began to ask me concerning myself, and I gave him my history at some length; at which the worthy gentleman laughed many times, saying, that I was a Barry all over. In the middle of my story he would stop me, to make me stand back to back, and measure with him (by which I ascertained that our heights were the same, and that my uncle had a stiff knee, moreover, which made him walk in a peculiar way), and uttered, during the course of the narrative, a hundred exclamations of pity, and kindness, and sympathy. It was 'Holy saints!' and 'Mother of Heaven!' and 'Blessed Mary!' continually, by which, and with justice, I concluded that he was still devotedly attached to the ancient faith of our family.

It was with some difficulty that I came to explain to him the last part of my history, viz., that I was put into his service as a watch upon his actions, of which I was to give information in a certain quarter. When I told him (with a great deal of hesitation) of this fact, he burst out laughing, and enjoyed the joke amazingly. 'The rascals!' said he; 'they think to catch me, do they? Why, Redmond, my chief conspiracy is a faro-bank.* But the king is so jealous that he will see a spy in every person who comes to his miserable capital in the great sandy desert here. Ah, my boy, I must show you Paris and Vienna!'

I said, there was nothing I longed for more than to see any city but Berlin, and should be delighted to be free of the odious military service. Indeed, I thought, from his splendour of appearance, the knick-knacks about the room, the gilded carriage in the *remise*,* that my uncle was a man of vast property; and that he would purchase a dozen, nay, a whole regiment of substitutes, in order to restore me to freedom.

But I was mistaken in my calculations regarding him, as his history of himself speedily showed me. 'I have been beaten about the world,' said he, 'ever since the year 1742, when my brother, your father, and Heaven forgive him, cut my family estate from under my heels, by turning heretic, in order to marry that scold of a mother of yours. Well, let bygones be bygones. 'Tis probable that I should have run through the little property as he did in my place, and I should have had to begin a year or two later the life I have been leading ever since I was compelled to leave Ireland. My lad, I have been in every service; and between ourselves, owe money in every capital in Europe. I made a campaign or two with the Pandours under Austrian Trenck.* I was captain in the Guard of his Holiness the Pope. I made the campaign of Scotland with the Prince of Wales*—a bad fellow, my dear, caring more for his mistress and his brandy-bottle than for the crowns of the three kingdoms. I have served in Spain and in Piedmont; but I have been a rolling stone, my good fellow. Play—play has been my ruin! that and beauty' (here he gave a leer which made him, I must confess, look anything but handsome; besides, his rouged cheeks were all beslobbered with the tears which he had shed on receiving me). 'The women have made a fool of me, my dear

Redmond. I am a soft-hearted creature, and this minute, at sixty-two, have no more command of myself than when Peggy O'Dwyer made a fool of me at sixteen.'

'Faith, sir,' says I, laughing, 'I think it runs in the family!' and described to him, much to his amusement, my romantic passion for my cousin, Nora Brady. He resumed his narrative.

'The cards now are my only livelihood. Sometimes I am in luck, and then I lay out my money in these trinkets you see. It's property, look you, Redmond, and the only way I have found of keeping a little about me. When the luck goes against me, why, my dear, my diamonds go to the pawnbrokers, and I wear paste. Friend Moses, the goldsmith, will pay me a visit this very day, for the chances have been against me all the week past, and I must raise money for the bank to-night. Do you understand the cards?'

I replied that I could play as soldiers do, but had no great skill.

'We will practise in the morning, my boy,' said he, 'and I'll put you up to a thing or two worth knowing.'

Of course I was glad to have such an opportunity of acquiring knowledge, and professed myself delighted to receive my uncle's instruction.

The chevalier's account of himself rather disagreeably affected me. All his show was on his back, as he said. His carriage, with the fine gilding, was a part of his stock-in-trade. He *had* a sort of mission from the Austrian court:—it was to discover whether a certain quantity of alloyed ducats which had been traced to Berlin, were from the King's treasury. But the real end of Monsieur de Balibari was play. There was a young *attaché* of the English embassy, my Lord Deuceace, afterwards Viscount and Earl of Crabs in the English peerage, who was playing high; and it was after hearing of the passion of this young English nobleman that my uncle, then at Prague, determined to visit Berlin and engage him. For there is a sort of chivalry among the knights of the dice-box: the fame of great players is known all over Europe. I have known the Chevalier de Casanova,* for instance, to travel six hundred miles, from Paris to Turin, for the purpose of meeting Mr. Charles Fox,* then only my Lord Holland's dashing son, afterwards the greatest of European orators and statesmen.

It was agreed that I should keep my character of valet, that in the presence of strangers I should not know a word of English, that I should keep a good look-out on the trumps when I was serving the champagne and punch about; and, having a remarkably fine eyesight, and a great natural aptitude, I was speedily able to give my dear uncle much assistance against his opponents at the green table. Some prudish persons may affect indignation at the frankness of these confessions, but Heaven pity them! Do you suppose that any man who has lost or won a hundred thousand pounds at play will not take the advantages which his neighbour enjoys? They are all the same. But it is only the clumsy fool who *cheats*, who resorts to the vulgar expedients of cogged dice and cut cards. Such a man is sure to go wrong some time or other, and is not fit to play in the society of gallant gentlemen; and my advice to people who see such a vulgar person at his pranks is, of course, to back him while he plays, but never—never to have anything to do with him. Play grandly, honourably. Be not, of course, cast down at losing; but above all, be not eager at winning, as mean souls are. And, indeed, with all one's skill and advantages that winning is often problematical; I have seen a sheer ignoramus that knows no more of play than of Hebrew, blunder you out of five thousand pounds in a few turns of the cards. I have seen a gentleman and his confederate play against another and *his* confederate. One never is secure in these cases: and when one considers the time and labour spent, the genius, the anxiety, the outlay of money required, the multiplicity of bad debts that one meets with (for dishonourable rascals are to be found at the play-table, as everywhere else in the world), I say, for my part, the profession is a bad one; and, indeed, have scarcely ever met a man who, in the end, profited by it. I am writing now with the experience of a man of the world. At the time I speak of I was a lad, dazzled by the idea of wealth, and respecting, certainly too much, my uncle's superior age and station in life.

There is no need to particularize here the little arrangements made between us; the play-men of the present day want no instruction, I take it, and the public have little interest in the matter. But simplicity was our secret. Everything successful is simple. If, for instance, I wiped the dust off a chair with my napkin, it was to show that the enemy was strong in diamonds; if I pushed it, he had ace, king; if I said, 'Punch or wine, my lord?' hearts was meant; if 'Wine or punch?' clubs. If I blew my nose, it was to indicate that there was another confederate employed by the adversary; and *then*, I warrant you, some pretty trials of skill would take place. My Lord Deuceace, although so young, had a very great skill and cleverness with the cards in every way; and it was only from hearing Frank Punter, who came with him, yawn three times when the chevalier had the ace of trumps, that I knew we were Greek to Greek, as it were.

My assumed dullness was perfect; and I used to make Monsieur de Potzdorff laugh with it, when I carried my little reports to him at the Garden-house outside the town where he gave me rendezvous. These reports, of course, were arranged between me and my uncle beforehand. I was instructed (and it is always far the best way) to tell as much truth as my story would possibly bear. When, for instance, he would ask me, 'What does the chevalier do of a morning?' 'He goes to church regularly' (he was very religious), 'and after hearing mass comes home to breakfast. Then he takes an airing in his chariot till dinner, which is served at noon. After dinner he writes his letters, if he have any letters to write: but he has very little to do in this way. His letters are to the Austrian envoy, with whom he corresponds, but who does not acknowledge him; and being written in English, of course I look over his shoulder. He generally writes for money. He says he wants it to bribe the secretaries of the treasury, in order to find out really where the alloyed ducats come from; but, in fact, he wants it to play of evenings, when he makes his party with Calsabigi, the lottery contractor, the Russian *attachés*, two from the English embassy, my Lords Deuceace and Punter, who play a *jeu d'enfer*, and a few more. The same set meet every night at supper: there are seldom any ladies; those who come are chiefly French ladies, members of the *corps de ballet*. He wins often, but not always. Lord Deuceace is a very fine player. The Chevalier Elliot,* the English minister, sometimes comes, on which occasion the secretaries do not play. Monsieur de Balibari dines at the missions, but *en petit comité*, not on grand days of reception. Calsabigi, I think, is his confederate at play.

He has won lately, but the week before last he pledged his *solitaire* for four hundred ducats.'

'Do he and the English *attachés* talk together in their own language?'

'Yes; he and the envoy spoke yesterday for half an hour about the new *danseuse* and the American troubles:* chiefly about the new *danseuse*.'

It will be seen that the information I gave was very minute and accurate, though not very important. But such as it was, it was carried to the ears of that famous hero and warrior the Philosopher of Sans Souci;* and there was not a stranger who entered the capital but his actions were similarly spied and related to Frederick the Great.

As long as the play was confined to the young men of the different embassies, his Majesty did not care to prevent it; nay, he encouraged play at all the missions, knowing full well that a man in difficulties can be made to speak, and that a timely *rouleau** of frederics would often get him a secret worth many thousands. He got some papers from the French house in this way: and I have no doubt that my Lord Deuceace would have supplied him with information at a similar rate, had his chief not known the young nobleman's character pretty well; and had (as is usually the case) the work of the mission performed by a steady *roturier*,* while the young brilliant bloods of the suite sported their embroidery at the balls, or shook their Mechlin ruffles* over the green tables at faro. I have seen many scores of these young sprigs since, of these and their principals, and *mon Dieu!* what fools they are! What dullards, what fribbles, what addle-headed simple coxcombs! This is one of the lies of the world, this diplomacy; or how could we suppose that, were the profession as difficult as the solemn red-box and tape-men would have us believe, they would invariably choose for it little pink-faced boys from school, with no other claim than mamma's title, and able, at most, to judge of a curricle, a new dance, or a neat boot?

When it became known, however, to the officers of the garrison that there was a faro-table in town, they were wild to be admitted to the sport; and, in spite of my entreaties to the contrary, my uncle was not averse to allow the young gentlemen their fling, and once or twice cleared a handsome sum out of their purses. It was in vain

I told him that I must carry the news to my captain, before whom his comrades would not fail to talk, and who would thus know of the intrigue even without my information.

'Tell him,' said my uncle.

'They will send you away,' said I, 'then what is to become of me?'

'Make your mind easy,' said the latter, with a smile; 'you shall not be left behind, I warrant you. Go take a last look at your barracks, make your mind easy, say a farewell to your friends in Berlin. The dear souls, how they will weep when they hear you are out of the country, and, as sure as my name is Barry, out of it you shall go!'

'But how, sir,' said I.

'Recollect Mr. Fakenham of Fakenham,' said he, knowingly. ''Tis you yourself taught me how. Go get me one of my wigs. Open my dispatch-box yonder, where the great secrets of the Austrian chancery lie; put your hair back off your forehead; clap me on this patch and these moustachios, and now look in the glass!'

'The Chevalier de Balibari,' said I, bursting with laughter, and began walking the room in his manner with his stiff knee.

The next day when I went to make my report to Monsieur de Potzdorff, I told him of the young Prussian officers that had been of late gambling; and he replied, as I expected, that the King had determined to send the chevalier out of the country.

'He is a stingy curmudgeon,' I replied; 'I have had but three frederics from him in two months, and I hope you will remember your promise to advance me!'

'Why, three frederics were too much for the news you have picked up,' said the captain, sneering.

'It is not my fault that there has been no more,' I replied. 'When is he to go, sir?'

'The day after to-morrow. You say he drives after breakfast and before dinner. When he comes out to his carriage, a couple of *gendarmes* will mount the box, and the coachman will get his orders to move on.'

'And his baggage, sir?' said I.

'Oh, that will be sent after him. I have a fancy to look into that red box which contains his papers, you say; and at noon, after parade, shall be at the inn. You will not say a word to any one there regarding the affair, and will wait for me at the chevalier's rooms until my arrival. We must force that box. You are a clumsy hound, or you would have got the key long ago!'

I begged the captain to remember me, and so took my leave of him. The next night I placed a couple of pistols under the carriage-seat; and I think the adventures of the following day are quite worthy of the honours of a separate chapter.

CHAPTER IX

I APPEAR IN A MANNER BECOMING MY NAME AND LINEAGE

FORTUNE, smiling at parting upon Monsieur de Balibari, enabled him to win a handsome sum with his faro bank.

At ten o'clock the next morning, the carriage of the Chevalier de Balibari drew up as usual at the door of his hotel; and the chevalier, who was at his window, seeing the chariot arrive, came down the stairs in his usual stately manner.

'Where is my rascal Ambrose?' said he, looking around and not finding his servant to open the door.

'I will let down the steps for your honour,' said a *gendarme*, who was standing by the carriage; and no sooner had the chevalier entered than the officer jumped in after him, another mounted the box by the coachman, and the latter began to drive.

'Good gracious!' said the chevalier, 'what is this?'

'You are going to drive to the frontier,' said the *gendarme*, touching his hat.

'It is shameful—infamous! I insist upon being put down at the Austrian ambassador's house!'

'I have orders to gag your honour if you cry out,' said the *gendarme*.

'All Europe shall hear of this!' said the chevalier, in a fury.

'As you please,' answered the officer, and then both relapsed into silence.

The silence was not broken between Berlin and Potsdam,

through which place the chevalier passed as his Majesty was reviewing his guards there, and the regiments of Bülow, Zitwitz, and Henkel de Donnersmark. As the chevalier passed his Majesty, the King raised his hat and said, 'Qu'il ne descende pas : je lui souhaite un bon voyage.' The Chevalier de Balibari acknowledged this courtesy by a profound bow.

They had not got far beyond Potsdam, when, boom! the alarm cannon began to roar.

'It is a deserter !' said the officer.

'Is it possible ?' said the chevalier, and sank back into his carriage again.

Hearing the sound of the guns, the common people came out along the road with fowling-pieces and pitchforks, in hopes to catch the truant. The *gendarmes* looked very anxious to be on the look-out for him too. The price of a deserter was fifty crowns to those who brought him in.

'Confess, sir,' said the chevalier to the police officer in the carriage with him, 'that you long to be rid of me from whom you can get nothing, and to be on the look-out for the deserter who may bring you in fifty crowns ? Why not tell the postilion to push on ? You may land me at the frontier and get back to your hunt all the sooner.' The officer told the postilion to get on, but the way seemed intolerably long to the chevalier. Once or twice he thought he heard the noise of horse galloping behind ; his own horses did not seem to go two miles an hour, but they *did* go. The black-and-white barriers came in view at last, hard by Brück, and opposite them the green-and-yellow of Saxony. The Saxon custom-house officers came out.

'I have no luggage,' said the chevalier.

'The gentleman has nothing contraband,' said the Prussian officers, grinning, and took their leave of their prisoner with much respect.

The Chevalier de Balibari gave them a frederic apiece.

'Gentlemen,' said he, 'I wish you a good day. Will you please to go to the house whence we set out this morning, and tell my man there to send on my baggage to the Three [Crowns]*at Dresden ?' Then ordering fresh horses, the chevalier set off on his journey for that capital. I need not tell you that *I* was the chevalier.

'FROM THE CHEVALIER DE BALIBARI TO REDMOND BARRY, ESQUIRE, GENTILHOMME ANGLAIS

'*A l'Hôtel des* 3 *Couronnes, à Dresde, en Saxe.*

'NEPHEW REDMOND,—This comes to you by a sure hand, no other than Mr. Lumpit of the English mission, who is acquainted, as all Berlin will be directly, with our wonderful story. They only know half as yet; they only know that a deserter went off in my clothes, and all are in admiration of your cleverness and valour.

'I confess that for two hours after your departure I lay in bed in no small trepidation, thinking whether his Majesty might have a fancy to send me to Spandau* for the freak of which we had both been guilty. But in that case I had taken my precautions; I had written a statement of the case to my chief, the Austrian minister, with the full and true story how you had been set to spy upon me, how you turned out to be my very near relative, how you had been kidnapped yourself into the service, and how we both had determined to effect your escape. The laugh would have been so much against the King that he never would have dared to lay a finger upon me. What would Monsieur de Voltaire* have said to such an act of tyranny?

'But it was a lucky day, and everything has turned out to my wish. As I lay in my bed two and a half hours after your departure, in comes your ex-captain Potzdorff. "Redmont!" says he, in his imperious High Dutch* way, "are you there?" No answer. "The rogue is gone out," said he; and straightway makes for my red box where I keep my love-letters, my glass eye which I used to wear, my favourite lucky dice with which I threw the thirteen mains* at Prague; my two sets of Paris teeth, and my other private matters that you know of.

'He first tried a bunch of keys, but none of them would fit the little English lock. Then my gentleman takes out of his pocket a chisel and hammer, and falls to work like a professional burglar, actually bursting open my little box!

'Now was my time to act. I advance towards him armed with an immense water-jug. I come noiselessly up to him just as he had broken the box, and, with all my might, I deal him such a blow over the head as smashes the water-jug to atoms, and sends my captain with a snort lifeless to the ground. I thought I had killed him.

'Then I ring all the bells in the house; and shout, and swear, and scream, "Thieves!—thieves!—landlord!—murder!—fire!" until the whole household come tumbling up the stairs. "Where is my servant?" roar I. "Who dares to rob me in open day? Look at the villain whom I find in the act of breaking my chest open! Send for the police, send for his Excellency the Austrian minister! all Europe shall know of this insult!'

'"Dear heaven!" says the landlord, "we saw you go away three hours ago!"

'"*Me!*" say I; "why, man, I have been in bed all the morning. I am ill—I have taken physic—I have not left the house this morning! Where is that scoundrel Ambrose? But, stop! where are my clothes and wig?" for I was standing before them in my chamber-gown and stockings, with my nightcap on.

'"I have it—I have it!" says a little chamber-maid; "Ambrose is off in your honour's dress."

'"And my money—my money!" says I; "where is my purse with forty-eight frederics in it? But we have one of the villains left. Officers, seize him!"

'"It's the young Herr von Potzdorff!" says the landlord, more and more astonished.

'"What! a gentleman breaking open my trunk with hammer and chisel—impossible!"

'Herr von Potzdorff was returning to life by this time, with a swelling on his skull as big as a saucepan; and the officers carried him off, and the judge who was sent for dressed a *procès-verbal** of the matter, and I demanded a copy of it, which I sent forthwith to my ambassador.

'I was kept a prisoner to my room the next day, and a judge, a general, and a host of lawyers, officers and officials were set upon me to bully, perplex, threaten, and cajole me. I said it was true you had told me that you had been kidnapped into the service, that I thought you were released from it, and that I had you with the best recommendations. I appealed to my minister, who was bound to come to my aid; and, to make a long story short, poor Potzdorff is now on his way to Spandau; and his uncle, the elder Potzdorff, has brought me five hundred louis, with a humble request that I would leave Berlin forthwith, and hush up this painful matter.

'I shall be with you at the Three Crowns the day after you receive this. Ask Mr. Lumpit to dinner. Do not spare your money—you are my son. Everybody in Dresden knows your loving uncle,

'THE CHEVALIER DE BALIBARI.'

And by these wonderful circumstances I was once more free again, and I kept my resolution then made, never to fall more into the hands of any recruiter, and thenceforth and for ever to be a gentleman.

With this sum of money, and a good run of luck which ensued presently, we were enabled to make no ungenteel figure. My uncle speedily joined me at the inn at Dresden, where, under pretence of illness, I had kept quiet until his arrival; and, as the Chevalier de Balibari was in particular good odour at the court of Dresden (having been an intimate acquaintance of the late monarch the Elector, King of Poland,[*] the most dissolute and agreeable of European princes), I was speedily in the very best society of the Saxon capital, where I may say that my own person and manners, and the singularity of the adventures in which I had been a hero, made me especially welcome. There was not a party of the nobility to which the two gentlemen of Balibari were not invited. I had the honour of kissing hands and being graciously received at court by the Elector, and I wrote home to my mother such a flaming description of my prosperity that the good soul very nearly forgot her celestial welfare and her confessor, the Rev. Joshua Jowls, in order to come after me to Germany, but travelling was very difficult in those days, and so we were spared the arrival of the good lady.

I think the soul of Harry Barry, my father, who was always so genteel in his turn of mind, must have rejoiced to see the position which I now occupied. All the women anxious to receive me, all the men in a fury; hobnobbing with dukes and counts at supper, dancing minuets with high-well-born baronesses (as they absurdly call themselves in Germany), with lovely excellencies, nay, with highnesses and transparencies[*] themselves—who could compete with the gallant young Irish noble? who would suppose that seven weeks before I had been a common—bah! I am ashamed to think of it! One of the pleasantest moments of my life was at a grand gala at the electoral palace, where I had the honour of walking a polonaise with no other than the Margravine of Bayreuth,[*] old Fritz's own sister; old Fritz, whose hateful blue baize livery I had worn, whose belts I had pipe-clayed, and whose abominable rations of small beer and sauerkraut I had swallowed for five years.

Having won an English chariot from an Italian gentleman at play, my uncle had our arms painted on the panels in a more splendid way than ever, surmounted (as we were descended from the ancient kings) with an Irish crown of the most splendid size and gilding. I had this crown in lieu of a coronet engraved on a large amethyst signet-ring worn on my forefinger; and I don't mind confessing that I used to say the jewel had been in my family for several thousand years, having originally belonged to my direct ancestor, his late Majesty King Brian Boru, or Barry.

I warrant the legends of the Heralds' College are not more authentic than mine was.

At first the minister and the gentlemen at the English hotel used to be rather shy of us two Irish noblemen, and questioned our pretensions to rank. The minister was a lord's son, it is true, but he was likewise a grocer's grandson, and so I told him at Count Lobkowitz's masquerade. My uncle, like a noble gentleman as he was, knew the pedigree of every considerable family in Europe. He said it was the only knowledge befitting a gentleman; and when we were not at cards, we would pass hours over Gwillim or D'Hozier, reading the genealogies, learning the blazons, and making ourselves acquainted with the relationships of our class. Alas! the noble science is going into disrepute now; so are cards, without which studies and pastimes I can hardly conceive how a man of honour can exist.

My first affair of honour with a man of undoubted fashion was on the score of my nobility with young Sir Rumford Bumford of the English embassy, my uncle at the same time sending a cartel to the minister, who declined to come. I shot Sir Rumford in the leg, amidst the tears of joy of my uncle, who accompanied me to the ground; and I promise you that none of the young gentlemen questioned the authenticity of my pedigree, or laughed at my Irish crown again.

What a delightful life did we now lead! I knew I was born a gentleman, from the kindly way in which I took to the business, as business it certainly is. For though it *seems* all pleasure, yet I assure any low-bred persons who may chance to read this, that we, their betters, have to work as well as they; though I did not rise until noon, yet had I not been up at play until long past midnight? Many a time have we come home to bed as the troops were marching out to early parade; and, oh! it did my heart good to hear the bugles blowing the *reveillé* before daybreak, or to see the regiments marching out to exercise, and think that I was no longer bound to that disgusting discipline, but restored to my natural station.

I came into it at once, and as if I had never done anything else all my life. I had a gentleman to wait upon me, a French *friseur* to dress my hair of a morning: I knew the taste of chocolate as by intuition almost, and could distinguish between the right Spanish and the French before I had been a week in my new position; I had rings on all my fingers, watches in both my fobs, canes, trinkets, and snuff-boxes of all sorts, and each outvying the other in elegance; I had the finest natural taste for lace and china of any man I ever knew. I could judge a horse as well as any Jew dealer in Germany; in shooting and athletic exercises I was unrivalled; I could not spell, but I could speak German and French cleverly; I had at the least twelve suits of clothes; three richly embroidered with gold, two laced with silver, a garnet-coloured velvet pelisse* lined with sable; one of French grey, silver-laced and lined with chinchilla. I had damask morning-robes. I took lessons on the guitar, and sang French catches exquisitely. Where, in fact, was there a more accomplished gentleman than Redmond de Balibari?

All the luxuries becoming my station could not, of course, be purchased without credit and money, to procure which, as our patrimony had been wasted by our ancestors, and we were above the vulgarity and slow returns and doubtful chances of trade, my uncle kept a faro bank. We were in partnership with a Florentine, well known in all the courts of Europe, the Count Alessandro Pippi, as skilful a player as ever was seen, but he turned out a sad knave latterly, and I have discovered that his countship was a mere impostor. My uncle was maimed, as I have said; Pippi, like all impostors, was a coward; it was my unrivalled skill with the sword, and readiness to use it, that maintained the reputation of the firm, so to speak, and silenced many a timid gambler who might have hesitated to pay his losings. We always played on parole with anybody; any person, that is, of honour and noble lineage. We never pressed for our winnings or declined to receive promissory notes in lieu of gold. But woe to the man who did not pay when the note became due! Redmond de Balibari was sure to wait upon him with his bill, and I promise you there were very few bad debts; on the contrary, gentlemen were grateful to us for our forbearance, and our character for honour stood unimpeached. In later times a vulgar national prejudice has chosen to cast a slur upon the character of men of honour engaged in the profession of play; but I speak of the good old days in Europe, before the cowardice of the French aristocracy (in the shameful

Revolution, which served them right) brought discredit and ruin upon our order. They cry fie now upon men engaged in play; but I should like to know how much more honourable *their* modes of livelihood are than ours. The broker of the Exchange who bulls and bears, and buys and sells, and dabbles with lying loans, and trades on state secrets, what is he but a gamester? The merchant who deals in teas and tallow, is he any better? His bales of dirty indigo are his dice, his cards come up every year instead of every ten minutes, and the sea is his green table. You call the profession of the law an honourable one, where a man will lie for any bidder, lie down poverty for the sake of a fee from wealth, lie down right because wrong is in his brief. You call a doctor an honourable man, a swindling quack, who does not believe in the nostrums which he prescribes, and takes your guinea for whispering in your ear that it is a fine morning; and yet, forsooth, a gallant man who sets him down before the baize and challenges all comers, his money against theirs, his fortune against theirs, is proscribed by your modern moral world. It is a conspiracy of the middle classes against gentlemen—it is only the shopkeeper cant which is to go down nowadays. I say that play was an institution of chivalry, it has been wrecked along with other privileges of men of birth.[1] When Seingalt* engaged a man for six-and-thirty hours without leaving the table, [I vow I think it was a glorious tournament, and what the ingenious person who has lately written *Ivanhoe* calls 'a *passage* of arms.'][2]* How have we had the best blood, and the brightest eyes, too, of Europe throbbing round the table as I and my uncle have held the cards and the bank against some terrible player, who was matching some thousands out of his millions against our all which was there on the baize! When we engaged that daring Alexis Kossloffsky,* and won seven thousand

[1] [Lest any weak minds should be perverted by the above tirade of Mr. Barry, it may be here observed that it was natural in this gentleman, who appears by his own confession to have been the fighting man or bully of a gambling firm, to defend himself, but that his manner of doing so is quite unsatisfactory; for to prove that others are rogues (and such possibly there may be in the recognized professions), is by no means to disprove his own roguery, and so the question stands exactly where it did previously.]—Footnote in *Fraser's Magazine*, omitted in later editions.

[2] Replaced in later editions by 'do you think he showed no courage?'

louis in a single coup, had we lost, we should have been beggars the next day; when *he* lost, he was only a village and a few hundred serfs in pawn the worse. When at Toeplitz, the Duke of Courland* brought fourteen lackeys each with four bags of florins, and challenged our bank to play against the sealed bags, what did we ask? 'Sir,' said we, 'we have but eighty thousand florins in bank, or two hundred thousand at three months; if your Highness's bags do not contain more than eighty thousand, we will meet you;' and we did, and after eleven hours' play, in which our bank was at one time reduced to two hundred and three ducats, we won seventeen thousand florins of him. Is *this* not something like boldness? does *this* profession not require skill, and perseverance, and bravery? Four crowned heads looked on at the game, and an imperial princess, when I turned up the ace of hearts and made Paroli,* burst into tears. No man on the European Continent held a higher position than Redmond Barry then; and when the Duke of Courland lost, he was pleased to say that we had won nobly: and so we had, and spent nobly what we won.

At this period my uncle, who attended mass every day regularly, always put ten florins into the box. Wherever we went, the tavern-keepers made us more welcome than royal princes. We used to give away the broken meat from our suppers and dinners to scores of beggars who blessed us. Every man who held my horse or cleaned my boots got a ducat for his pains. I was, I may say, the author of our common good fortune, by putting boldness into our play. Pippi was a faint-hearted fellow, who was always cowardly when he began to win. My uncle (I speak with great respect of him) was too much of a devotee, and too much of a martinet at play ever to win *greatly*. His moral courage was unquestionable, but his daring was not sufficient. Both of these my seniors very soon acknowledged me to be their chief, and hence the style of splendour I have described.

I have mentioned H.I.H. the Princess Frederica Amelia,* who was affected by my success, and shall always think with gratitude of the protection with which that exalted lady honoured me. She was passionately fond of play, as indeed were the ladies of almost all the courts in Europe in those days, and hence would often arise no small trouble to us; for the truth must be told, that ladies love to play, certainly, but not to *pay*. The point of honour is not understood by the charming sex; and it was with the greatest difficulty, in our peregrinations to the various courts of northern Europe, that we could keep them from the table, could get their money if they lost, or, if they paid, prevent them from using the most furious and extraordinary means of revenge. In those great days of our fortune, I calculate that we lost no less than fourteen thousand louis by such failures of payment. A princess of a ducal house gave us paste instead of diamonds, which she had solemnly pledged to us; another organized a robbery of the crown jewels, and would have charged the theft upon us, but for Pippi's caution, who had kept back a note of hand 'her High Transparency' gave us, and sent it to his ambassador, by which precaution I do believe our necks were saved. A third lady of high (but not princely) rank, after I had won a considerable sum in diamonds and pearls from her, sent her lover with a band of cut-throats to waylay me, and it was only by extraordinary courage, skill, and good luck that I escaped from these villains, wounded myself, but leaving the chief aggressor dead on the ground. My sword entered his eye and broke there, and the villains who were with him fled, seeing their chief fall. They might have finished me else, for I had no weapon of defence.

Thus it will be seen that our life, for all its splendour, was one of extreme danger and difficulty, requiring high talents and courage for success; and often, when we were in a full vein of success, we were suddenly driven from our ground on account of some freak of a reigning prince, some intrigue of a disappointed mistress, or some quarrel with the police minister. If the latter personage were not bribed or won over, nothing was more common than for us to receive a sudden order of departure, and so, perforce, we lived a wandering and desultory life.

Though the gains of such a life are, as I have said, very great, yet the expenses are enormous. Our appearance and retinue was too splendid for the narrow mind of Pippi, who was always crying out at my extravagance, though obliged to own that his own meanness and parsimony would never have achieved the great victories which my generosity had won. With all our success, our capital was not very great. That speech to the Duke of Courland, for instance, was a mere boast as far as the two hundred thousand florins at three months were concerned. We had no credit, and no money beyond that on our table, and should have been forced to fly if his Highness had won and accepted our bills. Sometimes, too, we were hit very hard. A bank is a certainty, *almost*, but now and then a bad day will come; and men who have the courage of good fortune, at least, ought to meet bad luck well: the former, believe me, is the harder task of the two.

One of these evil chances befell us in the Duke of Baden's territory, at Mannheim.* Pippi, who was always on the look-out for business, offered to make a bank at the inn where we put up, and where the officers of the Duke's cuirassiers supped; and some small play accordingly took place, and some wretched crowns and louis changed hands, I trust rather to the advantage of these poor gentlemen of the army, who are surely the poorest of all devils under the sun.

But, as ill luck would have it, a couple of young students from the neighbouring University of Heidelberg, who had come to Mannheim for their quarter's revenue, and so had some hundred of dollars between them, were introduced to the table, and, having never played before (as is always the case), began to win. As ill luck would have it, too, they were tipsy, and against tipsiness I have often found the best calculations of play fail entirely. They played in the most perfectly insane way, and yet won always. Every card they backed turned up in their favour. They had won a hundred louis from us in ten minutes; and, seeing that Pippi was growing angry and the luck against us, I was for shutting up the bank for the night, saying the play was only meant for a joke, and that now we had had enough.

But Pippi, who had quarrelled with me that day, was determined to proceed, and the upshot was, that the students played and won more; then they lent money to the officers, who began to win, too; and in this ignoble way, in a tavern room thick with tobacco-smoke, across a deal table besmeared with beer and liquor, and, to a parcel of hungry subalterns and a pair of beardless students, three of the most skilful and renowned players in Europe lost seventeen hundred louis. I blush now when I think of it. It was like Charles XII or Richard Cœur de Lion* falling before a petty fortress and an unknown hand (as my friend Mr. Johnson wrote), and was, in fact, a most shameful defeat.

Nor was this the only defeat. When our poor conquerors had gone off, bewildered with the treasure which fortune had flung in their way (one of these students was called the Baron de Clootz,* perhaps he who afterwards lost his head at Paris), Pippi resumed the quarrel of the morning, and some exceedingly high words passed between us. Among other things I recollect I knocked him down with a stool, and was for flinging him out of window; but my uncle, who was cool, and had been keeping Lent with his usual solemnity, interposed between us, and a reconciliation took place, Pippi apologizing and confessing he had been wrong.

I ought to have doubted, however, the sincerity of the treacherous Italian; indeed, as I never before believed a word that he said in his life, I know not why I was so foolish as to credit him now, and go to bed, leaving the keys of our cash-box with him. It contained, after our loss to the cuirassiers, in bills and money, near upon 8,000*l.* sterling. Pippi insisted that our reconciliation should be ratified over a bowl of hot wine, and I have no doubt put some soporific drug into the liquor, for my uncle and I both slept till very late the next morning, and woke with violent headaches and fever. We did not quit our beds till noon. He had been gone twelve hours, leaving our treasury empty; and behind him a sort of calculation, by which he strove to make out that this was his share of the profits, and that all the losses had been incurred without his consent.

Thus, after eighteen months, we had to begin the world again. But was I cast down? No. Our wardrobes still were worth a very large sum of money, for gentlemen did not dress like parish-clerks in those days, and a person of fashion would often wear a suit of clothes and a set of ornaments that would be a shop-boy's fortune; and, without repining for one single minute, or saying a single angry word (my uncle's temper in this respect was admirable), or allowing the secret of our loss to be known to a mortal soul, we pawned three-fourths of our jewels and clothes to Moses Löwe, the banker, and with produce of the sale, and our private pocket-money, amounting in all to something less than 800 louis, we took the field again.

CHAPTER X

MORE RUNS OF LUCK

I AM not going to entertain my readers with an account of my professional career as a gamester any more than I did with anecdotes of my life as a military man. I might fill volumes with tales of this kind were I so minded, but, at this rate, my recital would not be brought to a conclusion for years, and who knows how soon I may be called upon to stop? I have gout, rheumatism, gravel,* and a disordered liver. I have two or three wounds in my body, which break out every now and then, and give me intolerable pain, and a hundred more signs of breaking up. Such are the effects of time, illness, and free-living upon one of the strongest constitutions and finest forms the world ever saw. Ah! I suffered from none of these ills in the year '66, when there was no man in Europe more gay in spirits, more splendid in personal accomplishment, than young Redmond Barry.

Before the treachery of the scoundrel Pippi, I had visited many of the best courts of Europe, especially the smaller ones, where play was patronized, and the professors of that science always welcome. Among the ecclesiastical principalities of the Rhine we were particularly well received. I never knew finer or gayer courts than those of the Electors of Treves and Cologne,* where there was more splendour and gaiety than at Vienna, far more than in the wretched barrack-court of Berlin. The court of the Archduchess-Governess of the Netherlands* was, likewise, a royal place for us knights of the dice-box and gallant votaries of fortune, whereas in the stingy Dutch or the beggarly Swiss republics it was impossible for a gentleman to gain a livelihood unmolested. [Yes, the old times were the times for *gentlemen*, before Bonaparte brutalized Europe with his swaggering Grenadiers, and was conquered in his turn by our shopkeepers* and cheesemongers of England here. To return, however, to my personal adventure.][1]

After our mishap at Mannheim, my uncle and I made

[1] Omitted in later editions.

for the Duchy of X——.[1] [It has since been erected into a kingdom, and][2]* the reader may find out the place easily enough, but I do not choose to print at full the names of some illustrious persons in whose society I then fell, and among whom I was made the sharer in a very strange and tragical adventure.

There was no court in Europe at which strangers were more welcome than at that of the noble Duke of X——, none where pleasure was more eagerly sought after, and more splendidly enjoyed. The prince did not inhabit his capital of S——, but, imitating in every respect the ceremonial of the court of Versailles, built himself a magnificent palace at a few leagues from his chief city, and round about his palace a superb aristocratic town, inhabited entirely by his nobles, and the officers of his sumptuous court. The people were rather hardly pressed, to be sure, in order to keep up this splendour; for his Highness's dominions were small, and so he wisely lived in a sort of awful retirement from them, seldom showing his face in his capital, or seeing any countenances but those of his faithful domestics and officers. His palace and gardens of Ludwigslust* were exactly on the French model. Twice a week there were court receptions, and grand court galas twice a month. There was the finest opera out of France, and a ballet unrivalled in splendour, on which his Highness, a great lover of music and dancing, expended prodigious sums. It may be because I was then young, but I think I never saw such an assemblage of brilliant beauty as used to figure there on the stage of the court theatre, in the grand mythological ballets which were then the mode, and in which you saw Mars in red-heeled pumps and a periwig, and Venus in patches and a hoop. They say the costume was incorrect, and have changed it since, but, for my part, I have never seen a Venus more lovely than the Coralie, who was the chief dancer, and found no fault with the attendant nymphs, in their trains, and lappets, and powder. These operas used to take place twice a week, after which some great officer of the court would have his evening, and his brilliant supper, and the dice-box rattled everywhere, and all the world played. I have seen seventy play-tables set out in the grand gallery of Ludwigslust, besides the faro bank,

[1] In *Fraser's Magazine* the Duchy is called 'W——' throughout.
[2] Omitted in later editions.

where the Duke himself would graciously come and play, and win or lose with a truly royal splendour.

It was hither we came after the Mannheim misfortune. The nobility of the court were pleased to say our reputation had preceded us, and the two Irish gentlemen were made welcome. The very first night at court we lost 740 of our 800 louis; the next evening, at the court-marshal's table, I won them back, with 1,300 more. You may be sure we allowed no one to know how near we were to ruin on the first evening, but, on the contrary, I endeared every one to me by my gay manner of losing, and the finance-minister himself cashed a note for 400 ducats, drawn by me upon my steward of Ballybarry Castle in the kingdom of Ireland, which very note I won from his excellency the next day, along with a considerable sum in ready cash. In that noble court everybody was a gambler. You would see the lackeys in the ducal ante-rooms at work with their dirty packs of cards; the coach- and chair-men playing in the court, while their masters were punting in the saloons above; the very cook-maids and scullions, I was told, had a bank, where one of them, an Italian confectioner, made a handsome fortune. He purchased afterwards a Roman marquisate, and his son has figured as one of the most fashionable of the illustrious foreigners then in London. The poor devils of soldiers played away their pay, when they got it, which was seldom; and I don't believe there was an officer in any one of the Guard regiments but had his cards in his pouch, and no more forgot his dice than his sword-knot. Among such fellows it was diamond cut diamond. What you call fair play would have been a folly. The gentlemen of Ballybarry would have been fools, indeed, to appear as pigeons in such a hawk's nest. None but men of courage and genius could live and prosper in a society where every one was bold and clever; and here my uncle and I held our own, aye, and more than our own.

His Highness the Duke was a widower, or rather, since the death of the reigning Duchess, had contracted a morganatic marriage with a lady whom he had ennobled, and who considered it a compliment (such was the morality of those days) to be called the Northern Dubarry.* He had been married very young, and his son, the hereditary Prince, may be said to have been the political sovereign of the state, for the reigning Duke was fonder of pleasure than of politics, and loved to talk a great deal more with his grand huntsman, or the director of his opera, than with ministers and ambassadors.

The hereditary Prince, whom I shall call Prince Victor, was of a very different character from his august father. He had made the Wars of the Succession and Seven Years, with great credit, in the Empress's service, was of a stern character, seldom appeared at court, except when ceremony called him, but lived almost alone in his wing of the palace, where he devoted himself to the severest studies, being a great astronomer and chemist. He shared in the rage, then common throughout Europe, of hunting for the philosopher's stone; and my uncle often regretted that he had no smattering of chemistry, like Balsamo (who called himself Cagliostro), St. Germain,* and other individuals, who had obtained very great sums from Duke Victor by aiding him in his search after the great secret.* His amusements were hunting and reviewing the troops; but for him, and if his good-natured father had not had his aid, the army would have been playing at cards all day, and so it was well that the prudent Prince was left to govern.

Duke Victor was fifty years of age, and his Princess, the Princess Olivia, was scarce three-and-twenty. They had been married seven years, and, in the first years of their union the Princess had borne him a son and a daughter. The stern morals and manners, the dark and ungainly appearance of the husband, were little likely to please the brilliant and fascinating young woman, who had been educated in the south (she was connected with the ducal house of S——), who had passed two years at Paris under the guardianship of Mesdames, daughters of his Most Christian Majesty,* and who was the life and soul of the court of X——, the gayest of the gay, the idol of her august father-in-law, and, indeed, of the whole court. She was not beautiful, but charming; not witty, but charming too, in her conversation as in her person. She was extravagant beyond all measure; so false, that you could not trust her; but her very weaknesses were more winning than the virtues of other women, her selfishness more delightful than others' generosity. I never knew a woman whose faults made her so attractive. She used to ruin people, and yet they all loved her. My old uncle has seen her cheating at ombre,* and let her win 400 louis without resisting in the least.

Her caprices with the officers and ladies of her household were ceaseless, but they adored her. She was the only one of the reigning family whom the people worshipped. She never went abroad but they followed her carriage with shouts of acclamation, and, to be generous to them, she would borrow the last penny from one of her poor maids of honour, whom she would never pay. In the early days her husband was as much fascinated by her as all the rest of the world was; but her caprices had caused frightful outbreaks of temper on his part, and an estrangement which, though interrupted by almost mad returns of love, was still general. I speak of her Royal Highness with perfect candour and admiration, although I might be pardoned for judging her more severely, considering her opinion of myself. She said the elder Monsieur de Balibari was a finished old gentleman, and the younger one had the manners of a courier. The world has given a different opinion, and I can afford to chronicle this almost single sentence against me. Besides, she had a reason for her dislike to me, which you shall hear.

Five years in the army, long experience of the world, had, ere now, dispelled any of those romantic notions regarding love with which I commenced life; and I had determined, as is proper with gentlemen (it is only your low people who marry for mere affection), to consolidate my fortunes by marriage. In the course of our peregrinations, my uncle and I had made several attempts to carry this object into effect; but numerous disappointments had occurred, which are not worth mentioning here, and had prevented me hitherto from making such a match as I thought was worthy of a man of my birth, abilities, and personal appearance. Ladies are not in the habit of running away on the Continent, as is the custom in England (a custom whereby many honourable gentlemen of my country have much benefited); guardians and ceremonies, and difficulties of all kinds intervene; true love is not allowed to have its course, and poor women cannot give away their honest hearts to the gallant fellows who have won them. Now it was settlements that were asked for; now it was my pedigree and title-deeds that were not satisfactory, though I had a plan and rent-roll of the Ballybarry estates, and the genealogy of the family up to King Brian Boru, or Barry, most handsomely designed on paper; now it was a young lady who was whisked off to a convent, just as she was ready to fall into my arms; on another occasion, when a rich widow of the Low Countries was about to make me lord of a noble estate in Flanders, comes an order of the police which drives me out of Brussels at an hour's notice, and consigns my mourner to her château. But at X—— I had an opportunity of playing a great game, and had won it, too, but for the dreadful catastrophe which upset my fortune.

In the household of the hereditary Princess there was a lady nineteen years of age, and possessor of the greatest fortune in the whole duchy. The Countess Ida, such was her name, was daughter of a late minister and favourite of his Highness the Duke of X—— and his Duchess, who had done her the honour to be her sponsors at birth, and who, at the father's death, had taken her under their august guardianship and protection. At sixteen she was brought from her castle, where, up to that period, she had been permitted to reside, and had been placed with the Princess Olivia, as one of her Highness's maids of honour.

The aunt of the Countess Ida, who presided over her house during her minority, had foolishly allowed her to contract an attachment for her cousin-german, a penniless sub-lieutenant in one of the Duke's foot regiments, who had flattered himself to be able to carry off this rich prize; and if he had not been a blundering, silly idiot indeed, with the advantage of seeing her constantly, of having no rival near him, and the intimacy attendant upon close kinsmanship, might easily, by a private marriage, have secured the young Countess and her possessions. But he managed matters so foolishly that he allowed her to leave her retirement, to come to court for a year, and take her place in the Princess Olivia's household, and then what does my young gentleman do, but appear at the Duke's levee one day, in his tarnished epaulet and threadbare coat, and make an application in due form to his Highness, as the young lady's guardian, for the hand of the richest heiress in his dominions!

The weakness of the good-natured Prince was such that, as the Countess Ida herself was quite as eager for the match as her silly cousin, his Highness might have been induced to allow the match, had not the Princess Olivia been induced to interpose, and to procure from the Duke a peremptory veto to the hopes of the young man. The cause of this refusal was as yet unknown, no other suitor for the young lady's hand was mentioned, and the lovers continued to correspond, hoping that time might effect a change in his Highness's resolutions, when, of a sudden, the lieutenant was drafted into one of the regiments which the Prince was in the habit of selling to the great Powers then at war (this military commerce was a principal part of his Highness's and other princes' revenues in those days), and their connexion was thus abruptly broken off.

It was strange that the Princess Olivia should have taken this part against a young lady who had been her favourite; for, at first, with those romantic and sentimental notions which almost every woman has, she had somewhat encouraged the Countess Ida and her penniless lover, but now suddenly turned against them, and, from loving the Countess, as she previously had done, pursued her with every manner of hatred which a woman knows how to inflict; and there was no end to the ingenuity of her tortures, the venom of her tongue, the bitterness of her sarcasm and scorn. When I first came to court at X——, the young fellows there had nicknamed the young lady the *dumme Gräfin*, the stupid countess. She was generally silent, handsome, but pale, stolid-looking, and awkward, taking no interest in the amusements of the place, and appearing in the midst of the feasts as glum as the death's head which, they say, the Romans used to have at their tables.

It was rumoured that a young gentleman of French extraction, the Chevalier de Magny, equerry to the reigning Duke, and present at Paris when the Princess Olivia was married to him by proxy there, was the intended of the rich Countess Ida; but no official declaration of the kind was yet made, and there were whispers of a dark intrigue, which, subsequently, received frightful confirmation.

This Chevalier de Magny was the grandson of an old general officer in the Duke's service, the Baron de Magny. The Baron's father had quitted France at the expulsion of Protestants, after the revocation of the edict of Nantes,* and taken service in X——, where he died. The son succeeded him, and quite unlike most French gentlemen of birth whom I have known, was a stern and cold Calvinist, rigid in the performance of his duty, retiring in his manners, mingling little with the court, and a close friend and favourite of Duke Victor, whom he resembled in disposition.

The chevalier, his grandson, was a true Frenchman: he had been born in France, where his father held a diplomatic appointment in the Duke's service. He had mingled in the gay society of the most brilliant court in the world, and had endless stories to tell us of the pleasures of the *petites maisons*, of the secrets of the Parc aux Cerfs, and of the wild gaieties of Richelieu* and his companions. He had been almost ruined at play, as his father had been before him; for, out of the reach of the stern old baron in Germany, both son and grandson had led the most reckless of lives. He came back from Paris soon after the embassy which had been dispatched thither on the occasion of the marriage of the Princess, was received sternly by his old grandfather, who, however, paid his debts once more, and procured him the post in the Duke's household. The Chevalier de Magny rendered himself a great favourite of his august master; he brought with him the modes and the gaieties of Paris; he was the deviser of all the masquerades and balls, the recruiter of the ballet-dancers, and by far the most brilliant and splendid young gentleman of the court.

After we had been a few weeks at Ludwigslust, the old Baron de Magny endeavoured to have us dismissed from the duchy; but his voice was not strong enough to overcome that of the general public, and the Chevalier de Magny especially stood our friend with his Highness when the question was debated before him. The chevalier's love of play had not deserted him. He was a regular frequenter of our bank, where he played for some time with pretty good luck, and where, when he began to lose, he paid with a regularity surprising to all those who knew the smallness of his means, and the splendour of his appearance.

Her Highness the Princess Olivia was also very fond of play. On half a dozen occasions when we held a bank at court, I could see her passion for the game. I could see—that is, my cool-headed old uncle could see—much more. There was an intelligence between Monsieur de Magny and this illustrious lady. 'If her Highness be not in love with the little Frenchman,' my uncle said to me one night after play, 'may I lose the sight of my last eye!'

'And what then, sir?' said I.

'What then?' said my uncle, looking me hard in the

face. 'Are you so green as not to know what then? Your fortune is to be made, if you choose to back it now; and we may have back the Barry estates in two years, my boy.'

'How is that?' asked I, still at a loss.

My uncle dryly said, 'Get Magny to play; never mind his paying; take his notes of hand. The more he owes the better; but, above all, make him play.'

'He can't pay a shilling,' answered I. 'The Jews will not discount his notes at cent per cent.'

'So much the better. You shall see we will make use of them,' answered the old gentleman. And I must confess that the plan he laid was a gallant, clever, and fair one.

I was to make Magny play; in this there was no great difficulty. We had an intimacy together, for he was a good sportsman as well as myself; and we came to have a pretty considerable friendship for one another; and, if he saw a dice-box, it was impossible to prevent him from handling it; but he took to it as natural as a child does to sweetmeats.

At first he won of me; then he began to lose; then I played him money against some jewels that he brought, family trinkets, he said, and indeed of considerable value. He begged me, however, not to dispose of them in the duchy, and I gave and kept my word to him to this effect. From jewels he got to playing upon promissory notes; and, as they would not allow him to play at the court tables and in public upon credit, he was very glad to have an opportunity of indulging his favourite passion upon credit. I have had him for hours at my pavilion (which I had fitted up in the Eastern manner, very splendid), rattling the dice till it became time to go to his service at court, and we would spend day after day in this manner. He brought me more jewels,—a pearl necklace, an antique emerald breast ornament, and other trinkets, as a set-off against these losses,—for I need not say that I should not have played with him all this time had he been winning: but, after about a week, the luck set in against him, and he became my debtor in a prodigious sum. I do not care to mention the extent of it; it was such as I never thought the young man could pay.

Why, then, did I play for it? why waste days in private play with a mere bankrupt, when business seemingly much more profitable was to be done elsewhere? My reason, I boldly confess. I wanted to win from Monsieur de Magny not his money, but his intended wife, the Countess Ida. Who can say that I had not a right to use *any* stratagem in this matter of love ? Or, why say love ? I wanted the wealth of the lady ; I loved her quite as much as Magny did ; I loved her quite as much as yonder blushing virgin of seventeen does who marries an old lord of seventy. I followed the practice of the world in this, having resolved that marriage should achieve my fortune.

I used to make Magny, after his losses, give me a friendly letter of acknowledgement to some such effect as this :—

My dear Monsieur de Balibari, I acknowledge to have lost to you this day at lansquenet [or piquet,*or hazard, as the case may be : I was master of him at any game that is played] the sum of three hundred ducats, and shall hold it as a great kindness on your part if you will allow the debt to stand over until a future day, when you shall receive payment from your very grateful, humble servant.

With the jewels he brought me I also took the precaution (but this was my uncle's idea, and a very good one) to have a sort of invoice, and a letter begging me to receive the trinkets as so much part payment of a sum of money he owed me.

When I had put him in such a position as I deemed favourable to my intentions, I spoke to him candidly, and without any reserve, as one man of the world should speak to another. 'I will not, my dear fellow,' said I, 'pay you so bad a compliment as to suppose that you expect we are to go on playing at this rate much longer, and that there is any satisfaction to me in possessing more or less sheets of paper bearing your signature, and a series of notes of hand which I know you never can pay. Don't look fierce or angry, for you know Redmond Barry is your master at the sword ; besides, I would not be such a fool as to fight a man who owes me so much money ; but hear calmly what I have to propose.

'You have been very confidential to me during our intimacy of the last month ; and I know all your personal affairs completely. You have given your word of honour to your grandfather never to play upon parole, and you know how you have kept it, and that he will disinherit you if he hears the truth. Nay, suppose he dies to-morrow, his estate is not sufficient to pay the sum in which you are indebted to me ; and, were you to yield me up all, you would be a beggar, and a bankrupt too.

'Her Highness the Princess Olivia denies you nothing. I shall not ask why ; but give me leave to say, I was aware of the fact when we began to play together.'

'Will you be made baron—chamberlain, with the grand cordon of the order ?' gasped the poor fellow. 'The Princess can do anything with the Duke.'

'I shall have no objection,' said I, 'to the yellow riband and the gold key ; though a gentleman of the house of Ballybarry cares little for the titles of the German nobility. But this is not what I want. My good chevalier, you have hid no secrets from me. You have told me with what difficulty you have induced the Princess Olivia to consent to the project of your union with the Gräfin Ida, whom you don't love. I know whom you love very well.'

'Monsieur de Balibari !' said the discomfited chevalier ; he could get out no more. The truth began to dawn upon him.

'You begin to understand,' continued I. 'Her Highness the Princess' (I said this in a sarcastic way) 'will not be very angry, believe me, if you break off your connexion with the stupid Countess. I am no more an admirer of that lady than you are ; but I want her estate. I played you for that estate, and have won it ; and I will give you your bills and five thousand ducats on the day I am married to it.'

'The day *I* am married to the Countess,' answered the chevalier, thinking to have me, 'I will be able to raise money to pay your claim ten times over' (this was true, for the Countess's property may have been valued at near half a million of our money) ; 'and then I will discharge my obligations to you. Meanwhile, if you annoy me by threats, or insult me again as you have done, I will use that influence, which, as you say, I possess, and have you turned out of the duchy, as you were out of the Netherlands last year.'

I rang the bell quite quietly. 'Zamor,' said I to a tall negro fellow habited like a Turk, that used to wait upon me, 'when you hear the bell ring a second time, you will take this packet to the marshal of the court, this to his Excellency the General de Magny, and this you will place in the hands of one of the equerries of his Highness the hereditary Prince. Wait in the ante-room, and do not go with the parcels until I ring again.'

The black fellow having retired, I turned to Monsieur de Magny and said, 'Chevalier, the first packet contains a letter from you to me, declaring your solvency, and solemnly promising payment of the sums you owe me; it is accompanied by a document from myself (for I expected some resistance on your part), stating that my honour has been called in question, and begging that the paper may be laid before your august master, his Highness. The second packet is for your grandfather, enclosing the letter from you in which you state yourself to be his heir, and begging for a confirmation of the fact. The last parcel for his Highness the hereditary Duke,' added I, looking most sternly, 'contains the Gustavus Adolphus emerald, which he gave to his Princess, and which you pledged to me as a family jewel of your own. Your influence with her Highness must be great indeed,' I concluded, 'when you could extort from her such a jewel as that, and when you could make her, in order to pay your play-debts, give up a secret upon which both your heads depend.'

'Villain!' said the Frenchman, quite aghast with fury and terror, 'would you implicate the Princess?'

'Monsieur de Magny,' I answered with a sneer, 'no: I will say *you stole* the jewel.' It was my belief he did, and that the unhappy and infatuated Princess was never privy to the theft until long after it had been committed. How we came to know the history of the emerald is simple enough. As we wanted money (for my occupation with Magny caused our bank to be much neglected), my uncle had carried Magny's trinkets to Mannheim to pawn. The Jew who lent upon them knew the history of the stone in question; and when he asked how her Highness came to part with it, my uncle very cleverly took up the story where he found it, said that the Princess was very fond of play, that it was not always convenient to her to pay, and hence the emerald had come into our hands. He brought it wisely back with him to S——; and, as regards the other jewels which the chevalier pawned to us, they were of no particular mark; no inquiries have ever been made about them to this day; and I did not only not know then that they came from her Highness, but have only my conjectures upon the matter now.

The unfortunate young gentleman must have had a cowardly spirit, when I charged him with the theft, not to make use of my two pistols that were lying by chance before him, and to send out of the world his accuser and his own ruined self. With such imprudence and miserable recklessness on his part and that of the unhappy lady who had forgotten herself for this poor villain, he must have known that discovery was inevitable. But it was written that this dreadful destiny should be accomplished; instead of ending like a man, he now cowed before me quite spirit-broken, and, flinging himself down on the sofa, burst into tears, and calling wildly upon all the saints to help him, as if they could be interested in the fate of such a wretch as him!

I saw that I had nothing to fear from him; and, calling back Zamor, my black, said I would myself carry the parcels, which I returned to my *escritoire;* and, my point being thus gained, I acted, as I always do, generously towards him. I said that, for security's sake, I should send the emerald out of the country, but that I pledged my honour to restore it to the Duchess, without any pecuniary consideration, on the day when she should procure the sovereign's consent to my union with the Countess Ida.

This will explain pretty clearly, I flatter myself, the game I was playing; and, though some rigid moralist may object to its propriety, I say that anything is fair in love, and that men so poor as myself can't afford to be squeamish about their means of getting on in life. The great and rich are welcomed, smiling, up the grand staircase of the world; the poor but aspiring must clamber up the wall, or push and struggle up the back stair, or, *pardi*, crawl through any of the conduits of the house, never mind how foul and narrow, that lead to the top. The unambitious sluggard pretends that the eminence is not worth attaining, declines altogether the struggle, and calls himself a philosopher. I say he is a poor-spirited coward. What is life good for but for honour? and that is so indispensable, that we should attain it anyhow.

The manner to be adopted for Magny's retreat was proposed by myself, and was arranged so as to consult the feelings of delicacy of both parties. I made Magny take the Countess Ida aside, and say to her, 'Madam, though I have never declared myself your admirer, you and the Count have had sufficient proof of my regard for you; and my demand would, I know, have been backed by his Highness, your august guardian. I know the Duke's gracious wish is that my attentions should be received favourably; but, as time has not appeared to alter your attachment elsewhere, and as I have too much spirit to force a lady of your name and rank to be united to me against your will, the best plan is, that I should make you, for form's sake, a proposal *un*authorized by his Highness: that you should reply, as I am sorry to think your heart dictates to you, in the negative: on which I also will formally withdraw from my pursuit of you, stating that, after a refusal, nothing, not even the Duke's desire, should induce me to persist in my suit.'

The Countess Ida almost wept at hearing these words from Monsieur de Magny, and tears came into her eyes, he said, as she took his hand for the first time, and thanked him for the delicacy of the proposal. She little knew that the Frenchman was incapable of that sort of delicacy, and that the graceful manner in which he withdrew his addresses was of my invention.

As soon as he withdrew, it became my business to step forward, but cautiously and gently, so as not to alarm the lady, and yet firmly, so as to convince her of the hopelessness of her design of uniting herself with her shabby lover, the sub-lieutenant. The Princess Olivia was good enough to perform this necessary part of the plan in my favour, and solemnly to warn the Countess Ida that, though Monsieur de Magny had retired from paying his addresses, his Highness, her guardian, would still marry her as he thought fit, and that she must for ever forget her out-at-elbowed adorer. In fact, I can't conceive how such a shabby rogue as that could ever have had the audacity to propose for her: his birth was certainly good; but what other qualifications had he?

When the Chevalier de Magny withdrew, numbers of other suitors, you may be sure, presented themselves; and amongst these your very humble servant, the cadet of Ballybarry. There was a *carrousel*, or tournament, held at this period, in imitation of the antique meetings of chivalry, in which the chevaliers tilted at each other, or at the ring; and on this occasion I was habited in a splendid Roman dress (viz.: a silver helmet, a flowing periwig, a cuirass of gilt leather richly embroidered, a light blue velvet mantle, and crimson morocco half-boots): and in this habit I rode my bay horse Brian, and carried off three rings, and won the prize over all the Duke's gentry, and the nobility of surrounding countries who had come to the show. A wreath of gilded laurel was to be the prize of the victor, and it was to be awarded by the lady he selected. So I rode up to the gallery where the Countess Ida was seated behind the hereditary Princess, and, calling her name loudly, yet gracefully, begged to be allowed to be crowned by her, and thus proclaimed myself to the face of all Germany, as it were, her suitor. She turned very pale, and the Princess red, I observed: but the Countess Ida ended by crowning me; after which, putting spurs into my horse, I galloped round the ring, saluting his Highness the Duke at the opposite end, and performing the most wonderful exercises with my bay.

My success did not, as you may imagine, increase my popularity with the young gentry. They called me adventurer, bully, dice-loader, impostor, and a hundred pretty names; but I had a way of silencing these gentry. I took the Count de Schmetterling,* the richest and bravest of the young men who seemed to have a hankering for the Countess Ida, and publicly insulted him at the ridotto, flinging my cards into his face. The next day I rode thirty-five miles into the territory of the Elector of B——, and met Monsieur de Schmetterling, and passed my sword twice through his body; and rode back with my second, the Chevalier de Magny, and presented myself at the Duchess's whist that evening. Magny was very unwilling to accompany me at first; but I insisted upon his support, and that he should countenance my quarrel. Directly after paying my homage to her Highness, I went up to the Countess Ida, and made her a marked and low obeisance, gazing at her steadily in the face until she grew crimson red; and then staring round at every man who formed her circle, until, *ma foi*, I stared them all away. I instructed Magny to say, everywhere, that the Countess was madly in love with me; which commission, along with many others of mine, the poor devil was obliged to perform. He made rather a *sotte figure*,* as the French say, acting the pioneer for me, praising me everywhere, accompanying me always! he who had been the pink of the *mode* until my arrival; he who thought his pedigree of beggarly Barons of Magny was superior to the race of great Irish kings from which I descended; who had sneered at me a hundred times as a spadassin,* a deserter, and had called me a vulgar Irish upstart. Now I had my revenge of the gentleman, and took it too.

I used to call him, in the choicest societies, by his Christian name of Maxime. I would say, 'Bon jour, Maxime; comment vas-*tu*?'* in the Princess's hearing, and could see him bite his lips for fury and vexation. But I had him under my thumb, and her Highness too—I, poor private of Bülow's regiment. And this is a proof of what genius and perseverance can do, and should act as a warning to great people never to have *secrets*, if they can help it.

I knew the Princess hated me, but what did I care? She knew I knew all, and indeed, I believe, so strong was her prejudice against me, that she thought I was an indelicate villain, capable of betraying a lady, which I would scorn to do; so that she trembled before me as a child before its schoolmaster. She would, in her woman's way, too, make all sorts of jokes and sneers at me on reception days, and ask about my palace in Ireland, and the kings, my ancestors, and whether, when I was a private in Bülow's foot, my royal relatives had interposed to rescue me, and whether the cane was smartly administered there,—anything to mortify me. But Heaven bless you! I can make allowances for people, and used to laugh in her face. Whilst her gibes and jeers were continuing, it was my pleasure to look at poor Magny and see how *he* bore them. The poor devil was trembling lest I should break out under the Princess's sarcasms and tell all; but my revenge was, when the Princess attacked me, to say something bitter to *him*,—to pass it on as boys do at school. And *that* was the thing which used to make her Highness feel. She would wince just as much when I attacked Magny as if I had been saying anything rude to herself. And, though she hated me, she used to beg my pardon in private; and though her pride would often get the better of her, yet her prudence obliged this magnificent Princess to humble herself to the poor penniless Irish boy.

As soon as Magny had formally withdrawn from the Countess Ida, the Princess took the young lady into favour again, and pretended to be very fond of her. To do them justice I don't know which of the two disliked me most,—the Princess, who was all eagerness, and fire, and coquetry, or the Countess, who was all state and splendour. The latter, especially, pretended to be disgusted by me; and yet, after all, I have pleased her betters, was once one of the handsomest men in Europe, and would defy any heyduck of the court to measure a chest or a leg with me; but I did not care for any of her silly prejudices, and determined to win her and wear her in spite of herself. Was it on account of her personal charms or qualities? No. She was quite white, thin, short-sighted, tall, and awkward, and my taste is quite the contrary; and as for her mind, no wonder that a poor creature who had a hankering after a wretched ragged ensign could never appreciate *me*. It was her estate I made love to; as for herself, it would be a reflection on my taste as a man of fashion to own that I liked her.

CHAPTER XI

IN WHICH THE LUCK GOES AGAINST BARRY

My hopes of obtaining the hand of one of the richest heiresses in Germany were now, as far as all human probability went, and as far as my own merits and prudence could secure my fortune, pretty certain of completion. I was admitted whenever I presented myself at the Princess's apartments, and had as frequent opportunities as I desired of seeing the Countess Ida there. I cannot say that she received me with any particular favour; the silly young creature's affections were, as I have said, engaged ignobly elsewhere; and, however captivating my own person and manners may have been, it was not to be expected that she should all of a sudden forget her lover for the sake of the young Irish gentleman who was paying his addresses to her. But such little rebuffs as I got were far from discouraging me. I had very powerful friends, who were to aid me in my undertaking; and knew that, sooner or later, the victory must be mine. In fact, I only waited my time to press my suit. Who could tell the dreadful stroke of fortune which was impending over my illustrious protectress, and which was to involve me partially in her ruin ?

All things seemed for awhile quite prosperous to my wishes ; and, in spite of the Countess Ida's disinclination, it was much easier to bring her to her senses than, perhaps, may be supposed in a silly, constitutional country like England, where people are not brought up with those wholesome sentiments of obedience to royalty which were customary in Europe at the time when I was a young man.

I have stated how, through Magny, I had the Princess, as it were, at my feet. Her Highness had only to press the match upon the old Duke, over whom her influence was unbounded, and to secure the goodwill of the Countess of Liliengarten*(which was the romantic title of his Highness's morganatic spouse), and the easy old man would give an order for the marriage, which his ward would perforce obey. Madame de Liliengarten was too, from her position, extremely anxious to oblige the Princess Olivia, who might be called upon any day to occupy the throne. The old Duke was tottering, apoplectic, and exceedingly fond of good living. When he was gone, his relict would find the patronage of the Duchess Olivia most necessary to her. Hence there was a close mutual understanding between the two ladies, and the world said that the hereditary Princess was already indebted to the favourite for help on various occasions. Her Highness had obtained, through the Countess, several large grants of money for the payment of her multifarious debts ; and she was now good enough to exert her gracious influence over Madame de Liliengarten in order to obtain for me the object so near my heart. It is not to be supposed that my end was to be obtained without continual unwillingness and refusals on Magny's part, but I pushed my point resolutely and had means in my hands of overcoming the stubbornness of that feeble young gentleman. Also, I may say, without vanity, that if the high and mighty Princess detested me, the Countess (though she was of extremely low origin, it is said) had better taste and admired me. She often did us the honour to go partners with us in one of our faro banks, and declared that I was the handsomest man in the duchy. All I was required to prove was my nobility, and I got at Vienna such a pedigree as would satisfy the most greedy in that way. In fact, what had a man descended from the Barrys and the Bradys to fear before any *von* in Germany? By way of making assurance doubly sure, I promised Madame de Liliengarten ten thousand louis on the day of my marriage, and she knew that as a playman I had never failed in my word, and I vow that, had I paid fifty per cent for it, I would have got the money.

Thus by my talents, honesty, and acuteness I had, considering I was a poor patronless outcast, raised for myself very powerful protectors. Even his Highness the Duke Victor was favourably inclined to me, for, his favourite charger falling ill of the staggers, I gave him a ball such as my uncle Brady used to administer, and cured the horse, after which his Highness was pleased to notice me frequently. He invited me to his hunting and shooting parties, where I showed myself to be a good sportsman, and once or twice he condescended to talk to me about my prospects in life, lamenting that I had taken to gambling, and that I had not adopted a more regular means of advancement. 'Sir,' said I, 'if you will allow me to speak frankly to your Highness, play with me is only a means to an end. Where should I have been without it? A private still in King Frederick's grenadiers. I come of a race which gave princes to my country; but persecutions have deprived them of their vast possessions. My uncle's adherence to his ancient faith drove him from our country. I too resolved to seek advancement in the military service; but the insolence and ill treatment which I received at the hands of the English were not bearable by a high-born gentleman, and I fled their service. It was only to fall into another bondage to all appearance still more hopeless, when my good star sent a preserver to me in my uncle, and my spirit and gallantry enabled me to take advantage of the means of escape afforded me. Since then we have lived, I do not disguise it, by play; but who can say I have done him a wrong? Yet, if I could find myself in an honourable post, and with an assured maintenance, I would never, except for amusement, such as every gentleman must have, touch a card again. I beseech your Highness to inquire of your resident at Berlin if I did not on every occasion act as a gallant soldier. I feel that I have talents of a higher order, and should be proud to have occasion to exert them, if, as I do not doubt, my fortune shall bring them into play.'

The candour of this statement struck his Highness greatly, and impressed him in my favour, and he was pleased to say that he believed me, and would be glad to stand my friend.

Having thus the two Dukes, the Duchess, and the reigning favourite enlisted on my side, the chances certainly were that I should carry off the great prize; and I ought, according to all common calculations, to have been a prince of the empire at this present writing, but that my ill luck pursued me in a matter in which I was not the least to blame,—the unhappy Duchess's attachment to the weak, silly, cowardly Frenchman. The display of this love was painful to witness, as its end was frightful to think of. The Princess made no disguise of it. If Magny spoke a word to a lady of her household, she would be jealous, and attack with all the fury of her tongue the unlucky offender. She would send him a half-dozen of notes in the day: at his arrival to join her circle or the courts which she held, she would brighten up, so that all might perceive. It was a wonder that her husband had not long ere this been made aware of her faithlessness, but the Prince Victor was himself of so high and stern a nature that he could not believe in her stooping so far from her rank as to forget her virtue; and I have heard say, that when hints were given to him of the evident partiality which the Princess showed for the equerry, his answer was a stern command never more to be troubled on the subject. 'The Princess is light-minded,' he said; 'she was brought up at a frivolous court; but her folly goes not beyond coquetry: crime is impossible; she has her birth, and my name, and her children, to defend her.' And he would ride off to his military inspections and be absent for weeks, or retire to his suite of apartments, and remain closeted there whole days, only appearing to make a bow at her Highness's levee, or to give her his hand at the court galas, where ceremony required that he should appear. He was a man of vulgar tastes, and I have seen him in the private garden, with his great ungainly figure, running races or playing at ball with his little son and daughter, whom he would find a dozen pretexts daily for visiting. The serene children were brought to their mother every morning at her toilet, but she received them very indifferently, except on one occasion, when the young Duke Ludwig got his little uniform as colonel of hussars, being presented with a regiment by his godfather, the Emperor Leopold.* Then, for a day or two, the Duchess Olivia was charmed with the little boy; but she grew tired of him speedily, as a child does of a toy. I remember one day, in the morning circle, some of the Princess's rouge came off on the arm of her son's little white military jacket; on which she slapped the poor child's face, and sent him sobbing away. Oh, the woes that have been worked by women in this world! the misery into which men have lightly stepped with smiling faces, often not even with the excuse of passion, but from mere foppery, vanity, and bravado! Men play with these dreadful two-edged tools, as if no harm could come to them. I, who have seen more of life than most men, if I had a son, would go on my knees to him and beg him to avoid woman, who is worse than poison. Once intrigue, and your whole life is endangered; you never know when the evil may fall upon you, and the woe of whole families, and the ruin of innocent people perfectly dear to you, may be caused by a moment of your folly.

When I saw how entirely lost the unlucky Monsieur de Magny seemed to be, in spite of all the claims I had against him, I urged him to fly. He had rooms in the palace, in the garrets over the Princess's quarters (the building was a huge one, and accommodated almost a city of noble retainers of the family); but the infatuated young fool would not budge, although he had not even the excuse of love for staying. 'How she squints,' he would say of the Princess, 'and how crooked she is! She thinks no one can perceive her deformity. She writes me verses out of Gresset or Crébillon,* and fancies I believe them to be original. Bah! they are no more her own than her hair is!' It was in this way that the wretched lad was dancing over the ruin that was yawning under him. I do believe that his chief pleasure in making love to the Princess was that he might write about his victories to his friends of the *petites maisons* at Paris, where he longed to be considered as a wit and a *vainqueur de dames*.

Seeing the young man's recklessness, and the danger of his position, I became very anxious that *my* little scheme should be brought to a satisfactory end, and pressed him warmly on the matter.

My solicitations with him were, I need not say, from the nature of the connexion between us, generally pretty successful; and, in fact, the poor fellow could *refuse me nothing*, as I used often laughingly to say to him, very little to his liking. But I used more than threats, or the legitimate influence I had over him. I used delicacy and generosity; as a proof of which, I may mention that I promised to give back to the Princess the family emerald which I mentioned in the last chapter that I had won from her unprincipled admirer at play.

This was done by my uncle's consent, and was one of the usual acts of prudence and foresight which distinguish that clever man. 'Press the matter now, Redmond, my boy,' he would urge. 'This affair between her Highness and Magny must end ill for both of them, and that soon, and where will be your chance to win the Countess then? Now is your time! win her and wear her before the month is over, and we will give up the punting business, and go live like noblemen at our castle in Swabia. Get rid of that emerald, too,' he added; 'should an accident happen, it will be an ugly deposit found in our hand.' This it was that made me agree to forgo the possession of the trinket, which, I must confess, I was loath to part with. It was lucky for us both that I did, as you shall presently hear.

Meanwhile, then, I urged Magny: I myself spoke strongly to the Countess of Liliengarten, who promised formally to back my claim with his Highness the reigning Duke; and Monsieur de Magny was instructed to induce the Princess Olivia to make a similar application to the old sovereign in my behalf. It was done. The two ladies urged the Prince; his Highness (at a supper of oysters and champagne) was brought to consent, and her Highness the hereditary Princess did me the honour of notifying personally to the Countess Ida that it was the Prince's will that she should marry the young Irish nobleman, the Chevalier Redmond de Balibari. The notification was made in my presence; and though the young Countess said, 'Never!' and fell down in a swoon at her lady's feet, I was, you may be sure, entirely unconcerned at this little display of mawkish sensibility, and felt, indeed, now that my prize was secure.

That evening I gave the Chevalier de Magny the emerald,

which he promised to restore to the Princess; and now the only difficulty in my way lay with the hereditary Prince, of whom his father, his wife, and the favourite were alike afraid. He might not be disposed to allow the richest heiress in his duchy to be carried off by a noble, though not a wealthy, foreigner. Time was necessary in order to break the matter to Prince Victor. The Princess must find him at some moment of good humour. He had days of infatuation still, when he could refuse his wife nothing; and our plan was to wait for one of these, or for any other chance which might occur.

But it was destined that the Princess should never see her husband at her feet, as often as he had been. Fate was preparing a terrible ending to her follies, and my own hope. In spite of his solemn promises to me, Magny never restored the emerald to the Princess Olivia.

He had heard, in casual intercourse with me, that my uncle and I had been beholden to Mr. Moses Löwe, the banker of Heidelberg, who had given us a good price for our valuables; and the infatuated young man took a pretext to go thither, and offered the jewel for pawn. Moses Löwe recognized the emerald at once, gave Magny the sum the latter demanded, which the chevalier lost presently at play; never, you may be sure, acquainting us with the means by which he had made himself master of so much capital. We, for our parts, supposed that he had been supplied by his usual banker, the Princess; and many rouleaux of his gold pieces found their way into our treasury, when at the court galas, at our own lodgings, or at the apartments of Madame de Liliengarten (who on these occasions did us the honour to go halves with us) we held our bank of faro.

Thus Magny's money was very soon gone. But though the Jew held his jewel, of thrice the value, no doubt, of the sums he had lent upon it, that was not all the profit which he intended to have from his unhappy creditor, over whom he began speedily to exercise his authority. His Hebrew connexions at X——, money-brokers, bankers, horse-dealers, about the court there, must have told their Heidelberg brother what Magny's relations with the Princess were; and the rascal determined to take advantage of these, and to press to the utmost both victims. My uncle and I were, meanwhile, swimming upon the high tide of fortune, prospering with our cards, and with the still greater matrimonial game which we were playing; and we were quite unaware of the mine under our feet.

Before a month was passed, the Jew began to pester Magny. He presented himself at X——, and asked for further interest—hush-money, otherwise he must sell the emerald. Magny got money for him; the Princess again befriended her dastardly lover. The success of the first demand only rendered the second more exorbitant. I know not how much money was extorted and paid on this unlucky emerald; but it was the cause of the ruin of us all.

One night we were keeping our table as usual at the Countess of Liliengarten's, and Magny being in cash somehow kept drawing out rouleau after rouleau, and playing with his common ill-success. In the middle of the play a note was brought in to him, which he read, and turned very pale on perusing; but the luck was against him, and looking up rather anxiously at the clock, he waited for a few more turns of the cards, and having, I suppose, lost his last rouleau, he got up with a wild oath that scared some of the polite company assembled, and left the room. A great trampling of horses was heard without, but we were too much engaged with our business to heed the noise, and continued our play.

Presently some one came into the play-room and said to the Countess, 'Here is a strange story! A Jew has been murdered in the Kaiserwald. Magny was arrested when he went out of the room.' All the party broke up hearing this strange news, and we shut up our bank for the night. Magny had been sitting by me during the play (my uncle dealt and I paid and took the money), and, looking under the chair there was a crumpled paper, which I took up and read. It was that which had been delivered to him, and ran thus:—

If you have done it, take the orderly's horse who brings this. It is the best of my stable. There are a hundred louis in each holster, and the pistols are loaded. Either course lies open to you; you know what I mean. In a quarter of an hour I shall know our fate—whether I am to be dishonoured and survive you, whether you are guilty and a coward, or whether you are still worthy of the name of

M.

This was in the handwriting of the old General de Magny; and my uncle and I, as we walked home at night, having made and divided with the Countess de Liliengarten no inconsiderable profits that night, felt our triumphs greatly dashed by the perusal of the letter. 'Has Magny,' we asked, 'robbed the Jew, or has his intrigue been discovered ?' In either case, my claims on the Countess Ida were likely to meet with serious drawbacks ; and I began to feel that my 'great card' was played and perhaps lost.

Well, it *was* lost ; though I say, to this day, it was well and gallantly played. After supper (which we never for fear of consequences took during play) I became so agitated in my mind as to what was occurring that I determined to sally out about midnight into the town, and inquire what was the real motive of Magny's apprehension. A sentry was at the door, and signified to me that I and my uncle were under arrest.

We were left in our quarters for six weeks so closely watched that escape was impossible, had we desired it ; but, as innocent men, we had nothing to fear. Our course of life was open to all, and we desired and courted inquiry. Great and tragical events happened during those six weeks, of which, though we heard the outline, as all Europe did, when we were released from our captivity, we were yet far from understanding all the particulars, which were not much known to me for many years after. Here they are as they were told me by the lady who, of all the world perhaps, was most likely to know them. But the narrative had best form the contents of another chapter.

CHAPTER XII

CONTAINS THE TRAGICAL HISTORY OF THE PRINCESS OF X——

MORE than twenty years after the events described in the past chapters I was walking with my Lady Lyndon, in the Rotunda, at Ranelagh.* It was in the year 1790 ; the emigration from France* had already commenced, the old counts and marquises were thronging to our shores, not starving and miserable as one saw them a few years afterwards, but unmolested as yet, and bringing with them some token of their national splendour. I was walking with Lady Lyndon, who, proverbially jealous and always anxious to annoy me, spied out a foreign lady who was evidently remarking me, and of course asked who was the hideous fat Dutchwoman who was leering at me so? I knew her not in the least. I felt I had seen the lady's face somewhere (it was now, as my wife said, enormously fat and bloated), but I did not recognize in the bearer of that face one who had been among the most beautiful women in Germany in her day.

It was no other than Madame de Liliengarten, the mistress, or, as some said, the morganatic wife, of the old Duke of X——, Duke Victor's father. She had left X—— a few months after the elder Duke's demise, had gone to Paris, as I heard, where some unprincipled adventurer had married her for her money; but, however, had always retained her quasi-royal title, and pretended, amidst the great laughter of the Parisians who frequented her house, to the honours and ceremonial of a sovereign's widow. She had a throne erected in her state-room, and was styled by her servants and those who wished to pay court to her, or borrow money from her, 'Altesse.' Report said she drank rather copiously—certainly her face bore every mark of that habit, and had lost the rosy, frank, good-humoured beauty which had charmed the sovereign who had ennobled her.

Although she did not address me in the circle at Ranelagh, I was at this period as well known as the Prince of Wales, and she had no difficulty in finding my house in Berkeley Square, whither a note was next morning dispatched to me. 'An old friend of Monsieur de Balibari,' it stated (in extremely bad French) 'is anxious to see the Chevalier again and to talk over old happy times. Rosina de Liliengarten (can it be that Redmond Balibari has forgotten her?) will be at her house in Leicester Fields all the morning looking for one who would never have passed her by *twenty years* ago.'

Rosina of Liliengarten it was, indeed—such a full-blown Rosina I have seldom seen. I found her in a decent first-floor in Leicester Fields*(the poor soul fell much lower afterwards) drinking tea, which had somehow a very strong smell of brandy in it; and after salutations, which would be more tedious to recount than they were to perform, and after further straggling conversation, she gave me briefly the following narrative of the events in X——, which I may well entitle the 'Princess's Tragedy.'

'You remember Monsieur de Geldern, the police minister. He was of Dutch extraction, and, what is more, of a family of Dutch Jews. Although everybody was aware of this blot in his scutcheon, he was mortally angry if ever his origin was suspected; and made up for his father's errors by outrageous professions of religion, and the most austere practices of devotion. He visited church every morning, confessed once a week, and hated Jews and Protestants as much as an inquisitor could do. He never lost an opportunity of proving his sincerity, by persecuting one or the other whenever occasion fell in his way.

'He hated the Princess mortally; for her Highness in some whim had insulted him with his origin, caused pork to be removed from before him at table, or injured him in some such silly way; and he had a violent animosity to the old Baron de Magny, both in his capacity of Protestant, and because the latter in some haughty mood had publicly turned his back upon him as a sharper and a spy. Perpetual quarrels were taking place between them in council, where it was only the presence of his august masters that restrained the Baron from publicly and frequently expressing the contempt which he felt for the officer of police.

'Thus Geldern had hatred as one reason for ruining the Princess, and it is my belief he had a stronger motive still—interest. You remember whom the Duke married, after the death of his first wife?—a Princess of the house of F——. Geldern built his fine palace two years after, and, as I feel convinced, with the money which was paid to him by the F—— family for forwarding the match.

'To go to Prince Victor, and report to his Highness a case which everybody knew, was not by any means Geldern's desire. He knew the man would be ruined for ever in the Prince's estimation who carried him intelligence so disastrous. His aim, therefore, was, to leave the matter to explain itself to his Highness; and, when the time was ripe, he cast about for a means of carrying his point. He had spies in the houses of the elder and younger Magny; but this you know, of course, from your experience of Continental customs. We had all spies over each other. Your black (Zamor, I think, was his name) used to give me reports every morning; and I used to entertain the dear old Duke with stories of you and your uncle practising piquet and dice in the morning, and with your quarrels and intrigues. We levied similar contributions on everybody in X——, to amuse the dear old man. Monsieur de Magny's valet used to report both to me and Monsieur de Geldern.

'I knew of the fact of the emerald being in pawn; and it was out of my exchequer that the poor Princess drew the funds which were spent upon the odious Löwe, and the still more worthless young chevalier. How the Princess could trust the latter as she persisted in doing, is beyond my comprehension; but there is no infatuation like that of a woman in love: and you will remark, my dear Monsieur de Balibari, that our sex generally fix upon a bad man.'

'Not always, madam,' I interposed; 'your humble servant has created many such attachments.'

'I do not see that that affects the truth of the proposition,' said the old lady dryly, and continued her narrative. 'The Jew who held the emerald had had many dealings with the Princess, and at last was offered a bribe of such magnitude that he determined to give up the pledge. He committed the inconceivable imprudence of bringing the emerald with him to X——, and waited on Magny, who was provided by the Princess with the money to redeem the pledge, and was actually ready to pay it.

'Their interview took place in Magny's own apartments, when his valet overheard every word of their conversation. The young man, who was always utterly careless of money when it was in his possession, was so easy in offering it that Löwe rose in his demands, and had the conscience to ask double the sum for which he had previously stipulated.

'At this the chevalier lost all patience, fell on the wretch, and was for killing him, when the opportune valet rushed in and saved him. The man had heard every word of the conversation between the disputants, and the Jew ran flying with terror into his arms; and Magny, a quick and passionate, but not a violent man, bade the servant lead the villain downstairs, and thought no more of him.

'Perhaps he was not sorry to be rid of him, and to have in his possession a large sum of money, four thousand ducats, with which he could tempt fortune once more, as you know he did at your table that night.'

'Your ladyship went halves, madam,' said I; 'and you know how little I was the better for my winnings.'

'The man conducted the trembling Israelite out of the

palace, and no sooner had seen him lodged at the house of one of his brethren, where he was accustomed to put up, than he went away to the office of his excellency the minister of police, and narrated every word of the conversation which had taken place between the Jew and his master.

'Geldern expressed the greatest satisfaction at his spy's prudence and fidelity. He gave him a purse of twenty ducats, and promised to provide for him handsomely, as great men do sometimes promise to reward their instruments; but you, Monsieur de Balibari, know how seldom those promises are kept. "Now, go and find out," said Monsieur de Geldern, "at what time the Israelite proposes to return home again, or whether he will repent, and take the money." The man went on this errand. Meanwhile, to make matters sure, Geldern arranged a play-party at my house, inviting you thither with your bank, as you may remember; and finding means, at the same time, to let Maxime de Magny know that there was to be faro at Madame de Liliengarten's. It was an invitation the poor fellow never neglected.'

I remembered the facts, and listened on, amazed at the artifice of the infernal minister of police.

'The spy came back from his message to Löwe, and stated that he had made inquiries among the servants of the house where the Heidelberg banker lodged, and that it was the latter's intention to leave X—— that afternoon. He travelled by himself, riding an old horse, exceedingly humbly attired, after the manner of his people.

'"Johann," said the minister, clapping the pleased spy upon the shoulder, "I am more and more pleased with you. I have been thinking, since you left me, of your intelligence, and the faithful manner in which you have served me; and shall soon find an occasion to place you according to your merits. Which way does this Israelitish scoundrel take?"

'"He goes to R—— to-night."

'"And must pass by the Kaiserwald. Are you a man of courage, Johann Kerner?"

'"Will your excellency try me?" said the man, his eyes glittering; "I served through the Seven Years' War, and was never known to fail there."

'"Now, listen. The emerald must be taken from that Jew; in the very keeping it the scoundrel has committed high treason. To the man who brings me that emerald I swear I will give five hundred louis. You understand why it is necessary that it should be restored to her Highness. I need say no more."

'"You shall have it to-night, sir," said the man. "Of course your excellency will hold me harmless in case of accident."

'"Psha!" answered the minister; "I will pay you half the money beforehand; such is my confidence in you. Accident's impossible, if you take your measures properly. There are four leagues of wood; the Jew rides slowly. It will be night before he can reach, let us say, the old Powder-Mill in the wood. What's to prevent you from putting a rope across the road, and dealing with him there? Be back with me this evening at supper. If you meet any of the patrol, say, 'Foxes are loose,'—that's the word for to-night. They will let you pass them without questions."

'The man went off quite charmed with his commission, and when Magny was losing his money at our faro-table, his servant waylaid the Jew at the spot named the Powder-Mill, in the Kaiserwald. The Jew's horse stumbled over a rope which had been placed across the road; and, as the rider fell groaning to the ground, Johann Kerner rushed out on him, masked, and pistol in hand, and demanded his money. He had no wish to kill the Jew, I believe, unless his resistance should render extreme measures necessary.

'Nor did he commit any such murder; for, as the yelling Jew roared for mercy, and his assailant menaced him with the pistol, a squad of patrol came up, and laid hold of the robber and the wounded man.

'Kerner swore an oath. "You have come too soon," said he to the sergeant of the police. "*Foxes are loose.*" "Some are caught," said the sergeant, quite unconcerned; and bound the fellow's hands with the rope which he had stretched across the road to entrap the Jew. He was placed behind a policeman on a horse; Löwe was similarly accommodated, and the party thus came back into the town as the night fell.

'They were taken forthwith to the police quarter; and, as the chief happened to be there, they were examined by his excellency in person. Both were rigorously searched; the Jew's papers and cases taken from him; the jewel was found in a private pocket. As for the spy, the minister, looking at him angrily, said, "Why, this is the servant of the Chevalier de Magny, one of her Highness's equerries!"

and, without hearing a word in exculpation from the poor frightened wretch, ordered him into close confinement.

'Calling for his horse, he then rode to the Prince's apartments at the palace, and asked for an instant audience. When admitted, he produced the emerald. "This jewel," said he, "has been found on the person of a Heidelberg Jew, who has been here repeatedly of late, and has had many dealings with her Highness's equerry, the Chevalier de Magny. This afternoon the chevalier came from his master's lodgings, accompanied by the Hebrew; was heard to make inquiries as to the route the man intended to take on his way homewards; followed him, or preceded him rather, and was found in the act of rifling his victim by my police in the Kaiserwald. The man will confess nothing; but, on being searched, a large sum in gold was found on his person; and though it is with the utmost pain that I can bring myself to entertain such an opinion, and to implicate a gentleman of the character and name of Monsieur de Magny, I do submit that our duty is to have the chevalier examined relative to the affair. As Monsieur de Magny is in her Highness's private service, and in her confidence, I have heard, I would not venture to apprehend him without your Highness's permission."

'The Prince's master of the horse, a friend of the old Baron de Magny, who was present at the interview, no sooner heard the strange intelligence than he hastened away to the old general with the dreadful news of his grandson's supposed crime. Perhaps his Highness himself was not unwilling that his old friend and tutor in arms should have the chance of saving his family from disgrace; at all events, Monsieur de Hengst,* the master of the horse, was permitted to go off to the baron undisturbed, and break to him the intelligence of the accusation pending over the unfortunate chevalier.

'It is possible that he expected some such dreadful catastrophe, for, after hearing Hengst's narrative (as the latter afterwards told me), he only said, "Heaven's will be done!" for some time refused to stir a step in the matter, and then only by the solicitation of his friend was induced to write the letter which Maxime de Magny received at our play-table.

'Whilst he was there, squandering the Princess's money, a police visit was paid to his apartments, and a hundred proofs, not of his guilt with respect to the robbery, but of his guilty connexion with the Princess, were discovered there,—tokens of her giving, passionate letters from her, copies of his own correspondence to his young friends at Paris,—all of which the police minister perused, and carefully put together under seal for his Highness, Prince Victor. I have no doubt he perused them, for, on delivering them to the hereditary Prince, Geldern said that, *in obedience to his Highness's orders*, he had collected the chevalier's papers, but he need not say that, on his honour, he (Geldern) himself had never examined the documents. His difference with Messieurs de Magny was known; he begged his Highness to employ any other official person in the judgement of the accusation brought against the young chevalier.

'All these things were going on while the chevalier was at play. A run of luck—you had great luck in those days. Monsieur de Balibari—was against him. He stayed and lost his 4,000 ducats; he received his uncle's note, and, such was the infatuation of the wretched gambler, that, on receipt of it, he went down to the courtyard, where the horse was in waiting, absolutely took the money which the poor old gentleman had placed in the saddle-holsters, brought it upstairs, played it, and lost it, and when he issued from the room to fly, it was too late; he was placed in arrest at the bottom of my staircase, as you were upon entering your own home.

'Even when he came in under the charge of the soldiery sent to arrest him, the old general, who was waiting, was overjoyed to see him, and flung himself into the lad's arms, and embraced him, it was said, for the first time in many years. "He is here, gentlemen," he sobbed out,—"thank God he is not guilty of the robbery!" and then sank back in a chair in a burst of emotion, painful, it was said by those present, to witness on the part of a man so brave, and known to be so cold and stern.

'"Robbery!" said the young man, "I swear before Heaven I am guilty of none!" and a scene of almost touching reconciliation was passed between them, before the unhappy young man was led from the guard-house into the prison which he was destined never to quit.

'That night the Duke looked over the papers which Geldern had brought to him. It was at a very early stage of the perusal, no doubt, that he gave orders for your arrest;

for you were taken at midnight, Magny at ten o'clock, after which time the old Baron de Magny had seen his Highness, protesting of his grandson's innocence, and the Prince had received him most graciously and kindly: His Highness said he had no doubt the young man was innocent, his birth and his blood rendered such a crime impossible; but suspicion was too strong against him; he was known to have been that day closeted with the Jew; to have received a very large sum of money which he squandered at play, and of which the Hebrew had, doubtless, been the lender,—to have dispatched his servant after him, who inquired the hour of the Jew's departure, lay in wait for him, and rifled him. Suspicion was so strong against the chevalier that common justice required his arrest, and, meanwhile, until he cleared himself, he should be kept in not dishonourable durance, and every regard had for his name and the services of his honourable grandfather. With this assurance, and with a warm grasp of the hand, the Prince left old General de Magny that night, and the veteran retired to rest, almost consoled and confident in Maxime's eventual and immediate release.

'But in the morning, before daybreak, the Prince, who had been reading papers all night, wildly called to the page, who slept in the next room across the door, bade him get horses, which were always kept in readiness in the stables, and, flinging a parcel of letters into a box, told the page to follow him on horseback with these. The young man (Monsieur de Weissenborn) told this to a young lady who was then of my household, and who is now Madame de Weissenborn and a mother of a score of children.

'The page described that never was such a change seen as in his august master in the course of that single night. His eyes were bloodshot, his face livid, his clothes were hanging loose about him, and he who had always made his appearance on parade as precisely dressed as any sergeant of his troops, might have been seen galloping through the lonely streets at early dawn without a hat, his unpowdered hair streaming behind him like a madman.

'The page, with the box of papers, clattered after his master,—it was no easy task to follow him; and they rode from the palace to the town, and through it to the general's quarter. The sentinels at the door were scared at the strange figure that rushed up to the general's gate, and, not knowing him, crossed bayonets, and refused him admission. " Fools," said Weissenborn, " it is the Prince ! " And, jangling at the bell as if for an alarm of fire, it was at length opened by the porter, and his Highness ran up to the general's bedchamber, followed by the page with the box.

' " Magny—Magny," roared the Prince, thundering at the closed door, " get up ! " And to the queries of the old man from within, answered, " It is I—Victor—the Prince ! —get up ! " And presently the door was opened by the general in his *robe de chambre*, and the Prince entered. The page brought in the box, and was bidden to wait without, which he did ; but there led from Monsieur de Magny's bedroom into his antechamber two doors, the great one which formed the entrance into his room, and a smaller one which led, as the fashion is with our houses abroad, into the closet which communicates with the alcove where the bed is. The door of this was found by M. de Weissenborn to be open, and the young man was thus enabled to hear and see everything which occurred within the apartment.

' The general, somewhat nervously, asked what was the reason of so early a visit from his Highness ; to which the Prince did not for a while reply further than by staring at him rather wildly, and pacing up and down the room.

' At last he said, " Here is the cause ! " dashing his fist on the box ; and, as he had forgotten to bring the key with him, he went to the door for a moment, saying, " Weissenborn, perhaps, has it " ; but, seeing over the stove one of the general's *couteaux de chasse*, he took it down, and said, " That will do," and fell to work to burst the red trunk open with the blade of the forest-knife. The point broke, and he gave an oath, but continued haggling on with the broken blade, which was better suited to his purpose than the long, pointed knife, and finally succeeded in wrenching open the lid of the chest.

' " What is the matter ? " said he, laughing,—" Here's the matter—read that !—here's more matter—read that !—here's more — no, not that ; that's somebody else's picture—but here's hers !—Do you know that, Magny ?—My wife's—the Princess's !—Why did you and your cursed race ever come out of France, to plant your infernal wickedness wherever your foot fell and to ruin honest German homes ? What have you and yours ever had from my family but confidence and kindness ? We gave you a home when you had none, and here's our reward!" and he flung a parcel of papers down before the old general, who saw the truth at once,—he had known it long before, probably, and sank down on his chair, covering his face.

'The Prince went on gesticulating and shrieking almost. "If a man injured you so, Magny, before you begot the father of that gambling, lying villain yonder, you would have known how to revenge yourself. You would have killed him! Yes, would have killed him. But who's to help me to my revenge? I've no equal. I can't meet that dog of a Frenchman,—that pimp from Versailles,—and kill him as if he had played the traitor to one of his own degree."

'"The blood of Maxime de Magny," said the old gentleman, proudly, "is as good as that of any prince in Christendom."

'"Can I take it?" cried the Prince; "you know I can't. I can't have the privilege of any other gentleman of Europe. What am I to do? Look here, Magny; I was wild when I came here, I didn't know what to do. You've served me for thirty years, you've saved my life twice; they are all knaves and harlots about my poor old father here—no honest men or women—you are the only one—you saved my life; tell me what am I to do?" Thus, from insulting Monsieur de Magny, the poor distracted Prince fell to supplicating him, and, at last, fairly flung himself down, and burst out in an agony of tears.

'Old Magny, one of the most rigid and cold of men on common occasions, when he saw this outbreak of passion on the Prince's part, became, as my informant has described to me, as much affected as his master. The old man from being cold and high, suddenly fell, as it were, into the whimpering querulousness of extreme old age. He lost all sense of dignity; he went down on his knees, and broke out into all sorts of wild, incoherent attempts at consolation; so much so, that Weissenborn said he could not bear to look at the scene, and actually turned away from the contemplation of it.

'But, from what followed in a few days, we may guess the results of the long interview. The Prince, when he came away from the conversation with his old servant, forgot his fatal box of papers and sent the page back for them. The general was on his knees praying in the room when the young man entered, and only stirred and looked round wildly as the other removed the packet. The Prince rode away to his hunting-lodge at three leagues from X——, and three days after that Maxime de Magny died in prison, having made a confession that he was engaged in an attempt to rob the Jew, and that he had made away with himself, ashamed of his dishonour.

'But it is not known that it was the general himself who took his grandson poison; it was said even that he shot him in the prison. This, however, was not the case. General de Magny carried his grandson the draught which was to carry him out of the world, represented to the wretched youth that his fate was inevitable, that it would be public and disgraceful unless he chose to anticipate the punishment, and so left him. But *it was not of his own accord*, and not until he had used *every* means of escape, as you shall hear, that the unfortunate being's life was brought to an end.

'As for General de Magny, he quite fell into imbecility a short time after his nephew's death, and my honoured Duke's demise. After his Highness the Prince married the Princess Mary of F——, as they were walking in the English park together they once met old Magny riding in the sun in the easy chair, in which he was carried commonly abroad after his paralytic fits. "This is my wife, Magny," said the Prince, affectionately, taking the veteran's hand; and he added, turning to his Princess, "General de Magny saved my life during the Seven Years' War."

'"What, you've taken her back again?" said the old man. "I wish you'd send me back my poor Maxime." He had quite forgotten the death of the poor Princess Olivia, and the Prince, looking very dark indeed, passed away.

'And now,' said Madame de Liliengarten, 'I have only one more gloomy story to relate to you—the death of the Princess Olivia. It is even more horrible than the tale I have just told you.' With which preface the old lady resumed her narrative.

'The kind, weak Princess's fate was hastened, if not occasioned, by the cowardice of Magny. He found means to communicate with her from his prison, and her Highness, who was not in open disgrace yet (for the Duke, out of regard to the family, persisted in charging Magny with only robbery), made the most desperate efforts to relieve him and to bribe the jailers to effect his escape. She was so wild that she lost all patience and prudence in the conduct of any schemes she may have had for Magny's liberation, for her husband was inexorable, and caused the chevalier's prison to be too strictly guarded for escape to be possible. She offered the state jewels in pawn to the court banker, who of course was obliged to decline the transaction. She fell down on her knees, it is said, to Geldern, the police minister, and offered him Heaven knows what as a bribe. Finally, she came screaming to my poor dear Duke, who, with his age, diseases, and easy habits, was quite unfit for scenes of so violent a nature, and who, in consequence of the excitement created in his august bosom by her frantic violence and grief, had a fit in which I very nigh lost him. That his dear life was brought to an untimely end by these transactions I have not the slightest doubt, for the Strasburg pie,* of which they said he died, never, I am sure, could have injured him, but for the injury which his dear gentle heart received from the unusual occurrences in which he was forced to take a share.

'All her Highness's movements were carefully, though not ostensibly, watched by her husband, Prince Victor, who, waiting upon his august father, sternly signified to him that if his Highness (*my* Duke) should dare to aid the Princess in her efforts to release Magny, he, Prince Victor, would publicly accuse the Princess and her paramour of high treason, and take measures with the Diet for removing his father from the throne as incapacitated to reign. Hence interposition on our part was vain, and Magny was left to his fate.

'It came, as you are aware, very suddenly. Geldern, police minister, Hengst, master of the horse, and the colonel of the Prince's guard, waited upon the young man in his prison two days after his grandfather had visited him there and left behind him the phial of poison which the criminal had not the courage to use. And Geldern signified to the young man that unless he took of his own accord the laurel-water*provided by the elder Magny, more violent means of death would be instantly employed upon him, and that a file of grenadiers was in waiting in the courtyard to dispatch him. Seeing this, Magny, with the most dreadful self-abasement, after dragging himself round the room on his knees from one officer to another, weeping and screaming with terror, at last desperately drank off the potion and was a corpse in a few minutes. Thus ended this wretched young man.

'His death was made public in the *Court Gazette* two days after, the paragraph stating that Monsieur de M——, struck with remorse for having attempted the murder of the Jew, had put himself to death by poison in prison, and a warning was added to all young noblemen of the duchy to avoid the dreadful sin of gambling, which had been the cause of the young man's ruin, and had brought upon the grey hairs of one of the noblest and most honourable of the servants of the Duke irretrievable sorrow.

'The funeral was conducted with decent privacy, the General de Magny attending it. The carriages of the two Dukes and all the first people of the court made their calls upon the general afterwards. He attended parade as usual the next day on the Arsenal-Place, and Duke Victor, who had been inspecting the building, came out of it leaning on the brave old warrior's arm. He was particularly gracious to the old man, and told his officers the oft-repeated story how at Rosbach, when the X—— contingent served with the troops of the unlucky Soubise, the general had thrown himself in the way of a French dragoon who was pressing hard upon his Highness in the rout, had received the blow intended for his master and killed the assailant. And he alluded to the family motto of "Magny sans tache," and said, "It had been always so with his gallant friend and tutor in arms." This speech affected all present very much, with the exception of the old general, who only bowed and did not speak: but when he went home he was heard muttering, "Magny sans tache, Magny sans tache!" and was attacked with paralysis that night, from which he never more than partially recovered.

'The news of Maxime's death had somehow been kept from the Princess until now, a *Gazette* even being printed without the paragraph containing the account of his suicide; but it was at length, I know not how, made known to her. And when she heard it, her ladies tell me, she screamed and fell as if struck dead, then sat up wildly and raved like a madwoman, and was then carried to her bed, where her physician attended her, and where she lay of a brain fever. All this while the Prince used to send to make inquiries concerning her, and from his giving orders that his Castle of Schlangenfels* should be prepared and furnished, I make no doubt it was his intention to send her into confinement thither, as had been done with the unhappy sister of his Britannic Majesty at Zell.*

'She sent repeatedly to demand an interview with his Highness, which the latter declined, saying that he would communicate with her Highness when her health was sufficiently recovered. To one of her passionate letters he sent back for reply a packet, which, when opened, was found to contain the emerald that had been the cause round which all this dark intrigue moved.

'Her Highness at this time became quite frantic, vowed in the presence of all her ladies that one lock of her darling Maxime's hair was more precious to her than all the jewels in the world; rang for her carriage, and said she would go and kiss his tomb; proclaimed the murdered martyr's innocence, and called down the punishment of Heaven, the wrath of her family, upon his assassin. The Prince, on hearing these speeches (they were all, of course, regularly brought to him), is said to have given one of his dreadful looks (which I remember now), and to have said, "This cannot last much longer."

'All that day and the next the Princess Olivia passed in dictating the most passionate letters to the Prince her father, to the Kings of France, Naples, and Spain, her kinsmen, and to all other branches of her family, calling upon them in the most incoherent terms to protect her against the butcher and assassin, her husband, assailing his person in the maddest terms of reproach, and at the same time confessing her love for the murdered Magny. It was in vain that those ladies who were faithful to her pointed out to her the inutility of these letters, the dangerous folly of the confessions which they made; she insisted upon writing them, and used to give them to her second robe-woman, a Frenchwoman (her Highness always affectioned persons of that nation), who had the key of her cassette,* and carried every one of these epistles to Geldern.

'With the exception that no public receptions were held, the ceremony of the Princess's establishment went on as before. Her ladies were allowed to wait upon her and perform their usual duties about her person. The only men admitted were, however, her servants, her physician, and chaplain ; and one day when she wished to go into the garden, a heyduck, who kept the door, intimated to her Highness that the Prince's orders were that she should keep her apartments.

'They abut, as you remember, upon the landing of the marble staircase of Schloss X——, the entrance to Prince Victor's suite of rooms being opposite the Princess's on the same landing. This space is large, filled with sofas and benches, and the gentlemen and officers who waited upon the Duke used to make a sort of ante-chamber of the landing-place, and pay their court to his Highness there, as he passed out, at eleven o'clock, to parade. At such a time, the heyducks* within the Princess's suite of rooms used to turn out with their halberts and present to Prince Victor—the same ceremony being performed on his own side, when pages came out and announced the approach of his Highness. The pages used to come out and say, "The Prince, gentlemen !' and the drums beat in the hall, and the gentlemen rose who were waiting on the benches that ran along the balustrade.

'As if fate impelled her to her death, one day the Princess, as her guards turned out, and she was aware that the Prince was standing, as was his wont, on the landing, conversing with his gentlemen (in the old days, he used to cross to the Princess's apartment and kiss her hand), the Princess, who had been anxious all the morning, complaining of heat, insisting that all the doors of the apartments should be left open, and giving tokens of an insanity, which I think was now evident, rushed wildly at the doors when the guards passed out, flung them open, and before a word could be said, or her ladies could follow her, was in presence of Duke Victor, who was talking as usual on the landing, and placing herself between him and the stair, began apostrophizing him with frantic vehemence :—

' "Take notice, gentlemen !" she screamed out, "that this man is a murderer and a liar ; that he lays plots for honourable gentlemen, and kills them in prison ! Take notice that I too am in prison, and fear the same fate ; the same butcher who killed Maxime de Magny may, any night, put the knife to my throat. I appeal to you, and to all the Kings of Europe, my royal kinsmen. I demand to be set free from this tyrant and villain, this liar and traitor !

I adjure you all, as gentlemen of honour, to carry these letters to my relatives, and say from whom you had them ! " and with this the unhappy lady began scattering letters about among the astonished crowd.

'" *Let no man stoop !* " cried the Prince, in a voice of thunder. " Madame de Gleim, you should have watched your patient better. Call the Princess's physicians : her Highness's brain is affected. Gentlemen, have the goodness to retire." And the Prince stood on the landing as the gentlemen went down the stairs, saying fiercely to the guard, " Soldier, if she moves, strike with your halbert ! " on which the man brought the point of his weapon to the Princess's breast ; and the lady, frightened, shrank back and re-entered her apartments. " Now, Monsieur de Weissenborn," said the Prince, " pick up all those papers ; " and the Prince went into his own apartments, preceded by his pages, and never quitted them until he had seen every one of the papers burnt.

'The next day the *Court Gazette* contained a bulletin signed by the three physicians, stating that " Her Highness the hereditary Princess laboured under inflammation of the brain, and had passed a restless and disturbed night." Similar notices were issued day after day. The services of all her ladies, except two, were dispensed with. Guards were placed within and without her doors ; her windows were secured, so that escape from them was impossible, and you know what took place ten days after. The church-bells were ringing all night, and the prayers of the faithful asked for a person *in extremis*. A *Gazette* appeared in the morning, edged with black, and stating that the high and mighty Princess Olivia Maria Ferdinanda, consort of his Serene Highness Victor Louis Emanuel, Hereditary Prince of X——, had died in the evening of the 24th of January, 1769.

'But do you know *how* she died, sir ? That, too, is a mystery. Weissenborn, the page, was concerned in this dark tragedy ; and the secret was so dreadful that never, believe me, till Prince Victor's death did I reveal it.

'After the fatal *esclandre** which the Princess had made, the Prince sent for Weissenborn, and binding him by the most solemn adjuration to secrecy (he only broke it to his wife many years after ; indeed, there is no secret in the world that women cannot know if they will), dispatched him on the following mysterious commission.

' " There lives," said his Highness, " on the Kehl side of the river, opposite to Strasburg, a man whose residence you will easily find out from his name, which is *Monsieur de Strasbourg*. You will make your inquiries concerning him quietly, and without occasioning any remark; perhaps you had better go into Strasburg for the purpose, where the person is quite well known. You will take with you any comrade on whom you can perfectly rely; the lives of both, remember, depend on your secrecy. You will find out some period when Monsieur de Strasbourg is alone, or only in company of the domestic who lives with him (I myself visited the man by accident on my return from Paris five years since, and hence am induced to send for him now, in my present emergency). You will have your carriage waiting at his door at night; and you and your comrade will enter his house masked, and present him with a purse of a hundred louis, promising him double that sum on his return from his expedition. If he refuse, you must use force and bring him, menacing him with instant death should he decline to follow you. You will place him in the carriage with the blinds drawn, one or other of you never losing sight of him the whole way, and threatening him with death if he discover himself or cry out. You will lodge him in the old [Owl][1] Tower here, where a room shall be prepared for him; and his work being done, you will restore him to his home in the same speed and secrecy with which you brought him from it."

' Such were the mysterious orders Prince Victor gave his page; and Weissenborn, selecting for his comrade in the expedition Lieutenant Bartenstein, set out on his strange journey.

' All this while the palace was hushed as if in mourning, the bulletins in the *Court Gazette* appeared announcing the continuance of the Princess's malady; and though she had but few attendants, strange and circumstantial stories were told regarding the progress of her complaint. She was quite wild. She had tried to kill herself. She had fancied herself to be I don't know how many different characters. Expresses were sent to her family informing them of her state, and couriers dispatched *publicly* to

[1] Omitted in later editions.

Vienna and Paris to procure the attendance of physicians skilled in treating diseases of the brain. That pretended anxiety was all a feint: it was never intended that the Princess should recover.

'The day on which Weissenborn and Bartenstein returned from their expedition, it was announced that her Highness the Princess was much worse; that night the report through the town was that she was at the agony, and that night the unfortunate creature was endeavouring to make her escape.

'She had unlimited confidence in the French chamberwoman who attended her, and between her and this woman the plan of escape was arranged. The Princess took her jewels in a casket; a private door, opening from one of her rooms and leading into the outer gate, it was said, of the palace, was discovered for her; and a letter was brought to her purporting to be from the Duke, her father-in-law, and stating that a carriage and horses had been provided, and would take her to B——, the territory where she might communicate with her family and be safe.

'The unhappy lady, confiding in her guardian, set out on the expedition. The passages wound through the walls of the modern part of the palace and abutted in effect at the old Owl Tower, as it was called, on the outer wall; the tower was pulled down afterwards, and for good reason.

'At a certain place the candle, which the chamberwoman was carrying, went out; and the Princess would have screamed with terror, but her hand was seized, and a voice cried, "Hush!" and the next minute a man in a mask (it was the Duke himself) rushed forward, gagged her with a handkerchief, her hands and legs were bound, and she was carried swooning with terror into a vaulted room, where she was placed by a person there waiting and tied in an arm-chair. The same mask who had gagged her came and bared her neck and said, "It had best be done now she has fainted."

'Perhaps it would have been as well; for though she recovered from her swoon, and her confessor, who was present, came forward and endeavoured to prepare her for the awful deed which was about to be done upon her, and for the state into which she was about to enter—when she came to herself it was only to scream like a maniac, to curse the Duke as a butcher and tyrant, and to call upon Magny, her dear Magny.

'At this the Duke said, quite calmly, "May God have mercy on her sinful soul!" He, the confessor, and Geldern, who were present, went down on their knees; and, as his Highness dropped his handkerchief, Weissenborn fell down in a fainting fit, while *Monsieur de Strasbourg*, taking the back hair in his hand, separated the shrieking head of Olivia from the miserable, sinful body. May Heaven have mercy upon her soul!'

. . . . . .

This was the story told by Madame de Liliengarten, and the reader will have no difficulty in drawing from it that part which affected myself and my uncle; who, after six weeks of arrest, were set at liberty, but with orders to quit the duchy immediately; indeed, with an escort of dragoons to conduct us to the frontier. What property we had we were allowed to sell and realize in money, but none of our play debts were paid to us, and all of my hopes of the Countess Ida were thus at an end.

When Duke Victor came to the throne, which he did when, six months after, apoplexy carried off the old sovereign his father, all the good old usages of X—— were given up,—play forbidden; the opera and ballet sent to the right-about; and the regiments which the old Duke had sold recalled from their foreign service; with them came my countess's beggarly cousin, the ensign, and he married her. I don't know whether they were happy or not. It is certain that a woman of such a poor spirit did not merit any very high degree of pleasure.

The now reigning Duke of X—— himself married four years after his first wife's demise; and Geldern, though no longer police-minister, built the grand house of which Madame de Liliengarten spoke. What became of the minor actors in the great tragedy, who knows? Only *Monsieur de Strasbourg* was restored to his duties. Of the rest,—the Jew, the chamber-woman, the spy on Magny, I know nothing. Those sharp tools with which great people cut out their enterprises are generally broken in the using; nor did I ever hear that their employers had much regard for them in their ruin.

CHAPTER XIII

I CONTINUE MY CAREER AS A MAN OF FASHION

I FIND I have already filled up many scores of pages, and yet a vast deal of the most interesting portion of my history remains to be told, viz., that which describes my sojourn in the kingdoms of England and Ireland, and the great part I played there, moving among the most illustrious of the land, myself not the least distinguished of the brilliant circle. In order to give due justice to this portion of my memoirs, then,—which is more important than my foreign adventures can be (though I could fill volumes with interesting descriptions of the latter),—I shall cut short the account of my travels in Europe, and of my success at the Continental courts, in order to speak of what befell me at home. Suffice it to say that there is not a capital in Europe, except the beggarly one of Berlin, where the young Chevalier de Balibari was not known and admired, and where he has not made the brave, the high born, and the beautiful talk of him. I won 80,000 roubles from Potemkin* at the Winter Palace at Petersburg, which the scoundrelly favourite never paid me; I have had the honour of seeing his Royal Highness the Chevalier Charles Edward* as drunk as any porter at Rome; my uncle played several matches at billiards against the celebrated Lord C——* at Spa, and I promise you did not come off a loser. In fact, by a neat stratagem of ours, we raised the laugh against his lordship, and something a great deal more substantial. My lord did not know that the Chevalier Barry had a useless eye, and when, one day, my uncle playfully bet him odds at billiards that he would play him with a patch over one eye, the noble lord, thinking to bite us (he was one of the most desperate gamblers that ever lived), accepted the bet, and we won a very considerable amount of him.

Nor need I mention my successes among the fairer portion of the creation. One of the most accomplished, the tallest, the most athletic, and the handsomest gentlemen of Europe, as I was then, a young fellow of my figure could not fail of having advantages, which a person of my spirit knew very well how to use. But upon these subjects I am dumb. Charming Schuvaloff, black-eyed Sczotarska, dark Valdez, tender Hegenheim, brilliant Langeac !*—ye gentle hearts that knew how to beat in old times for the warm young Irish gentleman, where are ye now ? Though my hair has grown grey now, and my sight dim, and my heart cold with years, and ennui, and disappointment, and the treachery of friends, yet I have but to lean back in my arm-chair and think, and those sweet figures come rising up before me out of the past, with their smiles, and their kindnesses, and their bright tender eyes ! There are no women like them now—no manners like theirs ! Look you at a bevy of women at the Prince's, stitched up in tight white satin sacks, with their waists under their arms, and compare them to the graceful figures of the old time ! Why, when I danced with Coralie de Langeac at the fêtes on the birth of the first Dauphin* at Versailles, her hoop was eighteen feet in circumference, and the heels of her lovely little *mules* were three inches from the ground ; the lace of my *jabot* was worth a thousand crowns, and the buttons of my amaranth*-velvet coat alone cost eighty thousand livres. Look at the difference now ! The gentlemen are dressed like boxers, quakers, or hackney-coachmen ; and the ladies are not dressed at all. There is no elegance, no refinement, none of the chivalry of the old world, of which I form a portion. Think of the fashion of London being led by a Br-mm-ll ![1]* a nobody's son ; a low creature, who can no more dance a minuet than I can talk Cherokee ; who cannot even crack a bottle like a gentleman ; who never showed himself to be a man with his sword in his hand, as we used to approve ourselves in the good old times, before that vulgar Corsican* upset the gentry of the world ! Oh, to see the Valdez once again as on that day I met her first driving in state, with her eight mules, and her retinue of gentlemen by the side of yellow Mançanares !* Oh, for another drive with Hegenheim, in the gilded sledge, over the Saxon snow ! False as Schuvaloff was, 'twas better to be jilted by her than to be adored by any other woman. I can't think of any one of them without tenderness. I have ringlets of all their hair in my poor little museum of recollections. Do you keep mine, you dear souls that survive the turmoils and troubles of near half

[1] This manuscript must have been written at the time when Mr. Brummell was the leader of the London fashion.

a hundred years? How changed its colour is now, since the day Sczotarska wore it round her neck, after my duel with Count Bjernaski, at Warsaw!

I never kept any beggarly books of accounts in those days. I had no debts. I paid royally for everything I took, and I took everything I wanted. My income must have been very large. My entertainments and equipages were those of a gentleman of the highest distinction; nor let any scoundrel presume to sneer because I carried off and married my Lady Lyndon (as you shall presently hear), and call me an adventurer, or say I was penniless, or the match unequal. Penniless! I had the wealth of Europe at my command. Adventurer! So is a meritorious lawyer or a gallant soldier; so is every man who makes his own fortune an adventurer. My profession was play, in which I was then unrivalled. No man could play with me through Europe *on the square*;* and my income was just as certain (during health and the exercise of my profession) as that of a man who draws on his Three-per-cents, or any fat squire whose acres bring him revenue. Harvest is not more certain than the effect of skill is: a crop is a chance as much as a game of cards greatly played by a fine player; there may be a drought, or a frost, or a hail-storm, and your stake is lost: but one man is just as much an adventurer as another.

In evoking the recollection of these kind and fair creatures I have nothing but pleasure. I would I could say as much of the memory of another lady, who will henceforth play a considerable part in the drama of my life,—I mean the Countess of Lyndon, whose fatal acquaintance I made at Spa, very soon after the events described in the last chapter had caused me to quit Germany.

Honoria, Countess of Lyndon, Viscountess Bullingdon in England, Baroness Castle Lyndon of the kingdom of Ireland, was so well known to the great world in her day, that I have little need to enter into her family history, which is to be had in any Peerage that the reader may lay his hand on. She was, as I need not say, a countess, viscountess, and baroness in her own right. Her estates in Devon and Cornwall were among the most extensive in those parts; her Irish possessions not less magnificent, and they have been alluded to, in a very early part of these memoirs, as lying near to my own paternal property in the kingdom of Ireland: indeed, unjust confiscations in the time of Elizabeth and her father went to diminish *my* acres, while they added to the already vast possessions of the Lyndon family.

The countess, when I first saw her at the assembly at Spa, was the wife of her cousin, the Right Hon. Sir Charles Reginald Lyndon, Knight of the Bath, and minister to George II and George III at several of the smaller courts of Europe. Sir Charles Lyndon was celebrated as a wit and *bon vivant*; he could write love-verses against Hanbury Williams,* and make jokes with George Selwyn;* he was a man of *virtu*, like Horry Walpole, with whom and Mr. Gray* he had made a part of the grand tour, and was cited, in a word, as one of the most elegant and accomplished men of his time.

I made this gentleman's acquaintance as usual at the play-table, of which he was a constant frequenter. Indeed, one could not but admire the spirit and gallantry with which he pursued his favourite pastime; for, though worn out by gout and a myriad of diseases, a cripple wheeled about in a chair, and suffering pangs of agony, yet you would see him every morning and every evening at his post behind the delightful green cloth; and if, as it would often happen, his own hands were too feeble or inflamed to hold the box, he would call the mains, nevertheless, and have his valet or a friend to throw for him. I like this courageous spirit in a man; the greatest successes in life have been won by such indomitable perseverance.

I was by this time one of the best-known characters in Europe; and the fame of my exploits, my duels, my courage at play, would bring crowds around me in any public society where I appeared. I could show reams of scented paper to prove that this eagerness to make my acquaintance was not confined to the *gentlemen* only, but that I hate boasting, and only talk of myself in so far as it is necessary to relate myself's adventures, the most singular of any man's in Europe. Well, Sir Charles Lyndon's first acquaintance with me originated in the right honourable knight's winning 700 pieces of me at piquet (for which he was almost my match); and I lost them with much good humour, and paid them: and paid them, you may be sure, punctually. Indeed, I will say this for myself, that losing money at play never in the least put me out of good humour with the winner, and that wherever I found a superior, I was always ready to acknowledge and hail him.

Lyndon was very proud of winning from so celebrated a person, and we contracted a kind of intimacy, which, however, did not for awhile go beyond pump-room attentions, and conversations over the supper-table at play, but which gradually increased, until I was admitted into his more private friendship. He was a very free-spoken man (the gentry of those days were much prouder than at present), and used to say to me in his haughty, easy way, 'Hang it, Mr. Barry, you have no more manners than a barber, and I think my black footman has been better educated than you; but you are a young fellow of originality and pluck, and I like you, sir, because you seem determined to go to the deuce by a way of your own.' I would thank him laughingly for this compliment, and say that, as he was bound to the next world much sooner than I was, I would be obliged to him to get comfortable quarters arranged there for me. He used also to be immensely amused with my stories about the splendour of my family and the magnificence of Castle Brady; he would never tire of listening or laughing at those histories.

'Stick to the trumps, however, my lad,' he would say, when I told him of my misfortunes in the conjugal line, and how near I had been winning the greatest fortune in Germany. 'Do anything but marry, my artless Irish rustic' (he called me by a multiplicity of queer names). 'Cultivate your great talents in the gambling line, but mind this, that a woman will beat you.'

That I denied, mentioning several instances in which I had conquered the most intractable tempers among the sex.

'They will beat you in the long run, my Tipperary Alcibiades.* As soon as you are married, take my word of it, you are conquered. Look at me. I married my cousin, the noblest and greatest heiress in England—married her in spite of herself almost' (here a dark shade passed over Sir Charles Lyndon's countenance). 'She is a weak woman. You shall see her, sir, *how* weak she is; but she is my mistress. She has embittered my whole life. She is a fool, but she has got the better of one of the best heads in Christendom. She is enormously rich, but somehow I have never been so poor as since I married her. I thought to better myself, and she has made me miserable and killed me. And she will do as much for my successor when I am gone.'

'Has her ladyship a very large income?' said I. At which Sir Charles burst out into a yelling laugh, and made me blush not a little at my *gaucherie;* for the fact is, seeing him in the condition in which he was, I could not help speculating upon the chance a man of spirit might have with his widow.

'No, no!' said he, laughing. 'Waugh hawk,* Mr. Barry, don't think, if you value your peace of mind, to stand in my shoes when they are vacant. Besides, I don't think my Lady Lyndon would *quite* condescend to marry a ——'

'Marry a what, sir?' said I, in a rage.

'Never mind what; but the man who gets her will rue it, take my word on't. A plague on her! had it not been for my father's ambition and mine (he was her uncle and guardian, and we wouldn't let such a prize out of the family), I might have died peaceably, at least, carried my gout down to my grave in quiet, lived in my modest tenement* in Mayfair, had every house in England open to me, and now, now I have six of my own, and every one of them is a hell to me. Beware of greatness, Mr. Barry. Take warning by me. Ever since I have been married and have been rich, I have been the most miserable wretch in the world. Look at me. I am dying, a worn-out cripple at the age of fifty. Marriage has added forty years to my life. When I took off Lady Lyndon, there was no man of my years who looked so young as myself. Fool that I was! I had enough with my pensions, perfect freedom, the best society in Europe; and I gave up all these, and married, and was miserable. Take a warning by me, Captain Barry, and stick to the trumps.'

Though my intimacy with the knight was considerable, for a long time I never penetrated into any other apartments of his hotel but those which he himself occupied. His lady lived entirely apart from him, and it is only curious how they came to travel together at all. She was a goddaughter of old Mary Wortley Montagu,* and, like that famous old woman of the last century, made considerable pretensions to be a blue-stocking and a *bel esprit.* Lady Lyndon wrote poems in English and Italian, which still may be read by the curious in the pages of the magazines of the day. She entertained a correspondence with several of the European *savants*, upon history, science, and ancient languages, and especially theology. Her pleasure was to dispute controversial points with abbés and bishops, and her flatterers said she rivalled Madame Dacier* in learning. Every adventurer who had a discovery in chemistry, a new antique bust, or a plan for discovering the philosopher's stone, was sure to find a patroness in her. She had numberless works dedicated to her, and sonnets without end addressed to her by all the poetasters of Europe under the name of Lindonira or Calista.* Her rooms were crowded with hideous China magots,* and all sorts of objects of virtu.

No woman piqued herself more upon her principles, or allowed love to be made to her more profusely. There was a habit of courtship practised by the fine gentlemen of those days, which is little understood in our coarse, downright times; and young and old fellows would pour out floods of compliments in letters and madrigals, such as would make a sober lady stare were they addressed to her nowadays, so entirely has the gallantry of the last century disappeared out of our manners.

Lady Lyndon moved about with a little court of her own. She had half a dozen carriages in her progresses. In her own she would travel with her companion (some shabby lady of quality), her birds, and poodles, and the favourite *savant* for the time being. In another would be her female secretary and her waiting-women, who, in spite of their care, never could make their mistress look much better than a slattern. Sir Charles Lyndon had his own chariot, and the domestics of the establishment would follow in other vehicles.

Also must be mentioned the carriage in which rode her ladyship's chaplain, Mr. Runt, who acted in capacity of governor to her son, the little Viscount Bullingdon,—a melancholy, deserted little boy, about whom his father was more than indifferent, and whom his mother never saw, except for two minutes at her levee, when she would put to him a few questions of history or Latin grammar, after which he was consigned to his own amusements, or the care of his governor, for the rest of the day.

The notion of such a Minerva* as this, whom I saw in the

public places now and then, surrounded by swarms of needy abbés and schoolmasters, who flattered her, frightened me for some time, and I had not the least desire to make her acquaintance. I had no desire to be one of the beggarly adorers in the great lady's train,—fellows, half friend, half lackey, who made verses, and wrote letters, and ran errands, content to be paid by a seat in her ladyship's box at the comedy, or a cover at her dinner-table at noon. 'Don't be afraid,' Sir Charles Lyndon would say, whose great subject of conversation and abuse was his lady, 'my Lindonira will have nothing to do with you. She likes the Tuscan brogue, not that of Kerry. She says you smell too much of the stable to be admitted to ladies' society; and, last Sunday fortnight, when she did me the honour to speak to me last, said, "I wonder, Sir Charles Lyndon, a gentleman who has been the King's ambassador can demean himself by gambling and boozing with low Irish blacklegs!" Don't fly in a fury, I'm a cripple, and it was Lindonira said it, not I.'

This piqued me, and I resolved to become acquainted with Lady Lyndon, if it were but to show her ladyship that the descendant of those Barrys, whose property she unjustly held, was not an unworthy companion for any lady, were she ever so high. Besides, my friend the knight was dying, his widow would be the richest prize in the three kingdoms. Why should I not win her, and, with her, the means of making in the world that figure which my genius and inclination desired? I felt I was equal in blood and breeding to any Lyndon in Christendom, and determined to bend this haughty lady. When I determine, I look upon the thing as done.

My uncle and I talked the matter over, and speedily settled upon a method for making our approaches upon this stately lady of Castle Lyndon. Mr. Runt, young Lord Bullingdon's governor, was fond of pleasure, of a glass of Rhenish in the garden-houses in the summer evenings, and of a sly throw of the dice when the occasion offered; and I took care to make friends with this person, who, being a college tutor and an Englishman, was ready to go on his knees to any one who resembled a man of fashion. Seeing me with my retinue of servants, my *vis-à-vis* and chariots, my valets, my hussar, and horses, dressed in gold, and velvet, and sables, saluting the greatest people in

Europe as we met on the course or at the Spas, Runt was dazzled by my advances, and was mine by a beckoning of the finger. I shall never forget the poor wretch's astonishment when I asked him to dine, with two counts, off gold plate, at the little room in the casino; he was made happy by being allowed to win a few pieces of us, became exceedingly tipsy, sang Cambridge songs, and recreated the company by telling us, in his horrid Yorkshire French, stories about the gyps* and all the lords that had ever been in his college. I encouraged him to come and see me oftener and bring with him his little viscount, for whom, though the boy always detested me, I took care to have a good stock of sweetmeats, toys, and picture-books when he came.

I then began to enter into a controversy with Mr. Runt, and confided to him some doubts which I had, and a very, very earnest leaning towards the Church of Rome. I made a certain abbé whom I knew write me letters upon transubstantiation, &c., which the honest tutor was rather puzzled to answer, and I knew that they would be communicated to his lady, as they were; for, asking leave to attend the English service which was celebrated in her apartments, and frequented by the best English then at the Spa, on the second Sunday she condescended to look at me, on the third she was pleased to reply to my profound bow by a curtsy, the next day I followed up the acquaintance by another obeisance in the public walk, and, to make a long story short, her ladyship and I were in full correspondence on transubstantiation before six weeks were over. My lady came to the aid of her chaplain, and then I began to see the prodigious weight of his arguments, as was to be expected. The progress of this harmless little intrigue need not be detailed. I make no doubt every one of my readers has practised similar stratagems when a fair lady was in the case.

I shall never forget the astonishment of Sir Charles Lyndon when, on one summer evening, as he was issuing out to the play-table in his sedan-chair, according to his wont, her ladyship's barouche-and-four, with her outriders in the tawny livery of the Lyndon family, came driving into the courtyard of the house which they inhabited, and in that carriage, by her ladyship's side, sat no other than 'the vulgar Irish adventurer,' as she was pleased to call him, I mean Redmond Barry, Esquire.

He made the most courtly of his bows, and grinned and waved his hat in as graceful a manner as the gout permitted, and her ladyship and I replied to the salutation with the utmost politeness and elegance on our parts.

I could not go to the play-table for some time afterwards, for Lady Lyndon and I had an argument on transubstantiation, which lasted for three hours, in which she was, as usual, victorious, and in which her companion, the Honourable Miss Flint Skinner, fell asleep; but when, at last, I joined Sir Charles at the casino, he received me with a yell of laughter, as his wont was, and introduced me to all the company as Lady Lyndon's interesting young convert. This was his way. He laughed and sneered at everything. He laughed when he was in a paroxysm of pain, he laughed when he won money, or when he lost it; his laugh was not jovial or agreeable, but rather painful and sardonic.

'Gentlemen,' said he to Punter, Colonel Loder, Count du Carreau,* and several jovial fellows with whom he used to discuss a flask of champagne and a Rhenish trout or two after play, 'see this amiable youth! He has been troubled by religious scruples, and has flown for refuge to my chaplain, Mr. Runt, who has asked for advice from my wife, Lady Lyndon; and, between them both, they are confirming my ingenious young friend in his faith. Did you ever hear of such doctors and such a disciple?'

'Faith, sir,' said I, 'if I want to learn good principles it's surely better I should apply for them to your lady and your chaplain than to you!'

'He wants to step into my shoes!' continued the knight.

'The man would be happy who did so,' responded I, 'provided there were no chalk-stones* included!' at which reply Sir Charles was not very well pleased, and went on with increased rancour. He was always free-spoken in his cups, and, to say the truth, he was in his cups many more times in a week than his doctors allowed.

'Is it not a pleasure, gentlemen,' said he, 'for me, as I am drawing near the goal, to find my home such a happy one—my wife so fond of me, that she is even now thinking of appointing a successor? (I don't mean you precisely, Mr. Barry; you are only taking your chance with a score of others whom I could mention.) Isn't it a comfort to see her, like a prudent housewife, getting everything ready for her husband's departure?'

'I hope you are not thinking of leaving us soon, Knight?' said I, with perfect sincerity, for I liked him as a most amusing companion.

'Not so soon, my dear, as you may fancy, perhaps,' continued he. 'Why, man, I have been given over any time these four years, and there was always a candidate or two waiting to apply for the situation. Who knows how long I may keep you waiting?' and he *did* keep me waiting some little time longer than at that period there was any reason to suspect.

As I declared myself pretty openly, according to my usual way, and authors are accustomed to describe the persons of the ladies with whom their heroes fall in love; in compliance with this fashion, I perhaps should say a word or two respecting the charms of my Lady Lyndon. But though I celebrated them in many copies of verses of my own and other persons' writing, and though I filled reams of paper in the passionate style of those days with compliments to every one of her beauties and smiles, in which I compared her to every flower, goddess, or famous heroine ever heard of; truth compels me to say, that there was nothing divine about her at all. She was very well, but no more. Her shape was fine, her hair dark, her eyes good, and exceedingly active; she loved singing, but performed it as so great a lady should, very much out of tune. She had a smattering of half a dozen modern languages, and, as I have said before, of many more sciences than I even knew the name of. She piqued herself on knowing Greek and Latin, but the truth is that Mr. Runt used to supply her with the quotations which she introduced into her voluminous correspondence. She had as much love of admiration, as strong, uneasy a vanity, and as little heart as any woman I ever knew. Otherwise, when her son, Lord Bullingdon, on account of his differences with me, ran—but that matter shall be told in its proper time. Finally, my Lady Lyndon was about a year older than myself, though, of course, she would take her Bible oath that she was three years younger.

Few men are so honest as I am, for few will own to their real motives, and I don't care a button about confessing mine. What Sir Charles Lyndon said was perfectly true. I made the acquaintance with Lady Lyndon with ulterior views. 'Sir,' said I to him, when after the scene described and the jokes he made upon me, we met alone, 'let those laugh that win. You were very pleasant upon me a few nights since, and on my intentions regarding your lady. Well, if they *are* what you think they are;—if I *do* wish to step into your shoes, what then? I have no other intentions than you had yourself. I'll be sworn to muster just as much regard for my Lady Lyndon as you ever showed her; and if I win her and wear her when you're dead and gone, *corbleu*,* Knight, do you think it will be the fear of your ghost will deter me?'

Lyndon laughed as usual, but somewhat disconcertedly; indeed, I had clearly the best of him in the argument, and had just as much right to hunt my fortune as he had.

But one day, he said, 'If you marry such a woman as my Lady Lyndon, mark my words, you will regret it. You will pine after the liberty you once enjoyed. By George! Captain Barry,' he added with a sigh, 'the thing that I regret most in life, perhaps it is because I am old, *blasé*, and dying, is that I never had a virtuous attachment.'

'Ha, ha! a milkmaid's daughter!' said I, laughing at the absurdity.

'Well, why not a milkmaid's daughter? My good fellow, I *was* in love in youth, as most gentlemen are, with my tutor's daughter, Helena, a bouncing girl, of course older than myself' (this made me remember my own little love passages with Nora Brady, in the days of my early life), 'and do you know, sir, I heartily regret I didn't marry her? There's nothing like having a virtuous drudge at home, sir, depend upon that. It gives a zest to one's enjoyments in the world, take my word for it. No man of sense need restrict himself, or deny himself a single amusement for his wife's sake; on the contrary, if he select the animal properly, he will choose such a one as shall be no bar to his pleasure, but a comfort in his hours of annoyance. For instance, I have got the gout: who tends me? A hired valet, who robs me whenever he has the power. My wife never comes near me. What friend have I? None in the wide world. Men of the world, as you and I are, don't make friends, and we are fools for our pains. Get a friend, sir, and that friend a woman—a good household drudge, who loves you. *That* is the most precious sort of friendship, for the expense of it is all on the woman's side. The *man* needn't contribute anything. If he's a rogue, she'll vow he's an angel; if he is a brute, she will like him all the better for his ill-treatment of her. They like it, sir, these women. They are born to be our greatest comforts and conveniences; our—our moral bootjacks, as it were; and, to men in your way of life, believe me such a person would be invaluable. I'm only speaking for your bodily and mental comfort's sake, mind. Why didn't I marry poor Helena Flower, the curate's daughter?'

I thought these speeches the remarks of a weakly, disappointed man, although since, perhaps, I have had reason to find the truth of Sir Charles Lyndon's statements. The fact is, in my opinion, that we often buy money very much too dear. To purchase a few thousands a year at the expense of an odious wife, is very bad economy for a young fellow of any talent and spirit; and there have been moments of my life when, in the midst of my greatest splendour and opulence, with half a dozen lords at my levee, with the finest horses in my stables, the grandest house over my head, with unlimited credit at my banker's, and—Lady Lyndon to boot, I have wished myself back a private of Bülow's or anything so as to get rid of her. To return, however, to the story. Sir Charles, with his complication of ills, was dying before us by inches; and I've no doubt it could not have been very pleasant to him to see a young handsome fellow paying court to his widow before his own face, as it were. After I once got into the house on the transubstantiation dispute, I found a dozen more occasions to improve my intimacy, and was scarcely ever out of her ladyship's doors. The world talked and blustered, but what cared I? The men cried fie upon the shameless Irish adventurer, but I have told my way of silencing such envious people; and my sword had by this time got such a reputation through Europe that few people cared to encounter it. If I can once get my hold of a place, I keep it. Many's the house I have been to where I have seen the men avoid me. 'Faugh! the low Irishman,' they would say. 'Bah! the coarse adventurer!' 'Out on the insufferable blackleg and puppy!' and so forth. This hatred has been of no inconsiderable service to me in the world; for when I fasten on a man, nothing can induce me to release my hold: and I am left to myself, which is all the better. As I told Lady Lyndon in those days with perfect sincerity, 'Calista' (I used to call her Calista in my correspondence)—'Calista, I swear to thee, by the spotlessness of thy own soul, by the brilliancy of thy immitigable eyes, by everything pure and chaste in heaven and in thy own heart, that I will never cease from following thee! Scorn I can bear, and have borne at thy hands. Indifference I can surmount; 'tis a rock which my energy will climb over, a magnet which attracts the dauntless iron of my soul!' and it was true, I wouldn't have left her—no, though they had kicked me downstairs every day I presented myself at her door.

That is my way of fascinating women. Let the man who has to make his fortune in life remember this maxim. *Attacking* is his only secret. Dare, and the world always yields; or, if it beat you sometimes, dare again, and it will succumb. In those days my spirit was so great that if I had set my heart upon marrying a princess of the blood, I would have had her!

I told Calista my story, and altered very, very little of the truth. My object was to frighten her, to show her that what I wanted that I dared, that what I dared that I won; and there were striking passages enough in my history to convince her of my iron will and indomitable courage. 'Never hope to escape me, madam,' I would say: 'offer to marry another man, and he dies upon this sword, which never yet met its master. Fly from me, and I will follow you, though it were to the gates of Hades.' I promise you this was very different language to that she had been in the habit of hearing from her Jemmy-Jessamy* adorers. You should have seen how I scared the fellows from her!

When I said in this energetic way that I would follow Lady Lyndon across the Styx if necessary, of course I meant that I would do so provided nothing more suitable presented itself in the interim. If Lyndon would not die, where was the use of my pursuing the countess? And somehow, towards the end of the Spa season, very much to my mortification I do confess, the knight made another rally: it seemed as if nothing would kill him. 'I am sorry for you, Captain Barry,' he would say, laughing as usual. 'I'm grieved to keep you, or any gentleman, waiting. Had you not better arrange with my doctor, or get the cook to flavour my omelet with arsenic? What are the odds, gentlemen,' he would add, 'that I don't live to see Captain Barry hanged yet?'

In fact the doctors tinkered him up for a year. 'It's my usual luck,' I could not help saying to my uncle, who was my confidential and most excellent adviser in all matters of the heart; 'I've been wasting the treasures of my affections upon that flirt of a countess, and here's her husband restored to health and likely to live I don't know how many years!' And as if to add to my mortification, there came just at this period to Spa, an English tallow-chandler's heiress, with a plum to her fortune, and Madame Cornu, the widow of a Norman cattle-dealer and farmer-general,* with a dropsy and two hundred thousand livres a year.

'What's the use of my following the Lyndons to England,' says I, 'if the knight won't die?'

'Don't follow them, my dear simple child,' replied my uncle. 'Stop here and pay court to the new arrivals.'

'Yes, and lose Calista for ever, and the greatest estate in all England.'

'Pooh, pooh! youths like you easily fire and easily despond. Keep up a correspondence with Lady Lyndon. You know there's nothing she likes so much. There's the Irish abbé, who will write you the most charming letters for a crown apiece. Let her go, write to her, and meanwhile look out for anything else which may turn up. Who knows? you might marry the Norman widow, bury her, take her money, and be ready for the countess against the knight's death.'

And so with vows of the most profound respectful attachment, and having given twenty louis to Lady Lyndon's waiting-woman for a lock of her hair (of which fact, of course, the woman informed her mistress), I took leave of the countess when it became necessary for her return to her estates in England, swearing I would follow her as soon as an affair of honour I had in my hands could be brought to an end.

I shall pass over the events of the year that ensued before I again saw her. She wrote to me according to promise, with much regularity at first, with somewhat less frequency afterwards. My affairs, meanwhile, at the play-table went on not unprosperously, and I was just on the point of marrying the widow Cornu (we were at Brussels by this time, and the poor soul was madly in love with me) when the

*London Gazette** was put into my hands, and I read the following announcement :—

Died at Castle Lyndon, in the kingdom of Ireland, the Right Honourable Sir Charles Lyndon, Knight of the Bath, Member of Parliament for Lyndon in Devonshire, and many years his Majesty's representative at various European courts. He hath left behind him a name which is endeared to all his friends for his manifold virtues and talents, a reputation justly acquired in the service of his Majesty, and an inconsolable widow to deplore his loss. Her ladyship, the bereaved Countess of Lyndon, was at the Bath when the horrid intelligence reached her of her husband's demise, and hastened to Ireland immediately in order to pay her last sad duties to his beloved remains.

That very night I ordered my chariot and posted to Ostend, whence I freighted a vessel to Dover, and travelling rapidly into the West, reached Bristol, from which port I embarked for Waterford, and found myself, after an absence of eleven years, in my native country.

CHAPTER XIV

I RETURN TO IRELAND, AND EXHIBIT MY SPLENDOUR AND GENEROSITY IN THAT KINGDOM

How were times changed with me now! I had left my country a poor penniless boy—a private soldier in a miserable marching regiment. I returned an accomplished man, with property to the amount of five thousand guineas in my possession, with a splendid wardrobe and jewel-case worth two thousand more, having mingled in all the scenes of life a not undistinguished actor in them, having shared in war and in love, having by my own genius and energy won my way from poverty and obscurity to competence and splendour. As I looked out from my chariot windows as it rolled along over the bleak, bare roads, by the miserable cabins of the peasantry, who came out in their rags to stare as the splendid equipage passed, and huzzaed for his lordship's honour as they saw the magnificent stranger in the superb gilded vehicle, my huge body-servant Fritz lolling behind with curling moustaches and long queue, his green livery barred with silver lace, I could not help thinking of myself with considerable complacency, and thanking my stars that had endowed me with so many good qualities. But for my own merits I should have been a raw Irish squireen, such as those I saw swaggering about the wretched towns through which my chariot passed on its road to Dublin. I might have married Nora Brady (and though, thank Heaven, I did not, I have never thought of that girl but with kindness, and even remember the bitterness of losing her more clearly at this moment than any other incident of my life), I might have been the father of ten children by this time, or a farmer on my own account, or an agent to a squire, or a gauger, or an attorney, and here I was one of the most famous gentlemen of Europe! I bade my fellow get a bag of copper money and throw it among the crowd as we changed horses, and I warrant me there was as much shouting set up in praise of my honour as if my Lord Townsend,* the Lord Lieutenant himself, had been passing.

My second day's journey, for the Irish roads were rough in those days, and the progress of a gentleman's chariot terribly slow, brought me to Carlow, where I put up at the very inn which I had used eleven years back when flying from home after the supposed murder of Quin in the duel. How well I remember every moment of the scene! The old landlord was gone who had served me; the inn that I then thought so comfortable looked wretched and dismantled, but the claret was as good as in the old days, and I had the host to partake of a jug of it and hear the news of the country.

He was as communicative as hosts usually are; the crops and the markets, the price of beasts at last Castledermot fair, the last story about the vicar, and the last joke of Father Hogan the priest; how the Whiteboys* had burned Squire Scanlan's ricks, and the highwaymen had been beaten off in their attack upon Sir Thomas's house; who was to hunt the Kilkenny hounds next season, and the wonderful run entirely they had last March; what troops were in the town, and how Miss Biddy Toole had run off with Ensign Mullins; all the news of sport, assize, and quarter-sessions were detailed by this worthy chronicler of small-beer, who wondered that my honour hadn't heard of them in England or in foreign parts, where he seemed to think the world was as interested as he was about the doings of Kilkenny and Carlow. I listened to these tales with, I own, a considerable pleasure, for every now and then a name would come up in the conversation which I remembered in old days, and bring with it a hundred associations connected with them.

I had received many letters from my mother, which informed me of the doings of the Brady's Town family. My uncle was dead, and Mick, his eldest son, had followed him too to the grave. The Brady girls had separated from their paternal roof as soon as their elder brother came to rule over it. Some were married, some gone to settle with their odious old mother in out-of-the-way watering-places. Ulick, though he had succeeded to the estate, had come in for a bankrupt property, and Castle Brady was now inhabited only by the bats and owls and the old game-keeper. My mother, Mrs. Harry Barry, had gone to live at Bray, to sit under Mr. Jowls, her favourite preacher, who had a chapel there; and, finally, the landlord told me that Mrs. Barry's son had gone to foreign parts, enlisted in the Prussian service, and had been shot there as a deserter.

I don't care to own that I hired a stout nag from the landlord's stable after dinner, and rode back at nightfall, twenty miles to my old home. My heart beat to see it. Barryville had got a pestle and mortar over the door, and was called 'The Esculapian Repository,' by Doctor Mac-shane; a red-headed lad was spreading a plaster in the old parlour; the little window of my room, once so neat and bright, was cracked in many places, and stuffed with rags here and there; the flowers had disappeared from the trim garden-beds which my good orderly mother tended. In the churchyard there were two more names put into the stone over the family vault of the Bradys; they were those of my cousin, for whom my regard was small, and my uncle, whom I had always loved. I asked my old companion the blacksmith, who had beaten me so often in old days, to give my horse a feed and a litter: he was a worn, weary-looking man now, with a dozen dirty, ragged children paddling about his smithy, and had no recollection of the fine gentleman who stood before him. I did not seek to recall myself to his memory till the next day, when I put ten guineas into his hand, and bade him drink the health of English Redmond.

As for Castle Brady, the gates of the park were still there, but the old trees were cut down in the avenue, a black stump jutting out here and there, and casting long shadows as I passed in the moonlight over the worn, grass-grown old road. A few cows were at pasture there. The garden-gate was gone, and the place a tangled wilderness. I sat down on the old bench, where I had sat on the day when Nora jilted me; and I do believe my feelings were as strong then as they had been when I was a boy, eleven years before; and I caught myself almost crying again, to think that Nora Brady had deserted me. I believe a man forgets nothing. I've seen a flower, or heard some trivial word or two, which have awakened recollections that somehow had lain dormant for scores of years; and when I entered the house in Clarges Street where I was born (it was used as a gambling-house when I first visited London), all of a sudden the memory of my childhood came back to me—of my actual infancy; I recollected my father in green and gold, holding me up to look at a gilt coach which stood at the door, and my mother in a flowered sack,* with patches on her face. Some day, I wonder, will everything we have seen and thought and done come and flash across our minds in this way? I had rather not. I felt so as I sat upon the bench at Castle Brady, and thought of the bygone times.

The hall-door was open—it was always so at that house; the moon was flaring in at the long old windows, and throwing ghastly chequers upon the floors; and the stars were looking in on the other side, in the blue of the yawning window over the great stair; from it you could see the old stable-clock, with the letters glistening on it still. There had been jolly horses in those stables once; and I could see my uncle's honest face, and hear him talking to his dogs as they came jumping and whining and barking round about him of a gay winter morning. We used to mount there; and the girls looked out at us from the hall-window, where I stood and looked at the sad, mouldy, lonely old place. There was a red light shining through the crevices of a door at one corner of the building, and a dog presently came out baying loudly, and a limping man followed with a fowling-piece.

'Who's there?' said the old man.

'PHIL PURCELL, don't you know me?' shouted I; 'it's Redmond Barry.'

I thought the old man would have fired his piece at me

at first, for he pointed it at the window; but I called to him to hold his hand, and came down and embraced him. . . . Psha! I don't care to tell the rest: Phil and I had a long night, and talked over a thousand foolish old things that have no interest for any soul alive now; for what soul is there alive that cares for Barry Lyndon?

I settled a hundred guineas on the old man when I got to Dublin, and made him an annuity which enabled him to pass his old days in comfort.

Poor Phil Purcell was amusing himself at a game of exceedingly dirty cards with an old acquaintance of mine, no other than Tim, who was called my 'valet' in the days of yore, and whom the reader may remember as clad in my father's old liveries. They used to hang about him in those times, and lap over his wrists and down to his heels; but Tim, though he protested he had nigh killed himself with grief when I went away, had managed to grow enormously fat in my absence, and would have fitted almost into Daniel Lambert's coat,* or that of the vicar of Castle Brady, whom he served in the capacity of clerk. I would have engaged the fellow in my service but for his monstrous size, which rendered him quite unfit to be the attendant of any gentleman of condition; and so I presented him with a handsome gratuity, and promised to stand godfather to his next child, the eleventh since my absence. There is no country in the world where the work of multiplying is carried on so prosperously as in my native island. Mr. Tim had married the girls' waiting-maid, who had been a kind friend of mine in the early times; and I had to go salute poor Molly next day, and found her a slatternly wench in a mud hut, surrounded by a brood of children almost as ragged as those of my friend the blacksmith.

From Tim and Phil Purcell, thus met fortuitously together, I got the very last news respecting my family. My mother was well.

'Faith, sir,' says Tim, 'and you're come in time mayhap from preventing an addition to your family.'

'Sir!' exclaimed I, in a fit of indignation.

'In the shape of father-in-law, I *mane*, sir,' says Tim: 'the misthress is going to take on with Mister Jowls the *praacher*.'

Poor Nora, he added, had made many additions to the illustrious race of Quin; and my cousin Ulick was in Dublin, coming to little good, both my informants feared, and having managed to run through the small available remains of property which my good old uncle had left behind him.

I saw I should have no small family to provide for; and then, to conclude the evening, Phil, Tim, and I had a bottle of usquebaugh, the taste of which I had remembered for eleven good years, and did not part except with the warmest terms of fellowship, and until the sun had been some time in the sky. I am exceedingly affable: that has always been one of my characteristics. I have no false pride, as many men of high lineage like my own have, and, in default of better company, will hob and nob with a ploughboy or a private soldier just as readily as with the first noble in the land.

I went back to the village in the morning, and found a pretext for visiting Barryville under a device of purchasing drugs. The hooks were still in the wall where my silver-hilted sword used to hang; a blister* was lying on the window-sill, where my mother's *Whole Duty of Man** had its place; and the odious Doctor Macshane had found out who I was (my countrymen find out everything, and a great deal more besides), and sniggering, asked me how I left the King of Prussia, and whether my friend the Emperor Joseph* was as much liked as the Empress Maria Theresa had been. The bell-ringers would have had a ring of bells for me, but there was but one, Tim, who was too fat to pull, and I rode off before the vicar, Doctor Bolter (who had succeeded old Mr. Texter, who had the living in my time), had time to come out to compliment me; but the rapscallions of the beggarly village had assembled in a dirty army to welcome me, and cheered 'Hurrah for Masther Redmond!' as I rode away.

My people were not a little anxious regarding me by the time I returned to Carlow, and the landlord was very much afraid, he said, that the highwaymen had gotten hold of me. There, too, my name and station had been learned from my servant Fritz, who had not spared his praises of his master, and had invented some magnificent histories concerning me. He said it was the truth that I was intimate with half the sovereigns of Europe, and the prime favourite with most of them. Indeed I had made my uncle's Order of the Spur hereditary, and travelled under the name of the Chevalier Barry, chamberlain to the Duke of Hohenzollern-Sigmaringen.*

They gave me the best horses the stable possessed to carry me on my road to Dublin, and the strongest ropes for harness; and we got on pretty well, and there was no rencontre between the highwaymen and the pistols with which Fritz and I were provided. We lay that night at Kilcullen, and the next day I made my entry into the city of Dublin, with four horses to my carriage, five thousand guineas in my purse, and one of the most brilliant reputations in Europe, having quitted the city a beggarly boy, eleven years before.

The citizens of Dublin have as great and laudable a desire for knowing their neighbours' concerns as the country people have; and it is impossible for a gentleman, however modest his desires may be (and such mine have notoriously been through life), to enter the capital without having his name printed in every newspaper in town and mentioned in a number of societies. My name and titles were all over the town the day after my arrival. A great number of polite persons did me the honour to call at my lodgings, when I selected them; and this was a point very necessary of immediate care, for the hotels in the town were but vulgar holes, unfit for a nobleman of my fashion and elegance. I had been informed of the fact by travellers on the Continent; and determining to fix on a lodging at once, I bade the drivers go slowly up and down the streets with my chariot, until I had selected a place suitable to my rank. This proceeding, and the uncouth questions and behaviour of my German Fritz, who was instructed to make inquiries at the different houses until convenient apartments could be lighted upon, brought an immense mob round my coach; and by the time the rooms were chosen you might have supposed I was the new general of the forces, so great was the multitude following us.

I fixed at length upon a handsome suite of apartments in Capel Street, paid the ragged postilions who had driven me a splendid gratuity, and establishing myself in the rooms with my baggage and Fritz, desired the landlord to engage me a second fellow to wear my liveries, a couple of stout reputable chairmen and their machine, and a coachman who had handsome job-horses to hire for my chariot, and serviceable riding horses to sell. I gave him a handsome sum in advance; and I promise you the effect of my advertisement was such that next day I had a regular levee in my antechamber; grooms, valets, and maîtres d'hôtel offered themselves without number; I had proposals for the purchase of horses sufficient to mount a regiment, both from dealers and gentlemen of the first fashion. Sir Lawler Gawler came to propose to me the most elegant bay mare ever stepped; my Lord Dundoodle had a team of four that wouldn't disgrace my friend the Emperor; and the Marquis of Ballyragget sent his gentleman and his compliments, stating that if I would step up to his stables, or do him the honour of breakfasting with him previously, he would show me the two finest greys in Europe. I determined to accept the invitations of Dundoodle and Ballyragget, but to purchase my horses from the dealers. It is always the best way. Besides, in those days, in Ireland, if a gentleman warranted his horse, and it was not sound, or a dispute arose, the remedy you had was the offer of a bullet in your waistcoat. I had played at the bullet game too much in earnest to make use of it heedlessly: and I may say, proudly for myself, that I never engaged in a duel unless I had a real, available, and prudent reason for it.

There was a simplicity about this Irish gentry which amused and made me wonder. If they tell more fibs than their downright neighbours across the water, on the other hand they believe more; and I made myself in a single week such a reputation in Dublin as would take a man ten years and a mint of money to acquire in London. I had won five hundred thousand pounds at play; I was the favourite of the Empress Catherine of Russia; the confidential agent of Frederick of Prussia; it was I won the battle of Hochkirchen;* I was the cousin of Madame du Barry, the French king's favourite, and a thousand things beside. Indeed, to tell the truth, I hinted a number of these stories to my kind friends Ballyragget and Gawler, when they were not slow to improve the hints I gave them.

After having witnessed the splendours of civilized life abroad, the sight of Dublin in the year 1771, when I returned thither, struck me with anything but respect. It was as savage as Warsaw almost, without the regal grandeur of the latter city. The people looked more ragged than any race I have ever seen, except the gipsy hordes along the banks of the Danube. There was, as I have said, not an inn in the town fit for a gentleman of condition to dwell in. Those luckless fellows who could not keep carriage, and walked the streets at night, ran imminent risks of the knives of the women and ruffians who lay in wait there,—of a set of ragged, savage villains who neither knew the use of shoe nor razor; and as a gentleman entered his chair or his chariot, to be carried to his evening rout, or the play, the flambeaux of the footmen would light up such a set of wild, gibbering, Milesian* faces as would frighten a genteel person of average nerves. I was luckily endowed with strong ones; besides, had seen my amiable countrymen before.

I know this description of them will excite anger among some Irish patriots, who don't like to have the nakedness of our land abused, and are angry if the whole truth be told concerning it. But, bah! it was a poor provincial place, Dublin, in the old days of which I speak, and many a tenth-rate German residence is more genteel. There were, it is true, near three hundred resident peers at the period; and a House of Commons; and my Lord Mayor and his corporation; and a roystering, noisy university, whereof the students made no small disturbances nightly, patronized the roundhouse,* ducked obnoxious printers and tradesmen, and gave the law at the Crow Street Theatre.* But I had seen too much of the first society of Europe to be much tempted by the society of these noisy gentry, and was a little too much of a gentleman to mingle with the disputes and politics of my Lord Mayor and his aldermen. In the House of Commons there were some dozen of right pleasant fellows. I never heard in the English Parliament better speeches than from Flood and Daly, of Galway.* Dick Sheridan,* though not a well-bred person, was as amusing and ingenious a table-companion as ever I met; and, though during Mr. Edmund Burke's* interminable speeches in the English House I used always to go to sleep, I yet have heard from well-informed parties that Mr. Burke was a person of considerable abilities, and even reputed to be eloquent in his more favourable moments.

I soon began to enjoy to the full extent the pleasures that the wretched place affords, and which were within a gentleman's reach: Ranelagh* and the ridotto; Mr. Mossop,* at Crow Street; my Lord Lieutenant's parties, where there was a great deal too much boozing, and too little play, to suit a person of my elegant and refined habits; Daly's Coffee-house,* and the houses of the nobility, were soon open to me; and I remarked with astonishment in the higher circles, what I had experienced in the lower on my first unhappy visit to Dublin, an extraordinary want of money, and a preposterous deal of promissory notes flying about, for which I was quite unwilling to stake my guineas. The ladies, too, were mad for play, but exceeding unwilling to pay when they lost. Thus, when the old Countess of Trumpington lost ten pieces to me at quadrille, she gave me, instead of the money, her ladyship's note of hand on her agent in Galway; which I put, with a great deal of politeness, into the candle. But when the Countess made me a second proposition to play, I said, that as soon as her ladyship's remittances were arrived, I would be the readiest person to meet her; but till then was her very humble servant. And I maintained this resolution and singular character throughout the Dublin society: giving out at Daly's that I was ready to play any man, for any sum, at any game; or to fence with him, or to ride with him (regard being had to our weight), or to shoot flying, or at a mark; and in this latter accomplishment, especially if the mark be a live one, Irish gentlemen of that day had no ordinary skill.

Of course, I dispatched a courier in my liveries to Castle Lyndon with a private letter for Runt, demanding from him full particulars of the Countess of Lyndon's state of health and mind; and a touching and eloquent letter to her ladyship, in which I bade her remember ancient days, which I tied up with a single hair from the lock which I had purchased from her woman, and in which I told her that Sylvander remembered his oath, and could never forget his Calista. The answer I received from her was exceedingly unsatisfactory and inexplicit; that from Mr. Runt explicit enough, but not at all pleasant in its contents. My Lord George Poynings, the Marquess of Tiptoff's younger son, was paying very marked addresses to the widow, being a kinsman of the family, and having been called to Ireland relative to the will of the deceased Sir Charles Lyndon.

Now, there was a sort of rough-and-ready law in Ireland in those days which was of great convenience to persons desirous of expeditious justice, and of which the newspapers of the time contain a hundred proofs. Fellows with the nicknames of Captain Fireball, Lieutenant Buffcoat, and Ensign Steele were repeatedly sending warning letters to landlords, and murdering them if the notes were unattended to. The celebrated Captain Thunder* ruled in the southern counties, and his business seemed to be to procure wives for gentlemen who had not sufficient means to please the parents of the young ladies, or, perhaps, had not time for a long and intricate courtship.

I had found my cousin Ulick at Dublin, grown very fat, and very poor; hunted up by Jews and creditors; dwelling in all sorts of queer corners, from which he issued at nightfall to the Castle, or to his card-party at his tavern; but he was always the courageous fellow: and I hinted to him the state of my affections regarding Lady Lyndon.

'The Countess of Lyndon!' said poor Ulick; 'well, that *is* a wonder. I myself have been mightily sweet upon a young lady, one of the Kiljoys of Ballyhack, who has ten thousand pounds to her fortune, and to whom her ladyship is guardian; but how is a poor fellow without a coat to his back to get on with an heiress in such company as that? I might as well propose for the Countess myself.'

'You had better not,' said I, laughing; 'the man who tries runs a chance of going out of the world first.' And I explained to him my own intention regarding Lady Lyndon; and honest Ulick, whose respect for me was prodigious when he saw how splendid my appearance was, and heard how wonderful my adventures and great my experience of fashionable life had been, was lost in admiration of my daring and energy, when I confided to him my intention of marrying the greatest heiress in England.

I bade Ulick go out of town on any pretext he chose, and put a letter into a post-office near Castle Lyndon, which I prepared in a feigned hand, and in which I gave a solemn warning to Lord George Poynings to quit the country, saying that the great prize was never meant for the likes of him; and that there were heiresses enough in England, without coming to rob them out of the domains of Captain Fireball. The letter was written on a dirty piece of paper, in the worst of spelling; it came to my lord by the post-conveyance, and, being a high-spirited young man, he, of course, laughed at it.

As ill luck would have it for him, he appeared in Dublin a very short time afterwards; was introduced to the Chevalier Redmond Barry, at the Lord Lieutenant's table; adjourned with him and several other gentlemen to the club at Daly's, and there, in a dispute about the pedigree of a horse, in which everybody said I was in the right, words arose, and a meeting was the consequence. I had had no affair in Dublin since my arrival, and people were anxious to see whether I was equal to my reputation. I make no boast about these matters, but always do them when the time comes; and poor Lord George, who had a neat hand and a quick eye enough, but was bred in the clumsy English school, only stood before my point until I had determined where I should hit him.

My sword went in under his guard, and came out at his back. When he fell, he good-naturedly extended his hand to me, and said, '*Mr. Barry, I was wrong!*' I felt not very well at ease when the poor fellow made this confession, for the dispute had been of my making, and, to tell the truth, I had never intended it should end in any other way than a meeting.

He lay on his bed for four months with the effects of that wound; and the same post which conveyed to Lady Lyndon the news of the duel, carried her a message from Captain Fireball to say, 'This is NUMBER ONE!'

'You, Ulick,' said I, 'shall be *number two.*'

'Faith,' said my cousin, 'one's enough!' but I had my plan regarding him, and determined at once to benefit this honest fellow, and to forward my own designs upon the widow.

CHAPTER XV

I PAY COURT TO MY LADY LYNDON

As my uncle's attainder was not reversed for being out with the Pretender, in 1745, it would have been inconvenient for him to accompany his nephew to the land of our ancestors, where, if not hanging, at least a tedious process of imprisonment, and a doubtful pardon, would have awaited the good old gentleman. In any important crisis of my life, his advice was always of importance to me, and I did not fail to seek it at this juncture, and to implore his counsel as regarded my pursuit of the widow ; I told him the situation of her heart, as I have described it in the last chapter, of the progress that young Poynings had made in her affections, and of her forgetfulness of her old admirer, and I got a letter, in reply, full of excellent suggestions, by which I did not fail to profit.

The kind chevalier prefaced it by saying that he was for the present boarding in the Minorite convent at Brussels, that he had thoughts of making his *salut** there, and retiring for ever from the world, devoting himself to the severest practices of religion. Meanwhile he wrote with regard to the lovely widow. It was natural that a person of her vast wealth and not disagreeable person should have many adorers about her ; and that, as in her husband's lifetime, she had shown herself not at all disinclined to receive my addresses, I must make no manner of doubt I was not the first person whom she had so favoured, nor was I likely to be the last.

'I would, my dear child,' he added, 'that the ugly attainder round my neck, and the resolution I have formed of retiring from a world of sin and vanity altogether, did not prevent me from coming personally to your aid in this delicate crisis of your affairs ; for, to lead them to a good end, it requires not only the indomitable courage, swagger, and audacity, which you possess beyond any young man I have ever known' (as for the 'swagger,' as the chevalier calls it, I deny it *in toto*, being always most modest in my demeanour), 'but though you have the vigour to execute, you have not the ingenuity to suggest plans of conduct for the following out of a scheme that is likely to be long and difficult of execution. Would you have ever thought of the brilliant scheme of the Countess Ida, which so nearly made you the greatest fortune in Europe, but for the advice and experience of a poor old man, now making up his accounts with the world, and about to retire from it for good and all ?

'Well, with regard to the Countess of Lyndon, your manner of winning her is quite *en l'air* at present to me, nor can I advise day by day as I would I could, according to circumstances as they arise. But your general scheme should be this. If I remember the letters you used to have from her during the period of the correspondence which the silly woman entertained you with, much high-flown sentiment passed between you, and especially was written by her ladyship herself; she is a blue-stocking, and fond of writing; she used to make her griefs with her husband the continual theme of her correspondence (as women will do). I recollect several passages in her letters bitterly deploring her fate in being united to one so unworthy of her.

'Surely, in the mass of billets you possess from her, there must be enough to compromise her. Look them well over, select passages, and threaten to do so. Write to her at first in the undoubting tone of a lover who has every claim upon her. Then, if she is silent, remonstrate, alluding to former promises from her, producing proofs of her former regard for you, vowing despair, destruction, revenge, if she prove unfaithful. Frighten her—astonish her by some daring feat, which will let her see your indomitable resolution; you are the man to do it. Your sword has a reputation in Europe, and you have a character for boldness, which was the first thing that caused my Lady Lyndon to turn her eyes upon you. Make the people talk about you at Dublin. Be as splendid, and as brave, and as odd as possible. How I wish I were near you! You have no imagination to invent such a character as I would make for you—but why speak; have I not enough of the world and its vanities ?'

There was much practical good sense in this advice, which I quote, unaccompanied with the lengthened description of his mortifications and devotions which my uncle indulged in, finishing his letter, as usual, with earnest prayers for my conversion to the true faith. But he was constant to his form of worship ; and I, as a man of honour and principle, was resolute to mine, and have no doubt that the one, in this respect, will be as acceptable as the other.

Under these directions it was, then, I wrote to Lady Lyndon, to ask on my arrival when the most respectful of her admirers might be permitted to intrude upon her grief ? Then, as her ladyship was silent, I demanded, had she forgotten old times, and one whom she had favoured with her intimacy at a very happy period ? Had Calista forgotten Eugenio ? At the same time I sent down by my servant with this letter a present of a little sword for Lord Bullingdon, and a private note to his governor, whose note of hand, by the way, I possessed for a sum—I forget what—but such as the poor fellow would have been very unwilling to pay. To this an answer came from her ladyship's amanuensis, stating that Lady Lyndon was too much disturbed by grief at her recent dreadful calamity to see any one but her own relations ; and advices from my friend, the boy's governor, stating that my Lord George Poynings was the young kinsman who was about to console her.

This caused the quarrel between me and the young nobleman, whom I took care to challenge on his first arrival at Dublin.

When the news of the duel was brought to the widow at Castle Lyndon, my informant wrote me that Lady Lyndon shrieked and flung down the journal, and said, 'The horrible monster ! He would not shrink from murder, I believe' ; and little Lord Bullingdon, drawing his sword—the sword I had given him, the rascal !—declared he would kill with it the man who had hurt cousin George. On Mr. Runt telling him that I was the donor of the weapon, the little rogue still vowed that he would kill me all the same ! Indeed, in spite of my kindness to him, that boy always seemed to detest me.

Her ladyship sent up daily couriers to inquire after the health of Lord George ; and, thinking to myself that she would probably be induced to come to Dublin if she were to hear that he was in danger, I managed to have her informed that he was in a precarious state, that he grew worse, that Redmond Barry had fled in consequence; of this flight I caused the *Mercury** newspaper to give notice also, but indeed it did not carry me beyond the town of Bray, where my poor mother dwelt, and where, under the difficulties of a duel, I might be sure of having a welcome.

Those readers who have the sentiment of filial duty strong in their mind will wonder that I have not yet described my interview with that kind mother whose sacrifices for me in youth had been so considerable, and for whom a man of my warm and affectionate nature could not but feel the most enduring and sincere regard.

But a man, moving in the exalted sphere of society in which I now stood, has his public duties to perform before he consults his private affections: and so upon my first arrival I dispatched a messenger to Mrs. Barry, stating my arrival, conveying to her my sentiments of respect and duty, and promising to pay them to her personally so soon as my business in Dublin would leave me free.

This, I need not say, was very considerable. I had my horses to buy, my establishment to arrange, my *entrée* into the genteel world to make; and, having announced my intention to purchase horses, and live in a genteel style, was in a couple of days so pestered by visits of the nobility and gentry, and so hampered by invitations to dinners and suppers, that it became exceedingly difficult for me during some days to manage my anxiously desired visit to Mrs. Barry.

It appears that the good soul provided an entertainment as soon as she heard of my arrival, and invited all her humble acquaintances of Bray to be present; but I was engaged subsequently to my Lord Ballyragget on the day appointed, and was, of course, obliged to break the promise that I had made to Mrs. Barry to attend her humble festival.

I endeavoured to sweeten the disappointment by sending my mother a handsome satin sack and velvet robe, which I purchased for her at the best mercer's in Dublin (and indeed told her I had brought from Paris expressly for her); but the messenger whom I dispatched with the presents brought back the parcels, with the piece of satin torn half way up the middle: and I did not need his descriptions to be aware that something had offended the good lady, who came out, he said, and abused him at the door, and would have boxed his ears, but that she was restrained by a gentleman in black, who I concluded with justice was her clerical friend Mr. Jowls.

This reception of my presents made me rather dread than hope for an interview with Mrs. Barry, and delayed my visit to her for some days further. I wrote her a dutiful and soothing letter, to which there was no answer returned, although I mentioned that on my way to the capital I had been at Barryville, and revisited the old haunts of my youth.

I don't care to own that she is the only human being whom I am afraid to face. I can recollect her fits of anger as a child, and the reconciliations, which used to be still more violent and painful; and so, instead of going myself, I sent my factotum, Ulick Brady, to her, who rode back, saying that he had met with a reception he would not again undergo for twenty guineas; that he had been dismissed the house, with strict injunctions to inform me that my mother disowned me for ever. This parental anathema, as it were, affected me much, for I was always the most dutiful of sons, and I determined to go as soon as possible, and brave what I knew must be an inevitable scene of reproach and anger, for the sake, as I hoped, of as certain a reconciliation.

I had been giving one night an entertainment to some of the genteelest company in Dublin, and was showing my Lord Marquis downstairs with a pair of wax tapers, when I found a woman in a grey coat seated at my doorsteps, to whom, taking her for a beggar, I tendered a piece of money, and whom my noble friends, who were rather hot with wine, began to joke as my door closed, and I bade them all good night.

I was rather surprised and affected to find afterwards that the hooded woman was no other than my mother, whose pride had made her vow that she would not enter my doors, but whose natural maternal yearnings had made her long to see her son's face once again, and who had thus planted herself in disguise at my gate. Indeed, I have found in my experience that these are the only women who never deceive a man, and whose affection remains constant through all trials. Think of the hours that the kind soul must have passed, lonely in the street, listening to the din and merriment within my apartments, the clinking of the glasses, the laughing, the choruses, and the cheering.

When my affair with Lord George happened, and it became necessary to me, for the reasons I have stated, to be out of the way, now, thought I, is the time to make my peace with my good mother: she will never refuse me an asylum now that I seem in distress; and so sending to her a notice that I was coming, that I had had a duel which had brought me into trouble, and required I should go into hiding, I followed my messenger half an hour afterwards, and, I warrant me, there was no want of a good reception, for presently, being introduced into an empty room by the barefooted maid who waited upon Mrs. Barry, the door was opened, and the poor mother flung herself into my arms with a scream, and with transports of joy which I shall not attempt to describe—they are but to be comprehended by women who hold in their arms an only child after a twelve years' absence from him.

The Reverend Mr. Jowls, my mother's director, was the only person to whom the door of her habitation was opened during my sojourn, and he would take no denial. He mixed for himself a glass of rum-punch, which he seemed in the habit of drinking at my good mother's charge, groaned aloud, and forthwith began reading me a lecture upon the sinfulness of my past courses, and especially of the last horrible action I had been committing.

'Sinful,' said my mother, bristling up when her son was attacked, 'sure we're all sinners; and it's you, Mr. Jowls, who have given me the inexpressible blessing to let me know *that.* But how else would you have had the poor child behave?'

'I would have had the gentleman avoid the drink, and the quarrel, and this wicked duel altogether,' answered the clergyman.

But my mother cut him short, by saying such sort of conduct might be very well in a person of his cloth and his birth, but it neither became a Brady nor a Barry. In fact, she was quite delighted with the thought that I had pinked an English marquis's son in a duel; and so, to console her, I told her of a score more in which I had been engaged, and of some of which I have already informed the reader.

As my late antagonist was in no sort of danger when I spread that report of his perilous situation, there was no particular call that my hiding should be very close. But the widow did not know the fact as well as I did; and caused her house to be barricaded, and Becky, her barefooted serving-wench, to be a perpetual sentinel to give alarm, lest the officers should be in search of me.

The only person I expected, however, was my cousin, Ulick, who was to bring me the welcome intelligence of Lady Lyndon's arrival; and I own, after two days' close confinement at Bray, in which I narrated all the adventures of my life to my mother, and succeeded in making her accept the dresses she had formerly refused, and a considerable addition to her income which I was glad to make, I was very glad when I saw that reprobate, Ulick Brady, as my mother called him, ride up to the door in my carriage with the welcome intelligence for my mother that the young lord was out of danger, and for me, that the Countess of Lyndon had arrived in Dublin.

'And I wish, Redmond, that the young gentleman had been in danger a little longer,' said the widow, her eyes filling with tears, 'and you'd have stayed so much the more with your poor old mother.' But I dried her tears, embracing her warmly, and promised to see her often, and hinted I would have mayhap a house of my own and a noble daughter to welcome her.

'Who is she, Redmond dear?' said the old lady.

'One of the noblest and richest women in the empire, mother,' answered I. 'No more Brady, this time,' I added, laughing; with which hopes I left Mrs. Barry in the best of tempers.

No man can bear less malice than I do; and, when I have once carried my point, I am one of the most placable creatures in the world. I was a week in Dublin before I thought it necessary to quit that capital. I had become quite reconciled to my rival in that time; made a point of calling at his lodgings, and speedily became an intimate consoler of his bedside. He had a gentleman to whom I did not neglect to be civil, and towards whom I ordered my people to be particular in their attentions, for I was naturally anxious to learn what my Lord George's position with the lady of Castle Lyndon had really been, whether other suitors were about the widow, and how she would bear the news of his wound.

The young nobleman himself enlightened me somewhat upon the subjects I was most desirous to inquire into.

'Chevalier,' said he to me, one morning when I went to pay him my compliments, 'I find you are an old acquaintance with my kinswoman, the Countess of Lyndon. She writes me a page of abuse of you in a letter here; and the strange part of the story is this, that one day when there was talk about you at Castle Lyndon, and the splendid equipage you were exhibiting in Dublin, the fair widow vowed and protested she never had heard of you.

'"Oh! yes, mamma," said the little Bullingdon, "the tall dark man at Spa with the cast in his eye, who used to make my governor tipsy, and sent me the sword; his name is Mr. Barry."

'But my lady ordered the boy out of the room, and persisted in knowing nothing about you.'

'And are you a kinsman and acquaintance of my Lady Lyndon, my lord?' said I, in a tone of grave surprise.

'Yes, indeed,' answered the young gentleman. 'I left her house but to get this ugly wound from you. And it came at a most unlucky time too.'

'Why more unlucky now than at another moment?'

'Why, look you, chevalier. I think the widow was not impartial to me. I think I might have induced her to make our connexion a little closer: and faith, though she is older than I am, she is the richest party now in England.'

'My Lord George,' said I, 'will you let me ask you a frank but an odd question?—will you show me her letters?'

'Indeed I'll do no such thing,' replied he, in a rage.

'Nay, don't be angry. If *I* show you letters of Lady Lyndon's to me, will you let me see hers to you?'

'What, in Heaven's name, do you mean, Mr. Barry?' said the young nobleman.

'*I* mean that I passionately loved Lady Lyndon. I mean that I am a—that I rather was not indifferent to her. I mean that I love her to distraction at this present moment, and will die myself, or kill the man who possesses her before me.'

'*You* marry the greatest heiress and the noblest blood in England?' said Lord George, haughtily.

'There's no nobler blood in Europe than mine,' answered I; 'and I tell you, I don't know whether to hope or not. But this I know, that there were days in which, poor as I am, the great heiress did not disdain to look down upon my poverty; and that any man who marries her passes over my dead body to do it. It's lucky for you,' I added, gloomily, 'that on the occasion of my engagement with you, I did not know what were your views regarding my Lady Lyndon. My poor boy, you are a lad of courage, and I love you. Mine is the first sword in Europe, and you would have been lying in a narrower bed than that you now occupy.'

'Boy!' said Lord George, 'I am not four years younger than you are.'

'You are forty years younger than I am in experience. I have passed through every grade of life. With my own skill and daring I have made my own fortune. I have been in fourteen pitched battles as a private soldier, and have been twenty-three times on the ground, and never was touched but once, and it was by the sword of a French *maître d'armes*, whom I killed. I started in life at seventeen, a beggar, and am now at seven-and-twenty, with 20,000 guineas. Do you suppose a man of my courage and energy can't attain anything that he dares, and that, having claims upon the widow, I will not press them?'

This speech was not exactly true to the letter (for I had multiplied my pitched battles, my duels, and my wealth somewhat); but I saw that it made the impression I desired to effect upon the young gentleman's mind, who listened to my statement with peculiar seriousness, and whom I presently left to digest it.

A couple of days afterwards I called to see him again, when I brought with me some of the letters that had passed between me and my Lady Lyndon. 'Here,' said I, 'look, I show it you in confidence, it is a lock of her ladyship's hair; here are her letters signed Calista, and addressed to Eugenio. Here is a poem, "When Sol bedecks the Mead with Light, and pallid Cynthia sheds her ray," addressed, by her ladyship, to your humble servant.'

'Calista! Eugenio! Sol bedecks the mead with light,' cried the young lord. 'Am I dreaming? Why, my dear Barry, the widow has sent me the very poem herself! "Rejoicing in the sunshine bright, or musing in the evening grey."'

I could not help laughing as he made the quotation. They were, in fact, the very words *my* Calista had addressed to me. And we found, upon comparing letters, that whole passages of eloquence figured in the one correspondence which appeared in the other. See what it is to be a blue-stocking and have a love of letter-writing!

The young man put down the papers in great perturbation.

'Well, thank Heaven!' said he, after a pause of some duration,—'thank Heaven for a good riddance! Ah, Mr. Barry, what a woman I *might* have married had these lucky papers not come in my way! I thought my Lady Lyndon had a heart, sir, I must confess, though not a very warm one, and that, at least, one could *trust* her. But marry her now! I would as lief send my servant into the street to get me a wife, as put up with such an Ephesian matron* as that.'

'My Lord George,' said I, 'you little know the world. Remember what a bad husband Lady Lyndon had, and don't be astonished that she, on her side, should be indifferent. Nor has she, I will dare to wager, ever passed beyond the bounds of harmless gallantry, or sinned beyond the composing of a sonnet or a billet-doux.'

'My wife,' said the little lord, 'shall write no sonnets or billets-doux, and I'm heartily glad to think I have obtained, in good time, a knowledge of the heartless vixen with whom I thought myself for a moment in love.'

The wounded young nobleman was either, as I have said, very young and green in matters of the world—for to suppose that a man would give up forty thousand a year because, forsooth, the lady connected with it had written a few sentimental letters to a young fellow, is too absurd; or, as I am inclined to believe, he was glad of an excuse to quit the field altogether, being by no means anxious to meet the victorious sword of Redmond Barry a second time.

When the idea of Poynings' danger, or the reproaches probably addressed by him to the widow regarding myself, had brought this exceedingly weak and feeble woman up to Dublin, as I expected, and my worthy Ulick had informed me of her arrival, I quitted my good mother, who was quite reconciled to me (indeed the duel had done that), and found the disconsolate Calista was in the habit of paying visits to the wounded swain, much to the annoyance, the servants told me, of that gentleman. The English are often absurdly high and haughty upon a point of punctilio; and, after his kinswoman's conduct, Lord Poynings swore he would have no more to do with her.

I had this information from his lordship's gentleman, with whom, as I have said, I took particular care to be friends; nor was I denied admission by his porter, when I chose to call, as before.

Her ladyship had most likely bribed that person as I had, for she had found her way up, though denied admission; and, in fact, I had watched her from her own house to Lord George Poynings' lodgings, and seen her descend from her chair there and enter, before I myself followed her. I proposed to await her quietly in the ante-room, to make a scene there, and reproach her with infidelity, if necessary; but matters were, as it happened, arranged much more conveniently for me, and walking, unannounced, into the outer room of his lordship's apartments, I had the felicity of hearing in the next chamber, of which the door was partially open, the voice of my Calista. She was in full cry, appealing to the poor patient, as he lay confined in his bed, and speaking in the most passionate manner. 'What can lead you, George,' she said, 'to doubt of my faith? How can you break my heart by casting me off in this monstrous manner? Do you wish to drive your poor Calista to the grave? Well, well, I shall join there the dear departed angel.'

'Who entered it three months since,' said Lord George, with a sneer. 'It's a wonder you have survived so long.'

'Don't treat your poor Calista in this cruel, cruel manner, Antonio!' cried the widow.

'Bah!' said Lord George, 'my wound is bad. My doctors forbid me much talk. Suppose your Antonio tired, my dear. Can't you console yourself with somebody else?'

'Heavens, Lord George! Antonio!'

'Console yourself with Eugenio,' said the young nobleman, bitterly, and began ringing his bell; on which his valet, who was in an inner room, came out, and he bade him show her ladyship downstairs.

Lady Lyndon issued from the room in the greatest flurry. She was dressed in deep weeds, with a veil over her face, and did not recognize the person waiting in the outer apartment. As she went down the stairs, I stepped lightly after her, and as her chairman opened her door, sprang forward, and took her hand to place her in the vehicle. 'Dearest widow,' said I, 'his lordship spoke correctly. Console yourself with Eugenio!' She was too frightened even to scream, as her chairman carried her away. She was set down at her house, and you may be sure that I was at the chair-door, as before, to help her out.

'Monstrous man!' said she, 'I desire you to leave me.'

'Madam, it would be against my oath,' replied I; 'recollect the vow Eugenio sent to Calista.'

'If you do not quit me, I will call for the domestics to turn you from the door.'

'What! when I am come with my Calista's letters in my pocket, to return them mayhap? You can soothe, madam, but you cannot frighten Redmond Barry.'

'What is it you would have of me, sir?' said the widow, rather agitated.

'Let me come upstairs, and I will tell you all,' I replied; and she condescended to give me her hand, and to permit me to lead her from her chair to her drawing-room.

When we were alone I opened my mind honourably to her.

'Dearest madam,' said I, 'do not let your cruelty drive a desperate slave to fatal measures. I adore you. In former days you allowed me to whisper my passion to you unrestrained; at present you drive me from your door, leave my letters unanswered, and prefer another to me. My flesh and blood cannot bear such treatment; look upon the punishment I have been obliged to inflict, tremble at that which I may be compelled to administer to that unfortunate young man; so sure as he marries you, madam, he dies.'

'I do not recognize,' said the widow, 'the least right you have to give the law to the Countess of Lyndon; I do not in the least understand your threats, or heed them. What has passed between me and an Irish adventurer that should authorize this impertinent intrusion?'

'*These* have passed, madam,' said I,—'Calista's letters to Eugenio. They may have been very innocent, but will the world believe it? You may have only intended to play with the heart of the poor artless Irish gentleman who adored and confided in you. But who will believe the stories of your innocence against the irrefragable testimony of your own handwriting? Who will believe that you could write these letters in the mere wantonness of coquetry, and not under the influence of affection?'

'Villain!' cried my Lady Lyndon, 'could you dare to construe out of those idle letters of mine any other meaning than that which they really bear?'

'I will construe anything out of them,' said I, 'such is the passion which animates me towards you. I have sworn it—you must and shall be mine! Did you ever know me promise to accomplish a thing and fail? Which will you prefer to have from me—a love such as woman never knew from man before, or a hatred to which there exists no parallel?'

'A woman of my rank, sir, can fear nothing from the hatred of an adventurer like yourself,' replied the lady, drawing up stately.

'Look at your Poynings—was *he* of your rank? You are the cause of that young man's wound, madam, and, but that the instrument of your savage cruelty relented, would have been the author of his murder—yes, of his murder; for, if a wife is faithless, does not she arm the husband who punishes the seducer? And I look upon you, Honoria Lyndon, as my wife.'

'Husband! wife, sir!' cried the widow, quite astonished.

'Yes, wife! husband! I am not one of those poor souls with whom coquettes can play, and who may afterwards throw them aside. You would forget what passed between us at Spa; Calista would forget Eugenio, but I will not let you forget me. You thought to trifle with my heart, did you? When once moved, Honoria, it is moved for ever. I love you—love as passionately now as I did when my passion was hopeless, and, now that I can win you, do you think I will forgo you? Cruel, cruel Calista! you little know the power of your own charms if you think their effect is so easily obliterated—you little know the constancy of this pure and noble heart if you think that, having once loved, it can ever cease to adore you. No! I swear by your cruelty that I will revenge it, by your wonderful beauty that I will win it, and be worthy to win it. Lovely, fascinating, fickle, cruel woman! you shall be mine—I swear it! Your wealth may be great, but am I not of a generous nature enough to use it worthily? Your rank is lofty, but not so lofty as my ambition. You threw yourself away once on a cold and spiritless debauchee ; give yourself now, Honoria, to a *man*, and one who, however lofty your rank may be, will enhance it and become it ! '

As I poured words to this effect out on the astonished widow, I stood over her, fascinated her with the glance of my eye, saw her turn red and pale with fear and wonder, saw that my praise of her charms and the exposition of my passion were not unwelcome to her, and witnessed with triumphant composure the mastery I was gaining over her. Terror, be sure of that, is not a bad ingredient of love. A man who wills fiercely to win the heart of a weak and vapourish woman *must* succeed if he have opportunity enough.

' Terrible man ! ' said Lady Lyndon, shrinking from me as soon as I had done speaking (indeed, I was at a loss for words, and thinking of another speech to make to her)— ' terrible man ! leave me.'

I saw that I had made an impression on her from those very words. If she lets me into the house to-morrow, said I, she is mine.

As I went downstairs I put ten guineas into the hand of the hall-porter, who looked quite astonished at such a gift.

' It is to repay you for the trouble of opening the door to me,' said I ; ' you will have to do so often.'

CHAPTER XVI

I PROVIDE NOBLY FOR MY FAMILY AND ATTAIN THE HEIGHT OF MY (SEEMING) GOOD FORTUNE

THE next day when I went back, my fears were realized ; the door was refused to me—my lady was not at home. This I knew to be false : I had watched the door the whole morning from a lodging I took at a house opposite.

' Your lady is not out,' said I ; ' she has denied me, and I can't, of course, force my way to her. But listen, you are an Englishman ? '

' That I am,' said the fellow, with an air of the utmost superiority. ' Your honour could tell that by my *haccent*.'

I knew he was, and might therefore offer him a bribe.

An Irish family servant in rags, and though his wages were never paid him, would probably fling the money in your face.

'Listen, then,' said I. 'Your lady's letters pass through your hands, don't they? A crown for every one that you bring me to read. There is a whisky-shop in the next street: bring them there when you go to drink, and call for me by the name of Dermot.'

'I recollect your honour at *Spar*,' says the fellow, grinning; 'seven's the main, heh?'* and, being exceedingly proud of this reminiscence, I bade my inferior adieu.

I do not defend this practice of letter-opening in private life, except in cases of the most urgent necessity, when we must follow the examples of our betters, the statesmen of all Europe, and, for the sake of a great good, infringe a little matter of ceremony. My Lady Lyndon's letters were none the worse for being opened, and a great deal the better, the knowledge obtained from the perusal of some of her multifarious epistles enabling me to become intimate with her character in a hundred ways, and obtain a power over her by which I was not slow to profit. By the aid of the letters and of my English friend, whom I always regaled with the best of liquor, and satisfied with presents of money still more agreeable (I used to put on a livery in order to meet him, and a red wig, in which it was impossible to know the dashing and elegant Redmond Barry), I got such an insight into the widow's movements as astonished her. I knew beforehand to what public places she would go; they were, on account of her widowhood, but few: and wherever she appeared, at church or in the park, I was always ready to offer her her book, or to canter on horseback by the side of her chariot.

Many of her ladyship's letters were the most whimsical rhodomontades* that ever blue-stocking penned. She was a woman who took up and threw off a greater number of dear friends than any one I ever knew. To some of these female darlings she began presently to write about my unworthy self, and it was with a sentiment of extreme satisfaction I found at length that the widow was growing dreadfully afraid of me, calling me her *bête noire*, her dark spirit, her murderous adorer, and a thousand other names indicative of her extreme disquietude and terror. It was: 'the wretch has been dogging my chariot through the park,' or, ' my fate pursued me at church,' and ' my inevitable adorer handed me out of my chair at the mercer's,' or what not. My wish was to increase this sentiment of awe in her bosom, and to make her believe that I was a person from whom escape was impossible.

To this end I bribed a fortune-teller whom she consulted, along with a number of the most foolish and distinguished people of Dublin in those days, and who, although she went dressed like one of her waiting-women, did not fail to recognize her real rank, and to describe as her future husband her persevering adorer Redmond Barry, Esq. This incident disturbed her very much. She wrote about it in terms of great wonder and terror to her female correspondents. 'Can this monster,' she wrote, 'indeed do as he boasts, and bend even Fate to his will ?—can he make me marry him though I cordially detest him, and bring me a slave to his feet ? The horrid look of his black serpent-like eyes fascinates and frightens me ; it seems to follow me everywhere, and even when I close my own eyes, the dreadful gaze penetrates the lids, and is still upon me.'

When a woman begins to talk of a man in this way, he is an ass who does not win her ; and, for my part, I used to follow her about, and put myself in an attitude opposite her, ' and fascinate her with my glance,' as she said, most assiduously. Lord George Poynings, her former admirer, was meanwhile keeping his room with his wound, and had seemed determined to give up all claims to her favour ; for he denied her admittance when she called, sent no answer to her multiplied correspondence, and contented himself by saying generally that the surgeon had forbidden him to receive visitors or to answer letters. Thus, while he went into the background, I came forward, and took good care that no other rivals should present themselves with any chance of success ; for, as soon as I heard of one, I had a quarrel fastened on him, and, in this way pinked two more besides my first victim Lord George. I always took another pretext for quarrelling with them than the real one of attention to Lady Lyndon, so that no scandal or hurt to her ladyship's feelings might arise in consequence ; but she very well knew what was the meaning of these duels, and the young fellows of Dublin, too, by laying two and two together, began to perceive that there was a certain dragon in watch for the wealthy heiress, and that the dragon must be subdued first before they could get at the lady. I warrant that, after the first three, not many champions were found to address the lady, and have often laughed (in my sleeve) to see many of the young Dublin beaux riding by the side of her carriage scamper off as soon as my bay mare and green liveries made their appearance.

I wanted to impress her with some great and awful instance of my power, and to this end had determined to confer a great benefit upon my honest cousin Ulick, and carry off for him the fair object of his affections, Miss Kiljoy, under the very eyes of her guardian and friend, Lady Lyndon, and in the teeth of the squires, the young lady's brothers, who passed the season at Dublin, and made as much swagger and to-do about their sister's 10,000*l*. Irish as if she had had a plum to her fortune. The girl was by no means averse to Mr. Brady, and it only shows how faint-spirited some men are, and how a superior genius can instantly overcome difficulties which, to common minds, seem insuperable, that he never had thought of running off with her, as I at once and boldly did. Miss Kiljoy had been a ward in Chancery until she attained her majority (before which period it would have been a dangerous matter for me to put in execution the scheme I meditated concerning her), but, though now free to marry whom she liked, she was a young lady of timid disposition, and as much under fear of her brothers and relatives as though she had not been independent of them. They had some friend of their own in view for the young lady, and had scornfully rejected the proposal of Ulick Brady, the ruined gentleman, who was quite unworthy, as these rustic bucks thought, of the hand of such a prodigiously wealthy heiress as their sister.

Finding herself lonely in her great house in Dublin, the Countess of Lyndon invited her friend Miss Amelia to pass the season with her at Dublin, and, in a fit of maternal fondness, also sent for her son, the little Bullingdon, and my old acquaintance his governor, to come to the capital and bear her company. A family coach brought the boy, the heiress, and the tutor from Castle Lyndon, and I determined to take the first opportunity of putting my plan in execution.

For this chance I had not very long to wait. I have said, in a former chapter of my biography, that the kingdom of Ireland was at this period ravaged by various parties of banditti, who, under the name of Whiteboys, Oakboys, Steelboys,* with captains at their head, killed proctors,* fired stacks, houghed and maimed cattle, and took the law into their own hands. One of these bands, or several of them for what I know, was commanded by a mysterious personage called Captain Thunder, whose business seemed to be that of marrying people with, or without their own consent, or that of their parents. The *Dublin Gazettes* and *Mercuries** of that period (the year 1772) teem with proclamations from the Lord Lieutenant, offering rewards for the apprehension of this dreadful Captain Thunder and his gang, and describing at length various exploits of the savage aide de camp of Hymen. I determined to make use, if not of the services, at any rate of the name of Captain Thunder, and put my cousin Ulick in possession of his lady and her ten thousand pounds. She was no great beauty, and, I presume, it was the money he loved rather than the owner of it.

On account of her widowhood, Lady Lyndon could not as yet frequent the balls and routs which the hospitable nobility of Dublin were in the custom of giving; but her friend Miss Kiljoy had no such cause for retirement, and was glad to attend any parties to which she might be invited. I made Ulick Brady a present of a couple of handsome suits of velvet, and by my influence procured him an invitation to many of the most elegant of these assemblies. But he had not had my advantages or experience of the manners of court; was as shy with ladies as a young colt, and could no more dance a minuet than a donkey. He made very little way in the polite world [or] in his mistress's heart; in fact, I could see that she preferred several other young gentlemen to him, who were more at home in the ball-room than poor Ulick, who had made his first impression upon the heiress, and felt his first flame for her, in her father's house of Ballykiljoy, where he used to hunt and get drunk with the old gentleman.

'I could do *thim* two well enough, anyhow,' Ulick would say, heaving a sigh; 'and, if it's drinking or riding across country would do it, there's no man in Ireland would have a better chance with Amalia.'

'Never fear, Ulick,' was my reply; 'you shall have your Amalia, or my name is not Redmond Barry.'

My Lord Charlemont,* who was one of the most elegant and accomplished noblemen in Ireland in those days, a fine scholar and wit, a gentleman who had travelled much abroad, where I had the honour of knowing him, gave a magnificent masquerade at his house of Marino, some few miles from Dublin, on the Dunleary road. And it was at this entertainment that I was determined that Ulick should be made happy for life. Miss Kiljoy was invited to the masquerade, and the little Lord Bullingdon, who longed to witness such a scene; and it was agreed that he was to go under the guardianship of his governor, my old friend the Rev. Mr. Runt. I learned what was the equipage in which the party were to be conveyed to the ball, and took my measures accordingly.

Ulick Brady was not present; his fortune and quality were not sufficient to procure him an invitation to so distinguished a place, and I had it given out three days previous that he had been arrested for debt; a rumour which surprised nobody who knew him.

I appeared that night in a character with which I was very familiar, that of a private soldier in the King of Prussia's guard. I had a grotesque mask made, with an immense nose and moustachios, talked a jumble of broken English and German, in which the latter greatly predominated; and had crowds round me laughing at my droll accent, and whose curiosity was increased by a knowledge of my previous history. Miss Kiljoy was attired as an antique princess, with little Bullingdon as a page of the times of chivalry; his hair was in powder, his doublet rose-colour and pea-green and silver, and he looked very handsome and saucy as he strutted about with my sword by his side. As for Mr. Runt, he walked about very demurely in a domino,* and perpetually paid his respects to the beauffet, and ate enough cold chicken, and drank enough punch and champagne, to satisfy a company of grenadiers.

The Lord Lieutenant came and went in state—the ball was magnificent. Miss Kiljoy had partners in plenty, among whom was myself, who walked a minuet with her (if the clumsy waddling of the Irish heiress may be called by such a name), and I took occasion to plead my passion for Lady Lyndon in the most pathetic terms, and to beg her friend's interference in my favour.

It was three hours past midnight when the party for Lyndon House went away. Little Bullingdon had long since been asleep in one of Lady Charlemont's china closets. Mr. Runt was exceedingly husky in talk, and unsteady in gait. A young lady of the present day would be alarmed to see a gentleman in such a condition; but it was a common sight in those jolly old times, when a gentleman was thought a milksop unless he was occasionally tipsy. I saw Miss Kiljoy to her carriage, with several other gentlemen, and peering through the crowd of ragged linkboys, drivers, beggars, drunken men and women, who used invariably to wait round great men's doors when festivities were going on, saw the carriage drive off, with a hurra from the mob, and came back presently to the supper-room, where I talked German, favoured the three or four topers still there with a High-Dutch chorus, and attacked the dishes and wine with great resolution.

'How can you drink *ai*sy with that big nose on?' said one gentleman.

'Go an' be hangt!' said I, in the true accent, applying myself again to the wine; with which the others laughed, and I pursued my supper in silence.

There was a gentleman present who had seen the Lyndon party go off, with whom I had made a bet, which I lost; and the next morning I called upon him and paid it him. All which particulars the reader will be surprised at hearing enumerated; but the fact is, that it was *not* I who went back to the party, but my late German valet, who was of my size, and, dressed in my mask, could perfectly pass for me. We changed clothes in a hackney-coach that stood near Lady Lyndon's chariot, and driving after it, speedily overtook it.

The fated vehicle which bore the lovely object of Ulick Brady's affections had not advanced very far when, in the midst of a deep rut in the road, it came suddenly to with a jolt, and the footman, springing off the back, cried 'Stop' to the coachman, warning him that a wheel was off, and that it would be dangerous to proceed with only three. Wheel-caps had not been invented in those days, as they have since by the ingenious builders of Long Acre.*

And how the linchpin of the wheel had come out I do not pretend to say, but it possibly may have been extracted by some rogues among the crowd before Lord Charlemont's gate.

Miss Kiljoy thrust her head out of the window, screaming as ladies do; Mr. Runt the chaplain woke up from his boozy slumbers; and little Bullingdon, starting up and drawing his little sword, said, 'Don't be afraid, Miss Amelia; if it's footpads, I am armed.' The young rascal had the spirit of a lion, that's the truth, as I must acknowledge, in spite of all my after-quarrels with him.

The hackney-coach which had been following Lady Lyndon's chariot, by this time came up, and the coachman seeing the disaster, stepped down from his box, and politely requested her ladyship's honour to enter his vehicle, which was as clean and elegant as any person of tiptop quality might desire. This invitation was, after a minute or two, accepted by the passengers of the chariot: the hackney-coachman promising to drive them to Dublin 'in a hurry.' Thady, the valet, proposed to accompany his young master and the young lady; and the coachman, who had a friend seemingly drunk by his side on the box, with a grin told Thady to get up behind. However, as the footboard there was covered with spikes, as a defence against the street boys, who love a ride gratis, Thady's fidelity would not induce him to brave these, and he was persuaded to remain by the wounded chariot, for which he and the coachman manufactured a linchpin out of a neighbouring hedge.

Meanwhile, although the hackney-coachman drove on rapidly, yet the party within seemed to consider it was a long distance from Dublin; and what was Miss Kiljoy's astonishment, on looking out of the window, at length to see around her a lonely heath, with no signs of buildings or city. She began forthwith to scream out to the coachman to stop, but the man only whipped the horses the faster for her noise, and bade her ladyship 'hould on—'twas a short cut he was taking.'

Miss Kiljoy continued screaming, the coachman flogging, the horses galloping, until two or three men appeared suddenly from a hedge, to whom the fair one cried for assistance; and the young Bullingdon opening the coach door, jumped valiantly out, toppling over head and heels as he fell, but, jumping up in an instant, he drew his little sword, and, running towards the carriage, exclaimed, 'This way, gentlemen! stop the rascal!'

'Stop!' cried the men; at which the coachman pulled up with extraordinary obedience. Runt all the while lay tipsy in the carriage, having only a dreamy half-consciousness of all that was going on.

The newly arrived champions of female distress now held a consultation, in which they looked at the young lord, and laughed considerably.

'Do not be alarmed,' said their leader, coming up to the door; 'one of my people shall mount the box by the side of that treacherous rascal, and, with your ladyship's leave, I and my companion will get in and see you home. We are well armed, and can defend you in case of danger.'

With this, and without more ado, he jumped into the carriage, his companion following him.

'Know your place, fellow!' cried out little Bullingdon, indignantly: 'and give place to the Lord Viscount Bullingdon!' and put himself before the huge person of the newcomer, who was about to enter the hackney-coach.

'Get out of that, my lord,' said the man, in a broad brogue, and shoving him aside. On which the boy, crying, 'Thieves! thieves!' drew out his little hanger, and ran at the man, and would have wounded him (for a small sword will wound as well as a great one), but his opponent, who was armed with a long stick, struck the weapon luckily out of the lad's hands; it went flying over his head, and left him aghast and mortified at his discomfiture.

He then pulled off his hat, making his lordship a low bow, and entered the carriage, the door of which was shut upon him by his confederate who was to mount the box. Miss Kiljoy might have screamed, but I presume her shrieks were stopped by the sight of an enormous horse-pistol which one of her champions produced, who said, 'No harm is intended you, ma'am, but if you cry out, we must gag you'; on which she suddenly became as mute as a fish.

All these events took place in an exceedingly short space of time, and when the three invaders had taken possession of the carriage, the poor little Bullingdon being left bewildered and astonished on the heath, one of them putting his head out of the window, said,—

'My lord, a word with you.'

'What is it?' said the boy, beginning to whimper; he was but eleven years old, and his courage had been excellent hitherto.

'You are only two miles from Marino. Walk back till you come to a big stone, there turn to the right, and keep on straight till you get to the high road, when you will easily find your way back. And when you see her ladyship, your mamma, give CAPTAIN THUNDER's compliments, and say Miss Amelia Kiljoy is going to be married.'

'Oh, heavens!' sighed out that young lady.

The carriage drove swiftly on, and the poor little nobleman was left alone on the heath, just as the morning began to break. He was fairly frightened, and no wonder. He thought of running after the coach, but his courage and his little legs failed him, so he sat down upon a stone and cried for vexation.

It was in this way that Ulick Brady made what I call a Sabine marriage.* When he halted with his two groomsmen at the cottage where the ceremony was to be performed, Mr. Runt, the chaplain, at first declined to perform it. But a pistol was held at the head of that unfortunate preceptor, and he was told, with dreadful oaths, that his miserable brains would be blown out, when he consented to read the service. The lovely Amelia had, very likely, a similar inducement held out to her, but of that I know nothing; for I drove back to town with the coachman as soon as we had set the bridal party down, and had the satisfaction of finding Fritz, my German, arrived before me, who had come back in my carriage in my dress, having left the masquerade undiscovered, and done everything there according to my orders.

Poor Runt came back the next day in a piteous plight, keeping silence as to his share in the occurrences of the evening; and with a dismal story of having been drunk, of having been waylaid and bound, of having been left on the road and picked up by a Wicklow cart, which was coming in with provisions to Dublin, and found him helpless on the road. There was no possible means of fixing any share of the conspiracy upon me. Little Bullingdon, who, too, found his way home, was unable in any way to identify me. But Lady Lyndon knew that I was concerned in the plot, for I met her ladyship hurrying the next day to the Castle, all the town being up about the *enlèvement.** And I saluted her with a smile so diabolical that I knew she was aware that I had been concerned in the daring and ingenious scheme.

Thus it was that I repaid Ulick Brady's kindness to me in early days, and had the satisfaction of restoring the fallen fortunes of a deserving branch of my family. He took his bride into Wicklow, where he lived with her in the strictest seclusion until the affair was blown over, the Kiljoys striving everywhere in vain to discover his retreat. They did not for a while even know who was the lucky man who had carried off the heiress; nor was it until she wrote a letter some weeks afterwards, signed Amelia Brady, and expressing her perfect happiness in her new condition, and stating that she had been married by Lady Lyndon's chaplain Mr. Runt, that the truth was known, and my worthy friend confessed his share of the transaction. As his good-natured mistress did not dismiss him from his post in consequence, everybody persisted in supposing that poor Lady Lyndon was privy to the plot; and the story of her ladyship's passionate attachment for me gained more and more credit.

I was not slow, you may be sure, in profiting by these rumours. Every one thought I had a share in the Brady marriage, though no one could prove it. Every one thought I was well with the widowed countess, though no one could show that I said so. But there is a way of proving a thing even while you contradict it, and I used to laugh and joke so à propos that all men began to wish me joy of my great fortune, and look up to me as the affianced husband of the greatest heiress in the kingdom. The papers took up the matter, the female friends of Lady Lyndon remonstrated with her and cried 'Fie!' Even the English journals and magazines, which in those days were very scandalous, talked of the matter, and whispered that a beautiful and accomplished widow, with a title and the largest possessions in the two kingdoms, was about to bestow her hand upon a young gentleman of high birth and fashion, who had distinguished himself in the services of his M—y the K— of Pr——. I won't say who was the author of these paragraphs, or how two pictures, one representing myself under the title of 'The Prussian Irishman,' and the other Lady Lyndon as 'The Countess of Ephesus,' actually appeared in the *Town and Country*

Magazine,* published at London, and containing the fashionable tittle-tattle of the day.

Lady Lyndon was so perplexed and terrified by this continual hold upon her, that she determined to leave the country. Well, she did; and who was the first to receive her on landing at Holyhead? Your humble servant, Redmond Barry, Esq. And, to crown all, the *Dublin Mercury*, which announced her ladyship's departure, announced mine *the day before*. There was not a soul but thought she had followed me to England, whereas she was only flying me. Vain hope!—a man of my resolution was not thus to be balked in pursuit. Had she fled to the Antipodes, I would have been there; aye, and would have followed her as far as Orpheus did Eurydice!*

Her ladyship had a house in Berkeley Square, London, more splendid than that which she possessed in Dublin, and, knowing that she would come thither, I preceded her to the English capital, and took handsome apartments in Hill Street, hard by. I had the same intelligence in her London house which I had procured in Dublin. The same faithful porter was there to give me all the information I required. I promised to treble his wages as soon as a certain event should happen. I won over Lady Lyndon's companion by a present of 100 guineas down, and a promise of 2,000 when I should be married, and gained the favours of her favourite lady's-maid by a bribe of similar magnitude. My reputation had so far preceded me in London that, on my arrival, numbers of the genteel were eager to receive me at their routs. We have no idea in this humdrum age what a gay and splendid place London was then; what a passion for play there was among young and old, male and female; what thousands were lost and won in a night; what beauties there were—how brilliant, gay, and dashing! Everybody was delightfully wicked. The royal Dukes of Gloucester and Cumberland* set the example —the nobles followed close behind. Running away was the fashion: ah! it was a pleasant time; and lucky was he who had fire, and youth, and money, and could live in it! I had all these, and the old frequenters of White's, Wattier's, and Goosetree's* could tell stories of the gallantry, spirit, and high fashion of Captain Barry.

The progress of a love-story is tedious to all those who are not concerned, and I leave such themes to the hack novel-writers, and the young boarding-school misses for whom they write. It is not my intention to follow, step by step, the incidents of my courtship, or to narrate all the difficulties I had to contend with, and my triumphant manner of surmounting them. Suffice it to say, I *did* overcome these difficulties. I am of opinion, with my friend, the late ingenious Mr. Wilkes,* that such impediments are nothing in the way of a man of spirit; and that he can convert indifference and aversion into love, if he have perseverance and cleverness sufficient. By the time the Countess's widowhood was expired, I had found means to be received into her house; I had her women perpetually talking in my favour, vaunting my powers, expatiating upon my reputation, and boasting of my success and popularity in the fashionable world.

Also, the best friends I had in the prosecution of my tender suit were the Countess's noble relatives, who were far from knowing the service that they did me, and to whom I beg leave to tender my heartfelt thanks for the abuse with which they then loaded me, and to whom I fling my utter contempt for the calumny and hatred with which they have subsequently pursued me.

The chief of these amiable persons was the Marchioness of Tiptoff, mother of the young gentleman whose audacity I had punished at Dublin. This old harridan, on the Countess's first arrival in London, waited upon her, and favoured her with such a storm of abuse for her encouragement of me, that I do believe she advanced my cause more than six months' courtship could have done, or the pinking of a half-dozen of rivals. It was in vain that poor Lady Lyndon pleaded her entire innocence, and vowed she had never encouraged me. 'Never encouraged him!' screamed out the old fury; 'didn't you encourage the wretch at Spa during Sir Charles's own life? Didn't you marry a dependant of yours to one of this profligate's bankrupt cousins? When he set off for England, didn't you follow him, like a madwoman, the very next day? Didn't he take lodgings at your very door almost—and do you call this no encouragement? For shame, madam, shame! You might have married my son—my dear and noble George, but that he did not choose to interfere with your shameful passion for the beggarly upstart whom you caused to assassinate him; and the only counsel I have to give your ladyship is this, to legitimatize the ties which you have contracted with this shameless adventurer; to make that connexion legal which, real as it is now, is against both decency and religion; and to spare your family and your son the shame of your present line of life.'

With this the old fury of a Marchioness left the room, and Lady Lyndon in tears; and I had the whole particulars of the conversation from her ladyship's companion, and augured the best result from it in my favour.

Thus, by the sage influence of my Lady Tiptoff, the Countess of Lyndon's natural friends and family were kept from her society. Even when Lady Lyndon went to court, the most august lady in the realm received her with such marked coldness that the unfortunate widow came home and took to her bed with vexation. And thus, I may say, that royalty itself became an agent in advancing my suit, and helping the plans of the poor Irish soldier of fortune. So it is that Fate works with agents, great and small; and by means over which they have no control the destinies of men and women are accomplished.

I shall always consider the conduct of Mrs. Bridget (Lady Lyndon's favourite maid) at this juncture, as a masterpiece of ingenuity; and, indeed, had such an opinion of her diplomatic skill that, the very instant I became master of the Lyndon estates, and paid her the promised sum—I am a man of honour, and rather than not keep my word with the woman, I raised the money of the Jews, at an exorbitant interest—as soon, I say, as I achieved my triumph, I took Mrs. Bridget by the hand, and said, 'Madam, you have shown such unexampled fidelity in my service that I am glad to reward you, according to my promise; but you have given proofs of such extraordinary cleverness and dissimulation that I must decline keeping you in Lady Lyndon's establishment, and beg you will leave it this very day;' which she did, and went over to the Tiptoff faction, and has abused me ever since.

But I must tell you what she did which was so clever. Why, it was the simplest thing in the world, as all master-strokes are. When Lady Lyndon lamented her fate and my—as she was pleased to call it—shameful treatment of her, Mrs. Bridget said, 'Why should not your ladyship write this young gentleman word of the evil which he is causing you? Appeal to his feelings (which, I have heard say, are very good indeed—the whole town is ringing with accounts of his spirit and generosity), and beg him to desist from a pursuit which causes the best of ladies so much pain? Do, my lady, write: I know your style is so elegant that I, for my part, have many a time burst into tears in reading your charming letters, and I have no doubt Mr. Barry will sacrifice anything rather than hurt your feelings.' And, of course, the abigail swore to the fact.

'Do you think so, Bridget?' said her ladyship. And my mistress forthwith penned me a letter, in her most fascinating and winning manner.

> Why, sir, wrote she, will you pursue me? why environ me in a web of intrigue so frightful that my spirit sinks under it, seeing escape is hopeless, from your frightful, your diabolical art? They say you are generous to others—be so to me. I know your bravery but too well: exercise it on men who can meet your sword, not on a poor feeble woman, who cannot resist you. Remember the friendship you once professed for me. And now, I beseech you, I implore you, to give a proof of it. Contradict the calumnies which you have spread against me, and repair, if you can, and if you have a spark of honour left, the miseries which you have caused to the heart-broken
>
> H. LYNDON.

What was this letter meant for but that I should answer it in person? My excellent ally told me where I should meet Lady Lyndon, and accordingly, I followed, and found her at the Pantheon.* I repeated the scene at Dublin over again; showed her how prodigious my power was, humble as I was, and that my energy was still untired. 'But,' I added, 'I am as great in good as I am in evil; as fond and faithful as a friend as I am terrible as an enemy. I will do everything,' I said, 'which you ask of me, except when you bid me not to love you. That is beyond my power; and while my heart has a pulse I must follow you. It is *my* fate, your fate. Cease to battle against it, and be mine. Loveliest of your sex, with life alone can end my passion for you, and, indeed, it is only by dying at your command that I can be brought to obey you. Do you wish me to die?'

She said laughing (for she was a woman of a lively, humorous turn) that she did not wish me to commit self-murder, and I felt from that moment that she was mine.

. . . . . .

A year from that day, on the 15th of May, in the year 1773, I had the honour and happiness to lead to the altar Honoria Countess of Lyndon, widow of the late Right Hon. Sir Charles Lyndon, K.B. The ceremony was performed at St. George's, Hanover Square, by the Rev. Samuel Runt, her ladyship's chaplain. A magnificent supper and ball was given at our house in Berkeley Square, and the next morning I had a duke, four earls, three generals, and a crowd of the most distinguished people in London, at my levee. Walpole made a lampoon about the marriage, and Selwyn cut jokes at the Cocoa-tree. Old Lady Tiptoff, although she had recommended it, was ready to bite off her fingers with vexation; and as for young Bullingdon, who was grown a tall lad of fourteen, when called upon by the Countess to embrace his papa, he shook his fist in my face, and said, '*He* my father! I would as soon call one of your ladyship's footmen papa!'

But I could afford to laugh at the rage of the boy and the old woman, and at the jokes of the wits of St. James's. I sent off a flaming account of our nuptials to my mother, and my uncle, the good chevalier; and now, arrived at the pitch of prosperity, and having, at thirty years of age, by my own merits and energy, raised myself to one of the highest social positions that any man in England could occupy, I determined to enjoy myself as became a man of quality for the remainder of my life.

After we had received the congratulations of our friends in London—for in those days people were not ashamed of being married, as they seem to be now—I and Honoria (who was all complacency, and a most handsome, sprightly, and agreeable companion) set off to visit our estates in the west of England, where I had never as yet set foot. We left London in three chariots, each with four horses; and my uncle would have been pleased could he have seen painted on their panels the Irish crown and the ancient coat of the Barrys beside the Countess's coronet and the noble cognizance of the noble family of Lyndon.

Before quitting London, I procured his Majesty's gracious permission to add the name of my lovely lady to my own, and henceforward assumed the style and title of BARRY LYNDON, as I have written it in this autobiography.

CHAPTER XVII

I APPEAR AS AN ORNAMENT OF ENGLISH SOCIETY

[It is, perhaps, as well for the reader that in the following part of his Memoirs, which details the history of Mr. Lyndon's life after his marriage and during the first years of his fashionable life, the autobiographer has not been more explicit. His papers at this period contain a mass of very unedifying and uninteresting documents,—such as tavern-bills of the Star and Garter and the Covent Garden* houses of entertainment; paid I O U's, indicating gambling transactions with some of the most fashionable personages of the day; letters in female handwriting, which show that he was anything but constant to the wife whom he had won; drafts of letters to lawyers and money-brokers relative to the raising of money, the insuring of Lady Lyndon's life, and correspondence with upholsterers, decorators, cooks, housekeepers, bailiffs and stewards. Indeed, he appears to have docketed all these testimonials of his extravagance with the most extraordinary punctuality, and kept every possible voucher of his want of principle. What he says of himself in the present section of the Memoirs, 'that he was clever enough at gaining a fortune, but incapable of keeping one,' is a statement (not like all the statements he makes) worthy of entire credit; and a professional accountant, were he to go through the voluminous Lyndon papers, might, no doubt, trace every step which the adventurer took in the destruction of the splendid property which he acquired through his lady. But this is a calculation not in the least profitable or necessary here; it is only sufficient to know the process, without entering into the interminable particulars. And the editor of the Memoirs, in placing these few lines of preface before the second part of them,[1] is glad to think that the reader is speedily about to arrive at that period in the history where poetical justice overtakes the daring and selfish hero of the tale. After enumerating the bribes he

[1] This chapter commenced Part II in the original issue of the story in *Fraser's Magazine*.

paid his agents in consequence of their marriage, Mr. Lyndon proceeds as follows to recount the pleasures of their honeymoon :—][1]

All the journey down to Hackton Castle, the largest and most ancient of our ancestral seats in Devonshire, was performed with the slow and sober state becoming people of the first quality in the realm. An outrider in my livery went on before us, and bespoke our lodging from town to town; and thus we lay in state at Andover, Ilminster, and Exeter; and the fourth evening arrived in time for supper before the antique baronial mansion, of which the gate was in an odious Gothic taste that would have set Mr. Walpole wild with pleasure.*

The first days of a marriage are commonly very trying; and I have known couples, who lived together like turtle-doves for the rest of their lives, peck each other's eyes out almost during the honeymoon. I did not escape the common lot; in our journey westward my Lady Lyndon chose to quarrel with me because I pulled out a pipe of tobacco* (the habit of smoking which I had acquired in Germany when a soldier in Bülow's, and could never give it over), and smoked it in the carriage; and also her ladyship chose to take umbrage both at Ilminster and Andover, because in the evenings when we lay there I chose to invite the landlords of the Bell and the Lion to crack a bottle with me. Lady Lyndon was a haughty woman, and I hate pride, and I promise you that in both instances I overcame this vice in her. On the third day of our journey I had her to light my pipe-match with her own hands, and made her deliver it to me with tears in her eyes; and at the Swan Inn at Exeter I had so completely subdued her, that she asked me humbly whether I would not wish the landlady as well as the host to step up to dinner with us. To this I should have had no objection, for, indeed, Mrs. Bonnyface* was a very good-looking woman; but we expected a visit from my lord Bishop, a kinsman of Lady Lyndon, and the *bien-séances** did not permit the indulgence of my wife's request. I appeared with her at evening service to compliment our right reverend cousin, and put her name down for twenty-five guineas and my own for one hundred, to the famous new organ* which was then being built for the cathedral.

[1] Omitted in later editions.

This conduct, at the very outset of my career in the county, made me not a little popular; and the residentiary canon who did me the favour to sup with me at the inn, went away after the sixth bottle hiccuping the most solemn vows for the welfare of such a p-p-pious gentleman.

Before we reached Hackton Castle, we had to drive through ten miles of the Lyndon estates, where the people were out to visit us, the church-bells set a-ringing, the parson and the farmers assembled in their best by the roadside, and the school-children and the labouring people were loud in their hurrahs for her ladyship. I flung money among these worthy characters, stopped to bow and chat with his reverence and the farmers, and if I found that the Devonshire girls were among the handsomest in the kingdom is it my fault? These remarks my Lady Lyndon especially would take in great dudgeon: and I do believe she was made more angry by my admiration of the red cheeks of Miss Betsy Quarringdon of Clumpton,* than by any previous speech or act of mine in the journey. 'Ah, ah, my fine madam, you are jealous, are you?' thought I, and reflected, not without deep sorrow, how lightly she herself had acted in her husband's lifetime, and that those are most jealous who themselves give most cause for jealousy.

Round Hackton village the scene of welcome was particularly gay; and a band of music had been brought from Plymouth, and arches and flags had been raised, especially before the attorney's and the doctor's houses, who were both in the employ of the family. There were many hundreds of stout people at the great lodge, which, with the park-wall, bounds one side of Hackton Green, and from which, for three miles, goes, or rather went, an avenue of noble elms up to the towers of the old castle. I wished they had been oak when I cut the trees down in '79, for they would have fetched three times the money; and I know nothing more culpable than the carelessness of ancestors in planting their grounds with timber of small value, when they might just as easily raise oak. Thus I have always said that the Roundhead Lyndon of Hackton, who planted these elms in Charles II's time, cheated me of 10,000*l.*

For the first few days after our arrival, my time was agreeably spent in receiving the visits of the nobility and gentry who came to pay their respects to the noble new-married couple, and, like Bluebeard's wife in the fairy tale, in inspecting the treasures, the furniture, and the numerous chambers of the castle. It is a huge old place, built as far back as Henry V's time, besieged and battered by the Cromwellians in the Revolution, and altered and patched up, in an odious old-fashioned taste, by the Roundhead Lyndon, who succeeded to the property at the death of a brother whose principles were excellent and of the true Cavalier sort, but who ruined himself chiefly by drinking, dicing, and a dissolute life, and a little by supporting the King. The castle stands in a fine chase, which was prettily speckled over with deer; and I can't but own that my pleasure was considerable at first as I sat in the oak parlour of summer evenings, with the windows open, the gold and silver plate shining in a hundred dazzling colours on the sideboards, a dozen jolly companions round the table, and could look out over the wide green park and the waving woods, and see the sun setting on the lake, and hear the deer calling to one another.

The exterior was, when I first arrived, a quaint composition of all sorts of architecture, of feudal towers, and gable-ends in Queen Bess's style, and rough-patched walls built up to repair the ravages of the Roundhead cannon; but I need not speak of this at large, having had the place new-faced at a vast expense, under a fashionable architect, and the façade laid out in the latest French-Greek* and most classical style. There had been moats, and drawbridges, and outer walls; these I had shaved away into elegant terraces, and handsomely laid out in parterres according to the plans of M. Cornichon,* the great Parisian architect, who visited England for the purpose.

After ascending the outer steps, you entered an antique hall of vast dimensions, wainscoted with black carved oak, and ornamented with portraits of our ancestors, from the square beard of Brook Lyndon, the great lawyer in Queen Bess's time, to the loose stomacher and ringlets of Lady Saccharissa Lyndon, whom Van Dyck painted when she was a maid of honour to Queen Henrietta Maria, and down to Sir Charles Lyndon, with his ribbon as a Knight of the Bath; and my lady, as she was painted by Hudson,* in a white satin sack and family diamonds, as she was presented to the old King George II. These diamonds were very fine; I first had them reset by Boehmer,* when we appeared before their French Majesties at Versailles, and finally raised 18,000*l.* upon [them], after that infernal run of ill luck at Goosetree's, when Jemmy Twitcher*(as we called my Lord Sandwich), Carlisle,* Charley Fox, and I played ombre for four-and-forty hours, *sans désemparer.** Bows and pikes, huge stag-heads, and hunting implements, and rusty old suits of armour that may have been worn in the days of Gog and Magog,* for what I know, formed the other old ornaments of this huge apartment, and were ranged round a fireplace where you might have turned a coach-and-six. This I kept pretty much in its antique condition, but had the old armour eventually turned out and consigned to the lumber-rooms upstairs, replacing it with china monsters, gilded settees from France, and elegant marbles, of which the broken noses and limbs, and ugliness, undeniably proved their antiquity, and which an agent purchased for me at Rome. But such was the taste of the times (and, perhaps, the rascality of my agent), that 30,000*l.* worth of these gems of art only went for 300 guineas at a subsequent period, when I found it necessary to raise money on my collections.

From this main hall branched off on either side the long series of state-rooms, poorly furnished with high-backed chairs and long, queer Venice glasses, when first I came to the property, but afterwards rendered so splendid by me, with the gold damasks of Lyons, and the magnificent Gobelin tapestries I won from Richelieu* at play. There were thirty-six bedrooms *de maître*, of which I only kept three in their antique condition,—the haunted room, as it was called, where the murder was done in James II's time, the bed where William slept after landing at Torbay,* and Queen Elizabeth's state-room. All the rest were redecorated by Cornichon, in the most elegant taste, not a little to the scandal of some of the steady old country dowagers; for I had pictures of Boucher and Vanloo* to decorate the principal apartments, in which the Cupids and Venuses were painted in a manner so natural that I recollect the old wizened Countess of Frumpington pinning over the curtains of her bed, and sending her daughter, Lady Blanche Whalebone, to sleep with her waiting-woman, rather than allow her to lie in a chamber hung all over with looking-glasses, after the exact fashion of the Queen's closet at Versailles.

For many of these ornaments I was not so much answerable as Cornichon, whom Lauraguais* lent me, and who was the intendant of my buildings during my absence abroad. I had given the man *carte blanche*, and when he fell down and broke his leg, as he was decorating a theatre in the room which had been the old chapel of the castle, the people of the country thought it was a judgement of Heaven upon him. In his rage for improvement the fellow dared anything. Without my orders, he cut down an old rookery which was sacred in the country, and had a prophecy regarding it, stating, 'When the rook-wood shall fall, down goes Hackton Hall.' The rooks went over and colonized Tiptoff Woods, which lay near us (and be hanged to them!), and Cornichon built a temple to Venus, and two lovely fountains on their site. Venuses and Cupids were the rascal's adoration; he wanted to take down the Gothic screen and place Cupids in our pew there; but old Doctor Huff, the rector, came out with a large oak stick, and addressed the unlucky architect in Latin, of which he did not comprehend a word, yet made him understand that he would break his bones if he laid a single finger upon the sacred edifice. Cornichon made complaints about the 'Abbé Huff,' as he called him ('*Et quel abbé, grand Dieu!*' added he, quite bewildered, '*un abbé avec douze enfants!*'), but I encouraged the Church in this respect, and bade Cornichon exert his talents only in the castle.

There was a magnificent collection of ancient plate, to which I added much of the most splendid modern kind: a cellar which, however well furnished, required continual replenishing, and a kitchen which I reformed altogether. My friend, Jack Wilkes, sent me down a cook from the Mansion House,* for the English cookery,—the turtle and venison department; I had a *chef* (who called out the Englishman, by the way, and complained sadly of the *gros cochon*, who wanted to meet him with *coups de poing*) and a couple of *aides* from Paris, and an Italian confectioner as my *officiers de bouche*. All which natural appendages to a man of fashion, the odious, stingy old Tiptoff, my kinsman and neighbour, affected to view with horror, and he spread through the country a report that I had my victuals cooked by Papists, lived upon frogs, and, he verily believed, fricassée'd little children.

But the squires ate my dinners very readily, for all

that, and old Dr. Huff himself was compelled to allow that my venison and turtle were most orthodox. The former gentry I knew how to conciliate, too, in other ways. There had been only a subscription pack of fox-hounds in the country, and a few beggarly couples of mangy beagles, with which old Tiptoff pattered about his grounds; I built a kennel and stables, which cost 30,000*l.*, and stocked them in a manner which was worthy of my ancestors, the Irish kings. I had two packs of hounds, and took the field in the season four times a week, with three gentlemen in my hunt-uniform to follow me, and open house at Hackton for all who belonged to the hunt.

These changes and this *train de vivre** required, as may be supposed, no small outlay; and I confess that I have little of that base spirit of economy in my composition which some people practise and admire. For instance, old Tiptoff was hoarding up his money to repair his father's extravagance and disencumber his estates; a good deal of the money with which he paid off his mortgages my agent procured upon mine. And, besides, it must be remembered I had only a life-interest upon the Lyndon property, was always of an easy temper in dealing with the money-brokers, and had to pay heavily for insuring her ladyship's life.

At the end of a year Lady Lyndon presented me with a son—Bryan Lyndon I called him, in compliment to my royal ancestry;* but what more had I to leave him than a noble name? Was not the estate of his mother entailed upon the odious little Turk, Lord Bullingdon, and who, by the way, I have not mentioned as yet, though he was living at Hackton, consigned to a new governor. The insubordination of that boy was dreadful. He used to quote passages of *Hamlet* to his mother, which made her very angry. Once when I took a horsewhip to chastise him, he drew a knife, and would have stabbed me; and, faith, I recollected my own youth, which was pretty similar, and, holding out my hand, burst out laughing, and proposed to him to be friends. We were reconciled for that time, and the next, and the next; but there was no love lost between us, and his hatred for me seemed to grow as he grew, which was apace.

I determined to endow my darling boy, Bryan, with a property, and to this end cut down twelve thousand pounds' worth of timber on Lady Lyndon's Yorkshire and Irish estates; at which proceeding Bullingdon's guardian, Tiptoff, cried out, as usual, and swore I had no right to touch a stick of the trees; but down they went; and I commissioned my mother to re-purchase the ancient lands of Ballybarry and Barryogue, which had once formed part of the immense possessions of my house. These she bought back with excellent prudence, and extreme joy; for her heart was gladdened at the idea that a son was born to my name, and with the notion of my magnificent fortunes.

To say truth, I was rather afraid, now that I lived in a very different sphere to that in which she was accustomed to move, lest she should come to pay me a visit, and astonish my English friends by her bragging and her brogue, her rouge and her old hoops and furbelows of the time of George II, in which she had figured advantageously in her youth, and which she still fondly thought to be at the height of the fashion. So I wrote to her, putting off her visit; begging her to visit us when the left wing of the castle was finished, or the stables built, and so forth. There was no need of such precaution. 'A hint's enough for me, Redmond,' the old lady would reply. 'I'm not coming to disturb you among your great English friends with my old-fashioned Irish ways. It's a blessing to me to think that my darling boy has attained the position which I always knew was his due, and for which I pinched myself to educate him. You must bring me the little Bryan, that his grandmother may kiss him, one day. Present my respectful blessing to her ladyship, his mamma. Tell her she has got a treasure in her husband, which she couldn't have had had she taken a duke to marry her; and that the Barrys and the Bradys, though without titles, have the best of blood in their veins. I shall never rest until I see you Earl of Ballybarry, and my grandson Lord Viscount Barryogue.'

How singular it was that the very same ideas should be passing in my mother's mind and my own! The very titles she had pitched upon had also been selected (naturally enough) by me; and I don't mind confessing that I had filled a dozen sheets of paper with my signature, under the names of Ballybarry and Barryogue, and had determined with my usual impetuosity to carry my point. My mother went and established herself at Ballybarry, living with the priest there until a tenement could be erected, and dating from 'Ballybarry Castle,' which, you may be sure, I gave out to be a place of no small importance. I had a plan of the estate in my study, both at Hackton and in Berkeley Square, and the plans of the elevation of Ballybarry Castle, the ancestral residence of Barry Lyndon, Esq., with the projected improvements, in which the castle was represented as about the size of Windsor, with more ornaments to the architecture; and eight hundred acres of bog falling in handy, I purchased them at three pounds an acre, so that my estate upon the map looked to be no insignificant one.[1] I also in this year made arrangements for purchasing the Polwellan estate and mines in Cornwall from Sir John Trecothick, for 70,000*l.*—an imprudent bargain, which was afterwards the cause to me of much dispute and litigation. The troubles of property, the rascality of agents, the quibbles of lawyers, are endless. Humble people envy us great men, and fancy that our lives are all pleasure. Many a time in the course of my prosperity I have sighed for the days of my meanest fortune, and envied the boon-companions at my table, with no clothes to their backs but such as my credit supplied them, without a guinea but what came from my pocket, but without one of the harassing cares and responsibilities which are the dismal adjuncts of great rank and property.

I did little more than make my appearance, and assume the command of my estates, in the kingdom of Ireland, rewarding generously those persons who had been kind to me in my former adversities, and taking my fitting place among the aristocracy of the land. But, in truth, I had small inducements to remain in it after having tasted of the genteeler and more complete pleasures of English and Continental life; and we passed our summers at Buxton,

[1] On the strength of this estate, and pledging his honour that it was not mortgaged, Mr. Barry Lyndon borrowed 17,000*l.*, in the year 1786, from young Captain Pigeon, the city merchant's son, who had just come in for his property. As for the Polwellan estate and mines, 'the cause of endless litigation,' it must be owned that our hero purchased them; but he never paid more than the first 5,000*l.* of the purchase-money. Hence the litigation of which he complains, and the famous Chancery suit of 'Trecothick *v.* Lyndon,' in which Mr. John Scott*greatly distinguished himself.—Ed. *Fraser's Mag.*

the Bath, and Harrogate, while Hackton Castle was being beautified in the elegant manner already described by me, and the season at our mansion in Berkeley Square.

It is wonderful how the possession of wealth brings out the virtues of a man, or, at any rate, acts as a varnish or lustre to them, and brings out their brilliancy and colour in a manner never known when the individual stood in the cold grey atmosphere of poverty. I assure you, it was a very short time before I was a pretty fellow of the first class; made no small sensation at the coffee-houses in Pall Mall, and afterwards at the most famous clubs. My style, equipages, and elegant entertainments were in everybody's mouth, and were described in all the morning prints. The needier part of Lady Lyndon's relatives, and such as had been offended by the intolerable pomposity of old Tiptoff, began to appear at our routs and assemblies; and as for relations of my own, I found in London and Ireland more than I had ever dreamed of, of cousins who claimed affinity with me. There were, of course, natives of my own country (of which I was not particularly proud), and I received visits from three or four swaggering shabby Temple bucks, with tarnished lace and Tipperary brogue, who were eating their way to the Bar in London; from several gambling adventurers at the watering-places, whom I soon speedily let to know their place; and from others of more reputable condition. Among them I may mention my cousin, the Lord Kilbarry, who, on the score of his relationship, borrowed thirty pieces from me to pay his landlady in Swallow Street, and whom, for my own reasons, I allowed to maintain and credit a connexion for which the Heralds' College gave no authority whatsoever. Kilbarry had a cover at my table; punted at play, and paid when he liked, which was seldom; had an intimacy with, and was under considerable obligations to, my tailor; and always boasted of his cousin, the great Barry Lyndon of the west country.

Her ladyship and I lived, after a while, pretty separate when in London. She preferred quiet, or, to say the truth, I preferred it, being a great friend to a modest, tranquil behaviour in woman, and a taste for the domestic pleasures. Hence I encouraged her to dine at home with her ladies, her chaplain, and a few of her friends; admitted three or four proper and discreet persons to accompany her to her box at the Opera or play, on proper occasions; and, indeed, declined for her the too frequent visits of her friends and family, preferring to receive them only twice or thrice in a season on our grand reception days. Besides, she was a mother, and had great comfort in the dressing, educating, and dandling our little Bryan, for whose sake it was fit that she should give up the pleasures and frivolities of the world; so she left *that* part of the duty of every family of distinction to be performed by me. To say the truth, Lady Lyndon's figure and appearance were not at this time such as to make for their owner any very brilliant appearance in the fashionable world. She had grown very fat, was short-sighted, pale in complexion, careless about her dress, dull in demeanour; her conversations with me characterized by a stupid despair, or a silly, blundering attempt at forced cheerfulness still more disagreeable: hence our intercourse was but trifling, and my temptations to carry her into the world or to remain in her society of necessity exceedingly small. She would try my temper, at home, too, in a thousand ways. When requested by me (often, I own, rather roughly) to entertain the company with conversation, wit, and learning, of which she was a mistress; or music, of which she was an accomplished performer, she would as often as not begin to cry, and leave the room. My company from this, of course, fancied I was a tyrant over her; whereas, I was only a severe and careful guardian over a silly, bad-tempered, and weak-minded lady.

She was luckily very fond of her youngest son, and through him I had a wholesome and effectual hold of her; for if in any of her tantrums or fits of haughtiness—(this woman was intolerably proud, and repeatedly, at first, in our quarrels, dared to twit me with my own original poverty and low birth),—if, I say, in our disputes she pretended to have the upper hand, to assert her authority against mine, to refuse to sign such papers as I might think necessary for the distribution of our large and complicated property, I would have Master Bryan carried off to Chiswick for a couple of days; and I warrant me his lady-mother could hold out no longer, and would agree to anything I chose to propose. The servants about her I took care should be in my pay, not hers: especially the child's head nurse was under *my* orders, not those of my lady; and a very handsome, red-cheeked, impudent jade she was; and a great fool she made me make of myself. This woman was more mistress of the house than the poor-spirited lady who owned it. She gave the law to the servants: and if I showed any particular attention to any of the ladies who visited us, the slut would not scruple to show her jealousy, and to find means to send them packing. The fact is, a generous man is always made a fool of by some woman or other; and this one had such an influence over me, that she could turn me round her finger.[1]

Her infernal temper (Mrs. Stammer was the jade's name) and my wife's moody despondency made my house and home not over-pleasant; hence I was driven a good deal abroad, where, as play was the fashion at every club,

[1] From these curious confessions, it would appear that Mr. Lyndon maltreated his lady in every possible way; that he denied her society, bullied her into signing away her property, spent it in gambling and taverns, was openly unfaithful to her; and, when she complained, threatened to remove her children from her. Nor, indeed, is he the only husband who has done the like, and has passed for 'nobody's enemy but his own'; a jovial, good-natured fellow. The world contains scores of such amiable people; and, indeed, it is because justice has not been done them that we have edited this autobiography. Had it been that of a mere hero of romance,—one of those heroic youths who figure in the novels of Scott and James,*—there would have been no call to introduce the reader to a personage already so often and so charmingly depicted. Mr. Barry Lyndon is not, we repeat, a hero of the common pattern; but let the reader look round, and ask himself, Do not as many rogues succeed in life as honest men? more fools than men of talent? And is it not just that the lives of this class should be described by the student of human nature as well as the actions of those fairy-tale princes, those perfect impossible heroes, whom our writers love to describe? There is something *naïve* and simple in that time-honoured style of novel-writing by which Prince Prettyman,* at the end of his adventures, is put in possession of every worldly prosperity, as he has been endowed with every mental and bodily excellence previously. The novelist thinks that he can do no more for his darling hero than make him a lord. Is it not a poor standard that, of the *summum bonum?* The greatest good in life is not to be a lord, perhaps not even to be happy. Poverty, illness, a humpback, may be rewards and conditions of good, as well as that bodily prosperity which all of us unconsciously set up for worship. But this is a subject for an essay, not a note; and it is best to allow Mr. Lyndon to resume the candid and ingenious narrative of his virtues and defects.—O. Y.*

tavern, and assembly, I, of course, was obliged to resume my old habit, and to commence as an amateur those games at which I was once unrivalled in Europe. But whether a man's temper changes with prosperity, or his skill leaves him when deprived of a confederate, and pursuing the game no longer professionally, he joins in it, like the rest of the world, for pastime, I know not; but certain it is that in the seasons of 1774–5 I lost much money at White's and the Cocoa-tree, and was compelled to meet my losses by borrowing largely upon my wife's annuities, insuring her ladyship's life, and so forth. The terms at which I raised these necessary sums, and the outlays requisite for my improvements, were, of course, very onerous, and clipped the property considerably; and it was some of these papers which my Lady Lyndon (who was of a narrow, timid, and stingy turn) occasionally refused to sign, until I *persuaded* her, as I have before shown.

My dealings on the turf ought to be mentioned, as forming part of my history at this time; but, in truth, I have no particular pleasure in recalling my Newmarket doings. I was infernally bit and bubbled in almost every one of my transactions there; and though I could ride a horse as well as any man in England, was no match with the English noblemen at backing him. Fifteen years after my horse, Bay Bülow, by Eclipse, out of Sophy Hardcastle, lost the Newmarket stakes, for which he was the first favourite, I found that a noble earl, who shall be nameless, had got into his stable the morning before he ran, and the consequence was that an outside horse won, and your humble servant was out to the amount of fifteen thousand pounds. Strangers had no chance in those days on the heath; and, though dazzled by the splendour and fashion assembled there, and surrounded by the greatest persons of the land,—the royal dukes, with their wives and splendid equipages,—old Grafton,* with his queer bevy of company, and such men as Ancaster, Sandwich, Lorn,*—a man might have considered himself certain of fair play and have been not a little proud of the society he kept. Yet, I promise you that, exalted as it was, there was no set of men in Europe who knew how to rob more genteelly, to bubble a stranger, to bribe a jockey, to doctor a horse, or to arrange a betting-book. Even *I* couldn't stand against these accomplished gamesters of the highest families in

Europe. Was it my own want of style, or my want of a fortune? I know not. But now I was arrived at the height of my ambition both my skill and my luck seemed to be deserting me. Everything I touched crumbled in my hand; every speculation I had, failed; every agent I trusted deceived me. I am, indeed, one of those born to make, and not to keep fortunes; for the qualities and energy which lead a man to effect the first are often the very causes of his ruin in the latter case; indeed I know of no other reason for the misfortunes which finally befell me.[1]

I had always a taste for men of letters, and perhaps, if the truth must be told, have no objection to playing the fine gentleman and patron among the wits. Such people are usually needy, and of low birth, and have an instinctive awe and love of a gentleman and a laced coat, as all must have remarked who have frequented their society. Mr. Reynolds,* who was afterwards knighted, and certainly the most elegant painter of his day, was a pretty dexterous courtier of the wit tribe; and it was through this gentleman, who painted a piece of me, Lady Lyndon, and our little Bryan, which was greatly admired at the Exhibition* (I was represented as quitting my wife, in the costume of the Tippleton yeomanry, of which I was major: the child starting back from my helmet like what-d'ye-call-'em—Hector's son, as described by Mr. Pope, in his *Iliad*),* it was through Mr. Reynolds that I was introduced to a score of these gentlemen, and their great chief, Mr. Johnson. I always thought their great chief a great bear. He drank tea twice or thrice at my house, misbehaving himself most grossly, treating my opinions with no more respect than those of a schoolboy, and telling me to mind my horses and tailors, and not trouble myself about letters. His Scotch bear-leader, Mr. Boswell, was a butt of the first quality. I never saw such a figure as the fellow cut in what he called a Corsican habit,* at one of Mrs. Cornely's balls,* at Carlisle House, Soho. But that the stories connected with that same establishment are not the most profitable tales in the world, I could tell tales of scores of queer doings there. All the high and low demireps of the town gathered

[1] The Memoirs seem to have been written about the year 1814, in that calm retreat which Fortune had selected for the author at the close of his life.

there, from his Grace of Ancaster down to my countryman, poor Mr. Oliver Goldsmith,* the poet [(whom I never saw, by the way, for he died in the year of my appearance in town)],[1] and from the Duchess of Kingston* down to the Bird of Paradise, or Kitty Fisher.* Here I have met very queer characters, who came to queer ends too; poor Hackman,* that afterwards was hanged for killing Miss Reay, and (on the sly) his reverence Dr. Simony,* whom my friend Sam Foote,* of the Little Theatre, bade to live even after forgery and the rope cut short the unlucky parson's career.

It was a merry place, London, in those days, and that's the truth. I'm writing now in my gouty old age, and people have grown vastly more moral and matter-of-fact than they were at the close of the last century, when the world was young with me. There was a difference between a gentleman and a common fellow in those times. We wore silk and embroidery then. Now every man has the same coachman-like look in his belcher* and caped coat, and there is no outward difference between my lord and his groom. Then it took a man of fashion a couple of hours to make his toilet, and he could show some taste and genius in the selecting it. What a blaze of splendour was a drawing-room, or an opera, of a gala night! What sums of money were lost and won at the delicious faro-table! My gilt curricle and outriders, blazing in green and gold, were very different objects to the equipages you see nowadays in the ring, with the stunted grooms behind them. A man could drink four times as much as the milksops nowadays can swallow; but 'tis useless expatiating on this theme. Gentlemen are dead and gone. The fashion has now turned upon your soldiers and sailors, and I grow quite moody and sad when I think of thirty years ago.

This is a chapter devoted to reminiscences of what was a very happy and splendid time with me, but presenting little of mark in the way of adventure, as is generally the case when times are happy and easy. It would seem idle to fill pages with accounts of the every-day occupations of a man of fashion,—the fair ladies who smiled upon him, the dresses he wore, the matches he played, and won or lost. At this period of time, when youngsters are employed

[1] Omitted in later editions, perhaps as being inconsistent with p. 15.

cutting the Frenchmen's throats in Spain and France,* lying out in bivouacs, and feeding off commissariat beef* and biscuits, they would not understand what a life their ancestors led; and so I shall leave further discourse upon the pleasures of the times when even the Prince was a lad in leading-strings, when Charles Fox had not subsided into a mere statesman, and Bonaparte* was a beggarly brat in his native island.

Whilst these improvements were going on in my estates,—my house, from an antique Norman castle, being changed to an elegant Greek temple, or palace—my gardens and woods losing their rustic appearance to be adapted to the most genteel French style—my child growing up at his mother's knees, and my influence in the country increasing,—it must not be imagined that I stayed in Devonshire all this while, and that I neglected to make visits to London and my various estates in England and Ireland.

I went to reside at the Trecothick estate, and the Polwellan wheal, where I found, instead of profit, every kind of pettifogging chicanery; I passed over in state to our territories in Ireland, where I entertained the gentry in a style the Lord Lieutenant himself could not equal; gave the fashion to Dublin (to be sure it was a beggarly, savage city in those days, and, since the time there has been a pother about the Union,* and the misfortunes attending it, I have been at a loss to account for the mad praises of the old order of things, which the fond Irish patriots have invented), I say I set the fashion to Dublin, and small praise to me, for a poor place it was in those times, whatever the Irish party may say.

In a former chapter I have given you a description of it. It was the Warsaw of our part of the world; there was a splendid, ruined, half-civilized nobility, ruling over a half-savage population. I say half-savage advisedly. The commonalty in the streets were wild, unshorn, and in rags. The most public places were not safe after nightfall. The College, the public buildings, and the great gentry's houses were splendid (the latter unfinished for the most part); but the people were in a state more wretched than any vulgar I have ever known; the exercise of their religion was only half-allowed to them; their clergy were forced to be educated out of the country; their aristocracy was quite distinct from them; there was a Protestant nobility, and in the towns, poor, insolent Protestant corporations,* with a bankrupt retinue of mayors, aldermen, and municipal officers, all of whom figured in addresses, and had the public voice in the country ; but there was no sympathy and connexion between the upper and the lower people of the Irish. To one who had been bred so much abroad as myself, this difference between Catholic and Protestant was doubly striking ; and though as firm as a rock in my own faith, yet I could not help remembering my grandfather held a different one, and wondering that there should be such a political difference between the two. I passed among my neighbours for a dangerous leveller, for entertaining and expressing such opinions, and especially for asking the priest of the parish to my table at Castle Lyndon. He was a gentleman, educated at Salamanca,* and, to my mind, a far better bred and more agreeable companion than his comrade the rector, who had but a dozen Protestants for his congregation, who was a lord's son, to be sure, but he could hardly spell, and the great field of his labours was in the kennel and cockpit.

I did not extend and beautify the house of Castle Lyndon as I had done our other estates, but contented myself with paying an occasional visit there, exercising an almost royal hospitality, and keeping open house during my stay. When absent, I gave to my aunt, the widow Brady, and her six unmarried daughters (although they always detested me) permission to inhabit the place, my mother preferring my new mansion of Barryogue.

And as my Lord Bullingdon was by this time grown excessively tall and troublesome, I determined to leave him under the care of a proper governor in Ireland, with Mrs. Brady and her six daughters to take care of him ; and he was welcome to fall in love with all the old ladies if he were so minded, and thereby imitate his step-father's example. When tired of Castle Lyndon, his lordship was at liberty to go and reside at my house with my mamma ; but there was no love lost between him and her, and, on account of my son Bryan, I think she hated him as cordially as ever I myself could possibly do.

The county of Devon is not so lucky as the neighbouring county of Cornwall,* and has not the share of representatives which the latter possesses ; where I have known a moderate country gentleman, with a few score of hundreds per annum from his estate, treble his income by returning three or four members to Parliament, and by the influence with ministers which these seats gave him. The parliamentary interest of the house of Lyndon had been grossly neglected during my wife's minority, and the incapacity of the earl her father; or, to speak more correctly, it had been smuggled away from the Lyndon family altogether by the adroit old hypocrite of Tiptoff Castle, who acted as most kinsmen and guardians do by their wards and relatives, and robbed them. The Marquess of Tiptoff returned four members to Parliament: two for the borough of Tippleton, which, as all the world knows, lies at the foot of our estate of Hackton, bounded on the other side by Tiptoff Park. For time out of mind we had sent members for that borough, until Tiptoff, taking advantage of the late lord's imbecility, put in his own nominees. When his eldest son became of age, of course my lord was to take his seat for Tippleton; when Rigby (Nabob Rigby, who made his fortune under Clive in India)* died, the marquess thought fit to bring down his second son, my Lord George Poynings, to whom I have introduced the reader in a former chapter, and determined, in his high mightiness, that he, too, should go and swell the ranks of the Opposition—the big old Whigs, with whom the marquess acted.

Rigby had been for some time in an ailing condition previous to his demise, and you may be sure that the circumstance of his failing health had not been passed over by the gentry of the county, who were stanch Government men for the most part, and hated my Lord Tiptoff's principles as dangerous and ruinous. 'We have been looking out for a man to fight against him,' said the squires to me; 'we can only match Tiptoff out of Hackton Castle. You, Mr. Lyndon, are our man, and at the next county election we will swear to bring you in.'

I hated the Tiptoffs so, that I would have fought them at any election. They not only would not visit at Hackton, but declined to receive those who visited us; they kept the women of the county from receiving my wife; they invented half the wild stories of my profligacy and extravagance with which the neighbourhood was entertained; they said I had frightened my wife into marriage, and that she was a lost woman; they hinted that Bullingdon's life was not secure under my roof, that his treatment was odious, and that I wanted to put him out of the way to make place for Bryan my son. I could scarce have a friend to Hackton but they counted the bottles drunk at my table. They ferreted out my dealings with my lawyers and agents. If a creditor was unpaid, every item of his bill was known at Tiptoff Hall; if I looked at a farmer's daughter, it was said I had ruined her. My faults are many, I confess, and, as a domestic character, I can't boast of any particular regularity, or temper; but Lady Lyndon and I did not quarrel more than fashionable people do, and, at first, we always used to make it up pretty well. I am a man full of errors, certainly, but not the devil that these odious backbiters at Tiptoff represented me to be. For the first three years I never struck my wife but when I was in liquor. When I flung the carving-knife at Bullingdon I was drunk, as everybody present can testify;[1] but as for having any systematic scheme against the poor lad, I can declare solemnly that, beyond merely hating him (and one's inclinations are not in one's power), I am guilty of no evil towards him.

I had sufficient motives, then, for enmity against the Tiptoffs, and am not a man to let a feeling of that kind lie inactive. Though a Whig, or, perhaps, because a Whig, the marquess was one of the haughtiest men breathing, and treated commoners as his idol, the great earl,* used to treat them—after he came to a coronet himself—as so many low vassals, who might be proud to lick his shoe-buckle. When the Tippleton mayor and corporation waited upon him, he received them covered, never offered Mr. Mayor a chair, but retired when the refreshments were brought, or had them served to the worshipful aldermen

[1] [These domestic qualities, which our hero describes so *naïvely*, were much more common in the past century than at present, and in the innumerable letters and journals of the period drunkenness is spoken of as quite a common condition of men of the very highest fashion, and pleaded and admitted as an excuse for all sorts of outrages. If the crude way in which these matters are discussed should offend some delicate readers of the present day, let them remember this is an authentic description of a bygone state of society, not a dandy apology, or encomium, such as some of our rose-water novelists invent, whose works from their very charity, become untrustworthy, and are no more natural or veracious, than the legend of Prince Prettyman or the story of Aladdin.]—Note in *Fraser's Magazine*. omitted in later editions.

in the steward's room. These honest Britons never rebelled against such treatment, until instructed to do so by my patriotism. No, the dogs liked to be bullied, and, in the course of a long experience, I have met with but very few Englishmen who are not of their way of thinking.

It was not until I opened their eyes that they knew their degradation. I invited the mayor to Hackton, and Mrs. Mayoress (a very buxom, pretty groceress she was, by the way) I made sit by my wife, and drove them both out to the races in my curricle. Lady Lyndon fought very hard against this condescension, but I had a way with her, as the saying is, and though she had a temper, yet I had a better one. A temper, psha! A wild cat has a temper, but a keeper can get the better of it, and I know very few women in the world whom I could not master.

Well, I made much of the mayor and corporation, sent them bucks for their dinners, or asked them to mine, made a point of attending their assemblies, dancing with their wives and daughters, going through, in short, all the acts of politeness which are necessary in such occasions; and though old Tiptoff must have seen my goings on, yet his head was so much in the clouds that he never once condescended to imagine his dynasty could be overthrown in his own town of Tippleton, and issued his mandates as securely as if he had been the Grand Turk,* and the Tippletonians no better than so many slaves of his will.

Every post which brought us any account of Rigby's increasing illness was the sure occasion of a dinner from me; so much so, that my friends of the hunt used to laugh, and say, 'Rigby's worse; there's a corporation dinner at Hackton.'

It was in 1776, when the American war broke out, that I came into Parliament. My Lord Chatham, whose wisdom his party in those days used to call superhuman, raised his oracular voice in the House of Peers against the American contest; and my countryman, Mr. Burke,* a great philosopher, but a plaguy long-winded orator, was the champion of the rebels in the Commons, where, however, thanks to British patriotism, he could get very few to back him. Old Tiptoff would have sworn black was white, if the great earl had bidden him, and he made his son give up his commission in the Guards, in imitation of my

Lord Pitt,* who resigned his ensigncy rather than fight against what he called his American brethren.

But this was a height of patriotism extremely little relished in England, where, ever since the breaking out of hostilities, our people hated the Americans heartily, and where, when we heard of the fight of Lexington, and the glorious victory of Bunker's Hill* (as we used to call it in those days), the nation flushed out in its usual hot-headed anger. The talk was all against the philosophers after that, and the people most indómitably loyal. It was not until the land-tax* was increased, that the gentry began to grumble a little, but still my party in the west was very strong against the Tiptoffs, and I determined to take the field and win as usual.

The old marquess neglected every one of the decent precautions which are requisite in a parliamentary campaign. He signified to the corporation and freeholders his intention of presenting his son, Lord George, and his desire that the latter should be elected their burgess; but he scarcely gave so much as a glass of beer to whet the devotedness of his adherents, and I, as I need not say, engaged every tavern in Tippleton in my behalf.

There is no need to go over the twenty-times-told tale of an election. I rescued the borough of Tippleton from the hands of Lord Tiptoff and his son, Lord George. I had a savage sort of satisfaction, too, in forcing my wife, who had been at one time exceedingly smitten by her kinsman, as I have already related, to take part against him, and to wear and distribute my colours when the day of election came. And when we spoke at one another, I told the crowd that I had beaten Lord George in love, that I had beaten him in war, and that I would now beat him in Parliament; and so I did, as the event proved: for, to the inexpressible anger of the old marquess, Barry Lyndon, Esquire, was returned Member of Parliament for Tippleton, in place of John Rigby, Esquire, deceased; and I threatened him at the next election to turn him out of *both* his seats, and went to attend my duties in Parliament.

It was then I seriously determined on achieving for myself the Irish peerage, to be enjoyed after me by my beloved son and heir.

CHAPTER XVIII

IN WHICH MY GOOD FORTUNE BEGINS TO WAVER

AND now, if any people should be disposed to think my history immoral (for I have heard some assert that I was a man who never deserved that so much prosperity should fall to my share), I will beg those cavillers to do me the favour to read the conclusion of my adventures, when they will see it was no such great prize that I had won, and that wealth, splendour, thirty thousand per annum, and a seat in Parliament are often purchased at too dear a rate, when one has to buy those enjoyments at the price of personal liberty, and saddled with the charge of a troublesome wife.

They are the deuce, these troublesome wives, and that is the truth. No man knows until he tries how wearisome and disheartening the burthen of one of them is, and how the annoyance grows and strengthens from year to year, and the courage weaker to bear it; so that that trouble which seemed light and trivial the first year, becomes intolerable ten years after. I have heard of one of the classical fellows in the dictionary* who began by carrying a calf up a hill every day, and so continued until the animal grew to be a bull, which he still easily accommodated upon his shoulders; but take my word for it, young unmarried gentlemen, a wife is a very much harder pack to the back than the biggest heifer in Smithfield; and, if I can prevent one of you from marrying, the Memoirs of Barry Lyndon, Esq., will not be written in vain. Not that my lady was a scold or a shrew, as some wives are; I could have managed to have cured her of that; but she was of a cowardly, crying, melancholy, maudlin temper, which is to me still more odious; and, do what one would to please her, would never be happy or in good humour. I left her alone after a while, and because, as was natural in my case, where a disagreeable home obliged me to seek amusement and companions abroad, she added a mean, detestable jealousy to all her other faults; and I could not for some time pay the commonest attention to any other woman but my Lady Lyndon must weep, and wring her hands, and threaten to commit suicide, and I know not what.

Her death would have been no comfort to me, as I leave any person of common prudence to imagine; for that scoundrel of a young Bullingdon (who was now growing up a tall, gawky, swarthy lad, and about to become my greatest plague and annoyance) would have inherited every penny of the property, and I should have been left considerably poorer even than when I married the widow; for I spent my personal fortune as well as the lady's income in the keeping up of our rank, and was always too much a man of honour and spirit to save a penny of Lady Lyndon's income. Let this be flung in the teeth of my detractors, who say I never could have so injured the Lyndon property had I not been making a private purse for myself; and who believe that, even in my present painful situation, I have hoards of gold laid by somewhere, and could come out as a Croesus* when I choose. I never raised a shilling upon Lady Lyndon's property but I spent it like a man of honour; besides incurring numberless personal obligations for money, which all went to the common stock. Independent of the Lyndon mortgages and encumbrances, I owe myself at least one hundred and twenty thousand pounds, which I spent while in occupancy of my wife's estate: so that I may justly say that property is indebted to me in the above-mentioned sum.

Although I have described the utter disgust and distaste which speedily took possession of my breast as regarded Lady Lyndon; and although I took no particular pains (for I am all frankness and aboveboard) to disguise my feelings in general, yet she was of such a mean spirit that she pursued me with her regard in spite of my indifference to her, and would kindle up at the smallest kind word I spoke to her. The fact is, between my respected reader and myself, that I was one of the handsomest and most dashing young men of England in those days, and my wife was violently in love with me; and though I say it who shouldn't, as the phrase goes, my wife was not the only woman of rank in London who had a favourable opinion of the humble Irish adventurer. What a riddle these women are, I have often thought! I have seen the most elegant creatures at St. James's grow wild for love of the coarsest and most vulgar of men; the cleverest women passionately admire the most illiterate of our sex, and so on. There is no end to the contrariety in the foolish creatures; and though I don't mean to hint that *I* am vulgar or illiterate, as the persons mentioned above (I would cut the throat of any man who dared to whisper a word against my birth or my breeding), yet I have shown that Lady Lyndon had plenty of reason to dislike me if she chose; but, like the rest of her silly sex, she was governed by infatuation, not reason; and, up to the very last day of our being together, would be reconciled to me, and fondle me, if I addressed her a single kind word.

'Ah,' she would say, in these moments of tenderness, 'ah, *Redmond*, if you would always be so!' And in these fits of love she was the most easy creature in the world to be persuaded, and would have signed away her whole property, had it been possible. And, I must confess, it was with very little attention on my part that I could bring her into good humour. To walk with her on the Mall, or at Ranelagh, to attend her to church at St. James's,* to purchase any little present or trinket for her, was enough to coax her. Such is female inconsistency! The next day she would be calling me 'Mr. Barry,' probably, and be bemoaning her miserable fate that she ever should have been united to such a monster. So it was she was pleased to call one of the most brilliant men in his Majesty's three kingdoms; and I warrant me *other* ladies had a much more flattering opinion of me.

Then she would threaten to leave me; but I had a hold of her in the person of her son, of whom she was passionately fond, I don't know why, for she had always neglected Bullingdon her elder, and never bestowed a thought upon his health, his welfare, or his education.

It was our young boy, then, who formed the great bond of union between me and her ladyship; and there was no plan of ambition I could propose in which she would not join for the poor lad's behoof, and no expense she would not eagerly incur, if it might by any means be shown to tend to his advancement. I can tell you, bribes were administered, and in high places too,—so near the royal person of his Majesty, that you would be astonished were I to mention what great personages condescended to receive our loans. I got from the English and Irish heralds a description and detailed pedigree of the Barony of Barryogue, and claimed respectfully to be reinstated in my ancestral titles, and also to be rewarded with the Viscounty of Ballybarry. 'This head would become a coronet,' my lady would sometimes say, in her fond moments, smoothing down my hair; and, indeed, there is many a puny whipster in their lordships' House who has neither my presence nor my courage, my pedigree, nor any of my merits.

The striving after this peerage I consider to have been one of the most unlucky of all my unlucky dealings at this period. I made unheard-of sacrifices to bring it about. I lavished money here and diamonds there. I bought lands at ten times their value; purchased pictures and articles of virtu at ruinous prices. I gave repeated entertainments to those friends to my claims who, being about the royal person, were likely to advance it. I lost many a bet to the royal dukes, his Majesty's brothers; but let these matters be forgotten, and, because of my private injuries, let me not be deficient in loyalty to my sovereign.

The only person in this transaction whom I shall mention openly is that old scamp and swindler Gustavus Adolphus, thirteenth Earl of Crabs. This nobleman was one of the gentlemen of his Majesty's closet, and one with whom the revered monarch was on terms of considerable intimacy. A close regard had sprung up between them in the old king's time; when his royal Highness, playing at battledore and shuttlecock with the young lord on the landing-place of the great staircase at Kew,* in some moment of irritation, the Prince of Wales kicked the young earl downstairs, who, falling, broke his leg. The prince's hearty repentance for his violence caused him to ally himself closely with the person whom he had injured; and when his Majesty came to the throne there was no man, it is said, of whom the Earl of Bute* was so jealous as of my Lord Crabs. The latter was poor and extravagant, and Bute got him out of the way, by sending him on the Russian and other embassies; but on this favourite's dismissal Crabs sped back from the Continent, and was appointed almost immediately to a place about his Majesty's person.

It was with this disreputable nobleman that I contracted an unlucky intimacy when, fresh and unsuspecting, I first established myself in town, after my marriage with Lady Lyndon: and, as Crabs was really one of the most entertaining fellows in the world, I took a sincere pleasure in his company; besides the interested desire I had in cultivating the society of a man who was so near the person of the highest personage in the realm.

To hear the fellow, you would fancy that there was scarce any appointment made in which he had not a share. He told me, for instance, of Charles Fox being turned out of his place* a day before poor Charley himself was aware of the fact. He told me when the Howes* were coming back from America, and who was to succeed to the command there. Not to multiply instances, it was upon this person that I fixed my chief reliance for the advancement of my claim to the Barony of Barryogue, and the Viscounty which I proposed to get.

One of the main causes of expense which this ambition of mine entailed upon me was the fitting out and arming a company of infantry from the Castle Lyndon and Hackton estates, in Ireland, which I offered to my gracious sovereign for the campaign against American rebels. These troops, superbly equipped and clothed, were embarked at Portsmouth in the year 1778; and the patriotism of the gentleman who had raised them was so acceptable at court that, on being presented by my Lord North,* his Majesty condescended to notice me particularly, and said, 'That's right, Mr. Lyndon, raise another company, and go with them too!' But this was by no means, as the reader may suppose, to my notions. A man with thirty thousand pounds per annum is a fool to risk his life like a common beggar; and on this account I have always admired the conduct of my friend Jack Bolter, who had been a most active and resolute cornet of horse, and, as such, engaged in every scrape and skirmish which could fall to his lot; but just before the battle of Minden he received news that his uncle, the great army contractor, was dead, and had left him five thousand per annum. Jack that instant applied for leave; and, as it was refused him on the eve of a general action, my gentleman took it, and never fired a pistol again, except against an officer who questioned his courage, and whom he winged in such a cool and determined manner, as showed all the world that it was from prudence, and a desire of enjoying his money, not from cowardice, that he quitted the profession of arms.

When this Hackton company was raised, my stepson, who was now sixteen years of age, was most eager to be allowed to join it, and I would have gladly consented to have been rid of the young man; but his guardian, Lord Tiptoff, who thwarted me in everything, refused his permission, and the lad's military inclinations were balked. If he could have gone on the expedition, and a rebel rifle had put an end to him, I believe, to tell the truth, I should not have been grieved over much, and I should have had the pleasure of seeing my other son the heir to the estate which his father had won with so much pains.

The education of this young nobleman had been, I confess, some of the loosest; and perhaps the truth is, I *did* neglect the brat. He was of so wild, savage, and insubordinate a nature that I never had the least regard for him; and before me and his mother, at least, was so moody and dull that I thought instruction thrown away upon him, and left him for the most part to shift for himself. For two whole years he remained in Ireland, away from us; and when in England, we kept him mainly at Hackton, never caring to have the uncouth, ungainly lad in the genteel company in the capital in which we naturally mingled. My own poor boy, on the contrary, was the most polite and engaging child ever seen; it was a pleasure to treat him with kindness and distinction; and before he was five years old, the little fellow was the pink of fashion, beauty, and good breeding.

In fact, he could not have been otherwise, with the care both his parents bestowed upon him, and the attentions that were lavished upon him in every way. When he was four years old, I quarrelled with the English nurse who had attended upon him, and about whom my wife had been so jealous, and procured for him a French *gouvernante*, who had lived with families of the first quality in Paris, and who, of course, must set my Lady Lyndon jealous too. Under the care of this young woman my little rogue learned to chatter French most charmingly. It would have done your heart good to hear the dear rascal swear, '*Mort de ma vie!*' and to see him stamp his little foot, and send the *manants* and *canaille** of the domestics to the *trente mille diables*. He was precocious in all things: at a very early age he would mimic everybody; at five, he would sit at table, and drink his glass of champagne with the best of us; and his nurse would teach him little French catches, and the last Parisian songs of Vadé and Collard,*—pretty songs they were too; and would make such of his hearers as understood French burst with laughing, and I promise you, scandalize some of the old dowagers who were admitted into the society of his mamma; not that there were many of them, for I did not encourage the visits of what you call respectable people to Lady Lyndon. They are sad spoilers of sport,—tale-bearers, envious, narrow-minded people; making mischief between man and wife. Whenever any of these grave personages in hoops and high heels used to make their appearance at Hackton, or in Berkeley Square, it was my chief pleasure to frighten them off; and I would make my little Bryan dance, sing, and play the *diable à quatre*,* and aid him myself so as to scare the old frumps.

I never shall forget the solemn remonstrances of our old square-toes of a rector at Hackton, who made one or two vain attempts to teach little Bryan Latin, and with whose innumerable children I sometimes allowed the boy to associate. They learned some of Bryan's French songs from him, which their mother, a poor soul who understood pickles and custards much better than French, used fondly to encourage them in singing; but which their father one day hearing, he sent Miss Sarah to her bedroom and bread-and-water for a week, and solemnly horsed Master Jacob in the presence of all his brothers and sisters, and of Bryan, to whom he hoped that flogging would act as a warning. But my little rogue kicked and plunged at the old parson's shins until he was obliged to get his sexton to hold him down, and swore, *corbleu*, *morbleu*, *ventrebleu*, that his young friend Jacob should not be maltreated. After this scene, his reverence forbade Bryan the rectory-house; on which I swore that his eldest son, who was bringing up for the ministry, should never have the succession of the living of Hackton, which I had thoughts of bestowing on him; and his father said, with a canting, hypocritical air, which I hate, that Heaven's will must be done; that he would not have his children disobedient or corrupted for the sake of a bishopric: and wrote me a pompous and solemn letter, charged with Latin quotations, taking farewell of me and my house. 'I do so with regret,' added the old gentleman, 'for I have received so many kindnesses from the Hackton family that it goes to my heart to be disunited from them. My poor, I fear, may suffer in consequence of my separation from you, and my being henceforward unable to bring to your notice instances of distress and affliction, which, when they were known to you, I will do you the justice to say, your generosity was always prompt to relieve.'

There may have been some truth in this, for the old gentleman was perpetually pestering me with petitions, and I know for a certainty, from his own charities, was often without a shilling in his pocket; but I suspect the good dinners at Hackton had a considerable share in causing his regrets at the dissolution of our intimacy, and I know that his wife was quite sorry to forgo the acquaintance of Bryan's *gouvernante*, Mademoiselle Louison, who had all the newest French fashions at her fingers' ends, and who never went to the Rectory but you would see the girls of the family turn out in new sacks or mantles the Sunday after.

I used to punish the old rebel by snoring very loud in my pew on Sundays during sermon-time; and I got a governor presently for Bryan, and a chaplain of my own, when he became of age sufficient to be separated from the women's society and guardianship. His English nurse I married to my head gardener, with a handsome portion; his French *gouvernante* I bestowed upon my faithful German Fritz, not forgetting the dowry in the latter instance, and they set up a French dining-house in Soho, and I believe at the time I write they are richer in the world's goods than their generous and free-handed master.

For Bryan I now got a young gentleman from Oxford, the Rev. Edmund Lavender, who was commissioned to teach him Latin when the boy was in the humour, and to ground him in history, grammar, and the other qualifications of a gentleman. Lavender was a precious addition to our society at Hackton. He was the means of making a deal of fun there. He was the butt of all our jokes, and bore them with the most admirable and martyr-like patience. He was one of that sort of men who would rather be kicked by a great man than not to be noticed by him; and I have often put his wig into the fire in the face of the company, and he would laugh at the joke as well as any man there. It was a delight to put him on a high-mettled horse, and send him after the hounds,—pale, sweating, calling on us, for Heaven's sake, to stop, and holding on for the dear life by the mane and the crupper. How it happened that the fellow was never killed I know not, but I suppose hanging is the way in which *his* neck will be broke. He never met with any accident, to speak of, in our hunting-matches; but you were pretty sure to find him at dinner in his place at the bottom of the table making the punch, whence he would be carried off fuddled to bed before the night was over. Many a time have Bryan and I painted his face black on those occasions. We put him into a haunted room, and frightened his soul out of his body with ghosts; we let loose cargoes of rats upon his bed; we cried fire, and filled his boots with water; we cut the legs of his preaching-chair, and filled his sermon-book with snuff. Poor Lavender bore it all with patience; and at our parties, or when we came to London, was amply repaid by being allowed to sit with the gentlefolks, and to fancy himself in the society of men of fashion. It was good to hear the contempt with which he talked about our rector. 'He has a son, sir, who is a servitor,* and a servitor at a small college,' he would say. 'How *could* you, my dear sir, think of giving the reversion of Hackton to such a low-bred creature?'

I should now speak of my other son, at least my Lady Lyndon's—I mean the Viscount Bullingdon. I kept him in Ireland for some years, under the guardianship of my mother, whom I had installed at Castle Lyndon; and great, I promise you, was her state in that occupation, and prodigious the good soul's splendour and haughty bearing. With all her oddities the Castle Lyndon estate was the best managed of all our possessions; the rents were excellently paid, the charges of getting them in smaller than they would have been under the management of any steward. It was astonishing what small expenses the good widow incurred, although she kept up the dignity of the *two* families, as she would say. She had a set of domestics to attend upon the young lord; she never went out herself but in an old gilt coach-and-six; the house was kept clean and tight; the furniture and gardens in the best repair; and, in our occasional visits to Ireland, we never found any house we visited in such good condition as our own. There were a score of ready serving lasses, and half as many trim men about the castle; and everything in as fine condition as the best housekeeper could make it. All this she did with scarcely any charges to us: for she fed sheep and cattle in the parks, and made a handsome profit of them at Ballinasloe; she supplied I don't know how many towns with butter and bacon; and the fruit and vegetables from the gardens of Castle Lyndon got the highest prices in Dublin market. She had no waste in the kitchen, as there used to be in most of our Irish houses; and there was no consumption of liquor in the cellars, for the old lady drank water, and saw little or no company. All her society was a couple of the girls of my ancient flame, Nora Brady, now Mrs. Quin, who with her husband had spent almost all their property, and who came to see me once in London, looking very old, fat, and slatternly, with two dirty children at her side. She wept very much when she saw me, called me 'Sir' and 'Mr. Lyndon,' at which I was not sorry, and begged me to help her husband, which I did, getting him, through my friend, Lord Crabs, a place in the excise in Ireland, and paying the passage of his family and himself to that country. I found him a dirty, cast-down, snivelling drunkard; and, looking at poor Nora, could not but wonder at the days when I had thought her a divinity. But if ever I have had a regard for a woman, I remain through life her constant friend, and could mention a thousand such instances of my generous and faithful disposition.

Young Bullingdon, however, was almost the only person with whom she was concerned that my mother could not keep in order. The accounts she sent me of him at first were such as gave my paternal heart considerable pain. He rejected all regularity and authority. He would absent himself for weeks from the house on sporting or other expeditions. He was when at home silent and queer, refusing to make my mother's game at piquet of evenings, but plunging into all sorts of musty old books, with which he muddled his brains; more at ease laughing and chatting with the pipers and maids in the servants'-hall than with the gentry in the drawing-room; always cutting gibes and jokes at Mrs. Barry, at which she (who was rather a slow woman at repartee) would chafe violently; in fact, leading a life of insubordination and scandal. And, to crown all, the young scapegrace took to frequenting the society of the Romish priest of the parish—a threadbare rogue, from some Popish seminary in France or Spain—rather than the company of the vicar of Castle Lyndon, a gentleman of Trinity, who kept his hounds and drank his two bottles a day.

Regard for the lad's religion made me not hesitate then how I should act towards him. If I have any principle which has guided me through life, it has been respect for the Establishment, and a hearty scorn and abhorrence of all other forms of belief. I therefore sent my French body-servant, in the year 17—, to Dublin with a commission to bring the young reprobate over, and the report brought to me was that he had passed the whole of the last night of his stay in Ireland with his Popish friend at the mass-house; that he and my mother had a violent quarrel on the very last day; that, on the contrary, he kissed Biddy and Dosy, her two nieces, who seemed very sorry that he should go; and that being pressed to go and visit the rector, he absolutely refused, saying he was a wicked old Pharisee, inside whose doors he would never set his foot. The doctor wrote me a letter, warning me against the deplorable errors of this young imp of perdition, as he called him, and I could see that there was no love lost between them. But it appeared that, if not agreeable to the gentry of the country, young Bullingdon had a huge popularity among the common people. There was a regular crowd weeping round the gate when his coach took its departure. Scores of the ignorant, savage wretches ran for miles along by the side of the chariot, and some went even so far as to steal away before his departure, and appear at the Pigeon-house at Dublin to bid him a last farewell. It was with considerable difficulty that some of these people could be kept from secreting themselves in the vessel, and accompanying their young lord to England.

To do the young scoundrel justice, when he came among us, he was a manly, noble-looking lad, and everything in his bearing and appearance betokened the high blood from which he came. He was the very portrait of some of the dark cavaliers of the Lyndon race, whose pictures hung in the gallery at Hackton, where the lad was fond of spending the chief part of his time, occupied with the musty old books which he took out of the library, and which I hate to see a young man of spirit poring over. Always in my company he preserved the most rigid silence, and a haughty, scornful demeanour, which was so much the more disagreeable because there was nothing in his behaviour I could actually take hold of to find fault with, although his whole conduct was insolent and supercilious to the highest degree. His mother was very much agitated at receiving him on his arrival; if he felt any such agitation he certainly did not show it. He made her a very low and formal bow when he kissed her hand; and, when I held out mine, put both his hands behind his back, stared me full in the face, and bent his head, saying, 'Mr. Barry Lyndon, I believe;' turned on his heel, and began talking about the state of the weather to his mother, whom he always styled 'your ladyship.' She was angry at this pert bearing, and, when they were alone, rebuked him sharply for not shaking hands with his father.

'My father, madam?' said he; 'surely you mistake. My father was the Right Honourable Sir Charles Lyndon. *I* at least have not forgotten him, if others have.' It was a declaration of war to me, as I saw at once; though I declare I was willing enough to have received the boy well on his coming amongst us, and to have lived with him on terms of friendliness. But as men serve me I serve them. Who can blame me for my after-quarrels with this young reprobate, or lay upon my shoulders the evils which afterwards befell? Perhaps I lost my temper, and my subsequent treatment of him *was* hard. But it was he began the quarrel, and not I; and the evil consequences which ensued were entirely of his creating.

As it is best to nip vice in the bud, and for a master of a family to exercise his authority in such a manner as that there may be no question about it, I took the earliest opportunity of coming to close quarters with Master Bullingdon, and the day after his arrival among us, upon his refusal to perform some duty which I requested of him, I had him conveyed to my study, and thrashed him soundly. This process, I confess, at first, agitated me a good deal, for I had never laid a whip on a lord before; but I got speedily used to the practice, and his back and my whip became so well acquainted that I warrant there was very little *ceremony* between us after a while.

If I were to repeat all the instances of the insubordination and brutal conduct of young Bullingdon, I should weary the reader. His perseverance in resistance was, I think, even greater than mine in correcting him, for a man, be he ever so much resolved to do his duty as a parent, can't be flogging his children all day, or for every fault they commit; and though I got the character of being so cruel a step-father to him, I pledge my word I spared him correction when he merited it many more times than I administered it. Besides, there were eight clear months in the year when he was quit of me, during the time of my presence in London at my place in Parliament and at the court of my sovereign.

At this period I made no difficulty to allow him to profit by the Latin and Greek of the old rector, who had christened him, and had a considerable influence over the wayward lad. After a scene or a quarrel between us, it was generally to the rectory-house that the young rebel would fly for refuge and counsel, and I must own that the parson was a pretty just umpire between us in our disputes. Once he led the boy back to Hackton by the hand, and actually brought him into my presence, although he had vowed never to enter the doors in my lifetime again, and said, 'He had brought his lordship to acknowledge his error, and submit to any punishment I might think proper to inflict.' Upon which I caned him in the presence of two or three friends of mine, with whom I was sitting drinking at the time; and to do him justice, he bore a pretty severe punishment without wincing or crying in the least. This will show that I was not too severe in my treatment upon the lad, as I had the authority of the clergyman himself for inflicting the correction which I thought proper.

Twice or thrice, Lavender, Bryan's governor, attempted to punish my Lord Bullingdon; but I promise you the rogue was too strong for *him*, and levelled the Oxford man to the ground with a chair, greatly to the delight of little Bryan, who cried out 'Bravo, Bully! thump him, thump him!' And Bully certainly did, to the governor's heart's content, who never attempted personal chastisement afterwards, but contented himself by bringing the tales of his lordship's misdoings to me, his natural protector and guardian.

With the child Bullingdon was, strange to say, pretty tractable. He took a liking for the little fellow,—as, indeed, everybody who saw that darling boy did,—liked him the more, he said, because he was 'half a Lyndon.' And well he might like him, for many a time, at the dear angel's intercession of 'Papa, don't flog Bully to-day!' I have held my hand, and saved him a horsing which he richly deserved.

With his mother, at first, he would scarcely deign to

have any communication. He said she was no longer one of the family. Why should he love her, as she had never been a mother to him ? But it will give the reader an idea of the dogged obstinacy and surliness of the lad's character, when I mention one trait regarding him. It has been made a matter of complaint against me that I denied him the education befitting a gentleman, and never sent him to college or to school ; but the fact is, it was of his own choice that he went to neither. He had the offer repeatedly from me (who wished to see as little of his impudence as possible), but he as repeatedly declined, and, for a long time, I could not make out what was the charm which kept him in a house where he must have been far from comfortable.

It came out, however, at last. There used to be very frequent disputes between my Lady Lyndon and myself, in which sometimes she was wrong, sometimes I was ; and which, as neither of us had very angelical tempers, used to run very high. I was often in liquor ; and when in that condition, what gentleman is master of himself ? Perhaps I *did*, in this state, use my lady rather roughly, fling a glass or two at her, and call her by a few names that were not complimentary. I may have threatened her life (which it was obviously my interest not to take), and have frightened her, in a word, considerably.

After one of these disputes, in which she ran screaming through the galleries, and I, as tipsy as a lord, came staggering after, it appears Bullingdon was attracted out of his room by the noise ; as I came up with her, the audacious rascal tripped up my heels, which were not very steady, and, catching his fainting mother in his arms, took her into his own room, where he, upon her entreaty, swore he would never leave the house as long as she continued united with me. I knew nothing of the vow, or indeed of the tipsy frolic which was the occasion of it ; I was taken up 'glorious,' as the phrase is, by my servants, and put to bed, and in the morning had no recollection of what had occurred any more than of what happened when I was a baby at the breast. Lady Lyndon told me of the circumstance years after ; and I mention it here, as it enables me to plead honourably 'not guilty' to one of the absurd charges of cruelty trumped up against me with respect to my step-son. Let my detractors apologize, if they dare, for the conduct of a graceless ruffian who trips up the heels of his own natural guardian and step-father after dinner.

This circumstance served to unite mother and son for a little, but their characters were too different. I believe she was too fond of me ever to allow him to be sincerely reconciled to her. As he grew up to be a man, his hatred towards me assumed an intensity quite wicked to think of (and which I promise you I returned with interest); and it was at the age of sixteen, I think, that the impudent young hang-dog, on my return from Parliament one summer, and on my proposing to cane him as usual, gave me to understand that he would submit to no further chastisement from me, and said, grinding his teeth, that he would shoot me if I laid hands on him. I looked at him; he was grown, in fact, to be a tall young man, and I gave up that necessary part of his education.

It was about this time that I raised the company which was to serve in America; and my enemies in the country (and since my victory over the Tiptoffs I scarce need say I had many of them) began to propagate the most shameful reports regarding my conduct to that precious young scapegrace, my son-in-law, and to insinuate that I actually wished to get rid of him. Thus my loyalty to my sovereign was actually construed into a horrid, unnatural attempt on my part on Bullingdon's life; and it was said that I had raised the American corps for the sole purpose of getting the young viscount to command it, and so of getting rid of him. I am not sure that they had not fixed upon the name of the very man in the company who was ordered to dispatch him at the first general action, and the bribe I was to give him for this delicate piece of service.

But the truth is, I was of opinion then (and though the fufilment of my prophecy has been delayed, yet I make no doubt it will be brought to pass ere long) that my Lord Bullingdon needed none of *my* aid in sending him into the other world, but had a happy knack of finding the way thither himself, which he would be sure to pursue. In truth, he began upon this way early; of all the violent, daring, disobedient scapegraces that ever caused an affectionate parent pain, he was certainly the most incorrigible; there was no beating him, or coaxing him, or taming him.

For instance, with my little son, when his governor brought him into the room as we were over the bottle after dinner, my lord would begin his violent and undutiful sarcasms at me.

'Dear child,' he would say, beginning to caress and fondle him, 'what a pity it is I am not dead for thy sake! The Lyndons would then have a worthier representative, and enjoy all the benefit of the illustrious blood of the Barrys of Barryogue; would they not, Mr. Barry Lyndon?' He always chose the days when company, or the clergy or gentry of the neighbourhood, were present, to make these insolent speeches to me.

Another day (it was Bryan's birthday) we were giving a grand ball and gala at Hackton, and it was time for my little Bryan to make his appearance among us, as he usually did in the smartest little court-suit you ever saw (ah, me! but it brings tears into my old eyes now to think of the bright looks of that darling little face); there was a great crowding and tittering when the child came in, led by his half-brother, who walked into the dancing-room (would you believe it?) in his stocking-feet, leading little Bryan by the hand, paddling about in the great shoes of the elder! 'Don't you think he fits my shoes very well, Sir Richard Wargrave?' says the young reprobate; upon which the company began to look at each other and to titter, and his mother coming up to Lord Bullingdon with great dignity, seized the child to her breast, and said, 'From the manner in which I love this child, my lord, you ought to know how I would have loved his elder brother, had he proved worthy of any mother's affection!' and, bursting into tears, Lady Lyndon left the apartment, and the young lord rather discomfited for once.

At last, on one occasion, his behaviour to me was so outrageous (it was in the hunting-field and in a large public company) that I lost all patience, rode at the urchin straight, wrenched him out of his saddle with all my force, and, flinging him roughly to the ground, sprang down to it myself, and administered such a correction across the young caitiff's head and shoulders with my horsewhip as might have ended in his death had I not been restrained in time, for my passion was up, and I was in a state to do murder or any other crime.

The lad was taken home and put to bed, where he lay

for a day or two in a fever, as much from rage and vexation as from the chastisement I had given him ; and three days afterwards, on sending to inquire at his chamber whether he would join the family at table, a note was found on his table, and his bed was empty and cold. The young villain had fled, and had the audacity to write in the following terms regarding me to my wife, his mother :—

'Madam,' he said, 'I have borne as long as mortal could endure the ill-treatment of the insolent Irish upstart whom you have taken to your bed. It is not only the lowness of his birth and the general brutality of his manners which disgust me, and must make me hate him so long as I have the honour to bear the name of Lyndon, which he is unworthy of, but the shameful nature of his conduct towards your ladyship, his brutal and ungentlemanlike behaviour, his open infidelity, his habits of extravagance, intoxication, his shameless robberies and swindling of my property and yours. It is these insults to you which shock and annoy me more than the ruffian's infamous conduct to myself. I would have stood by your ladyship as I promised, but you seem to have taken latterly your husband's part ; and, as I cannot personally chastise this low-bred ruffian who, to our shame be it spoken, is the husband of my mother, and as I cannot bear to witness his treatment of you, and loathe his horrible society as if it were the plague, I am determined to quit my native country, at least during his detested life, or during my own. I possess a small income from my father, of which I have no doubt Mr. Barry will cheat me if he can, but which, if your ladyship has some feelings of a mother left, you will, perhaps, award to me. Messrs. Childs, the bankers, can have orders to pay it to me when due ; if they receive no such orders, I shall be not in the least surprised, knowing you to be in the hands of a villain who would not scruple to rob on the highway, and shall try to find out some way in life for myself more honourable than that by which the penniless Irish adventurer has arrived to turn me out of my rights and home.'

This mad epistle was signed 'Bullingdon,' and all the neighbours vowed that I had been privy to his flight, and would profit by it ; though I declare on my honour my true and sincere desire, after reading the above infamous letter, was to have the author within a good arm's length of me, that I might let him know my opinion regarding him.

But there was no eradicating this idea from people's minds, who insisted that I wanted to kill Bullingdon, whereas murder, as I have said, was never one of my evil qualities; and even had I wished to injure my young enemy ever so much, common prudence would have made my mind easy, as I knew he was going to ruin his own way.

It was long before we heard of the fate of the audacious young truant; but after some fifteen months had elapsed, I had the pleasure of being able to refute some of the murderous calumnies which had been uttered against me, by producing a bill with Bullingdon's own signature, drawn from General Tarleton's army* in America, where my company was conducting itself with the greatest glory, and with which my lord was serving as a volunteer. There were some of my kind frends who persisted still in attributing all sorts of wicked intentions to me. Lord Tiptoff would never believe that I would pay any bill, much more any bill of Lord Bullingdon's; old Lady Betty Grimsby, his sister, persisted in declaring the bill was a forgery, and the poor dear lord dead, until there came a letter to her ladyship from Lord Bullingdon himself, who had been at New York at head quarters, and who described at length the splendid festival given by the officers of the garrison to our distinguished chieftains, the two Howes.

In the meanwhile, if I *had* murdered my lord, I could scarcely have been received with more shameful obloquy and slander than now followed me in town and country. 'You will hear of the lad's death, be sure,' exclaimed one of my friends. 'And then his wife's will follow,' added another. 'He will marry Jenny Jones,' added a third; and so on. Lavender brought me the news of these scandals about me: the country was up against me. The farmers on market-days used to touch their hats sulkily, and get out of my way; the gentlemen who followed my hunt now suddenly seceded from it, and left off my uniform; at the county ball, where I led out Lady Susan Capermore, and took my place third in the dance after the duke and the marquis, as was my wont, all the couples turned away as we came to them, and we were left to dance alone. Sukey Capermore has a love of dancing which would make her dance at a funeral if anybody asked her, and I had too much spirit to give in at this signal instance of insult towards me, so we danced with some of the very commonest low people at the bottom of the set—your apothecaries, wine-merchants, attorneys, and such scum as are allowed to attend our public assemblies.

The bishop, my Lady Lyndon's relative, neglected to invite us to the palace at the assizes; and, in a word, every indignity was put upon me which could by possibility be heaped upon an innocent and honourable gentleman.

My reception in London, whither I now carried my wife and family, was scarcely more cordial. On paying my respects to my sovereign at St. James's, his Majesty pointedly asked me when I had news of Lord Bullingdon. On which I replied, with no ordinary presence of mind, 'Sir, my Lord Bullingdon is fighting the rebels against your Majesty's crown in America. Does your Majesty desire that I should send another regiment to aid him?' On which the King turned on his heel, and I made my bow out of the presence-chamber. When Lady Lyndon kissed the Queen's hand at the Drawing-room, I found that precisely the same question had been put to her ladyship, and she came home much agitated at the rebuke which had been administered to her. Thus it was that my loyalty was rewarded, and my sacrifice, in favour of my country, viewed! I took away my establishment abruptly to Paris, where I met with a very different reception, but my stay amidst the enchanting pleasures of that capital was extremely short; for the French Government, which had been long tampering with the American rebels, now openly acknowledged the independence of the United States. A declaration of war* ensued, all we happy English were ordered away from Paris, and I think I left one or two fair ladies there inconsolable. It is the only place where a gentleman can live as he likes without being incommoded by his wife. The countess and I during our stay scarcely saw each other except upon public occasions, at Versailles, or at the Queen's play-table; and our dear little Bryan advanced in a thousand elegant accomplishments, which rendered him the delight of all who knew him.

I must not forget to mention here my last interview with my good uncle, the Chevalier de Ballybarry, whom I left at Brussels with strong intentions of making his *salut*, as the phrase is, and who had gone into retirement at a convent there. Since then he had come into the world again, much to his annoyance and repentance, having fallen desperately in love in his old age with a French actress, who had done as most ladies of her character do, ruined him, left him, and laughed at him. His repentance was very edifying. Under the guidance of Messieurs of the Irish College,* he once more turned his thoughts towards religion, and his only prayer to me when I saw him and asked in what I could relieve him, was to pay a handsome fee to the convent into which he proposed to enter.

This I could not, of course, do, my religious principles forbidding me to encourage superstition in any way; and the old gentleman and I parted rather coolly in consequence of my refusal, as he said, to make his old days comfortable.

I was very poor at the time, that is the fact; and *entre nous*, the Rosemont of the French opera, an indifferent dancer, but a charming figure and ankle, was ruining me in diamonds, equipages, and furniture bills;[1] added to which, I had a run of ill luck at play, and was forced to meet my losses by the most shameful sacrifices to the money-lenders, by pawning part of Lady Lyndon's diamonds (that graceless little Rosemont wheedled me out of some of them), and by a thousand other schemes for raising money. But when honour is in the case, was I ever found backward at her call? and what man can say that Barry Lyndon lost a bet which he did not pay?

As for my ambitious hopes regarding the Irish peerage, I began, on my return, to find out that I had been led wildly astray by that rascal Lord Crabs, who liked to take my money, but had no more influence to get me a coronet than to procure for me the Pope's tiara. The sovereign was not a whit more gracious to me on returning from the Continent than he had been before my departure; and I had it from one of the aides de camp of the royal Dukes, his brothers, that my conduct and amusements at Paris had been odiously misrepresented by some spies there, and had formed the subject of royal comment, and that the King

[1] [The Memoirs of Mr. Barry Lyndon abound in allusions to ladies of all names and nations, with whom he seems to have lived under his wife's eyes, and even in her very house. We have taken the liberty to expunge numerous passages of this nature from his memoirs, but it is necessary for the due understanding of this amiable character that occasional accounts of such proceedings should be allowed to remain.]—Note in *Fraser's Magazine*, omitted in later editions.

had, influenced by these calumnies, actually said I was the most disreputable man in the three kingdoms. I disreputable! I a dishonour to my name and country! When I heard these falsehoods, I was in such a rage that I went off to Lord North at once to remonstrate with the minister, to insist upon being allowed to appear before his Majesty and clear myself of the imputations against me, to point out my services to the Government in voting with them, and to ask when the reward that had been promised to me, viz., the title held by my ancestors, was again to be revived in my person?

There was a sleepy coolness in that fat Lord North, which was the most provoking thing that the Opposition had ever to encounter from him. He heard me with half-shut eyes. When I had finished a long, violent speech, which I made striding about his room in Downing Street, and gesticulating with all the energy of an Irishman, he opened one eye, smiled, and asked me gently if I had done. On my replying in the affirmative, he said, 'Well, Mr. Barry, I'll answer you, point by point. The King is exceedingly averse to make peers, as you know. Your claims, as you call them, *have* been laid before him, and his Majesty's gracious reply was that you were the most impudent man in his dominions, and merited a halter rather than a coronet. As for withdrawing your support from us, you are perfectly welcome to carry yourself and your vote whithersoever you please. And now, as I have a great deal of occupation, perhaps you will do me the favour to retire.' So saying, he raised his hand lazily to the bell, and bowed me out, asking blandly if there was any other thing in the world in which he could oblige me.

I went home in a fury which can't be described, and having Lord Crabs to dinner that day, assailed his lordship by pulling his wig off his head, and smothering it in his face, and by attacking him in that part of the person where, according to report, he had been formerly assaulted by Majesty. The whole story was over the town the next day, and pictures of me were hanging in the clubs and print-shops performing the operation alluded to. All the town laughed at the picture of the lord and the Irishman, and I need not say recognized both. As for me, I was one of the most celebrated characters in London in those days; my dress, style, and equipages being as well known as those of any leader of the fashion; and my popularity, if not great in the highest quarters, was at least considerable elsewhere. The people cheered me in the Gordon rows,* at the time they nearly killed my friend, Jemmy Twitcher, and burned Lord Mansfield's house down. Indeed, I was known as a staunch Protestant, and after my quarrel with Lord North veered right round to the Opposition, and vexed him with all the means in my power.

These were not, unluckily, very great, for I was a bad speaker, and the House would not listen to me, and presently, in 1780, after the Gordon disturbance, was dissolved, when a general election took place. It came on me, as all my mishaps were in the habit of coming, at a most unlucky time. I was obliged to raise more money, at most ruinous rates, to face the confounded election, and had the Tiptoffs against me in the field more active and virulent than ever.

My blood boils even now when I think of the rascally conduct of my enemies in that scoundrelly election. I was held up as the Irish Bluebeard, and libels of me were printed, and gross caricatures drawn representing me flogging Lady Lyndon, whipping Lord Bullingdon, turning him out of doors in a storm, and I know not what. There were pictures of a pauper cabin in Ireland, from which it was pretended I came; others in which I was represented as a lackey and shoeblack. A flood of calumny was let loose upon me, in which any man of less spirit would have gone down.

But though I met my accusers boldly, though I lavished sums of money in the election, though I flung open Hackton Hall, and kept champagne and burgundy running there and at all my inns in the town as commonly as water, the election went against me. The rascally gentry had all turned upon me and joined the Tiptoff faction; it was even represented that I held my wife by force, and though I sent her into the town alone, wearing my colours, with Bryan in her lap, and made her visit the mayor's lady and the chief women there, nothing would persuade the people but that she lived in fear and trembling of me, and the brutal mob had the insolence to ask her why she dared to go back, and how she liked horsewhip for supper.

I was thrown out of my election, and all the bills came down upon me together—all the bills I had been contracting for the years of my marriage, which the creditors, with a rascally unanimity, sent in until they lay upon my table in heaps. I won't cite their amount; it was frightful. My stewards and lawyers made matters worse. I was bound up in an inextricable toil of bills and debts, of mortgages and insurances, and all the horrible evils attendant upon them. Lawyers upon lawyers posted down from London: composition after composition was made, and Lady Lyndon's income hampered almost irretrievably to satisfy these cormorants. To do her justice, she behaved with tolerable kindness at this season of trouble; for whenever I wanted money I had to coax her, and whenever I coaxed her I was sure of bringing this weak and light-minded woman to good humour, who was of such a weak, terrified nature that to secure an easy week with me she would sign away a thousand a year. And when my troubles began at Hackton, and I determined on the only chance left, viz., to retire to Ireland and retrench, assigning over the best part of my income to the creditors until their demands were met, my lady was quite cheerful at the idea of going, and said, if we would be quiet, she had no doubt all would be well; indeed, was glad to undergo the comparative poverty in which we must now live, for the sake of the retirement and the chance of domestic quiet which she hoped to enjoy.

We went off to Bristol pretty suddenly, leaving the odious and ungrateful wretches at Hackton to vilify us, no doubt, in our absence. My stud and hounds were sold off immediately; the harpies would have been glad to pounce upon my person, but that was out of their power. I had raised by cleverness and management to the full as much on my mines and private estates as they were worth; so the scoundrels were disappointed in *this* instance; and as for the plate and property in the London house, they could not touch that, as it was the property of the heirs of the house of Lyndon.

I passed over to Ireland, then, and took up my abode at Castle Lyndon for a while, all the world imagining that I was an utterly ruined man, and that the famous and dashing Barry Lyndon would never again appear in the circles of which he had been an ornament. But it was not so. In the midst of my perplexities, Fortune reserved a great consolation for me still. Dispatches came home from America announcing Lord Cornwallis's defeat of

General Gates* in Carolina, and the death of Lord Bullingdon, who was present as a volunteer.

For my own desires to possess a paltry Irish title I cared little. My son was now heir to an English earldom, and I made him assume forthwith the title of Lord Viscount Castle-Lyndon, the third of the family titles. My mother went almost mad with joy at saluting her grandson as 'my lord,' and I felt that all my sufferings and privations were repaid by seeing this darling child advanced to such a post of honour.

[It must be manifest to the observer of human nature that the honourable subject of these Memoirs has never told the whole truth regarding himself, and, as his career comes to a close, perhaps is less to be relied on than ever. We have been obliged to expunge long chapters of his town and Paris life, which were by no means edifying; to omit numbers of particulars of his domestic career, which he tells with much *naïveté*. But though, in one respect, he communicates a great deal too much, he by no means tells all, and it must be remembered that we are only hearing his, the autobiographer's, side of the story. Even that is sufficient to show that Mr. Barry Lyndon is as unprincipled a personage as ever has figured at the head of a history, and as the public will persist in having a moral appended to such tales, we beg here respectfully to declare that we take the moral of the story of Barry Lyndon, Esquire, to be,—that worldly success is by no means the consequence of virtue; that if it is effected by honesty sometimes, it is attained by selfishness and roguery still oftener; and that our anger at seeing rascals prosper and good men frequently unlucky, is founded on a gross and unreasonable idea of what good fortune really is. When we fancy that we reward Virtue by saying 'King Pepin* was a good boy *and* rode in a gold coach,' we put virtue and the gold coach on a par of excellence, which is absurd and immoral. It is that gold coach which we respect vastly too much, and our homage to which we are showing daily in a thousand unconscious ways, by setting it up as the great reward of merit. With which protest let those critics be reassured, whose moral sense has been in any way offended by the success and advancement of the hero of this history. It is they who demoralize history who set up Luck as the great criterion of merit; and the Editor of the foregoing and ensuing pages persists in maintaining that his is the real, true, and original moral, and that all others are pinchbeck*and spurious.][1]

CHAPTER XIX

CONCLUSION

If the world were not composed of a race of ungrateful scoundrels, who share your prosperity while it lasts, and, even when gorged with your venison and burgundy, abuse the generous giver of the feast, I am sure I merit a good name and a high reputation in Ireland, at least, where my generosity was unbounded, and the splendour of my mansion and entertainments unequalled by any other nobleman of my time. As long as my magnificence lasted, all the country was free to partake of it; I had hunters sufficient in my stables to mount a regiment of dragoons, and butts of wine in my cellar which would have made whole counties drunk for years. Castle Lyndon became the head quarters of scores of needy gentlemen, and I never rode a-hunting but I had a dozen young fellows of the best blood of the country riding as my squires and gentlemen of the horse. My son, little Castle-Lyndon, was a prince; his breeding and manners, even at his early age, showed him to be worthy of the two noble families from whom he was descended, and I don't know what high hopes I had for the boy, and indulged in a thousand fond anticipations as to his future success and figure in the world. But stern Fate had determined that I should leave none of my race behind me, and ordained that I should finish my career, as I see it closing now—poor, lonely, and childless. I may have had my faults, but no man shall dare to say of me that I was not a good and tender father. I loved that boy passionately, perhaps with a blind partiality; I denied him nothing. Gladly, gladly, I swear, would I have died that his premature doom might have been averted. I think there is not a day since I lost him but his bright face and beautiful smiles look down

[1] Omitted in later editions.

on me out of heaven where he is, and that my heart does not yearn towards him. That sweet child was taken from me at the age of nine years, when he was full of beauty and promise; and so powerful is the hold his memory has of me that I have never been able to forget him; his little spirit haunts me of nights on my restless, solitary pillow; many a time, in the wildest and maddest company, as the bottle is going round, and the song and laugh roaring about, I am thinking of him. I have got a lock of his soft brown hair hanging round my breast now; it will accompany me to the dishonoured pauper's grave, where soon, no doubt, Barry Lyndon's worn-out old bones will be laid.

My Bryan was a boy of amazing high spirit (indeed, how, coming from such a stock, could he be otherwise?), impatient even of my control, against which the dear little rogue would often rebel gallantly; how much more, then, of his mother's and the women's, whose attempts to direct him he would laugh to scorn. Even my own mother ('Mrs. Barry of Lyndon' the good soul now called herself, in compliment to my new family) was quite unable to check him, and hence you may fancy what a will he had of his own. If it had not been for that, he might have lived to this day: he might—but why repine? Is he not in a better place? would the heritage of a beggar do any service to him? It is best as it is—Heaven be good to us!—Alas! that I, his father, should be left to deplore him.

It was in the month of October I had been to Dublin in order to see a lawyer and a moneyed man, who had come over to Ireland to consult with me about some sales of mine and the cut of Hackton timber, of which, as I hated the place and was greatly in want of money, I was determined to cut down every stick. There had been some difficulty in the matter. It was said I had no right to touch the timber. The brute peasantry about the estate had been roused to such a pitch of hatred against me that the rascals actually refused to lay an axe to the trees, and my agent (that scoundrel Larkins) declared that his life was in danger among them if he attempted any further despoilment (as they called it) of the property. Every article of the splendid furniture was sold by this time, as I need not say, and, as for the plate, I had taken good care to bring it off to Ireland, where it now was in the best of keeping, my banker's, who had advanced six thousand pounds on it, which sum I soon had occasion for.

I went to Dublin, then, to meet the English man of business, and so far succeeded in persuading Mr. Splint, a great shipbuilder and timber-dealer of Plymouth, of my claim to the Hackton timber, that he agreed to purchase it off-hand at about one-third of its value, and handed me over 5,000*l*., which, being pressed with debts at the time, I was fain to accept. *He* had no difficulty in getting down the wood, I warrant. He took a regiment of shipwrights and sawyers from his own and the King's yards at Plymouth, and in two months Hackton Park was as bare of trees as the Bog of Allen.

I had but ill luck with that accursed expedition and money. I lost the greater part of it in two nights' play at Daly's, so that my debts stood just as they were before; and before the vessel sailed for Holyhead, which carried away my old sharper of a timber-merchant, all that I had left of the money he brought me was a couple of hundred pounds, with which I returned home very disconsolately, and very suddenly, too, for my Dublin tradesmen were hot upon me, hearing I had spent the loan, and two of my wine-merchants had writs out against me for some thousands of pounds.

I bought in Dublin, according to my promise, however—for when I give a promise I will keep it at any sacrifices—a little horse for my dear little Bryan, which was to be a present for his tenth birthday, that was now coming on. It was a beautiful little animal and stood me in a good sum. I never regarded money for that dear child. But the horse was very wild. He kicked off one of my horse-boys, who rode him at first, and broke the lad's leg, and, though I took the animal in hand on the journey home, it was only my weight and skill that made the brute quiet.

When we got home I sent the horse away with one of my grooms to a farmer's house to break him thoroughly in, and told Bryan, who was all anxiety to see his little horse, that he would arrive by his birthday, when he should hunt him along with my hounds, and I promised myself no small pleasure in presenting the dear fellow to the field that day, which I hoped to see him lead some time or other in place of his fond father. Ah, me! never was that gallant boy to ride a fox-chase, or to take the place amongst the gentry of his country which his birth and genius had pointed out for him!

Though I don't believe in dreams and omens, yet I can't but own that when a great calamity is hanging over a man he has frequently many strange and awful forebodings of it. I fancy now I had many. Lady Lyndon, especially, twice dreamed of her son's death; but, as she was now grown uncommonly nervous and vapourish, I treated her fears with scorn, and my own, of course, too. And in an unguarded moment, over the bottle after dinner, I told poor Bryan, who was always questioning me about the little horse, and when it was to come, that it was arrived, that it was in Doolan's farm, where Mick the groom was breaking him in. 'Promise me, Bryan,' screamed his mother, 'that you will not ride the horse except in company of your father.' But I only said, 'Pooh, madam, you are an ass!' being angry at her silly timidity, which was always showing itself in a thousand disagreeable ways now; and, turning round to Bryan, said, 'I promise your lordship a good flogging if you mount him without my leave.'

I suppose the poor child did not care about paying this penalty for the pleasure he was to have, or possibly thought a fond father would remit the punishment altogether, for the next morning, when I rose rather late, having sat up drinking the night before, I found the child had been off at day-break, having slipped through his tutor's room (this was Redmond Quin, our cousin, whom I had taken to live with me), and I had no doubt but that he was gone to Doolan's farm.

I took a great horsewhip and galloped off after him in a rage, swearing I would keep my promise. But, Heaven forgive me! I little thought of it, when at three miles from home I met a sad procession coming towards me, peasants moaning and howling as our Irish do, the black horse led by the hand, and, on a door that some of the folks carried, my poor dear, dear little boy. There he lay in his little boots and spurs, and his little coat of scarlet and gold. His dear face was quite white, and he smiled as he held a hand out to me, and said, painfully, 'You won't whip me, will you, papa?' I could only burst out into tears in reply. I have seen many and many a man dying, and there's a look about the eyes which you cannot mistake. There was a little drummer-boy I was fond of who was hit down before my company at Kühnersdorf ;* when I ran up to give him some water, he looked exactly like my dear Bryan then did—there's no mistaking that awful look of the eyes. We carried him home and scoured the country round for doctors to come and look at his hurt.

But what does a doctor avail in a contest with the grim, invincible enemy ? Such as came could only confirm our despair by their account of the poor child's case. He had mounted his horse gallantly, sat him bravely all the time the animal plunged and kicked, and, having overcome his first spite, ran him at a hedge by the roadside. But there were loose stones at the top, and the horse's foot caught among them, and he and his brave little rider rolled over together at the other side. The people said they saw the noble little boy spring up after his fall and run to catch the horse, which had broken away from him, kicking him on the back, as it would seem, as they lay on the ground. Poor Bryan ran a few yards and then dropped down as if shot. A pallor came over his face, and they thought he was dead. But they poured whisky down his mouth, and the poor child revived ; still he could not move, his spine was injured, the lower half of him was dead when they laid him in bed at home. The rest did not last long, God help me ! He remained yet for two days with us, and a sad comfort it was to think he was in no pain.

During this time the dear angel's temper seemed quite to change ; he asked his mother and me pardon for any act of disobedience he had been guilty of towards us ; he said often he should like to see his brother Bullingdon. 'Bully was better than you, papa,' he said ; 'he used not to swear so, and he told and taught me many good things while you were away.' And, taking a hand of his mother and mine in each of his little clammy ones, he begged us not to quarrel so, but love each other, so that we might meet again in heaven, where Bully told him quarrelsome people never went. His mother was very much affected by these admonitions from the poor, suffering angel's mouth, and I was so too. I wish she had enabled me to keep the counsel which the dying boy gave us.

At last, after two days, he died. There he lay, the hope of my family, the pride of my manhood, the link which had kept me and my Lady Lyndon together. 'O Redmond,' said she, kneeling by the sweet child's body, 'do, do let us listen to the truth out of his blessed mouth, and do you amend your life, and treat your poor, loving, fond wife as her dying child bade you.' And I said I would; but there are promises which it is out of a man's power to keep, especially with such a woman as her. But we drew together after that sad event, and were for several months better friends.

I won't tell you with what splendour we buried him. Of what avail are undertakers' feathers and heralds' trumpery? I went out and shot the fatal black horse that had killed him at the door of the vault where we laid my boy. I was so wild that I could have shot myself too. But for the crime, it would have been better that I should, perhaps, for what has my life been since that sweet flower was taken out of my bosom? A succession of miseries, wrongs, disasters, and mental and bodily sufferings, which never fell to the lot of any other man in Christendom.

Lady Lyndon, always vapourish and nervous, after our blessed boy's catastrophe became more agitated than ever, and plunged into devotion with so much fervour that you would have fancied her almost distracted at times. She imagined she saw visions. She said an angel from heaven had told her that Bryan's death was as a punishment to her for her neglect of her first-born. Then she would declare Bullingdon was alive; she had seen him in a dream. Then again she would fall into fits of sorrow about his death, and grieve for him as violently as if he had been the last of her sons who had died, and not our darling Bryan, who, compared to Bullingdon, was what a diamond is to a vulgar stone. Her freaks were painful to witness, and difficult to control. It began to be said in the country that the countess was going mad. My scoundrelly enemies did not fail to confirm and magnify the rumour, and would add that I was the cause of her insanity, I had driven her to distraction, I had killed Bullingdon, I had murdered my own son; I don't know what else they laid to my charge. Even in Ireland their hateful calumnies reached me; my friends fell away from me. They began to desert my hunt as they did in England, and when I went to race or market found sudden reasons for getting out of my neighbourhood. I got the name of Wicked Barry, Devil Lyndon, which you please; the country-folks used to make marvellous legends about me; the priests said I had massacred I don't know how many German nuns in the Seven Years' War; that the ghost of the murdered Bullingdon haunted my house. Once at a fair in a town hard by, when I had a mind to buy a waistcoat for one of my people, a fellow standing by, said, ''Tis a strait-waistcoat he's buying for my Lady Lyndon.' And from this circumstance arose a legend of my cruelty to my wife, and many circumstantial details were narrated regarding my manner and ingenuity of torturing her.

The loss of my dear boy pressed not only on my heart as a father, but injured my individual interests in a very considerable degree, for as there was now no direct heir to the estate, and Lady Lyndon was of a weak health, and supposed to be quite unlikely to leave a family, the next in succession, that detestable family of Tiptoff, began to exert themselves in a hundred ways to annoy me, and were at the head of the party of enemies who were raising reports to my discredit. They interposed between me and my management of the property [1] in a hundred different ways, making an outcry if I cut a stick, sunk a shaft, sold a picture, or sent a few ounces of plate to be remodelled. They harassed me with ceaseless lawsuits, got injunctions from Chancery, hampered my agents in the execution of their work, so much so that you would have fancied my own was not my own, but theirs, to do as they liked with. What is worse, as I have reason to believe, they had tamperings and dealings with my own domestics under my own roof, for I could not have a word with Lady Lyndon but it somehow got abroad, and I could not be drunk with my chaplain and friends but some sanctified rascals would get hold of the news, and reckon up all the bottles I drank and all the oaths I swore. That these were not few, I acknowledge. I am of the old school, was always a free liver and speaker, and, at least, if I did and said what I liked, was not so bad as many a canting scoundrel I know of who covers his foibles and sins, unsuspected, with a mask of holiness.

As I am making a clean breast of it, and am no hypocrite,

[1] [The reader will perceive, by Mr. Lyndon's own showing, that his method of managing the property was to raise all he could get from it.]—Note in *Fraser's Magazine*, omitted in later editions.

I may as well confess now that I endeavoured to ward off the devices of my enemies by an artifice which was not, perhaps, strictly justifiable. Everything depended on my having an heir to the estate; for if Lady Lyndon, who was of weakly health, had died, the next day I was a beggar; all my sacrifices of money, &c., on the estate would not have been held in a farthing's account; all the debts would have been left on my shoulders; and my enemies would have triumphed over me, which, to a man of my honourable spirit, was 'the unkindest cut of all,'* as some poet says.

I confess, then, it was my wish to supplant these scoundrels, and, as I could not do so without an heir to my property, *I determined to find one*. If I had him near at hand, and of my own blood too, though with the bar sinister, is not here the question. It was then I found out the rascally machinations of my enemies, for, having broached this plan to Lady Lyndon, whom I made to be, outwardly at least, the most obedient of wives,—although I never let a letter from her or to her go or arrive without my inspection,—although I allowed her to see none but those persons who I thought, in her delicate health, would be fitting society for her, yet the infernal Tiptoffs got wind of my scheme, protested instantly against it, not only by letter, but in the shameful libellous public prints, and held me up to public odium as a 'child-forger,' as they called me. Of course I denied the charge—I could do no otherwise, and offered to meet any one of the Tiptoffs on the field of honour, and prove him a scoundrel and a liar, as he was, though, perhaps, not in this instance. But they contented themselves by answering me by a lawyer, and declined an invitation which any man of spirit would have accepted. My hopes of having an heir were thus blighted completely; indeed, Lady Lyndon (though, as I have said, I take her opposition for nothing) had resisted the proposal with as much energy as a woman of her weakness could manifest, and said she had committed one great crime in consequence of me, but would rather die than perform another. I could easily have brought her ladyship to her senses, however: but my scheme had taken wind, and it was now in vain to attempt it. We might have had a dozen children in honest wedlock, and people would have said they were false.

As for raising money on annuities, I may say I had used her life interest up. There were but few of those assurance societies* in my time which have since sprung up in the city of London; underwriters did the business, and my wife's life was as well known among them as, I do believe, that of any woman in Christendom. Latterly, when I wanted to get a sum against her life, the rascals had the impudence to say my treatment of her did not render it worth a year's purchase,—as if my interest lay in killing her! Had my boy lived, it would have been a different thing; he and his mother might have cut off the entail of a good part of the property between them, and my affairs have been put in better order. Now they were in a bad condition indeed. All my schemes had turned out failures; my lands, which I had purchased with borrowed money, made me no return, and I was obliged to pay ruinous interest for the sums with which I had purchased them. My income, though very large, was saddled with hundreds of annuities, and thousands of lawyers' charges; and I felt the net drawing closer and closer round me, and no means to extricate myself from its toils.

To add to all my perplexities, two years after my poor child's death, my wife, whose vagaries of temper and wayward follies I had borne with for twelve years, wanted to leave me, and absolutely made attempts at what she called escaping from my tyranny.

My mother, who was the only person that, in my misfortunes, remained faithful to me (indeed, she has always spoken of me in my true light, as a martyr to the rascality of others and a victim of my own generous and confiding temper), found out the first scheme that was going on, and of which those artful and malicious Tiptoffs were, as usual, the main promoters. Mrs. Barry, indeed, though her temper was violent and her ways singular, was an invaluable person to me in my house, which would have been at wrack and ruin long before but for her spirit of order and management, and for her excellent economy in the government of my numerous family. As for my Lady Lyndon, she, poor soul! was much too fine a lady to attend to household matters—passed her days with her doctor, or her books of piety, and never appeared among us except at my compulsion, when she and my mother would be sure to have a quarrel.

Mrs. Barry, on the contrary, had a talent for management in all matters. She kept the maids stirring, and the footmen to their duty; had an eye over the claret in the cellar, and the oats and hay in the stable; saw to the salting and pickling, the potatoes and the turf-stacking, the pig-killing and the poultry, the linen-room and the bakehouse, and the ten thousand minutiae of a great establishment. If all Irish housewives were like her, I warrant many a hall-fire would be blazing where the cobwebs only grow now, and many a park covered with sheep and fat cattle where the thistles are at present the chief occupiers. If anything could have saved me from the consequences of villany in others, and (I confess it, for I am not above owning to my faults) my own too easy, generous, and careless nature, it would have been the admirable prudence of that worthy creature. She never went to bed until all the house was quiet and all the candles out; and you may fancy that this was a matter of some difficulty with a man of my habits, who had commonly a dozen of jovial fellows (artful scoundrels and false friends most of them were!) to drink with me every night, and who seldom, for my part, went to bed sober. Many and many a night, when I was unconscious of her attention, has that good soul pulled my boots off, and seen me laid by my servants snug in bed, and carried off the candle herself, and been the first in the morning, too, to bring me my drink of small-beer. Mine were no milksop times, I can tell you. A gentleman thought no shame of taking his half-dozen bottles; and, as for your coffee and slops,* they were left to Lady Lyndon, her doctor, and the other old women. It was my mother's pride that I could drink more than any man in the country,—as much, within a pint, as my father before me, she said.

That Lady Lyndon should detest her was quite natural. She is not the first of woman or mankind either that has hated a mother-in-law. I set my mother to keep a sharp watch over the freaks of her ladyship, and this, you may be sure, was one of the reasons why the latter disliked her. I never minded that, however. Mrs. Barry's assistance and surveillance were invaluable to me; and, if I had paid twenty spies to watch my lady, I should not have been half so well served as by the disinterested care and watchfulness of my excellent mother. She slept with the house-keys under her pillow, and had an eye everywhere. She followed all the Countess's movements like a shadow; she managed to know, from morning till night, everything that my lady did. If she walked in the garden, a watchful eye was kept on the wicket; and, if she chose to drive out, Mrs. Barry accompanied her, and a couple of fellows in my liveries rode alongside of the carriage to see that she came to no harm. Though she objected, and would have kept her room in sullen silence, I made a point that we should appear together at church in the coach-and-six every Sunday, and that she should attend the race-balls in my company, whenever the coast was clear of the rascally bailiffs who beset me. This gave the lie to any of those maligners who said that I wished to make a prisoner of my wife. The fact is, that, knowing her levity, and seeing the insane dislike to me and mine which had now begun to supersede what, perhaps, had been an equally insane fondness for me, I was bound to be on my guard that she should not give me the slip. Had she left me I was ruined the next day. This (which my mother knew) compelled us to keep a tight watch over her; but, as for imprisoning her, I repel the imputation with scorn. Every man imprisons his wife to a certain degree; the world would be in a pretty condition if women were allowed to quit home and return to it whenever they had a mind. In watching over my wife, Lady Lyndon, I did no more than exercise the legitimate authority which awards honour and obedience to every husband.

Such, however, is female artifice that, in spite of all my watchfulness in guarding her, it is probable my lady would have given me the slip, had I not had quite as acute a person as herself as my ally; for, as the proverb says that 'the best way to catch one thief is to set another after him,' so the best way to get the better of a woman is to engage one of her own artful sex to guard her. One would have thought that, followed as she was, all her letters read, and all her acquaintances strictly watched by me, living in a remote part of Ireland away from her family, Lady Lyndon could have had no chance of communicating with her allies, or of making her wrongs, as she was pleased to call them, public; and yet, for a while, she carried on a correspondence under my very nose, and acutely organized a conspiracy for flying from me, as shall be told.

She always had an inordinate passion for dress, and, as she was never thwarted in any whimsey she had of this kind (for I spared no money to gratify her, and among my debts are milliners' bills to the amount of many thousands), boxes used to pass continually to and fro from Dublin, with all sorts of dresses, caps, flounces, and furbelows, as her fancy dictated. With these would come letters from her milliner, in answer to numerous similar injunctions from my lady, all of which passed through my hands, without the least suspicion, for some time. And yet in these very papers, by the easy means of sympathetic ink, were contained all her ladyship's correspondence, and Heaven knows (for it was some time, as I have said, before I discovered the trick) what charges against me.

But clever Mrs. Barry found out that always, before my lady-wife chose to write letters to her milliner, she had need of lemons to make her drink, as she said ; and this fact, being mentioned to me, set me a-thinking, and so I tried one of the letters before the fire, and the whole scheme of villany was brought to light. I will give a specimen of one of the horrid artful letters of this unhappy woman. In a great hand, with wide lines, were written a set of directions to her mantua-maker,* setting forth the articles of dress for which my lady had need, the peculiarity of their make, the stuffs she selected, &c. She would make out long lists in this way, writing each article in a separate line, so as to have more space for detailing all my cruelties and her tremendous wrongs. Between these lines she kept the journal of her captivity ; it would have made the fortune of a romance-writer in those days but to have got a copy of it, and to have published it under the title of the 'Lovely Prisoner, or the Savage Husband,' or by some name equally taking and absurd. The journal would be as follows :—

. . . . . .

'*Monday.*—Yesterday I was made to go to church. My odious, *monstrous*, *vulgar*, *she-dragon of a mother-in-law*, in a yellow satin and red ribbons, taking the first place in the coach ; Mr. L. riding by its side, on the horse he never paid for to Captain Hurdlestone. The wicked hypocrite led me to the pew, with hat in hand and a smiling countenance, and kissed my hand as I entered the coach after service, and patted my Italian greyhound,—all that the few people collected might see. He made me come downstairs in the evening to make tea for his company, of whom three-fourths, he himself included, were, as usual, drunk.

They painted the parson's face black, when his reverence had arrived at his seventh bottle, and at his usual insensible stage, and they tied him on the grey mare, with his face to the tail. The she-dragon read the *Whole Duty of Man* all the evening till bedtime, when she saw me to my apartments, locked me in, and proceeded to wait upon her abominable son, whom she adores for his wickedness, I should think, *as Sycorax did Caliban*.'*

. . . .

You should have seen my mother's fury as I read her out this passage! Indeed, I have always had a taste for a joke (that practised on the parson, as described above, is, I confess, a true bill), and used carefully to select for Mrs. Barry's hearing all the *compliments* that Lady Lyndon passed upon her. The dragon was the name by which she was known in this precious correspondence, or sometimes she was designated by the title of the 'Irish Witch.' As for me, I was denominated 'my jailer,' 'my tyrant,' 'the dark spirit which has obtained the mastery over my being,' and so on, in terms always complimentary to my power, however little they might be so to my amiability. Here is another extract from her 'Prison Diary,' by which it will be seen that my lady, although she pretended to be so indifferent to my goings on, had a sharp woman's eye, and could be as jealous as another:—

. . . .

'*Wednesday*.—This day two years my last hope and pleasure in life was taken from me, and my dear child was called to heaven. Has he joined his neglected brother there, whom I suffered to grow up unheeded by my side, and whom the tyranny of the monster to whom I am united drove to exile, and, perhaps, to death? Or is the child alive, as my fond heart sometimes deems? Charles Bullingdon! come to the aid of a wretched mother, who acknowledges her crimes, her coldness towards thee, and now bitterly pays for her error! But, no, he cannot live! I am distracted! My only hope is in you, my cousin—you whom I had once thought to salute by a *still fonder title*, my dear George Poynings! Oh, be my knight and my preserver, the true chivalric being thou ever wert, and rescue me from the thrall of the felon caitiff who holds me captive,—rescue me from him, and from Sycorax, the vile Irish witch, his mother!'

(Here follow some verses, such as her ladyship was in the habit of composing by reams, in which she compares herself to Sabra, in the *Seven Champions*,* and beseeches her George to rescue her from *the dragon*, meaning Mrs. Barry. I omit the lines, and proceed) :—

'Even my poor child, who perished untimely on this sad anniversary, the tyrant who governs me had taught to despise and dislike me. 'Twas in disobedience to my orders, my prayers, that he went on the fatal journey. What sufferings, what humiliations have I had to endure since then! I am a prisoner in my own halls. I should fear poison, but that I know the wretch has a sordid interest in keeping me alive, and that my death would be the signal for his ruin. But I dare not stir without my odious, hideous, vulgar jailer, the horrid Irishwoman, who pursues my every step. I am locked into my chamber at night, like a felon, and only suffered to leave it when *ordered* into the presence of my lord (*I* ordered!), to be present at his orgies with his boon companions, and to hear his odious converse as he lapses into the disgusting madness of intoxication! He has given up even the semblance of constancy—he, who swore that I alone could attach or charm him! And now he brings his vulgar mistresses before my very eyes, and would have had me acknowledge, as heir to my own property, his child by another!

'No, I never will submit! Thou, and thou only, my George, my early friend, shalt be heir to the estates of Lyndon. Why did not Fate join me to thee, instead of to the odious man who holds me under his sway, and make the poor Calista happy!'

. . . . . .

So the letters would run on for sheets upon sheets, in the closest cramped handwriting; and I leave any unprejudiced reader to say whether the writer of such documents must not have been as silly and vain a creature as ever lived, and whether she did not want being taken care of? I could copy out yards of rhapsody to Lord George Poynings, her old flame, in which she addressed him by the most affectionate names, and implored him to find a refuge for her against her oppressors; but they would fatigue the reader to peruse, as they would me to copy. The fact is, that this unlucky lady had the knack of writing a great deal more than she meant. She was always reading novels and trash; putting herself into imaginary characters, flying off into heroics and sentimentalities, and, with as little heart as any woman I ever knew, yet showing the most violent disposition to be in love. She wrote always as if she was in a flame of passion. I have an elegy on her lap-dog, the most tender and pathetic piece she ever wrote; and most tender notes of remonstrance to Betty, her favourite maid; to her housekeeper, on quarrelling with her; to half a dozen acquaintances, each of whom she addressed as the dearest friend in the world, and forgot, the very moment she took up another fancy. As for her love for her children, the above passage will show how much she was capable of true maternal feeling; the very sentence in which she records the death of one child serves to betray her egotisms, and to wreak her spleen against myself; and she only wishes to recall another from the grave, in order that he may be of some personal advantage to her. If I *did* deal severely with this woman, keeping her from her flatterers, who would have bred discord between us, and locking her up out of mischief, who shall say that I was wrong? If any woman deserved a strait-waistcoat, it was my Lady Lyndon; and I have known people in my time manacled, and with their heads shaved, in the straw, who had not committed half the follies of that foolish, vain, infatuated creature.[1]

My mother was so enraged by the charges against me and herself which these letters contained, that it was with the utmost difficulty I could keep her from discovering our knowledge of them to Lady Lyndon, whom it was, of course, my object to keep in ignorance of our knowledge of her designs; for I was anxious to know how far they went, and to what pitch of artifice she would go. The letters increased in interest (as they say of the novels) as they

[1] [Whatever her ladyship's faults were, and, indeed, she seems, according to her own showing, to have been as vain and silly a creature as ever lived, yet she seems to have had, from Mr. Barry's own account, a very sincere attachment for that amiable individual; to have come to him whenever he gave her the slightest encouragement; and, if she wrote silly letters to other persons, they appear to have been quite harmless, in intention at least, and to have had no further culpability than that resulting from an exceedingly strong vanity and feeble head. Those letters to Lord George Poynings, which her husband made use of against her subsequently, her husband here acknowledges to have been written without the slightest culpable design.] – Note in *Fraser's Magazine*, omitted in later editions.

proceeded. Pictures were drawn of my treatment of her which would make your heart throb. I don't know of what monstrosities she did not accuse me, and what miseries and starvation she did not profess herself to undergo, all the while she was living exceedingly fat and contented, to outward appearances, at our house at Castle Lyndon. Novel-reading and vanity had turned her brain. I could not say a rough word to her (and she merited many thousands a day, I can tell you) but she declared I was putting her to the torture; and my mother could not remonstrate with her but she went off into a fit of hysterics of which she would declare the worthy old lady was the cause.

At last she began to threaten to kill herself; and, though I by no means kept the cutlery out of the way, did not stint her in garters, and left her doctor's shop at her entire service,—knowing her character full well, and that there was no woman in Christendom less likely to lay hands on her precious life than herself, yet these threats had an effect evidently in the quarter to which they were addressed; for the milliner's packets now began to arrive with great frequency, and the bills sent to her contained assurances of coming aid. The chivalrous Lord George Poynings was coming to his cousin's rescue, and did me the compliment to say that he hoped to free his dear cousin from the clutches of the most atrocious villain that ever disgraced humanity, and that, when she was free, measures should be taken for a divorce, on the ground of cruelty and every species of ill-usage on my part.

I had copies of all these precious documents on one side and the other carefully made, by my before-mentioned relative, godson, and secretary, Mr. Redmond Quin, at present the *worthy* agent of the Castle Lyndon property. This was a son of my old flame Nora, whom I had taken from her in a fit of generosity, promising to care for his education at Trinity College, and provide for him through life. But after the lad had been for a year at the University the tutors would not admit him to commons or lectures until his college bills were paid; and, offended by this insolent manner of demanding the paltry sum due, I withdrew my patronage from the place, and ordered my gentleman to Castle Lyndon, where I made him useful to me in a hundred ways. In my dear little boy's lifetime he tutored the poor child as far as his high spirit would let him; but

I promise you it was small trouble poor dear Bryan ever gave the books. Then he kept Mrs. Barry's accounts; copied my own interminable correspondence with my lawyers and the agents of all my various property; took a hand at piquet or backgammon of evenings with me and my mother; or, being an ingenious lad enough (though of a mean, boorish spirit, as became the son of such a father, accompanied my Lady Lyndon's spinet with his flageolet; or read French and Italian with her, in both of which languages her ladyship was a fine scholar, and in which he also became perfectly conversant. It would make my watchful old mother very angry to hear them conversing in these languages; for, not understanding a word of either of them, Mrs. Barry was furious when they were spoken, and always said it was some scheming they were after. It was Lady Lyndon's constant way of annoying the old lady, when the three were alone together, to address Quin in one or other of these tongues.

I was perfectly at ease with regard to his fidelity, for I had bred the lad, and loaded him with benefits, and, besides, had had various proofs of his trustworthiness. He it was who brought me three of Lord George's letters, in reply to some of my lady's complaints, which were concealed between the leather and the boards of a book which was sent from the circulating library for her ladyship's perusal. He and my lady too had frequent quarrels. She mimicked his gait in her pleasanter moments; in her haughty moods she would not sit down to table with a tailor's grandson. 'Send me anything for company but that odious Quin,' she would say, when I proposed that he should go and amuse her with his books and his flute; for, quarrelsome as we were, it must not be supposed we were always at it; I was occasionally attentive to her. We would be friends for a month together, sometimes; then we would quarrel for a fortnight; then she would keep her apartments for a month; all of which domestic circumstances were noted down, in her ladyship's peculiar way, in her journal of captivity, as she called it: and a pretty document it is! Sometimes she writes, 'My monster has been almost kind to-day,' or 'My ruffian has deigned to smile.' Then she will break out into expressions of savage hate; but for my poor mother it was *always* hatred. It was, 'The she-dragon is sick to-day; I wish to Heaven she would die!' or, 'The hideous old Irish basket-woman has been treating me to some of her Billingsgate* to-day,' and so forth; all which expressions, read to Mrs. Barry, or translated from the French and Italian, in which many of them were written, did not fail to keep the old lady in a perpetual fury against her charge; and so I had my watch-dog, as I called her, always on the alert. In translating these languages, young Quin was of great service to me; for I had a smattering of French; and High Dutch, when I was in the army, of course, I knew well; but Italian I knew nothing of, and was glad of the services of so faithful and cheap an interpreter.

This cheap and faithful interpreter, this godson and kinsman, on whom and on whose family I had piled up benefits, was actually trying to betray me, and for several months, at least, was in league with the enemy against me. I believe that the reason why they did not move earlier was the want of the great mover of all treasons—money, of which, in all parts of my establishment, there was a woful scarcity; but of this they also managed to get a supply through my rascal of a godson, who could come and go quite unsuspected; and the whole scheme was arranged under our very noses, and the post-chaise ordered, and the means of escape actually got ready, while I never suspected their design.

A mere accident made me acquainted with their plan. One of my colliers had a pretty daughter; and this pretty lass had for her bachelor, as they call them in Ireland, a certain lad who brought the letter-bag for Castle Lyndon (and many a dunning letter for me was there in it, God wot!); and this letter-boy told his sweetheart how he brought a bag of money from the town for Master Quin; and how that Tim, the post-boy, had told him that he was to bring a chaise down to the water at a certain hour; and Miss Rooney, who had no secrets from me, blurted out the whole story, asked me what scheming I was after, and what poor, unlucky girl I was going to carry away with the chaise I had ordered, and bribe with the money I had got from town?

Then the whole secret flashed upon me, that the man I had cherished in my bosom was going to betray me. I thought at one time of catching the couple in the act of escape; half drowning them in the ferry which they had to cross to get to their chaise, and of pistolling the young traitor before Lady Lyndon's eyes; but, on second thoughts, it was quite clear that the news of the escape would make a noise through the country, and rouse the confounded justice's people about my ears, and bring me no good in the end. So I was obliged to smother my just indignation, and to content myself by crushing the foul conspiracy just at the moment it was about to be hatched.

I went home, and in half an hour, and with a few of my terrible looks, I had Lady Lyndon on her knees, begging me to forgive her; confessing all and everything; ready to vow and swear she would never make such an attempt again; and declaring that she was fifty times on the point of owning everything to me, but that she feared my wrath against the poor young lad, her accomplice, who was indeed the author and inventor of all the mischief. This, though I knew how entirely false the statement was, I was fain to pretend to believe; so I begged her to write to her cousin, Lord George, who had supplied her with money, as she admitted, and with whom the plan had been arranged, stating, briefly, that she had altered her mind as to the trip to the country proposed; and that, as her dear husband was rather in delicate health, she preferred to stay at home and nurse him. I added a dry postscript, in which I stated that it would give me great pleasure if his lordship would come and visit us at Castle Lyndon; and that I longed to renew an acquaintance which in former times gave me so much satisfaction. 'I should seek him out,' I added, 'so soon as ever I was in his neighbourhood, and eagerly anticipated the pleasure of a meeting with him.' I think he must have understood my meaning perfectly well, which was, that I would run him through the body on the very first occasion I could come at him.

Then I had a scene with my perfidious rascal of a nephew, in which the young reprobate showed an audacity and a spirit for which I was quite unprepared. When I taxed him with ingratitude, 'What do I owe you?' said he. 'I have toiled for you as no man ever did for another, and worked without a penny of wages. It was you yourself who set me against you, by giving me a task against which my soul revolted,—by making me a spy over your unfortunate wife, whose weakness is as pitiable as are her misfortunes and your rascally treatment of her. Flesh and blood could not bear to see the manner in which you used her. I tried to help her to escape from you; and I would do it again if the opportunity offered, and so I tell you to your teeth!' When I offered to blow his brains out for his insolence, 'Pooh!' said he,—'kill the man who saved your poor boy's life once, and who was endeavouring to keep him out of the ruin and perdition into which a wicked father was leading him, when a Merciful Power interposed, and withdrew him from this house of crime? I would have left you months ago, but I hoped for some chance of rescuing this unhappy lady. I swore I would try, the day I saw you strike her. Kill me, you woman's bully! You would, if you dared, but you have not the heart. Your very servants like me better than you. Touch me, and they will rise and send you to the gallows you merit!'

I interrupted this neat speech by sending a water-bottle at the young gentleman's head, which felled him to the ground; and then I went to meditate upon what he had said to me. It was true the fellow had saved poor little Bryan's life, and the boy to his dying day was tenderly attached to him. 'Be good to Redmond, papa,' were almost the last words he spoke; and I promised the poor child, on his death-bed, that I would do as he asked. It was also true that rough usage of him would be little liked by my people, with whom he had managed to become a great favourite; which, somehow, though I got drunk with the rascals often, and was much more familiar with them than a man of my rank commonly is, yet I knew I was by no means liked by them, and the scoundrels were murmuring against me perpetually.

But I might have spared myself the trouble of debating what his fate should be, for the young gentleman took the disposal of it out of my hands in the simplest way in the world, viz., by washing and binding up his head so soon as he came to himself, by taking his horse from the stables; and, as he was quite free to go in and out of the house and park as he liked, he disappeared without the least let or hindrance; and, leaving the horse behind him at the ferry, went off in the very post-chaise which was waiting for Lady Lyndon. I saw and heard no more of him for a considerable time, and, now that he was out of the house did not consider him a very troublesome enemy.

But the cunning artifice of woman is such that, I think, in the long run, no man, were he Machiavel himself, could escape from it; and though I had ample proofs in the above transaction (in which my wife's perfidious designs were frustrated by my foresight, and under her own handwriting) of the deceitfulness of her character and her hatred for me, yet she actually managed to deceive me, in spite of all my precautions and the vigilance of my mother in my behalf. Had I followed that good lady's advice, who scented the danger from afar off, as it were, I should never have fallen into the snare prepared for me, and which was laid in a way that was as successful as it was simple.

My Lady Lyndon's relation with me was a singular one. Her life was passed in a crack-brained sort of alternation between love and hatred for me. If I was in a good humour with her (as occurred sometimes), there was nothing she would not do to propitiate me further, and she would be as absurd and violent in her expressions of fondness as, at other moments, she would be in her demonstrations of hatred. It is not your feeble, easy husbands, who are loved best in the world, according to my experience of it. I do think the women like a little violence of temper, and think no worse of a husband who exercises his authority pretty smartly. I had got my lady into such a terror about me that when I smiled it was quite an era of happiness to her; and, if I beckoned to her, she would come fawning up to me like a dog. I recollect how, for the few days I was at school, the cowardly, mean-spirited fellows would laugh if ever our schoolmaster made a joke. It was the same in the regiment whenever the bully of a sergeant was disposed to be jocular—not a recruit but was on the broad grin. Well, a wise and determined husband will get his wife into this condition of discipline; and I brought my high-born wife to kiss my hand, to pull off my boots, to fetch and carry for me like a servant, and always to make it a holiday, too, when I was in good humour. I confided, perhaps, too much in the duration of this disciplined obedience, and forgot that the very hypocrisy which forms a part of it (all timid people are liars in their hearts) may be exerted in a way that may be far from agreeable in order to deceive you.

After the ill-success of her last adventure, which gave me endless opportunities to banter her, one would have thought I might have been on my guard as to what her real intentions were, but she managed to mislead me with an art of dissimulation quite admirable, and lulled me into a fatal security with regard to her intentions: for, one day, as I was joking her, and asking her whether she would take the water again, whether she had found another lover, and so forth, she suddenly burst into tears, and, seizing hold of my hand, cried passionately out,—

'Ah, Barry, you know well enough that I have never loved but you! Was I ever so wretched that a kind word from you did not make me happy? ever so angry, but the least offer of goodwill on your part did not bring me to your side? Did I not give a sufficient proof of my affection for you, in bestowing one of the first fortunes in England upon you? have I repined or rebuked you for the way you have wasted it? No, I loved you too much and too fondly; I have always loved you. From the first moment I saw you, I felt irresistibly attracted towards you. I saw your bad qualities, and trembled at your violence; but I could not help loving you. I married you, though I knew I was sealing my own fate in doing so, and in spite of reason and duty. What sacrifice do you want from me? I am ready to make any, so you will but love me, or, if not, that at least, you will gently use me.'

I was in a particularly good humour that day, and we had a sort of reconciliation; though my mother, when she heard the speech, and saw me softening towards her ladyship, warned me solemnly, and said, 'Depend on it, the artful hussy has some other scheme in her head now.' The old lady was right, and I swallowed the bait which her ladyship had prepared to entrap me as simply as any gudgeon takes a hook.

I had been trying to negotiate with a man for some money, for which I had pressing occasion; but since our dispute regarding the affair of the succession, my lady had resolutely refused to sign any papers for my advantage, and without her name, I am sorry to say, my own was of little value in the market, and I could not get a guinea from any money-dealer in London or Dublin. Nor could I get the rascals from the latter place to visit me at Castle Lyndon, owing to that unlucky affair I had with Lawyer Sharp, when I made him lend me the money he brought down, and old Solomons the Jew being robbed of the bond I gave him after leaving my house,[1] the people would not trust themselves within my walls any more. Our rents, too, were in the hands of receivers by this time, and it was as much as I could do to get enough money from the rascals to pay my wine-merchants their bills. Our English property, as I have said, was equally hampered, and, as often as I applied to my lawyers and agents for money, would come a reply demanding money of me, for debts and pretended claims which the rapacious rascals said they had on me.

It was, then, with some feelings of pleasure that I got a letter from my confidential man in Gray's Inn, London, saying (in reply to some ninety-ninth demand of mine) that he thought he could get me some money; and enclosing a letter from a respectable firm in the City of London, connected with the mining interest, which offered to redeem the incumbrance in taking a long lease of certain property of ours, which was still pretty free, upon the Countess's signature, and provided they could be assured of her free will in giving it. They said they heard she lived in terror of her life from me, and meditated a separation, in which case she might repudiate any deeds signed by her while in durance, and subject them, at any rate, to a doubtful and expensive litigation, and demanded to be made assured of her ladyship's perfect free will in the transaction before they advanced a shilling of their capital.

Their terms were so exorbitant that I saw at once their offer must be sincere, and, as my lady was in her gracious mood, had no difficulty in persuading her to write a letter, in her own hand, declaring that the accounts of our misunderstandings were utter calumnies, that we lived in perfect union, and that she was quite ready to execute any deed which her husband might desire her to sign.

This proposal was a very timely one, and filled me with great hopes. I have not pestered my readers with many accounts of my debts and law affairs, which were by this time so vast and complicated that I never thoroughly knew them myself, and was rendered half wild by their urgency. Suffice it to say, my money was gone—my credit was done.

[1] These exploits of Mr. Lyndon are not related in the narrative. He probably, in the cases above alluded to, took the law into his own hands.

I was living at Castle Lyndon off my own beef and mutton, and the bread, turf, and potatoes off my own estate; I had to watch Lady Lyndon within, and the bailiffs without. For the last two years, since I went to Dublin to receive money, which I unluckily lost at play there, to the disappointment of my creditors, I did not venture to show in that city, and could only appear at our own county town at rare intervals, and because I knew the sheriffs, whom I swore I would murder if any ill chance happened to me. A chance of a good loan, then, was the most welcome prospect possible to me, and I hailed it with all the eagerness imaginable.

In reply to Lady Lyndon's letter came, in course of time, an answer from the confounded London merchants, stating that if her ladyship would confirm by word of mouth, at their counting-house in Birchin Lane, London, the statement of her letter, they, having surveyed her property, would no doubt come to terms; but they declined incurring the risk of a visit to Castle Lyndon to negotiate, as they were aware how other respectable parties, such as Messrs. Sharp and Salmon of Dublin, had been treated there. This was a hit at me; but there are certain situations in which people can't dictate their own terms, and, faith, I was so pressed now for money, that I could have signed a bond with Old Nick himself, if he had come provided with a good round sum.

I resolved to go and take the Countess to London. It was in vain that my mother prayed and warned me. 'Depend on it,' says she, 'there is some artifice. When once you get into that wicked town, you are not safe. Here you may live for years and years, in luxury and splendour, barring claret and all the windows broken; but as soon as they have you in London, they'll get the better of my poor innocent lad; and the first thing I shall hear of you will be that you are in trouble.'

'Why go, Redmond?' said my wife. 'I am happy here, as long as you are kind to me, as you are now. We can't appear in London as we ought; the little money you will get will be spent, like all the rest has been. Let us turn shepherd and shepherdess, and look to our flocks and be content.' And she took my hand, and kissed it, while my mother only said, 'Humph! I believe she's at the bottom of it—the wicked *schamer!*'

I told my wife she was a fool; bade Mrs. Barry not be uneasy, and was hot upon going, and would take no denial from either party. How I was to get the money to go was the question; but that was solved by my good mother, who was always ready to help me on a pinch, and who produced sixty guineas from a stocking, which was all the ready money that Barry Lyndon, of Castle Lyndon, and married to a fortune of twenty thousand a year, could command, such had been the havoc made in this fine fortune by my own extravagance (as I must confess), but chiefly by my misplaced confidence and the rascality of others.

We did not start in state, you may be sure. We did not let the country know we were going, or leave notice of adieu with our neighbours. The famous Mr. Barry Lyndon and his noble wife travelled in a hack-chaise and pair to Waterford, under the name of Mr. and Mrs. Jones, and thence took shipping for Bristol, where we arrived quite without accident. When a man is going to the deuce, how easy and pleasant the journey is! The thought of the money quite put me in a good humour, and my wife, as she lay on my shoulder in the post-chaise going to London, said it was the happiest ride she had taken since our marriage.

One night we stayed at Reading, whence I dispatched a note to my agent at Gray's Inn, saying I would be with him during the day, and begging him to procure me a lodging, and to hasten the preparations for the loan. My lady and I agreed that we would go to France, and wait there for better times, and that night, over our supper, formed a score of plans both for pleasure and retrenchment. You would have thought it was Darby and Joan* together over their supper. Oh, woman! woman! when I recollect Lady Lyndon's smiles and blandishments, how happy she seemed to be on that night! what an air of innocent confidence appeared in her behaviour, and what affectionate names she called me! I am lost in wonder at the depth of her hypocrisy. Who can be surprised that an unsuspecting person like myself should have been a victim to such a consummate deceiver?

We were in London at three o'clock, and half an hour before the time appointed our chaise drove to Gray's Inn. I easily found out Mr. Tapewell's apartments—a gloomy den it was, and in an unlucky hour I entered it! As we went up the dirty back-stair, lighted by a feeble lamp and the dim sky of a dismal London afternoon, my wife seemed agitated and faint. 'Redmond,' said she, as we got up to the door, 'don't go in: I am sure there is danger. There's time yet, let us go back—to Ireland—anywhere!' And she put herself before the door, in one of her theatrical attitudes, and took my hand.

I just pushed her away to one side. 'Lady Lyndon,' said I, 'you are an old fool!'

'Old fool!' said she; and she jumped at the bell, which was quickly answered by a mouldy-looking gentleman, in an unpowdered wig, to whom she cried, 'Say Lady Lyndon is here;' and stalked down the passage, muttering, 'Old fool.' It was '*old*' which was the epithet that touched her. I might call her anything but that.

Mr. Tapewell was in his musty room, surrounded by his parchments and tin boxes. He advanced and bowed; begged her ladyship to be seated; pointed towards a chair for me, which I took, rather wondering at his insolence; and then retreated to a side-door, saying he would be back in one moment.

And back he *did* come in one moment, bringing with him—whom do you think? Another lawyer, six constables in red waistcoats, with bludgeons and pistols, my Lord George Poynings, and his aunt, Lady Jane Peckover.

When my Lady Lyndon saw her old flame, she flung herself into his arms in a hysterical passion. She called him her saviour, her preserver, her gallant knight, and then, turning round to me, poured out a flood of invective which quite astonished me.

'Old fool as I am,' said she, 'I have outwitted the most crafty and treacherous monster under the sun. Yes, I *was* a fool when I married you, and gave up other and nobler hearts for your sake—yes, I was a fool when I forgot my name and lineage to unite myself with a base-born adventurer—a fool to bear, without repining, the most monstrous tyranny that ever woman suffered; to allow my property to be squandered; to see women, as base and low-born as yourself——'

'For Heaven's sake, be calm!' cries the lawyer; and then bounded back behind the constables, seeing a threatening look in my eye, which the rascal did not like. Indeed,

I could have torn him to pieces had he come near me. Meanwhile, my lady continued in a strain of incoherent fury, screaming against me, and against my mother especially, upon whom she heaped abuse worthy of Billingsgate, and always beginning and ending the sentence with the word fool.

'You don't tell all, my lady,' says I, bitterly; 'I said *old* fool.'

'I have no doubt you said and did, sir, everything that a blackguard could say or do,' interposed little Poynings. 'This lady is now safe under the protection of her relations and the law, and need fear your infamous persecutions no longer.'

'But *you* are not safe,' roared I; 'and, as sure as I am a man of honour, and have tasted your blood once, I will have your heart's blood now.'

'Take down his words, constables; swear the peace against him!' screamed the little lawyer, from behind his tipstaffs.

'I would not sully my sword with the blood of such a ruffian,' cried my lord, relying on the same doughty protection. 'If the scoundrel remains in London another day, he will be seized as a common swindler.' And this threat indeed made me wince, for I knew that there were scores of writs out against me in town, and that once in prison, my case was hopeless.

'Where's the man will seize me?' shouted I, drawing my sword, and placing my back to the door. 'Let the scoundrel come. You—you cowardly braggart, come first, if you have the soul of a man!'

'We're not going to seize you!' said the lawyer; my ladyship, her aunt, and a division of the bailiffs moving off as he spoke. 'My dear sir, we don't wish to seize you; we will give you a handsome sum to leave the country, only leave her ladyship in peace!'

'And the country will be well rid of such a villain,' says my lord, retreating too, and not sorry to get out of my reach; and the scoundrel of a lawyer followed him, leaving me in possession of the apartment, and in company of the three bullies from the police-office,* who were all armed to the teeth. I was no longer the man I was at twenty, when I should have charged the ruffians sword in hand, and have sent at least one of them to his account.

I was broken in spirit, regularly caught in the toils, utterly baffled and beaten by that woman. Was she relenting at the door when she paused and begged me turn back? Had she not a lingering love for me still? Her conduct showed it, as I came to reflect on it. It was my only chance now left in the world, so I put down my sword upon the lawyer's desk.

'Gentlemen,' said I, 'I shall use no violence; you may tell Mr. Tapewell I am quite ready to speak with him when he is at leisure!' and I sat down and folded my arms quite peaceably. What a change from the Barry Lyndon of old days! but, as I have read in an old book about Hannibal the Carthaginian* general, when he invaded the Romans, his troops, which were the most gallant in the world, and carried all before them, went into cantonments in some city where they were so sated with the luxuries and pleasures of life that they were easily beaten in the next campaign. It was so with me now. My strength of mind and body were no longer those of the brave youth who shot his man at fifteen, and fought a score of battles within six years afterwards. Now, in the Fleet Prison,* where I write this, there is a small man who is always jeering me and making game of me, who asks me to fight, and I haven't the courage to touch him. But I am anticipating the gloomy and wretched events of my history of humiliation, and had better proceed in order.

I took a lodging in a coffee-house near Gray's Inn, taking care to inform Mr. Tapewell of my whereabouts, and anxiously expecting a visit from him. He came and brought me the terms which Lady Lyndon's friends proposed,—a paltry annuity of 300*l.* a year, to be paid on the condition of my remaining abroad out of the three kingdoms, and to be stopped on the instant of my return. He told me what I very well knew, that my stay in London would infallibly plunge me in jail, that there were writs innumerable taken out against me here and in the west of England, that my credit was so blown upon that I could not hope to raise a shilling, and he left me a night to consider of his proposal, saying that if I refused it, the family would proceed; if I acceded, a quarter's salary should be paid to me at any foreign port I should prefer.

What was the poor, lonely, and broken-hearted man to do? I took the annuity, and was declared outlaw in the course of next week. The rascal Quin had, I found, been, after all, the cause of my undoing. It was he devised the scheme for bringing me up to London, sealing the attorney's letter with a seal which had been agreed upon between him and the countess formerly; indeed, he had always been for trying the plan, and had proposed it at first, but her ladyship, with her inordinate love of romance, preferred the project of elopement. Of these points my mother wrote me word in my lonely exile, offering at the same time to come over and share it with me, which proposal I declined. She left Castle Lyndon a very short time after I had quitted it, and there was silence in that hall where, under my authority, had been exhibited so much hospitality and splendour. She thought she would never see me again, and bitterly reproached me for neglecting her; but she was mistaken in that and in her estimate of me. She is very old, and is sitting by my side at this moment in the prison working, and has a bedroom in Fleet Market* over the way; and, with the fifty-pound annuity which she has kept with a wise prudence, we manage to eke out a miserable existence, quite unworthy of the famous and fashionable Barry Lyndon.

Mr. Barry Lyndon's personal narrative finishes here, for the hand of death interrupted the ingenious author soon after the period at which the Memoir was compiled, after he had lived nineteen years an inmate of the Fleet Prison, where the prison records state he died of delirium tremens. His mother attained a prodigious old age, and the inhabitants of the place in her time can record with accuracy the daily disputes which used to take place between mother and son, until the latter, from habits of intoxication, falling into a state of almost imbecility, was tended by his tough old parent as a baby almost, and would cry if deprived of his necessary glass of brandy.

His life on the Continent we have not the means of following accurately, but he appears to have resumed his former profession of a gambler without his former success.

He returned secretly to England after some time, and made an abortive attempt to extort money from Lord George Poynings, under a threat of publishing his correspondence with Lady Lyndon, and so preventing his lordship's match with Miss Driver, a great heiress, of strict principles, and immense property in slaves in the West Indies. Barry narrowly escaped being taken prisoner by the bailiffs who were dispatched after him by his lordship, who would have stopped his pension, but his wife would never consent to that act of justice and, indeed, broke with my Lord George the very moment he married the West India lady.

The fact is, the old countess thought her charms were perennial, and was never out of love with her husband. She was living at Bath, her property being carefully nursed by her noble relatives the Tiptoffs, who were to succeed to it in default of direct heirs; and such was the address of Barry, and the sway he still held over the woman, that he actually had almost persuaded her to go and live with him again, when his plan and hers were interrupted by the appearance of a person that had been deemed dead for several years.

This was no other than Viscount Bullingdon, who started up to the surprise of all, and especially to that of his kinsman of the house of Tiptoff. This young nobleman made his appearance at Bath, with the letter from Barry to Lord George in his hand, in which the former threatened to expose his connexion with Lady Lyndon—a connexion, we need not state, which did not reflect the slightest dishonour upon either party, and only showed that her ladyship was in the habit of writing exceedingly foolish letters, as many ladies, nay, gentlemen, have done ere this. For calling the honour of his mother in question, Lord Bullingdon assaulted his step-father (living at Bath under the name of Mr. Jones), and administered to him a tremendous castigation in the Pump-room.

His lordship's history, since his departure, was a romantic one, which we do not feel bound to narrate. He had been wounded in the American War, reported dead, left prisoner, and escaped. The remittances which were promised him were never sent; the thought of the neglect almost broke the heart of the wild and romantic young man, and he determined to remain dead to the world at least, and to the mother who had denied him. It was in the woods of Canada, and three years after the event had occurred, that he saw the death of his half-brother chronicled in the *Gentleman's Magazine*,* under the title of 'Fatal Accident to Lord Viscount Castle-Lyndon,' on which he determined to return to England, where, though he made himself known, it was with very great difficulty indeed that he satisfied Lord Tiptoff of the authenticity of his claim. He was about to pay a visit to his lady-mother at Bath, when he recognized the well-known face of Mr. Barry Lyndon, in spite of the modest disguise which that gentleman wore, and revenged upon his person the insults of former days.

Lady Lyndon was furious when she heard of the rencounter, declined to see her son, and was for rushing at once to the arms of her adored Barry; but that gentleman had been carried off, meanwhile, from jail to jail, until he was lodged in the hands of Mr. Bendigo, of Chancery Lane, an assistant to the Sheriff of Middlesex, from whose house he went to the Fleet Prison. The sheriff and his assistant, the prisoner, nay, the prison itself, are now no more.

As long as Lady Lyndon lived, Barry enjoyed his income, and was perhaps as happy in prison as at any period of his existence; when her ladyship died, her successor sternly cut off the annuity, devoting the sum to charities, which, he said, would make a nobler use of it than the scoundrel who had enjoyed it hitherto. At his lordship's death, in the Spanish campaign,* in the year 1811, his estate fell into the family of the Tiptoffs, and his title merged in their superior rank; but it does not appear that the Marquis of Tiptoff (Lord George succeeded to the title on the demise of his brother) renewed either the pension of Mr. Barry or the charities which the late lord had endowed. The estate has vastly improved under his lordship's careful management. The trees in Hackton Park are all about forty years old, and the Irish property is rented in exceedingly small farms to the peasantry, who still entertain the stranger with stories of the daring, and the devilry, and the wickedness, and the fall of Barry Lyndon.

[When that famous character lost his income, his spirits entirely fell. He was removed into the paupers' ward, where he was known to black boots for wealthier prisoners, and where he was detected in stealing a tobacco-box. It was in this plight his staunch old mother found him, and from it she withdrew him; and if, upon being restored to bread-and-cheese, he despised blacking boots and no longer stole snuff-boxes, the reader must not fancy that he was a whit more virtuous than when, under the strong temptation of necessity, he performed those actions unworthy of a man and a gentleman. If the tale of his life have any moral (which I sometimes doubt), it is that honesty is *not* the best policy. That was a pettifogger's maxim, who half admits he would be a rogue if he found his profit in it, and has led astray scores of misguided people both in novels and the world, who forthwith set up the worldly prosperity or adversity of a man as standards by which his worth should be tried. Novelists especially make a most profuse, mean use of this pedlar's measure, and mete out what they call poetical justice.

Justice, forsooth! Does human life exhibit justice after this fashion? Is it the good always who ride in gold coaches, and the wicked who go to the workhouse? Is a humbug never preferred before a capable man? Does the world always reward merit, never worship cant, never raise mediocrity to distinction? never crowd to hear a donkey braying from a pulpit, nor ever buy the tenth edition of a fool's book? Sometimes the contrary occurs, so that fools and wise, bad men and good, are more or less lucky in their turn, and honesty is 'the best policy,' or not, as the case may be.

If this be true of the world, those persons who find their pleasure or get their livelihood by describing its manners and the people who live in it are bound surely to represent to the best of their power life as it really appears to them to be; not to foist off upon the public figures pretending to be delineations of human nature,—gay and agreeable cut-throats, otto-of-rose murderers, amiable hackney-coachmen, Prince Rodolphs* and the like, being representatives of beings that never have or could have existed. At least, if not bounden to copy nature, they are justified in trying; and hence in describing not only what is beautiful, but what is ill-favoured too, faithfully, so that each may appear as like as possible to nature. It is as right to look at a beauty as at a hunchback; and, if to look, to describe too: nor can the most prodigious genius improve upon the original. Who knows, then, but the old style of Molière and Fielding, who drew from nature, may come into fashion again, and replace the terrible, the humorous, always the genteel impossible now in vogue? Then, with the sham characters, the sham *moral* may disappear. The one is a sickly humbug as well as the other. I believe for my part Hogarth's pictures of 'Mariage à la Mode' in Trafalgar Square* to be more moral and more beautiful than West's* biggest heroic piece, or Angelica Kaufmann's* most elegant allegory!

G. S. FITZ-BOODLE.][1]

[1] Omitted in later editions.

APPENDIX

THE LUCK OF BARRY LYNDON AND ITS SERIAL PUBLICATION IN FRASER'S MAGAZINE

The Luck of Barry Lyndon; A Romance of the Last Century. By Fitz-Boodle, first published serially in *Fraser's Magazine* in 1844, was divided into two parts, the first part containing Chapters I–XVII and the second the three final chapters. When Thackeray revised the novel in 1856 he abandoned its division into parts and reduced the number of chapters by amalgamating Chapters I and II into a single unit. As part of his revision he also altered, and in some cases added, the chapter titles which are used throughout the present edition. The following table gives the original chapter titles together with the details of their serial publication in *Fraser's*. Barry's own narrative was printed in double columns of type; the supposed editorial comments by Fitz-Boodle, such as the opening comments in Part II Chapter I (the revised Chapter XVII) and the conclusion to the final chapter (the revised Chapter XIX), were printed in a single block of type.

Chapter No.	*Chapter Title*	*Volume, Month and Page*
Chapter I	none	Vol. 29 January 1844 pp. 35–51
Chapter II	none	
Chapter III	In which Barry Lyndon shews himself to be a Man of Spirit.	Vol. 29 February 1844 pp. 187–202
Chapter IV	In which the hero makes a false start in the Genteel World.	
Chapter V	In which Barry takes a near view of Military Glory	Vol. 29 March 1844 pp. 318–330
Chapter VI	In which Barry tries to remove as far from Military Glory as possible.	

Chapter No.	*Chapter Title*	*Volume, Month and Page*
Chapter VII	The Crimp Wagon—Military Episodes.	Vol. 29 April 1844 pp. 391–410
Chapter VIII	Barry leads a Garrison Life, and finds many Friendships.	
Chapter IX	Barry bids adieu to the Military Profession.	
Chapter X	none	Vol. 29 May 1844 pp. 548–563
Chapter XI	More runs of Luck.	
Chapter XII	In which the Luck goes against Barry.	Vol. 29 June 1844 pp. 723–738
Chapter XIII	The Princess's Tragedy.	
Chapter XIV	none	Vol. 30 July 1844 pp. 93–108
Chapter XV	none	
Chapter XVI	Barry in Love.	Vol. 30 August 1844 pp. 227–242
Chapter XVII	Barry provides for his Family and attains the Height of his Luck.	
PART II		
Chapter I	Barry appears at the Summit of Fortune.	Vol. 30 September 1844 pp. 353–364
	NO SERIAL PART	Vol. 30 October 1844
Chapter II	In which the Luck of Barry Lyndon begins to waver.	Vol. 30 November 1844 pp. 584–597
Chapter III	Conclusion.	Vol. 30 December 1844 pp. 666–683

EXPLANATORY NOTES

3 *Gwillim or D'Hozier*: John Guillim (1565–1621) systematized and illustrated the science of heraldry in his *A Display of Heraldrie* first published in 1610. Louis Pierre D'Hozier (1685–1767) published his *Armorial général ou registre de la noblesse de France* in ten volumes between 1738 and 1768.

adhesion to the old faith and monarch: Irish Catholics faithful to Charles I were dispossessed after Cromwell's campaign of 1649–50. Following the defeat of James II at the Boyne in 1690 and at Aughrim in 1691 more than one million acres of Irish land were forfeited especially by Catholics loyal to the Stuart cause.

the Irish crown: fantastic claims of descent both from the High Kings of Tara and from provincial kings were common among the dispossessed Irish catholic gentry.

4 *King Richard II . . . Oliver Cromwell*: Richard II's two expeditions to Ireland in 1394 and 1399 respectively had little long-term effect though both resulted in a temporary submission of the island. Cromwell's civil policy in his ruthless campaign of 1649–50 was described by Macaulay as 'able, straightforward, and cruel'. Of his massacre at Drogheda Thackeray commented in Chapter xxv of *The Irish Sketch Book*, 'is not the recollection of this butchery almost enough to make an Irishman turn rebel?'.

the murderous brewer: Oliver Cromwell was the great-great-grandson of Morgan Williams, an ale-brewer and innkeeper of Putney.

gallowglasses: mounted and armed retainers of the ancient Irish chieftains. Thackeray was probably familiar with the word from *Macbeth*, I, ii, 13.

5 *Sackville Street*: now O'Connell Street.

6 *Chevalier Borgne*: i.e. one-eyed.

Scotch disturbances in '45: Prince Charles Edward Stuart, the 'Young Pretender', landed in Scotland on 5 April 1745 in support of his father's claim to the throne. He was finally defeated at Culloden on 16 April 1746.

the good old laws being then in force: i.e. the Penal Laws affecting the civil rights of Roman Catholics. Under the Act of I Geo II (1727), a younger brother conforming to the established religion could deprive the elder of the legal right of primogeniture. The Catholic Relief Act (17 & 18 Geo III, 1778) enabled Catholics to purchase land, take leases for 999 years, and inherit without disability.

faro: a card-game in which players bet on the order in which certain cards will appear when taken from the top of the pack.

the Pigeon House: formerly the chief landing-place for visitors to Dublin. The Pigeon House (named for an overseer of the Ballast Office) is situated on the great breakwater known as the South Wall which extends from Ringsend into Dublin Bay.

7 *married at the Savoy*: i.e. illicitly. The Chapel of the Savoy is extra-parochial. The most notorious of the so-called 'Savoy parsons' was the Revd John Wilkinson who in 1755 married some 1,190 couples. Wilkinson was eventually arrested and sentenced to fourteen years' transportation.

Montague House . . . White's: to the north of Montague House in Bloomsbury (now the site of the British Museum) were open fields. The area was much used as a duelling-ground and is referred to as such by Mrs. Steele in Chapter XV of *Henry Esmond*; White's Club was first established in St. James's Street in 1698.

8 *mutes sent by Mr. Plumer*: paid attendants dispatched by the undertaker to attend the funeral. Plumer's name is a play on the black ostrich plumes once regarded as essential decoration to the hearse.

11 *plaster*: a composition used to disguise both a sallow complexion and skin defects such as pock-marks and wrinkles.

13 *a true blue Nassauite*: i.e. a Protestant determined to maintain the constitution of Church and State as established by William III, Prince of Orange-Nassau.

14 *taw, prison-bars*: taw is an alternative name for the game of

marbles, the taw being the fancy marble with which the player shoots. Prison-bars also known as prisoner's-base, is played with two teams, each occupying distinct 'bases'. The aim of each side is to take 'prisoners' by touching a player from the opposite side who runs out of his base.

15 *Johnson*: Samuel Johnson lived at 17 Gough Square 1748–59, at 7 Johnson's Court 1765–76, and at 8 Bolt Court from 1776 until his death in 1784. All these addresses lie to the north of Fleet Street.

Button's Coffee-house: an empty boast of Barry's. Button's Coffee-house was established in Russell Street, Covent Garden, in 1712. It was much frequented by early eighteenth-century wits but seems to have declined after *c.*1719. Button himself died, impoverished, in 1731.

Mr. Buswell: the spelling reflects a common pronunciation of James Boswell's surname.

Mr. Goldsmith: Oliver Goldsmith was born *c.*1730 either at Pallasmore, Co. Longford or at Elphin, Co. Roscommon. He arrived in London in 1756.

16 *Cocoa-tree*: like White's, the Cocoa-tree was a famous Tory coffee-house of Queen Anne's reign. The St. James's Street premises were converted into a club-house by 1746 when the club was a centre of the Jacobite party in Parliament. Later both Gibbon and Byron were members.

Staggerite: Richard Brinsley Sheridan (1751–1816) is punning on the term Stagirite, an inhabitant of Stagira in Macedonia, an epithet commonly applied to Aristotle.

served the French king at Fontenoy: i.e., in one of the Irish regiments of the French army. The battle of Fontenoy, in which the French defeated the British and their allies, was fought on 11 May 1745 during the War of the Austrian Succession.

Marshal Saxe: Maurice, comte de Saxe (1696–1750), marshall of France and commander at Fontenoy.

17 *St. George's, Hanover Square*: consecrated in 1724. Once celebrated for its fashionable marriages.

19 *run like the British out of Carthagena*: in 1741 a British expedition under Admiral Edward Vernon attempted to seize the important port of Cartagena in Spanish-held

Colombia. Forts at the entrance to the harbour were captured but the siege and assault on the city proved a failure and the force was withdrawn after enduring substantial losses, mainly as a result of fever. There was consequently considerable rancour between the army and navy. The episode is wryly described in Chapter 31 of Smollett's *Roderick Random* (1748).

the Old Hundredth: i.e the setting of the metrical version of Psalm 100 in the Genevan Psalter of 1551. It is marked 'Old Hundredth' in Nahum Tate and Nicholas Brady's Psalter of 1696 and sets the words 'All people that on earth do dwell'.

21 *a Persian song-book*: this is a burlesque of the growing fashion for oriental poetry in the mid-eighteenth century. William Collins's *Persian Eclogues* of 1742 demonstrate little knowledge of original Persian verse, an acquaintance with which might later have been formed through John Richardson's *A Specimen of Persian Poetry* of 1774. Richardson included paraphrases as well as verse translations. One of the Odes of Hafez begins:

> With sullen pace stern winter leaves the plain,
> And blooming spring trips gaily o'er the meads,
> Sweet Philomel now swells her plaintive strain,
> And her lov'd rose his blushing beauties spreads.

22 *Dr. Swift*: Jonathan Swift was Dean of St. Patrick's Cathedral, Dublin, from 1713 until his death in 1745.

23 *Alfonso . . . Lindamira*: this novel would appear to be an invention, or at best a conflation, on Barry's part. The name 'Alfonso' was commonly used in the minor fiction of the period and especially in novels with a Spanish setting (e.g. Le Sage's *Gil Blas of Santillane*). Lindamira (*Sp.* 'fair face') is the name of the heroine of *The Lover's Secretary* or *The Adventures of Lindamira, A Lady of Quality* of 1702 but no Alfonso appears in the story. The name is also employed in *Spectator* 41 and Thackeray himself refers to 'the Lindamiras and Ardelias of the poets' in Chapter VII of *Henry Esmond*.

24 *The Pretender*: James Francis Edward Stuart (1688–1766) had lived in exile in Rome since 1719. During the Seven Years' War, however, the French Government again

endeavoured to make use of the Stuarts, and, in 1759, an expedition was fitted out in Brittany for the invasion of England. In anticipation of victory Prince Charles Edward Stuart even went so far as to renounce his allegiance to the Roman Church. Concern lest the expedition should be directed against Ireland was expressed by the Lord Lieutenant in an address to the two Houses of Parliament on 29 November 1759 (as reported in the *Annual Register* for that year). Admiral Hawke's victory at Quiberon Bay (see n. to p. 27 below) dashed the hopes of both the French and the Pretender by rendering an invasion impossible.

the Duke of Cumberland: William Augustus, Duke of Cumberland (1721–65). Second son of George II and Captain-General of British land forces from 1745.

Bellona: in Roman mythology the goddess of War.

the Fencibles: volunteers enlisted for defensive service.

27 *King Frederick . . . Monsieur Thurot . . . Conflans*: Frederick II, King of Prussia (1712–86) was regarded as the champion of the Protestant cause in Germany during the Seven Years' War, his major opponents being the great Catholic powers, France and Austria; Commodore François Thurot (1727–60), a French naval officer of Irish descent, was given the command of a small squadron which, having eluded British ships, threatened the coast of Scotland and northern Ireland in the closing months of 1759 (see *Annual Register* for 1759). In February 1760 Thurot landed at Carrickfergus in Co. Antrim with one thousand men but was obliged to retreat. He was killed in action off the Isle of Man later that month. A further series of 'Anecdotes of the celebrated Thurot' was published in the *Annual Register* for 1760. It would appear to be to this account that Thackeray refers in his description of Carrickfergus in Chapter XXVIII of *The Irish Sketch Book*; on 20 November 1759 a French Fleet under the command of Admiral Hubert de Brienne, comte de Conflans (1712–86) was pursued into Quiberon Bay on the south coast of Brittany by Admiral Sir Edward Hawke (1705–81). The French were defeated in the brief engagement and many of their ships were wrecked by running

aground on the dangerous coastline thereby destroying all hope of an invasion of England. The victory at Quiberon Bay restored British confidence in the navy after the disaster three years earlier at Minorca where the British garrison had fallen to the French in May 1756 after the withdrawal of Admiral Byng's fleet. Byng had subsequently been court-martialled and shot, accused of an error of judgement, in March 1757. Much British activity in the Seven Years' War was successfully directed against French possessions in North America. Quebec fell on 13 September 1759.

31 *'Roast Beef of Old England'*: a song from Act 3 of Henry Fielding's *The Grub Street Opera* (1731):

When mighty roast beef was the Englishman's food
It ennobled our hearts and enriched our blood,
Our soldiers were brave and our courtiers were good
On the roast beef of England
And old England's roast beef.

Norelia . . . Eugenio: fanciful hispano-italianate names were common in eighteenth-century popular fiction.

39 *Freeny's people*: for the highwayman Captain James Freeny, see n. to p. 51 below, and Introduction, p. x above.

42 *shagreen*: a variety of untanned leather frequently used for covering cases.

43 *Lord George Sackville, at Minden*: the Battle of Minden was fought on 1 August 1759, a date that does not quite tally with the events described in Chapter I. Barry now tells us that his duel takes place in January or February 1759; the discussion of Thurot's squadron off the Irish coast *ought* to have taken place in October or November of the same year. For Lord George Sackville's conduct at Minden, see n. to p. 69 below.

47 *the police*: perhaps a loose use of the term for 1759, implying the constables and watchmen appointed for the parish by the magistracy. In 1732 Jonathan Swift used the word in a preciser manner: 'Nothing is held more commendable in all great cities . . . than what the French

call the *police*: by which word is meant the government thereof.'

50 *these days of stage-coaches*: a reminder of the supposed date of Barry's narrative, i.e. *c.*1800. Stage-coach travel was a late eighteenth-century development. A stage-coach duty act was passed in 1785 and coaches were made subject to provisions for the safety of passengers by an act of 1809.

a one-horse chair: a light vehicle or chaise.

51 *the famous Captain Freeny*: on a wet evening in Galway, during his visit to Ireland in 1842, Thackeray read and enjoyed 'eighteen-pennyworth of little books . . . these yellow-covered books are prepared for the people chiefly; and have been sold for many long years before the march of knowledge began to banish Fancy out of the world'. He quotes substantial sections of Captain Freeny's 'Autobiography' in Chapter XV of *The Irish Sketch Book* including Freeny's account of his action at Kilkenny. The title 'Captain' was frequently adopted by highwaymen.

52 *ridottos and routs*: both fashionable evening receptions consisting of music and dancing. Byron describes a ridotto in *Beppo*:

> 'They went to the Ridotto—'tis a hall
> Where people dance, and sup, and dance again;
> Its proper name, perhaps, were a masked ball.'

54 *Lord Lieutenant . . . sillery*: the Lord Lieutenant of Ireland at this date was John, fourth Duke of Bedford. Sillery is a white wine produced at Sillery in Champagne.

56 *jabot*: an ornamental frill worn on the shirt front.

drab: a grey woollen cloth.

57 *the Granby Somersets . . . Hampshire*: Barry had earlier been told that the Granby Somersets were from Worcestershire.

63 *link-boy*: a boy employed to carry a torch (link) to light passengers along a street.

64 *Gale's Foot*: an invention on Thackeray's part. No such regiment existed.

65 *married to Brown Bess*: 'Brown Bess' was an affectionate

military name applied to the Land Pattern series of flintlock musket. The expressions 'married to Brown Bess' or 'hugging Brown Bess' meant serving as a private soldier.

66 *halbert . . . ensigncy*: the halbert denoted the rank of sergeant in an Infantry Regiment. The ensign was formerly the lowest grade of commissioned officer in the infantry; the rank survives in the Foot Guards.

67 *the causes of the famous Seven Years' War*: the war was initially the result of a secret coalition between Austria, France, Russia, Sweden and Saxony aimed at crippling the power of Frederick II's Prussia. The *casus belli* was Frederick's pre-emptive invasion of Saxony on 29 August 1756. Active British support for Prussia was partly determined by George II's desire to protect his Hanoverian domains. Thackeray's attribution to Barry of a confusion over the War's causes perhaps reflects that of the *Annual Register* for 1758, which, in attempting to sum up the progress of the various campaigns, admitted: 'It would be difficult perfectly to understand the operations of the several powers at war . . . without reviewing the transaction of the preceding years; nor would it be easy to enter into the spirit of these without examining the causes which more nearly or remotely operated to produce these troubles that have involved so many parts of the world in one common distraction.'

Mr. Pitt: William Pitt (1708–78), created Earl of Chatham in 1766, had been dismissed from his secretaryship of state in April 1757 on account of his opposition to the King's continental policy. A political deadlock ensued during which a popular campaign on Pitt's behalf, partially orchestrated by his closest supporters, gradually obliged the Prime Minister, the Duke of Newcastle, to include 'the Great Commoner' in his administration. During this period Horace Walpole noted that it literally rained gold boxes upon Pitt's head. In the new administration Newcastle remained the nominal head of the cabinet but its real direction was decided by Pitt who was appointed secretary of state with the management of the war and of foreign affairs. Thackeray's uncle, the Revd Francis Thackeray had published his *A History of the Right Honorable William Pitt Earl of Chatham* in 2 volumes in

1827. The book was the subject of one of Macaulay's finest reviews (*Edinburgh Review*, January 1834).

Dettingen and Crefeld: a confusion on Barry's part. The Battle of Dettingen, the last in which an English monarch had commanded his forces, had taken place during the War of the Austrian Succession (1741–8) on 16 June 1743. George II's British, Hanoverian and Hessian forces defeated the French. At the Battle of Crefeld, 23 June 1758, a Hanoverian army under Prince Ferdinand of Brunswick defeated a French army under Louis de Bourbon-Condé, comte de Clermont.

alliance with the empress-queen: the alliance of Britain and Prussia survived until 1761, when Britain attempted to negotiate a separate peace with France at what seemed to Frederick II the expense of his interests. The friction between Britain and Prussia was accentuated in 1762 when negotiations began with Prussia's old enemy, Austria. Maria-Theresa, wife of the Holy Roman Emperor Francis I, was Queen of Hungary and Bohemia in her own right.

the battle of Lissa: now more familiarly known as the Battle of Leuthen (5 December 1757). Frederick II inflicted a massive defeat on the Austrians.

Cuxhaven . . . the Electorate: Cuxhaven is situated at the mouth of the Elbe bordering on what was formerly the Electorate of Hanover.

69 *Prince Ferdinand of Brunswick*: Field-Marshal Prince Ferdinand of Brunswick-Lüneburg (1721–82).

Duke of Broglio, at Bergen: Prince Ferdinand of Brunswick's offensive against the French under Victor François, duc de Broglie (1718–1804) was repulsed at Bergen, near Frankfurt, on 13 April 1759. Broglie's success won him the title of Marshall of France from Louis XV. Thackeray has taken the distinctive spelling of his name from the *Annual Register*.

the capitulation of Closter Zeven: following his defeat by the French under Louis-César Letellier, comte d'Estrées, at Hastenbeck the Duke of Cumberland was obliged to sign a capitulation at Kloster Zeven on 8 September 1757. Under the terms of the capitulation 38,000 Hanoverian troops were obliged to lay down their arms and disperse.

Lord George Sackville: Lord George Sackville, commander of the British cavalry at the Battle of Minden (1 August 1759) three times refused to obey the order to advance issued by his commanding officer, Prince Ferdinand of Brunswick. Sackville was later court-martialled and cashiered. His conduct has never been properly explained.

70 *regiments of Lorraine and Royal Cravate*: the Cavalry regiment of the Royal-Cravattes was routed at Minden. It had first been raised in 1643 from Croatian recruits. There is no record of the regiment of Lorraine serving at Minden.

72 *the provost-marshal*: the officer appointed as the head of the military police.

the year in which George II died . . .: George II died on 25 October 1760. The battle of Warburg, in which an Anglo-Hanoverian army under Prince Ferdinand of Brunswick defeated the French, was fought on 31 July. The battle was already virtually won when the British cavalry arrived, but the spectacular charge, led by John Manners, Marquis of Granby, served to restore its reputation tarnished by Lord George Sackville's inaction at Minden in 1759.

73 *Jagd-meister of the Duke of Cassel*: the *Jagd-meister* (Master of the Hunt) was a minor court official. Cassel is eight miles from Warburg.

75 *Aesculapius*: the Greek god of medicine, hence, figuratively, a doctor.

1814 . . . Brixton: Thackeray probably dropped this reference due to the conflict with the note in Chapter I, which claims that the narrative was written *c.*1800. In Chapter XVII, however, we are told that Barry is in the Fleet Prison in 1814. In the early years of the nineteenth century Brixton was still a village detached from London. Its church, St. Matthew's, was only started in 1822 but 'the prodigious increase of houses' by 1844 was noted in the *Builder*. The note would have had a certain piquancy when the novel first appeared.

79 *Hesse-Cassel territory*: Hessen-Cassel remained an inde-

pendent state until 1866. Its sovereign bore the title of Landgrave until 1803 when the title of Elector was conferred.

Prince Henry: Frederick II's youngest brother and one of his ablest commanders.

Wilhelmshöhe, the Elector's palace: the Landgrave's summer palace outside Cassel was celebrated for its gardens. Thackeray had visited the city during his German trip of 1830. The *Hofmarschall* was the official charged with the administration and ceremonial of the Court.

80 *O'Grady*: the British minister in Berlin 1760–4 was Andrew Mitchell.

the most ruthless seller of men in Germany: in 1755 the Landgrave of Hessen-Cassel entered into a treaty of Defensive Alliance with Great Britain which was invoked in 1757 when eight battalions were despatched to England. 5,000 Hessian troops had formerly served in the campaign of 1745–6 against the Young Pretender and some 12,000 would be used in North America in 1776–84.

giant regiment that our present monarch disbanded . . . Morgan Prussia: King Frederick William I of Prussia had developed a mania for tall soldiers and had assembled a Grenadier Regiment of giants from all parts of Europe. As Thomas Campbell noted in 1842 in his *Frederick the Great*, 'it had become a fixed idea with the king that the Almighty had made all tall men expressly for him'. The regiment was disbanded by Frederick William's successor, Frederick II, in 1740 on his accession to the throne. Frederick nevertheless retained his father's interest in tall soldiers, drafting a cabinet order in 1744 instructing his recruiters of the rates payable to such men. Men of six feet received 300 dollars, while those of five feet nine inches received 100 dollars (an inch shorter and the rate sank to 40 dollars).

The story of 'Morgan Prussia' is possibly based on that of the Irishman James Kirkland for whom Frederick William paid £1000.

81 *Clonmel*: Thackeray did not visit Clonmel, county town of the south riding of Tipperary, during his Irish trip.

82 *General Rolls*: there is no record of a General Rolls in the period.

84 *the Irish brigade, Roche's*: this may be an error for Rothe's or Roth's brigade, commanded by the Irish exile Charles Edward, comte de Roth, who died in 1766. A John Roche went into exile in 1691 and found service with the King of Sardinia but did not serve in the French army.

85 *Monsieur de Galgenstein*: this M. de Galgenstein must be a relative, or a descendant, of Count Gustavus Adolphus Maximilian von Galgenstein who figures prominently in Thackeray's earlier story *Catherine* (published in *Fraser's Magazine* between May 1839 and February 1840). The Count first appears at the age of twenty-six in the year 1705 which would seem to preclude his being the Prussian recruiting officer in *Barry Lyndon*. The name *Galgenstein* means 'gallows-stone'.

87 *'O Gretchen, mein Täubchen . . .' 'Prinz Eugen der edle Ritter'*: 'O Gretchen, my little dove, my heart's trumpet, my canon, my kettledrum, and my musket'; 'Prince Eugene the noble knight' is the opening line of an Austrian song commemorating the capture of Belgrade by Prince Eugene of Savoy in 1719.

88 *'Ein' feste Burg ist unser Gott'*: the opening line of Martin Luther's celebrated paraphrase of Psalm 46.

89 *the bishopric and town of Fulda*: Fulda was an independent prince-bishopric from 1752 to 1802.

90 *Japhet . . . Partholans and Nemedians*: according to Irish legend, Partholan, of the family of Japhet, son of Noah, landed in Ireland in 2048 BC. His race survived some three hundred years and was then superseded by that of Nemedius which had established itself in Ulster at about the time of the patriarch Jacob.

Joseph of Arimathea, and King Brute: ancient British tradition, recorded by Geoffrey of Monmouth in his *Historia Britonum*, states that the island of Britain was first colonized by Brutus, or Brute, the great-grandson of Aeneas. Legend also states that the Britons were first converted to Christianity by Joseph of Arimathea who landed at Glastonbury in AD 63 and established the monastery there. There was a considerable revival of interest in these stories during the Tudor period.

Phoenicians . . . and King MacNeil: in 1772 Colonel Charles Vallancey had posited the theory that Ireland was first settled by Phoenician traders from whom was derived the Irish language. The Tuatha Dé Dannan, descendants of Nemedius, arrived in Ireland from Scandinavia. They were succeeded by the Scythian Milesians, Heremon and Heber, who landed in Ireland from Spain in 1300 BC, both Princes being descendants of the Goth, Milesius. King MacNeil is probably the king Niall of the Nine Hostages, who ruled at Tara from AD 380 to 405. From him were descended the High Kings of Ireland known as the Ui Néill.

Tacitus briefly mentions Ireland, or Hibernia, in his *Agricola* (xxiv).

As in praesenti perfectum fumat in avi: a garbled quotation from the section of the old Eton Latin Grammar dealing with verbs of the first conjugation. The same line is cited in Chapter V of *Vanity Fair*.

Pfannkuchen: (Ger.) pancake.

rixdalers: from the German *Reichsthaler*, a silver coin worth about 4s 6d in English currency of the period.

91 *curriculum*: a play on 'curricle', a light two-wheeled carriage.

Strumpff: (Ger.) stocking.

92 *Nasenbrumm*: (Ger.) nosegrowl.

Pfarrer of Rumpelwitz: (Ger.) Pastor of Rumblewitz.

Ignatius: a reference to the writings of *either* Ignatius of Antioch (martyred AD 107) *or* Ignatius Loyola (1491–1556). Both writers might have proved apposite to the 'Babylonian question', in identification of the Church of Rome with the Whore of Babylon.

94 *M. de Soubise*: Charles de Rohan, prince de Soubise (1715–87), Marshall of France.

crushed under Frederick's heel: Frederick the Great's Prussian army crossed the Saxon frontier on 29 August 1756. Dresden was occupied on 10 September and Saxony finally capitulated on 14 October.

Grand Mogul: the Emperor of Delhi, the ruler of the Mughal Empire in India.

a complete Mensch: 'a full human-being'.

95 *the Bülow regiment*: the regiment under the command of the Prussian general Christoph Karl von Bülow (1716–88).

lighted matches: i.e. with the match ignited in the matchlock of a musket.

96 *Mr. Gillray*: James Gillray (1756–1815), the English caricaturist and engraver.

crimps: recruiting-party.

97 *Neiss*: properly Neisse in Silesia. Now Nysa in Poland.

98 *générale*: the call to arms.

100 *a fancy to Silesia*: Frederick the Great seized the Austrian province of Silesia in 1741–2.

master of Russia: Napoleon entered Moscow on 14 September 1812.

102 *one head or two*: the arms of the Kings of Prussia bear a single-headed eagle; those of the Austrian monarchy a double-headed imperial eagle.

103 *Uhlans*: Lancers.

frédérics-d'or: Prussian gold coins bearing the head of Frederick II.

groschen . . . dollar: a *groschen* was originally 1/30th of a *thaler* or dollar.

106 *Madame de Kameke*: the Kameckes were a distinguished Prussian family. A Frau von Kamecke had been Frederick II's chief governess as a child, as Thackeray probably knew from Thomas Campbell's *Frederick the Great and his Times* (1842).

107 *Tabaks-Rat von Dose*: a double play on the German *Tabaks-Rat*, Minister of Tobacco, and *Tabaksdose*, a snuff-box.

108 *a precious box of spikenard*: spikenard is a precious aromatic oil. The reference is to Mark 14: 3: 'There came a woman having an alabaster box of ointment of spikenard very precious; and she brake the box, and poured it on his head.'

109 *in spite of his name*: *Kurz* is the German for short.

110 *Marquis d'Argens*: Jean Baptiste de Boyer, marquis d'Argens (1704–71), Frederick the Great's chamberlain and Director of his Academy. Disgraced after his marriage to the Berlin actress Mlle Cochois. He returned to France in 1759.

112 *the Pope's order of the Spur*: the Military Order of the Spur (Ordine dello Speron d'oro) was suppressed by Gregory XVI in 1841.

116 *faro-bank*: the banker's desposit of money against which other players put their stakes in the game of faro.

remise: coach-house.

the Pandours under Austrian Trenck: originally a force raised on his Croatian estates by Baron Franz von Trenck, later incorporated as a regiment in the Austrian army under Trenck's command. Proverbial for their ferocity.

the Prince of Wales: Prince Charles Edward Stuart, the 'Young Pretender'.

117 *Chevalier de Casanova*: Giacomo Girolamo Casanova (1725–98) was granted the Dutch title of Chevalier de Seingalt in 1760. Casanova's memoirs were published in Leipzig in 1826–38.

Mr. Charles Fox: Charles James Fox (1749–1806) was the third son of the first Lord Holland. In 1763, when Charles was still at Eton, his father took him on a continental tour introducing him to gambling and other adult pleasures. Fox became MP for Midhurst in 1768 and made his mark with speeches against Wilkes in 1769.

119 *Chevalier Elliot*: Hugh Elliot was British envoy in Berlin from 1777 to 1782.

120 *the American troubles*: the British parliament passed an Act imposing heavy duties on imported American merchandise in March 1764 and followed it a year later with the obnoxious Stamp Act. The first American Congress met at New York in June 1765.

the Philosopher of Sans Souci: Frederick the Great fancied himself as a philosopher and man of letters and had begun a correspondence with Voltaire in 1736. He built the Palace of Sans Souci at Potsdam 1745–7.

rouleau: a number of gold coins made up into a cylindrical packet.

roturier: plebeian, common-man.

Mechlin ruffles: fine lace produced at Mechelen (Malines) in Belgium.

123 *the Three Crowns*: Thackeray has 'Three Kings' here. The correction is Saintsbury's. An inn near the Dreikönigskirche in Dresden-Neustadt on the right bank of the Elbe.

124 *Spandau*: the important garrison-town five miles from the centre of Berlin.

Monsieur de Voltaire: after a long correspondence, Frederick the Great had finally persuaded Voltaire to visit Berlin in July 1751. The philosopher's relationship with the king steadily deteriorated, reaching a crisis point in 1752 with a dispute over Frederick's president of the council, Maupertuis, whom Voltaire satirized in his *Diatribe de Docteur Akakia*. In March 1753 Voltaire left Berlin only to be arrested by one of Frederick's agents at Frankfurt on the pretext that he had removed some of the king's unpublished poems. Voltaire finally left Germany in July 1753. Thackeray would have been familiar with the story from Campbell's *Frederick the Great* and from Macaulay's essay, both of 1842.

High Dutch: German.

mains: the number called by the thrower before the dice are thrown in the game of hazard.

125 *procès-verbal*: the written statement of facts in support of a criminal charge.

126 *the Elector, King of Poland*: Frederick Augustus of Saxony (1696–1763), elected King of Poland as Augustus III in 1753.

transparencies: Thackeray's play with the German title *Durchlaucht* generally translated as 'Serene Highness.'

the Margravine of Bayreuth: Friederike Sophia Wilhelmine (1709–58) elder sister of Frederick the Great and wife of Frederick, Margrave of Brandenburg-Kulmbach. In his *The Four Georges* (1861) Thackeray recommended the

Margravine's memoirs (published in England in 1812) to 'those who are curious about European Court history of the last age'. As the Margravine died in 1758 Barry's boast of having danced with her is empty.

128 *pelisse*: a long fur-lined cloak or mantle.

129 *Seingalt*: Casanova.

Ivanhoe . . . 'a passage of arms': *Ivanhoe: A Romance* by 'the Author of Waverley' was published in three volumes in 1820. The famous 'passage of arms', or tournament, takes place at Ashby-de-la-Zouche and is described by Scott in his first volume. Unless we post-date Barry's memoirs to 1820 his acquaintance with Scott's novel is obviously impossible, a fact which explains Thackeray's replacement of the sentence in his revised edition.

Alexis Kossloffsky: possibly Prince Fedor Alexeivich Kozlovsky, sent by Catherine the Great to Fernay with presents for Voltaire in 1768. He was killed at the battle of Chesme in 1770. A Prince A. S. Kozlovsky was Procurator of the Holy Synod *c.* 1762–3.

130 *Toeplitz, the Duke of Courland*: the Empress Anne of Russia bestowed the Duchy of Courland on her favourite Ernst Johann Bühren or Biron who held it 1737–40. On the Empress's death Biron was disgraced and only regained his duchy under Catherine II in 1763. He died in 1772. Toeplitz, or Toplitz (Czech: Teplice) is a spa in Bohemia.

made Paroli: winning on a double stake at faro.

H.I.H. the Princess Frederica Amelia: no princess of the house of Habsburg with these Christian names existed in the period.

132 *the Duke of Baden's territory, at Mannheim*: Mannheim was until 1803 the capital of the Rhineland Palatinate. It was only annexed to Baden in that year. Baden itself was raised from a Margravate to a Grand Duchy in 1806.

Charles XII or Richard Coeur de Lion: the reference is to the account of the death of Charles XII of Sweden in Samuel Johnson's *The Vanity of Human Wishes* (1749):

> His fall was destin'd to a barren Strand,
> A petty Fortress, and a dubious hand.

133 *Baron de Clootz*: Jean Baptiste du Val de Grace, Baron de Clootz (1755–94) was born into a Prussian noble family but abandoned his title at the outbreak of the French Revolution. In 1790 he declared himself to be 'the orator of the human race' in Paris and changed his baptismal names to Anarcharsis. He was guillotined on 24 March 1794.

134 *gravel*: the presence in the bladder of accretions of crystal causing pain or difficulty in passing urine.

the Electors of Treves and Cologne: both Treves (Ger. Trier) and Cologne were independent bishoprics during the eighteenth century. The Archbishops of both were Electors of the Empire.

the Archduchess-Governess of the Netherlands: the Archduchess Marie-Christine, wife of the Duke of Saxe-Teschen, governor of the Austrian Netherlands.

shopkeepers: a reference to Napoleon's jibe against the English as 'a nation of shopkeepers'.

135 *the Duchy of X—*: Thackeray drew his story of 'The Tragical History of the Princess of X——' from Baron de la Mothe-Langon's *L'Empire, ou dix ans sous Napoléon* (Paris, 1836), though elements of it are based on the story of Princess Sophia Dorothea of Hanover and Philip von Königsmarck (which Thackeray retells in *The Four Georges*). Several German states, most notably Hanover and Bavaria, were elevated to the status of kingdom during the Napoleonic and post-Napoleonic era. In 1844 Thackeray had referred to the Duchy as 'W'.

Ludwigslust: (Ger.) 'Louis' pleasure'. An anticipation of the comment in *The Four Georges* concerning the suburban palaces of German princelings: 'Hard by, but away from the noise and brawling of the citizens and buyers, is Wilhelmslust, or Ludwigsruhe, or Monbijou, or Versailles—it scarcely matters which.'

136 *the Northern Dubarry*: so-named with reference to Louis XV's official mistress, Marie Jeanne Bécu, comtesse du Barry (1743–93).

137 *Balsamo . . . Cagliostro . . . St. Germain*: both Cagliostro and St. Germain were celebrated adventurers. Giuseppe Balsamo, who adopted the title 'Count Cagliostro' (1743–95), learned the rudiments of alchemy on the island of

Rhodes and thereafter made a highly successful business of selling love-philtres, elixirs and alchemical powders throughout Europe. He was imprisoned in the Bastille in 1785 and in the Fleet Prison in London in 1788. He died in prison in Rome.

The obscure alchemist who called himself the comte de St. Germain (*c.*1710–*c.*1780) was nicknamed *der Wundermann* in Germany where he frequented the princely courts. He claimed to have a secret formula for removing flaws from diamonds and to have discovered the elixir of life. According to Cagliostro, St. Germain was also the founder of freemasonry. St. Germain was finally patronized by the Landgrave Karl of Hesse with whom he pursued the study of 'secret sciences' in Schleswig-Holstein.

the great secret: the elixir of life.

Most Christian Majesty: the title *Majesté très Chrétienne* was first granted to the kings of France in 1469.

ombre: a card game for three players.

140 *the revocation of the edict of Nantes*: the edict of toleration of French protestants granted at Nantes in 1598 by Henri IV was revoked in 1685 by Louis XIV. Many Huguenots took refuge in the protestant states of Germany.

141 *Richelieu*: Louis François Armand du Plessis, duc de Richelieu (1696–1788), of whom Macaulay noted 'he was in truth the most eminent of that race of seducers by profession, who furnished Crébillon the younger and La Clos with models for their heroes'. Richelieu's supposed *Mémoires* were published 1790–1.

143 *lansquenet or piquet*: both card-games.

148 *Schmetterling*: (Ger.) butterfly.

sotte figure: a sorry figure.

149 *a spadassin*: a bully.

comment vas-tu?: the insulting use of the second person singular in a formal situation.

151 *Liliengarten*: (Ger.) Lilygarden.

154 *the Emperor Leopold*: Joseph II's brother did not succeed to the Austrian throne as Leopold II until 1790. He died in 1792.

Gresset or Crébillon: Jean Baptiste Louis Gresset (1709–77) trained as a Jesuit but was obliged to leave the order following the success of his *louche* verse such as *Vert-Vert* (1734) which celebrates the adventures of a parrot in a convent; Claude Prosper Jolyot de Crébillon (1707–77) was the son of the dramatist Prosper Crébillon and the author of a string of immoral novels. He nevertheless held the office of Censor from 1759.

158 *the Rotunda, at Ranelagh*: the Ranelagh gardens were opened at Chelsea in 1742. The famous Rotunda, 185 feet in diameter, was demolished in 1804.

the emigration from France: the so-called 'First Emigration' during the first year of the French Revolution.

159 *Leicester Fields*: Leicester Fields were laid out as a garden in the centre of Leicester Square in the 1720s. The Square itself was still, just, a respectable residential area in the late-eighteenth century though it had long been known as a resort of foreigners.

164 *Hengst*: (Ger.) stallion.

170 *Strasburg pie*: pâté de foie gras.

laurel-water: a distillation of laurel leaves containing a high proportion of prussic acid.

172 *Schlangenfels*: (Ger.) Snakescliff.

as had been done . . . at Zell: George III's sister Caroline Matilda, wife of Christian VII of Denmark, was accused of adultery in 1772. Her marriage was dissolved and she was condemned to confinement for life. At George III's insistence Matilda was removed to the Castle of Celle, or Zell, in Hanover where she died in 1775.

cassette: casket.

173 *heyducks*: armed life-guards originating in Hungary and Poland.

174 *esclandre*: scandalous scene.

178 *Potemkin*: Grigori Aleksandrovich Potemkin (1739–91). Statesman, favourite and lover of Catherine II of Russia.

Chevalier Charles Edward: after the failure of the Forty-Five the Prince had steadily become addicted to 'the nasty bottle' (as his brother Cardinal York phrased it).

Lord C——: almost certainly a reference to Philip Dormer, fourth Earl of Chesterfield (1694–1773).

179 *Schuvaloff . . . Langeac*: inventions on Thackeray's part.

the birth of the first Dauphin: Louis Joseph Xavier François, Dauphin of France, eldest son of Louis XVI, was born at Versailles on 22 October 1781. He died in June 1789 and was succeeded by his brother Louis Charles (born 1785).

amaranth: a dark blue or purple.

Br–mm–ll: George Bryan Brummell (1778–1840), familiarly known as 'Beau Brummell', was said to be the grandson of a servant. He was certainly the son of a civil servant. From *c.* 1798 he was acknowledged as the leader of London fashion and an associate of the Prince of Wales. He was obliged to retire to Calais in 1816 because of his debts.

that vulgar Corsican: Napoleon. First Consul in 1799; Emperor of France from 1804 until his abdication in 1814.

Mançanares: the river on which Madrid stands. Now more familiarly spelt 'Manzanares'.

180 *on the square*: honestly, 'on the level'.

181 *Hanbury Williams*: Sir Charles Hanbury Williams (1708–59). Diplomat and satirist.

George Selwyn: George Augustus Selwyn (1719–91). A contemporary of Gray and Walpole at Eton and later a noted wit, conversationalist and gambler.

Horry Walpole . . . Mr. Gray: Horace Walpole (1717–97), the antiquary, connoisseur, collector and great letter-writer, had been accompanied on the Grand Tour in 1739 by his old school-fellow, the poet Thomas Gray (1716–71). On the return journey from Florence in 1741 the two had separated after a quarrel.

182 *Alcibiades*: the Athenian statesman and general, Alcibiades (450–404 BC) had a reputation for capriciousness, opportunism and self-indulgence.

183 *'Waugh hawk'*: this instance is noted by the Oxford Dictionary as 'a perversion or misunderstanding' of 'ware-hawk', a hunting call denoting a need for care.

tenement: here a house held by tenure.

Mary Wortley Montagu: daughter of the first Duke of Kingston and wife of Edward Wortley Montagu, ambassador to Turkey. Lady Mary (1689–1762) was a poet and avid letter-writer.

184 *Madame Dacier*: Anne Lefebvre, Madame Dacier (*c.* 1651–1720). Wife of the scholar André Dacier and the quintessential *femme savante*. She edited Terence and Marcus Aurelius and translated Callimachus, Anacreon and Homer into French.

Calista: probably an allusion to the heroine of Nicholas Rowe's play *The Fair Penitent* (1703). Hazlitt described Calista as 'a virago, fair, a woman of high spirit and violent resolutions, anything but a penitent'.

magots: grotesque porcelain figures.

Minerva: the Roman goddess of wisdom and the arts.

186 *gyps*: college servants at Cambridge.

187 *Carreau*: (Fr.) the suit of diamonds at cards.

chalk-stones: the white concretions formed around the joints in chronic gout.

189 *corbleu*: (Fr.) Heavens!

191 *Jemmy-Jessamy*: dandy, foppish.

192 *farmer-general*: one who, under the *ancien régime*, 'farmed' or collected taxes.

193 *London Gazette*: the official journal issued twice weekly since the late seventeenth century and containing lists of government appointments, promotions and other public notices.

194 *Lord Townsend*: George Townshend, Viscount Townshend, the Lord Lieutenant of Ireland from October 1767 until November 1772.

Whiteboys: members of secret societies organized amongst the Irish tenantry determined to redress grievances by threatening landlords. Whiteboys, so called from their donning white shirts over their clothes, were active in Munster from the 1760s.

196 *a flowered sack*: a loose gown.

197 *Daniel Lambert's coat*: Daniel Lambert died at the age of forty at Stamford in 1809, weighing $52\frac{3}{4}$ stones.

198 *a blister*: a plaster used for raising blisters.

Whole Duty of Man: this enormously popular devotional work was first published in 1658 and is often ascribed to Richard Allestree.

the Emperor Joseph: Joseph II succeeded to the Austrian throne in 1765.

199 *the Duke of Hohenzollern-Sigmaringen*: Karl Friedrich, Prince of Hohenzollern-Sigmaringen (1769–85), head of the senior branch of the Hohenzollern family.

200 *the battle of Hochkirchen*: an Austrian victory against Prussia fought on 14 October 1758 before Barry had even left Ireland.

201 *Milesian*: i.e. descended from the Milesian tribes supposed to have invaded Ireland in 1070 BC.

the roundhouse: the Round Room at the Rotunda Assembly Rooms opened in 1764.

the Crow Street Theatre: Dublin's second theatre opened in 1758.

Flood and Daly, of Galway: Henry Flood (1732–91) MP for Kilkenny and from 1783 the representative for Winchester at the Westminster parliament. Denis Daly (1747–91) was elected MP for Galway in 1768.

Dick Sheridan: Richard Brinsley Sheridan, the son of the Dublin actor Thomas Sheridan, left Dublin in 1762 at the age of eleven.

Mr. Edmund Burke: Edmund Burke (1729–97) was born and educated in Dublin but was elected to the Westminster parliament as MP for Wendover in 1766. He was member for Bristol in 1774 and for Malton in 1781. Dr. Johnson remarked of him that 'he is never humdrum, never unwilling to talk, nor in haste to leave off'.

Ranelagh: Dublin's Ranelagh Gardens were not opened until 1776, a mile to the south of the city centre.

Mr. Mossop: Thomas Mossop, who was nicknamed 'Teapot' from his favourite way of standing on stage, was actor-manager of the Crow Street Theatre.

202 *Daly's Coffee-house*: Daly's in Dame Street opened early in the reign of George III and became Daly's Club in 1791.

According to the *Hibernian Magazine*, it was 'the most superb gambling house in the world'.

203 *Captain Thunder*: the title assumed by the leader of a secret society like the Whiteboys.

205 *making his salut*: retiring from the world and making his profession as a Franciscan.

208 *the Mercury*: the *Dublin Mercury* was first published in 1726.

214 *an Ephesian matron*: a reference to the story told by Eumolpus in Petronius's *Satyricon* of a supposedly inconsolable Ephesian widow who watches, fasting, by her husband's grave for five nights. She is finally distracted from her grief by the sexual advances of a soldier who has been set to guard the bodies of criminals crucified nearby. When one of the criminal's bodies is stolen the widow suggests the substitution of her dead husband's corpse.

219 *'seven's the main, heh'*: a reference to the winning call of 'seven' in a game of hazard.

rhodomontades: letters full of extravagant phrases and boasts.

222 *Whiteboys, Oakboys, Steelboys*: all secret agrarian societies. In 1763 the Oakboys (so named from their wearing a sprig of oak in their hats) rose against the imposition of forced labour on the roads and against heavy tithes. The Steelboys, or the 'Hearts of Steel', were active from *c.* 1772. Both were Ulster Protestant groups as opposed to the Catholic Whiteboys of Munster (for whom, see n. to p. 194 above).

proctors: agents or stewards.

Dublin Gazettes and Mercuries: the *Dublin Gazette* first appeared in the reign of James II but was restarted in 1705. The *Mercury* began in 1726.

223 *My Lord Charlemont*: James Caulfield, Earl of Charlemont (1728–99) was the doyen of Dublin's intellectual and social life in the mid-eighteenth century. He had a substantial house in Rutland Square (now Parnell Square) which now houses the Municipal Gallery of Modern Art. At his demesne at Marino near Clontarf Charlemont built

the famous Casino to the designs of Sir William Chambers in 1761–2. Marino is *not* on the Dunleary road.

a domino: a long black-silk cloak with a hood.

224 *the ingenious builders of Long Acre*: Long Acre was celebrated throughout the eighteenth and nineteenth centuries as a centre of the coachbuilding trade.

227 *a Sabine marriage*: a reference to the forcible abduction of women of the Sabine tribe by Romulus and the first Romans who were short of wives.

228 *enlèvement*: abduction.

229 *Town and Country Magazine*: published 1769–96.

as far as Orpheus did Eurydice: i.e. as far as Hades itself.

The royal Dukes of Gloucester and Cumberland: William Henry, Duke of Gloucester (1743–1805), the third son of Frederick, Prince of Wales, had secretly married Maria, Countess of Waldegrave, in 1766 but the validity of the marriage was not acknowledged until 1773. Henry Frederick, Duke of Cumberland (1745–90), the fourth son of Frederick, Prince of Wales, alienated his elder brother, George III, by his clandestine marriage to Mrs. Horton in 1771.

White's, Wattier's, and Goosetree's: all London clubs. James Goosetree opened a club-house at 51 Pall Mall in 1773. Wattier's, however, functioned only between *c.* 1807 and 1819. For White's, see n. to p. 7 above.

230 *Mr. Wilkes*: John Wilkes (1725–97), though notoriously ugly, was a great womaniser. The 'Essay on Woman' (a parody of Pope's 'Essay on Man'), co-written by Wilkes, but not published by him, was denounced in the House of Lords by Lord Sandwich (see n. to p. 238 below) as 'filthy', 'atrocious' 'impious' and 'indecent'. Wilkes was obliged to flee to Paris to escape prosecution. Apropos of 'strange inexplicable passions' Thackeray notes in his *Catherine* (1839–40), 'Was not Wilkes, the ugliest, charmingest, most successful man in the world?'

232 *the Pantheon*: the assembly room in Oxford Street built to the designs of James Wyatt in 1772.

234 *Star and Garter . . . Covent Garden*: the old Star and

Garter Hotel on Richmond Hill was renowned for its parties, dinners and wines. The north and east sides of Covent Garden were formerly noted for their hotels and taverns.

235 *Mr. Walpole*: Horace Walpole had declared in his *Anecdotes of Painting* of 1762 that 'one must have taste to be sensible of the beauties of Grecian architecture; one only wants passions to feel Gothic'. He had begun constructing his own 'little gothic castle' at Strawberry Hill in 1750.

a pipe of tobacco: as Dr. Johnson noted in 1773 during his Scottish tour, 'smoking is gone out'.

Mrs. Bonnyface: 'Boniface', the name of the landlord in Farquhar's comedy *The Beaux' Stratagem* (1707), was often applied generally to innkeepers.

bienséances: proprieties.

the famous new organ: the Loosemore organ at Exeter Cathedral of 1655 was repaired, and not replaced, in 1768 and again in 1782 by Paul Micheau.

236 *Clumpton*: possibly Cullompton, near Exeter.

237 *the latest French-Greek*: in September 1764 Horace Walpole noted of the French that 'they begin to see beauties in the antique—everything must be *à la grecque*'.

M. Cornichon: a play on the French words *corniche*, a cornice, and *cornichon*, a gherkin.

Hudson: the English portraitist, Thomas Hudson (1701–79).

Boehmer: the firm of Boehmer and Bassange were Court Jewellers to Louis XV and Louis XVI. It was they who made the famous 'Diamond Necklace' in 1780, the subject of Carlyle's essay first published in *Fraser's Magazine* in 1837.

238 *Jemmy Twitcher*: John Montagu, fourth Earl of Sandwich (1718–92) received considerable public opprobrium for his role in the prosecution of John Wilkes in 1763. At a performance at Covent Garden of Gay's *The Beggar's Opera* the house rose at Macheath's words 'That Jemmy Twitcher should peach, I own surprises me'. From then on Sandwich was commonly known as Jemmy Twitcher.

Carlisle: Frederick Howard, fifth Earl of Carlisle (1748–1825). A passionate gambler.

sans désemparer: without intermission.

the days of Gog and Magog: according to tradition the giant Gogmagog, or two giants Gog and Magog, were found in Britain at the landing of Brutus. Wooden effigies of the two giants have stood in Guildhall in London since at least the seventeenth century.

Richelieu: not the cardinal but his grand-nephew, the duc de Richelieu for whom see n. to p. 141 above.

William . . . Torbay: William of Orange landed at Brixham in Devon on 5 November 1688.

Boucher and Vanloo: François Boucher (1703–70) and Carle van Loo (1705–65) had both been awarded the title *premier peintre du roi*. Both painters were very much out of fashion in the 1840s. In his *Handbook of the History of the Spanish and French Schools of Painting* (1848) Sir Edmund Head dismissed Boucher with the words 'an artist whose indecency was such as to shock Diderot may well deserve to be treated as the type of the age and court of Louis XV'. Of van Loo he remarks 'his fame has gone on decreasing since the day of his death, when it stood very high'.

239 *Lauraguais*: Louis-Léon Félicité, comte de Lauraguais (1733–1824). A friend and patron of Voltaire, a man of letters and an amateur scientist. He was created duc de Brancas by Louis XVIII in 1814.

Jack Wilkes . . . the Mansion House: John Wilkes was elected Lord Mayor of London in October 1774.

240 *train de vivre*: grand style of living.

my royal ancestry: a compliment to Brian Boiromhe, or Boru, crowned at Tara in 1002.

242 *Mr. John Scott*: John Scott (1751–1838), created Baron Eldon of Eldon in 1799, was called to the bar in 1776.

245 *the novels of Scott and James*: in spite of his early admiration of the historical novels of Sir Walter Scott, Thackeray was critical of Scott's tendency to romanticize character and setting. He was to remark in his *Notes of a*

Journey from Cornhill to Grand Cairo (1846): 'When shall we have a real account of those times and heroes [the Crusades and the Crusaders]—no good-humoured pageant, like those of the Scott romances—but a real authentic story to instruct and frighten honest people of the present day, and make them thankful that the grocer governs the world now in place of the baron?.' Thackeray's opinion of the historical romances of G. P. R. James (1799–1860) was even lower as is evident in his burlesque of one of James's novels in his series 'Punch's Prize Novelists' of 1847.

Prince Prettyman: a character in George Villiers's play *The Rehearsal* (1672) who is seen shifting between the status of a fisherman and a prince.

O.Y.: Oliver Yorke, the fictitious editor of *Fraser's Magazine*.

246 *old Grafton*: Augustus Henry Fitzroy, third Duke of Grafton (1735–1811). Prime Minister from December 1767 to January 1770.

Ancaster, Sandwich, Lorn: Peregrine Bertie, third Duke of Ancaster and Kesteven (1713–78), and John Montagu, fourth Earl of Sandwich (1718–92), served in Grafton's cabinet. 'Lorn' must be John Campbell, Marquis of Lorn (1723–1806), who succeeded as fifth Duke of Argyle in 1770.

247 *Mr. Reynolds*: Joshua Reynolds (1723–92) became President of the Royal Academy on its foundation in 1768 and the King's principal painter in 1784. He was knighted in 1769.

the Exhibition: the first Royal Academy Exhibition was held in Pall Mall in 1769. From 1771 the Academy and its exhibitions were housed in Somerset House.

Mr. Pope, in his Iliad: the instance cited is from Book VI of the *Iliad*, Pope's translation of which appeared in 1715:

> 'Thus having spoke, th'illustrious Chief of *Troy*
> Stretch'd his fond Arms to clasp the lovely Boy.
> The Babe clung crying to his Nurse's Breast,
> Scar'd at the Dazzling Helm, and nodding Crest.'
> (ll. 594–7)

Mr. Boswell . . . a Corsican habit: Boswell's 'Corsican

habit' was a tribute to his active interest in Corsican nationalism. He had worn the costume at the Shakespeare Jubilee at Stratford in 1769 on which occasion the *London Magazine* noted that 'on the front of his cap was embroidered in gold letters '*Viva la Libertà*'—and on one side of it was a handsome blue feather and cockade, so that it had an elegant as well as a warlike appearance'.

Mrs. Cornely's balls: Theresa Cornelys (1723–97) organized subscription balls, masquerades and concerts at Carlisle House in Soho Square from 1760 until 1772. In the latter year she was declared bankrupt and, after a period as a hotelier in Southampton and as a huckstress under an assumed name, she died (like Barry himself) in the Fleet Prison.

248 *Mr. Oliver Goldsmith*: Goldsmith died in April 1774.

the Duchess of Kingston: Elizabeth Chudleigh (1720–88) secretly married Augustus John Hervey in 1744 but separated from him soon afterwards and denied the marriage on oath in 1769. In this latter year she married the second Duke of Kingston (whose mistress she had been for some time). She was accused of bigamy and found guilty of the offence in 1776. Her marriage to Augustus Hervey being declared still valid, and he succeeding to his brother's title, she became the Countess of Bristol.

Kitty Fisher: Catherine Maria Fisher (d. 1767), courtesan, was painted several times by Sir Joshua Reynolds.

poor Hackman: James Hackman (1752–79), vicar of Wiveton in Norfolk, was infatuated with Lord Sandwich's mistress, Martha Ray. He shot Martha outside Covent Garden Theatre on her refusal to marry him, and was hanged at Tyburn on 18 April 1779.

Dr. Simony: Dr. William Dodd (1729–77) was ordained deacon in 1751 and thereafter rose steadily through church preferment. He was appointed to a royal chaplaincy in 1763 and in the same year became a chaplain to the Bishop of St. David's and a prebend of Brecon. He opened his own chapel in Pimlico in the following year, ministering to a fashionable congregation, and by 1772 had obtained the valuable livings of Hockliffe and Chalgrave in Bedfordshire. In 1774 Dodd's ambition got the better of him. His wife wrote anonymously to the Lord Chancellor asking that the living of St. George's, Hanover Square be presented to her husband. The letter was traced back to the Dodds, and Dr. Dodd was struck off the list of royal chaplains as well as being pilloried by Samuel Foote (see below) in his farce *The Cozeners* (where he was referred to as Dr. Simony). In 1777 Dodd was tried for forging a bond in the name of his former pupil and patron, Lord Chesterfield, and despite pleas from Dr. Johnson was executed for forgery at Tyburn on 22 June.

Sam Foote: Samuel Foote (1720–77), actor and dramatist, was manager of the Haymarket Theatre (known in the eighteenth century as the Little Theatre) from 1747. He had satirized Dr. and Mrs. Dodd in his farce *The Cozeners* in 1774.

belcher: a belcher is a blue and white spotted neckerchief named after the pugilist Jim Belcher. It was worn from *c.* 1812 as were the soberer 'coachman-like' fashions Thackeray describes.

249 *Spain and France*: this reference carefully dates the supposed composition of Barry's memoirs at 1813–14. Wellington had defeated Soult's French army at Vittoria on 21 July 1813 and had driven the French across the Pyrenees. Wellington remained in the peninsula storming San Sebastian on 31 August and relieving the siege of Pamplona in October. He crossed the French frontier in November. Soult was defeated at Toulouse on 10 April 1814, four days after Napoleon's abdication.

commissariat beef: army issue.

the Prince . . . Fox . . . Bonaparte: in 1773, the date to which Barry refers, George, Prince of Wales, would have been well out of leading-strings, having reached his eleventh birthday in August. Charles James Fox had entered parliament in 1768 at the age of nineteen. Napoleon, who was born in August 1769, did not leave Corsica until he left for school at Autun at the end of 1779.

a pother about the Union: Britain and Ireland were united by the Act which became effective on 1 January 1801. The fragility of the Union was exemplified, however, by Robert Emmett's attempted *coup d'état* of July 1803.

250 *Protestant corporations*: Roman Catholics were not permitted to hold civil office until the repeal of the Test and Corporation Acts in May 1828 and the Roman Catholic Emancipation Bill of April 1829.

Salamanca: the Irish College at Salamanca in Spain (El Real Colegio de Nobles Irlandeses) was founded in 1592. It trained many eminent Irish bishops and priests.

The county of Devon . . . Cornwall: until 1821 Cornwall, notorious for its 'rotten boroughs', sent 44 members to Westminster. Devon, by contrast, returned only 26 members. By the Reform Act of 1832 Cornwall was reduced to 28 members and Devon to 18.

251 *Clive in India*: Robert Clive was Governor of Bengal 1758–60 and again 1765–7.

252 *the great earl*: William Pitt, created Earl of Chatham in 1766.

253 *the Grand Turk*: the Sultan.

Lord Chatham . . . Mr. Burke: in 1775 Chatham moved an address to the King, praying him to adopt a conciliatory policy towards America. He remained a firm advocate of conciliation in the Lords but opposed American independence from Britain. Edmund Burke made a succession of eloquent speeches in the House of Commons between 1775 and 1782 urging conciliation with the Colonists.

254 *Lord Pitt*: the Earl of Chatham's eldest son.

Lexington . . . Bunker's Hill: the first action between British and American forces took place at Lexington, Massachusetts, on 18 April 1775. The 'battle' of Bunker Hill (generally referred to as Bunker's Hill in eighteenth-century accounts) took place on 17 June. After the action American forces were obliged to withdraw, but it could scarcely be described as a 'glorious victory'.

land-tax: Land Tax was raised to 4*s*. in the £ in 1776. It was made permanent (at the 4*s*. rate) with the introduction of Income Tax in 1798.

255 *one of the classical fellows in the dictionary*: probably a reference to the athlete Milo of Crotona who according to Dr. John Lemprière's *Bibliotheca Classica or a Classical Dictionary* (1788, 1792) 'early accustomed himself to carry

the greatest burdens, and by degrees became a monster of strength. It is said that he carried on his shoulders a young bullock 4 years old, for above 40 yards, and afterwards killed it with one blow of his fist, and ate it up in one day.'

256 *Croesus*: the last king of the ancient kingdom of Lydia in Asia Minor. Famed for his riches.

257 *St. James's*: the fashionable church of St. James, Piccadilly.

258 *Kew*: Frederick Prince of Wales took a long lease on Kew House *c.*1730. He died there in 1751. Old Kew House was demolished in 1803. The Prince of Wales referred to here is Frederick's oldest son and successor, the future George III.

the Earl of Bute: John Stewart, third Earl of Bute (1713–92) had been a close friend of Frederick Prince of Wales and of Princess Augusta: he also acted as instructor in matters constitutional to their son, the future George III. In May 1762 he was appointed Prime Minister by his former pupil but held office for under a year. He continued to advise George III, much to the annoyance of his ministers, until 1765 when the two sharply disagreed.

259 *Fox being turned out of his place*: Fox, who had joined Lord North's administration as a junior lord of the treasury, was dismissed from office by the King in June 1774.

the Howes: Richard Howe, Earl Howe (1726–99) was appointed commander-in-chief in North America in February 1776. His brother, General Sir William Howe, had the command of the army. Both men asked to be relieved of their command in November 1777 but permission was not officially granted until the following spring.

Lord North: Frederick, Lord North (1726–92) became Prime Minister in January 1770. His administration lasted until 1782.

260 *manants and canaille*: boors and rascals.

songs of Vadé and Collard: Jean-Joseph Vadé (1719–57) was celebrated as a song-writer, dramatist and composer of *opéras-comiques*. No eighteenth-century musician of the name of Collard exists. It is possible, however, that

Thackeray is thinking of the composer François Collin (or Collin de Blamont) (1690–1760) who was *maître de la musique de la chambre* at Versailles from 1726.

261 *diable à quatre*: the devil incarnate, or possibly in this context a noisy devil.

263 *a servitor*: an undergraduate at certain of the Oxford colleges who was formerly permitted to pay reduced fees for lectures and board in exchange for menial services such as serving at table in Hall. The word 'servitor' was defined in Johnson's Dictionary as 'one of the lowest order in the university'.

272 *General Tarleton's army*: Sir Banastre Tarleton (1754–1833) served first in America as a cornet in 1776. He was promoted a captain in 1778 and a brevet major in 1779 and distinguished himself in the campaign in the Carolinas under Cornwallis. He was not promoted to the rank of Lieutenant General until 1801.

273 *a declaration of war*: France declared war on 6 February 1778.

274 *the Irish College*: the Irish College of St. Isidore at Rome was founded in 1625.

276 *the Gordon rows*: the riots of June 1780 inspired by the fanatic Lord George Gordon and intended to compel Parliament to repeal the Act for the Relief of Roman Catholics. During the riots Lord Sandwich ('Jemmy Twitcher') was dragged from his coach at Westminster and assaulted by the mob. Lord Mansfield's house on the north-east corner of Bloomsbury Square was burnt out.

278 *Lord Cornwallis's defeat of General Gates*: Cornwallis defeated an American army under the command of Horatio Gates at Camden, South Carolina, on 16 August 1780.

King Pepin: Pepin, or Pippin, seems to have been a familiar nursery figure as is witnessed by a nursery rhyme and by Elizabeth Newbery's *The History of Little King Pippin* of 1786.

279 *pinchbeck*: counterfeit, spurious.

283 *Kühnersdorf*: at the battle of Kunersdorf (12 August 1759) the Prussians were routed by an Austrian and Russian

army. Barry could not possibly have been at the battle for he was serving in the British army at the time.

286 *'the unkindest cut of all'*: *Julius Caesar*, III. ii.

287 *assurance societies*: the earliest known life insurance office 'The Society of Assurance for Widows and Orphans' was established in 1699. Many of its slightly later rivals collapsed at the bursting of the South Sea Bubble in 1720, though that year also marked the beginnings of the London Assurance Company and the Royal Exchange Assurance Company. In the first half of the nineteenth century, as Thackeray notes, the number of such companies rapidly increased.

288 *slops*: weak liquor, or as Johnson's Dictionary has it 'generally some nauseous or useless medicinal liquor'.

290 *mantua-maker*: dressmaker.

291 *as Sycorax did Caliban*: the witch Sycorax gave birth to the 'freckled whelp', Caliban, on the island on which Shakespeare's *The Tempest* is set.

292 *Sabra in the Seven Champions*: Sabra is the name of the princess rescued from the dragon by St. George. The legend was recorded in the popular, and often-printed, collection *The Seven Champions of Christendom* which recounted the stories of the patron-saints of Western Europe.

296 *Billingsgate*: foul and vituperative language, deriving from Billingsgate market in London, defined by Johnson's Dictionary as 'a place where there is always a crowd of low people, and frequent brawls and foul language'.

303 *Darby and Joan*: these traditional names for an affectionate husband and wife date back to the early eighteenth century.

305 *the police-office*: at this stage constables appointed by the local magistrate's office.

306 *Hannibal the Carthaginian*: a reference to the sojourn of Hannibal's army at Capua in 216 BC. According to the eighteenth chapter of Book XXIII of Livy's *History of Rome* it was a different army that left Capua: 'all trace of the old morale was gone . . . as soon as the army began to

live under canvas again . . . they lost all heart and gave out physically, like new recruits'.

the Fleet Prison: a debtors' prison rebuilt after its destruction by fire during the Gordon Riots of 1780. The prison had figured prominently in Dickens's *Pickwick Papers* of 1836–7 but was closed by act of parliament in 1842 and demolished in 1846.

307 *Fleet Market*: developed in 1737 as a meat, fish and vegetable market. It was adjacent to the prison, the inmates of which delicately referred to their address as 'No. 9 Fleet Market'.

308 *the Gentleman's Magazine*: first published in 1731.

309 *the Spanish campaign*: by the end of 1811 Portugal was lost to the French and Wellington was poised to pursue his campaign into Spain.

310 *Prince Rodolphs*: presumably a pantomime or fairy-tale hero. The substance of Thackeray's complaint echoes the theme of *Catherine* of 1839–40.

311 *Trafalgar Square*: Hogarth's six pictures which form the series 'Mariage à la Mode' (1743) were acquired by the newly-founded National Gallery in 1824. The Gallery itself moved to its Trafalgar Square premises in 1838.

West: the American-born painter Benjamin West (1738–1820) settled in England in 1763. He was Historical Painter to George III and the second president of the Royal Academy from 1792. His reputation was based on paintings of classical and modern history.

Angelica Kaufmann: the Swiss-born Angelica Kaufmann (1740–1807) was a friend of Sir Joshua Reynolds and a founder-member of the Royal Academy. She specialized in allegorical subjects. Much of her work was incorporated into the decorative schemes of the Adam brothers.